Jacko

Tom Keneally was born in 1935 and was educated in Sydney. He trained for several years for the Catholic priesthood but did not take orders.

In a distinguished writing life his work includes *Bring Larks and Heroes*, which won the Miles Franklin Award (1967); *The Survivor*, joint winner of the 1970 Captain Cook Award; *The Chant of Jimmie Blacksmith*, shortlisted for the Booker Prize; *Gossip from the Forest*, runner-up for the 1975 Booker Prize; *Confederates*, shortlisted for the 1979 Booker Prize; *Schindler's Ark*, winner of the 1982 Booker Prize and the *LA Times* Book Award for Fiction, and now a major motion picture; *Towards Asmara*; *Flying Hero Class*; and *Woman of the Inner Sea*. His latest book, *Our Republic*, is an account of both a personal and national quest for an Australian republic.

Tom Keneally is Founding Chair of the Australian Republican Movement. He presently teaches in the graduate writing program at the University of California at Irvine, where he holds a Distinguished Professorship. Recently he was made a fellow of the prestigious American Academy of Arts and Sciences.

Other books by Tom Keneally

Jacko

TOM KENEALLY

Published 1994 by Mandarin
a part of Reed Books Australia
22 Salmon Street, Port Melbourne, Victoria 3207
a division of Reed International Books Australia Pty Ltd
First published by William Heinemann, Australia, 1994

Reprinted 1994

Typeset in Sabon by Bookset Pty Ltd, Melbourne
Printed and bound in Australia by Griffin Paperbacks

National Library of Australia
cataloguing-in-publication data:

Keneally, Thomas, 1935– .
Jacko.

ISBN 1 86330 354 5.

I. Title.

A823.3

Gordon Elliott kindly told me
many tales of TV Gothic in America.
Some of them appear transmuted in this account.

If people ever wondered how Jacko Emptor was the video trespasser he became, they should have seen where he came from. In the country in which Jacko spent his childhood, a person could have travelled five hundred miles in all available directions without encountering a single locked door.

Those who, against the odds, understood and loved big Jacko were aware of how this childhood want of locked doors, this paucity of barriers to entry, so drastically directed his later life.

You could argue that factors other than locked-door deprivation governed the direction Jacko later took. You could claim, for example, that Jacko would not have come to the most crowded and locked-up city of the western world, to the Rome of its day, if Basil Sutherland, the Australian media colossus, had not raided America. Sutherland chose to found his own network in the United States, and invited in the television producer Durkin and his friend Jacko to bring peculiarly Australian tele-mayhem to an already vulgarized medium.

Starting a new network was, on the face of it, an extraordinary thing even for Sutherland to attempt. It had certainly occurred to no American to try it. It was a *given* of American culture that the soul was made up of three networks, three apish and like brains, with a little supernumerary cerebellum on the side called the Public Broadcasting System. These were fixed deities: The Trinity and the Virgin Mary.

Basil Sutherland, who had never been governed by such a cosmology, came from the irreverent city of Perth on the Indian Ocean. Perth, after all, had a tradition of doing racy, hectic, barely legal business.

Even so, no seer leaning over Basil Sutherland's birthcot in the Perth Presbyterian Hospital could have predicted it. That he *would* try to break the hegemony and balance of power of the three electronic sisters who held America's, and thus a large part of the world's, mind in bondage.

But back to Jacko, who worked for Sutherland. If you were a friend of Jacko Emptor's, you would have seen Sutherland's electronic ambitions as a fore-ordained mechanism to bring Jacko to the Mecca of locks. I could certainly have foretold it. That Basil would go to all that expansionary trouble just so that Jacko could come to a populous city in a populous nation, a city choked with doors, doors barred not once, but multiply barred, triple-locked, and electronically guarded. Not to mention doormen! The city of most bolts, most bars, most locks, most guards.

Basil Sutherland existed as a mere trigger to bring Jacko to it.

* * *

Behold Jacko Emptor then. Far from his home and his kin, he is at his work in New York: trying with his cameraman to get inside someone's walls. He wears a silly porkpie hat of a kind never found in all his Northern Territory father's millions of acres.

Though on Jacko's great loaf, a Stetson might look like a porkpie! He is also wearing earmuffs and a mohair overcoat and a Burberry scarf rustically knotted. The uninformed might say that he dresses in tune with the flippancy of his vocation: the comic but utterly serious business of circumventing doors.

The earmuffs and the mohair coat aren't all for comic effect though. It's bloody cold, brass monkeys this morning, especially in the cherrypicker bucket which is rising up the face of the Second Avenue apartment block he has chosen for a target. The cameraman and the cable handler who share with him the cramped bucket of the thing are both dressed like skiers. The wind is — as it always is around these big city buildings — subtle and circular. A cornering and recurring demon.

This is the building he wants to get into, and the cherrypicker, paid for by Sutherland, his implement of entry.

If Jacko wants to bring a peculiar, cold astringency to his genitals, he can look down, over the waist high parapet, and see the aimed white dish of the microwave truck looking homely: an electronic hearth more than a hundred feet below. Ecstatic to be trying this new method, and drunk with fear, he does, however, in his early thirties carry a disadvantage: the beginnings of the same gut which ten years ago he'd hated in his father, Stammer Jack. He is concerned about how, once he has parlayed entry to someone's apartment, he will get from the cherrypicker over a fourteenth floor windowsill.

* * *

The unwieldy, belly-freezing prospect that morning caused Jacko Emptor to begin muttering his bush mantra:

—And the man from Snowy River never shifted in
    his seat—
  It was grand to see that mountain horseman
    ride.
  Through the stringybarks and saplings on the
    rough and broken ground,
  Down the hillside at a racing pace he went;
  And he never drew the bridle till he landed
    safe and sound,
  At the bottom of that terrible descent.

—Give me a break, said the cameraman, when Jacko finished. The man's smoky disdain rose in a cloud above the cherrypicker. He was such a sour bugger, this freelancer. Vixen Six — Basil Sutherland's New York channel — had used him only once or twice before, and he told you as fast as he could that he had five kids by two marriages — this to explain why he considered some jobs too risky or ill-paid. He wouldn't have been here if poor old Clayton didn't have the flu. Clayton would, of course, try anything Jacko or Jacko's producer Dannie suggested, even at the pain of having his camera and his person attacked. Whereas this bloke! Anything other than straight camera work in clear weather on a flat surface, and he was up to the corner to call Durkin in the studio and negotiate an extra fee.

—I'm freelance, was his cry.

—He doesn't belong to anyone, Jacko had murmured to Dannie, his producer. Especially not to himself.

Arrived on location this morning and, having seen

the cherrypicker rig come down the dawn street, the cameraman said in his tight, convinced-of-malice way, No one said cherrypicker.

And then he was off to the corner. Could have used Dannie's phone, but did not want anyone overhearing his negotiations.

Three jobs past, Jacko had christened him Fartfeatures. Now the bugger was complaining about *The Man From Snowy River*.

—That's Banjo Paterson, said Jacko. Great Australian balladist, you ignorant bastard.

And Jacko persisted then:

—He was right among the horses as they climbed
     the further hill,
   And the watchers on the mountain standing
     mute,
   Saw him ply the stockwhip fiercely, he was
     right among them still,
   As he raced across the clearing in pursuit.
   Then they lost him for a moment where two
     mountain gullies met . . .

This, Jacko's talismanic verse, was better not intruded upon. He uttered the verse with a big, forced smile, apparently genial, in Fartfeatures' direction. Jacko had some special gifts, and the sparing use of contempt was powerful amongst them.

The unhappy camera oaf would, however, be responsible for guiding Jacko over the window sill and into the chosen room, so that a certain fraternal feeling had to be maintained in the bucket of the cherrypicker.

* * *

I am for the moment being dishonest, relaying events from Jacko's point of view, as if I knew quite what that was. I am, as you'll see, his friend and confidant in two cities, and have enough vanity to believe I know him. So for a time I will persist in it.

I know how delighted he was with the cherry-picker: the supreme device of trespass. I was always attracted by the hubris and triumphalism of all this! Jacko in a bucket on a hydraulic arm, going vertical in his desire to bypass all the locks.

Under my H-1 visa, I lived a more orderly life than Jacko. I was allowed to teach at NYU — holding seminars in a room above a deli in University Place — for as long as I wanted to. I had a reputation for being good at teaching graduate writing classes, the sort of class which is rare in my native land but is found everywhere in the United States. I had no internal knowledge of how my reputation had been achieved. I shared the city with a wife as tolerant and generous as Jacko's wife Lucy appeared to be to Jacko.

We — my wife Maureen and I — were not in New York all the time either. We returned to Sydney every year for at least five months. Given that Sydney was such a pristine city, I should have been a very contented man with my two wonderful locations. But I was unhappy somehow with my own writing, with my publisher, and with my purely literary prospects.

This is typical of people who follow my craft. There are only a few novelists of my acquaintance who are pleasant human beings meant for inhabiting families. For most, the measure of their happiness is the perceived state of their present work or the likely critical and commercial response to their last. Even delusions concerning the quality of what they are writing utterly govern their sense of well-being or their lack of contentment. We are therefore like alcoholics, and some of us make the comparison incarnate by drinking to celebrate or to soothe ourselves for shifts in talent.

In that winter I found comfort in the company of unreading, berserk Jacko, and in the mornings would get up unrefreshed by a furry, starting, unsettling whisky sleep, another rewrite of my novel on China awaiting me. And I would scratch myself and watch *Morning Manhattan* for a distracting sight of my turbulent friend Jacko.

* * *

Though vertigo and his bulk might make him graceless at the sill that morning, he possessed as his spiritual model the Man from Snowy River, who had ridden up and down vertical descents for characteristically antipodean motives: the approval of his mates in the male world.

Things were of course different in New York. The approval that counted here was the approval of hardnosed, talented young women — the kind Jacko was always in trouble for calling *girls* — who were the centurion producers of New York morning television. Jacko would speak to me of how they had watched their strenuous mothers expose the vein of fatuousness in their fathers, quite successful men outside the home, but eunuchs within. These girls had an eye for that seam of stupidity in every man they met from the age of five onwards.

Dannie (short for Danuta), Jacko's producer, seated

now in the production van below, was the paradigm of such wonderful but well-armoured women. She was barely twenty-five, a graduate of a communications school in Southern California, and full of acrid ambition. It was worth your while not to be indeliberately flippant with Dannie.

Generally, as site producer, she accompanied Jacko past the doors and barriers, but there wasn't room even for someone as small-boned as Dannie in the cherrypicker bucket. Video was the technology she seemed to have been born to and which operated today: she would talk to the cameraman, who had earphones; she would have two pictures to choose from when they went to air, the one provided by Fartfeatures, once he started running the tape, and one from the camera crew on the roof of the opposite building; and both she and Jacko had little plugs in their ears through which Durkin, producer-in-chief back at the Vixen Six studio, could speak to Dannie and Jacko.

The age of tongues had come. The age of many voices in the head. It had supplanted for Jacko the age of his father's cattle, the outrageous proteins of beef amongst which Jacko had been born and, sometimes in adolescence, feared he would be sunk and lost.

*　*　*

Here — in view of his producer Dannie's feelings for him — we have to look flatly at the truth which will be richly validated by this account: Jacko had not even addressed himself to the earnest struggle for self perception which most really modern people were embarked upon, especially in this city of locks. It had not yet come to him that men who *said* persistently and in all company how much they loved women were in fact misogynists.

Jacko took not only his bones from Stammer Jack Emptor and from Australian maledom, but, as well, a sort of half-chosen incompetence at sorting out the apparent polarities: desire and fellow-pilgrimhood, which connected and confused man and woman. He shared with and inherited from Stammer Jack the habit of confusing lust with tolerance, but then between peaks of sexual frenzy, of being frankly bewildered.

Urban and urbane men in New York applied themselves to the mystery. In Jacko's tradition, though, you knew you couldn't get anywhere with the mystery, and you went away and drank instead.

In New York, the Jacko in the cherrypicker bucket had actually been encouraged in these habits. Irrespective of his marriage of a year and a half and the bride named Lucy he had brought with him from Australia, he had found time to become a novelty in a city whose women normally praised men of a different sensibility from Jacko's. He was pleased to find himself so anachronistically incorrect that someone like Dannie had either never met anyone like him, or even, perversely, against all the rules, admired him for the integrity of his brashness. (I'm not being hard — I suppose I'm trying to be an anthropologist.)

Jacko himself both exulted in and was frightened by Dannie. He frequently noted both to me and to others that you didn't know why these New York girls wasted time on you. He feared they might have a missionary fervour, a task of consciousness-raising in mind.

* * *

The cherrypicker was ten floors up now, its great lazy forearm traversing the face of largely opaque or draped windows. The cable handler was coiling cable on the floor of the bucket so that it could in turn be played out into whatever apartment they were successful in penetrating. If any, of course, given all this stoically tinted and draped glass.

It was not until about the eleventh floor that Jacko began to think, This cherrypicker thing might return a dividend. At that height he was more prepared to focus on the face of the building than on the gulf below, and was gratified to be swung across a window which gave him a view into a kitchen.

The kitchen was rather well done — copper fittings, blond panelling, microwave. A woman of indeterminate age held the door jamb with one hand and was calling down the corridor to somebody. The primal mother summoning to nutriment.

—Ah, murmured Jacko as the yearning for such a maternal call struck him.

—What'd you say? asked the despised cameraman.

—I was thinking of my old mum, Jacko confessed.

—Okay, said the despised cameraman.

Now a living room on the twelfth. Wonders beyond the glass. Very heavy mittel-European sofas. Poles or Hungarians dwelt there for sure. A gilt-framed still life. Could be Corot, only this wasn't a Corot district.

This was a district chosen by Jacko as one of mid-rent and mid-intent, the sort of building whose tenants and owners did not have a law firm on a retainer. Ordinary, genial, tentative New Yorkers.

By the thirteenth floor Jacko loved this middle class tenement for yielding him so much already. For warming to him. For distracting him from the space below and from the curmudgeonly technician with whom he shared the cherrypicker.

—And the Snowy River riders on the mountains
         make their home,
      Where the river runs those giant hills between;
      I have seen full many horsemen since I first
         commenced to roam,
      But nowhere yet such horsemen have I seen.

This time Fartfeatures said nothing. For Jacko could hear an echo of Dannie's fluent, muscular commands coming through the despised cameraman's earphones.

—We're doing the intro, said the cameraman.

—The name's Jacko, Jacko reminded him.

But the cameraman ignored him. Bending over his viewfinder, he said, On the nod.

Durkin was telling Jacko the same thing through the nodule in his ear.

—Intro five seconds, said Durkin from the studio eight blocks south and two blocks west of the bucket.

Jacko counted in his head and then the cameraman gave a marginal, negligent nod. Jacko knew he thought, This is just light television anyhow. Who gives a damn about crass morning timing. Jacko smiled with a poisonous brilliance therefore. Just for the mongrel. Just for the drongo bastard.

—Good morning all you tousled, dressing-gowned,

somnolent and bemused inhabitants of Babylon-upon-Hudson, Jacko began. This is the Australian invader, Jacko Emptor. The nightmare of the dawn. Weary of doormen who lack the correct sporting attitudes, I am at the twelfth floor of the Delancey Apartments, and although there doesn't seem to be much of interest going on beyond the glass, I hope to be able to talk my way into the window of someone on the fourteenth floor, which is as high as we can go.

In the nodule in his ear, Jacko heard Dannie briefly conversing with Durkin. They were going first to a shot from the building across the road. Then cut back to the studio for news and an interview with an actor.

—We're off, said the cameraman.

Above him, Jacko could see a male face looking down from a closed window. It was curiously aged and yet firm-chinned and composed. It had the cropped hair which generally went with muscular men.

—Tell the operator to slow down, Jacko ordered the cameraman. See, that window. There. There's a feller.

Casually, Fartfeatures spoke into his mike.

—Stop, fourteenth floor. Ten o'clock.

—Steady as she goes, said Jacko.

They slid a little way past the man's window. He regarded his visitors curiously yet without surprise.

This is the fellow, Jacko knew. The cameraman gave instructions which eased them back until the balustrade of the cherrypicker stood level with the man's window.

—We're live, the cameraman muttered, and Durkin said the same thing into Jacko's ear. Jacko beamed his yokel smile.

—We're fourteen floors up now, he said. Colder than the nether extremity of a witch, and where I come from they never make a morning as braw and mean as this one is.

Dannie would be undercutting shots from the building opposite so that people would see that Jacko Emptor stopped at nothing.

He said, We hang beyond the window glass of an apparently intelligent and communicative male New Yorker. Let's talk to him eh. Let's give her a burl.

New Yorkers were growing accustomed to Jacko's argot, to the idiom of Stammer Jack's unutterably remote cattle duchy. *Give her a burl* was a modest item from Jacko's Australian lexicon.

Jacko turned to the window. He never wore quite as demented a smile as when he was asking for entry. He knocked on the glass by the man's right shoulder. The man nodded a little and looked at him. Indeed, a muscular fellow who wore a T-shirt in a way which made you think of ageing Marine NCOs. America was full of such military types, yet you never spotted an equivalent back home in Oz.

This fellow — a tough, stricken man, Jacko thought, rat-tat-tatting merrily away with kid gloves supplied by Barney's of Seventh Avenue in return for a mention in the credits.

The aged, tough man regarded Jacko's gloved knuckles without prejudice. Jacko leaned towards the inset glass and roared, Good morning, Sir! I'm Jacko Emptor from the Vixen Six Network, making my first airborne attempt at penetrating an American household. Are you a tolerant man, sir? Would you be willing to open your window and admit us to your home?

It was the astounding moment of consent. The man moved warily to open the window lock. Not, however, with the sort of wariness which had causes outside his own body — causes such as that a lunatic in a cherrypicker, a lunatic wearing earmuffs and a porkpie hat, was hammering on your glass. It was more the wariness caused by, say, a boil on the back of the neck.

* * *

And there was the problem now that the window opened out sideways. Jacko and the cameraman and cable handler had to crouch so that it would clear their heads. Jacko played this for comedy, but in the way he had learned: that he did not have to overdo things; that his large, meaty face, his reliably startled eyes, and his silly combination of hat and earmuffs could be depended upon for their own fair efficacy.

When he was a boy he would have tried too hard and people would have disliked him for it. Now he was a man and had put aside the things of boys: he had discovered timing.

His joy in being aware that some twenty-five million people in the eastern United States were now saying to their spouses, He's a lunatic, that Jacko Emptor!, was nothing beside his intimate joy when the man opened up his window.

The wind seemed to have grown in force, in its intent to tear big Jacko away from the gritty, kindly, exposed sill of the husky man in the T-shirt. Jacko nonetheless managed to roar, What a decent feller!

Barely breathing, he launched himself over the balustrade of the cherrypicker bucket. Employing a strong grip, the man in the T-shirt helped him. Higher than any star above Stammer Jack's and Chloe Emptor's cattle station, their son Jacko committed himself ecstatically to the grip of a stranger. It took a lot of wriggling of the hips to get into the man's apartment, a lot of stomach-grinding endeavour, a lot of damage to the fabric of his overcoat, but at no point did Jacko feel terror.

No sooner inside and standing than Jacko had to turn, panting, to receive the camera. But in the act of turning, he learned things he considered, in their way, prodigious. On an early version of a colour television set, which sat in the far corner, Jacko had seen himself enter the dimness of the man's living room. Proof if he needed it that others were parties to his spoliation of hearths. The furniture was of the kind that Jacko had first seen in a June Allyson/James Stewart film set on a Cold War air-force base: one ovoid coffee table, another boomerang-shaped. Both had thin, angled metal legs. The chairs had floral cushions and angular arms and lightly varnished legs. The very look of them evoked images in Jacko's mind of James Stewart's sober, brave, magisterial visage, of June's prehensilely aggrieved lips as her husband took off in a bomber from some desert airstrip to be democracy's sentinel and to crash-land in the Arctic.

There were stores where this sort of thing would be valued, what Jacko thought of as old people's Florida furniture. The big buy of 1955 washed up here to the fourteenth floor, on winter's high tide.

Fartfeatures was more than ready to throw his camera in at Jacko. Jacko kept one eye on the ancient television set to see that Dannie let this camera's jiggling images of hectic entry go out to the viewer.

For stealth, cunning and intrusion were nothing without these confused, jolting, blurred images. A cat burglar saw the world this way. Dannie refused to make the naive choice of the smoother images from Camera Two on the roof across the road.

As the despised cameraman tumbled in, Jacko handed back the camera, looked at its aimed eye, spread his arms and sang, We're in! The cable handler had also arrived, making the most athletic entry of the three of them, and was uncoiling cable out of the cherrypicker and into the living room, to give the camera the chance to roam. He pulled the window all but shut to keep the vicious air out.

In his ear, Jacko heard Durkin state that that was it. Dannie might have cut it there even if the studio hadn't told her. The belief was people would hang on in celebration of Jacko Emptor's one-hundred-and-forty-foot-high success and deliverance. They would want to know, above all, who this husky and impassive old man was.

Shivering, Fartfeatures said, Okay. We're dead.

—Oh mate, said Jacko to the man in the T-shirt, you wouldn't have any coffee, would you?

Jacko's host put his hand to his throat. A robot's voice, very mechanical, electronically spiky and utterly without intonation, answered.

—I can get you some, it said. Can't drink it myself. Had you been there, and been more interested in Jacko than the cameraman was, you would have thought, Yes, this is an utterly characteristic Jacko smile. It was broad as the yawn of a mastiff on the — for now — untransmitted and therefore unselfconscious dial of Jacko. Jacko — discoverer of new rooms, empowerer of new voices, and native of wide and silent Burren Waters, two hundred miles west of Hector in the remote Northern Territory.

* * *

Jacko and the cameraman, attended at some distance by the cable puller who was now running cable across the floor, amongst the archaic furniture, all followed their host into the hallway and so into the narrow kitchen. There was just enough room here for the three of them. The man bent to a cupboard and found a can of coffee.

—How long since you had the op. eh? Jacko asked. You know, the operation.

The man straightened himself. His hand went to his throat, where Jacko noticed now a small black hole. The fellow had in his fingers a minute microphone which he must, between speeches, conceal in his fist. Every sentence was a deliberate exercise. The fellow hadn't been catatonic at all. He had been concentrating on his breath and the muscles of his diaphragm.

The man said, Six weeks back. I wrote to you a week after the surgeon first pulled the cords. I'm grateful you came.

—Wrote to us?

—Yeah, said the monotone squawk. CBS news.

—Oh shit, mate. We're not CBS news. We're Vixen Six. You know, Basil Sutherland.

The man squared his aged NCO shoulders.

—I wondered why you'd come in a cherrypicker, the man conceded in his unearthly diction.

Jacko said, Haven't you heard of Basil Sutherland?

The biggest bastard ever to come out of Australia. Aside from me eh.

The man raised his hand and said, I don't watch much morning television.

—A proud boast, mate. And I don't blame you. Makes hair grow on the palms of your hands. Why'd you write to the news?

The cameraman said, We're going live again on ten.

—What's your name? Jacko asked the man in a hurried murmur.

—Sondquist, said the man, again raising his hand. Bob.

He had put the electric kettle on and was spooning coffee into a glass plunger. Did he not know that they were going live, or did he not care? The despised cameraman said they were live on the count of two, and tried to dominate Jacko and the man with two strokes of his index finger.

For going live, Jacko cranked up his old, ingenuous Australian smile, a cliché in its own terms, but fresh news on this coastline.

—We're in Mr Bob Sondquist's kitchen, built in the '40s or '50s, I'd say. The era before we average fellers took up cooking and turned it into a fancy activity. As far as I can tell, Bob was expecting us to be someone else with more pretensions. This is a common experience for Vixen Six. He thought we were CBS news, to whom he's apparently written. Why them, Bob?

Bob stood up straight and faced Jacko and resonated.

—I wrote to them about my daughter, Sunny.

There was a little scar tissue on Bob's throat. But

apart from that you could rarely see the aperture, and — given Bob's deft hand movements — barely catch sight of the mechanical device. Jacko did not choose to rush the issue of the daughter Bob had just raised. Never a linear man, he wanted to know all about Bob's means of talk.

—And Bob, you lost your oesophagus, did you, mate?

—It was the larynx I believe, said Bob.

—You'd know, son. Painful operation?

—Had worse, said Bob Sondquist in a flat, urgent, unboastful way. He held up the little mike.

—God bless technology. Are you married, Bob? asked Jacko, the bush vaudevillian. Handy little implement for a spouse, that one. Turn your husband on and off!

But Bob was a straight man.

—My wife departed this life a year after Sunny went missing.

The kettle hooted and Bob switched it off and made the coffee. Through Dannie's microwave dish on the truck far below, Bob Sondquist's deft coffee making reached the morning's millions. He handed a mug to Jacko, who savoured it on behalf of the caffeine-hungry populations of the Atlantic shores.

Bob Sondquist said, I thought I was a goner with this voice box problem, and something happened to make me realize I hadn't done enough about her. I'd gone to Missing Persons and filled out all the papers, but that wasn't enough. And they're useless anyhow. But when I face my wife in the next life, I want to be able to look her squarely in the face and say I tried everything I knew. So CBS was everything I knew.

In his head, Jacko could hear Durkin telling Dannie and himself that this was good stuff.

—Sadly, said Jacko, they're not in business for humanity's sake, Mr Sondquist. Neither are we, but we let you know that upfront. No pretensions with us, Bob. But at least we're here, and the others aren't. Do you have a picture of your daughter?

Sondquist said, In the other room, Mr Emptor.

The cameraman made urgent and peevish circles with his left hand, and Durkin said tenderly in Jacko's ear that they were crossing back to the studio. Jacko told the camera that he would just have his coffee while Mr Sondquist went and got the picture, and that they would come back to Bob Sondquist's apartment soon.

—Over to you Phil, said Jacko sweetly, giving control of the show back to the studio presenter, the so-called *anchorman*, Phil Maloney.

* * *

My wife slept while I watched this from my cherished apartment above Tower Records, on the corner of East Fourth and Broadway. Somewhat like Bob Sondquist, till recently I had not been a morning television watcher. I believed that, like liquor, the flippancy of the medium could only be decently resorted to after sunset, and could only be justified even then by a day of keen endeavours. But Jacko, my friend and a study of mine, had told me the night before that he was going up into the blue-grey air in his cherrypicker.

They have probably never constructed a human august enough *not* to be somehow flattered by being made privy to the smallest video secret. Michael Bickham, the great modernist writer back in Sydney might, perhaps, be proof against such silliness. There would of course also be literary theorists and deconstructionists at NYU who would have contempt for Jacko's high jinks. Yet perhaps they secretly watched him. For the figures showed that some of them must. At least some of the tenured giants of English, History, German, Political Science and Biochemistry must have liked and secretly watched Jacko a lot.

Jacko had been confiding in me shortly after midnight in a restaurant named Le Zinc in Duane Street. I, typically having little resistance to the centripetal pull of Jacko's hectic taste for brotherhood, regularly stayed up with him longer than I should.

And like the rest of his family, Jacko had an heroic liver. A metabolism, he both boasted and complained, which could have been depended upon to de-nature uranium. In Burren Waters there were visible signs of the Emptors' facility with booze. Fifty yards from the back door of their kitchen lay a pyramid of whisky, rum, beer, port and red and white wine bottles begun by Jacko's Liverpudlian grandfather Laurie Emptor in 1927 when he took the Burren Waters cattle leasehold. I knew too that Jacko's father Stammer Jack drank heinous quantities of dark, sugary Queensland rum, Red Mill and Bundaberg.

New York is a fatal city, therefore, for someone with antecedents like Jacko's. Everywhere the atmospheric bar — from the authentic squalid to the squalid chic to the period-varnished-and-mirrored to the unutterably chi-chi and the unconscionable — and never the responsibility afterwards of driving home two hundred miles from the Brahma Breeders Ball in

Hector, as Stammer Jack and his wife Chloe had to do, barefoot in evening dress. Once, rolling their Landrover on the way and waiting with bloodied faces and a last bottle of rum for dawn, they were stuck until some blacks up from the Tanami Desert came along and gleefully helped them get their vehicle upright again so that they could drive home for a steak and eggs breakfast.

In the season in which Jacko proposed to go up in the cherrypicker, and told me about it the night before in Le Zinc, he was under the sort of pressure Laurence Emptor and Stammer Jack had never experienced: to slim down, to present a better image for the young, to look lither. Grandfather Laurie and Stammer Jack had, in any case, lived a more aerobic and strenuous life in the saddle, though Stammer Jack had recently become lazier and begun to muster his cattle by helicopter.

Jacko had never been a gifted horseman, had never wanted to be. To judge from his childhood photographs, he had been a hefty and even soft boy. He had developed muscles exercising with a trainer who came to his loft in Tribeca, but still he readily gained weight. As a distant ambition he spoke of giving up booze, but on a daily basis he relished the bars of Soho and Tribeca, as — I confess — did I. We had become accustomed to drinking together either at mid-to-late afternoon or late at night in some bar or other on that blighted and magical isle. Sometimes we did both sessions on the one day.

I was twenty years older than Jacko, and the angels of abstention were certainly sending their messages to me. So, though I too loved New York for the fact that I could ride or walk home so easily uptown to

East Fourth, always counting in the normal footpad perils, I knew I had to stop these boyish sessions soon, because they were endangering my chemistry. But the end of drinking with Jacko would need to be the beginning of spiritual exercises: the examination of what to make of my career; of my sometimes minuscule, sometimes flaring, never consistent literary fame; of my howling failures; of my generous spouse; and of the occasional eccentric voices (none of them from my homeland, Australia) who said I might one day be worth a Nobel. I knew I would not reach a *modus vivendi* with all that until I gave up at least spirits and possibly wine. And doing so seemed as remote and unlikely as the chastity and penance of Egyptian saints of the sixth century.

In Le Zinc, Jacko and I were, in part, drinking for all the drinking we wouldn't be able to do in the future.

My wife Maureen, who came from an Australian working class family and so was forgiving of long night boozing, had excused herself and already gone home. Jacko's young wife, sipping at white wine, leniently attended him too, although according to Jacko's confidences to me, she made subtle attempts to improve him. It seemed to be Jacko's greatest fear: that women tried — of their nature — to improve men.

Jacko and I were, in fact, the worst sort of inebriates: the kind who did not suffer adequately — at least in the morning-after sense — for their misuse of themselves. To watch Jacko ascend by cherrypicker in the morning, I was no more bleary-eyed than many a sober citizen. Jacko himself was nimble enough to

survive the device, and to handle Bob Sondquist
exactly as Durkin's and Dannie's instincts and broadcasting policies dictated.

* * *

Jacko's wife was only twenty-three and — according
even to his friends — more than he deserved: the
beautiful snow-white Norman child of Northern Italian migrants to Australia, both of them accomplished
musicians. They occasionally turned up on Jacko's
doorstep when they came to New York with Musica
Viva — separately, however, for they were long
divorced.

The first good thing I noticed about Jacko's wife
was that she did not regard television with any particular seriousness. But she seemed quietly to relish
Jacko's tricks just the same.

—A cherrypicker, she had said earlier. That's
the go!

And the word *go*, as uttered by Lucy's lovely,
symmetric lips, would resonate with Australian vowels ancient as *The Man from Snowy River*, evocative
of *The Drover's Wife*. The Australian vowel, which
had waited basking like a lizard on the Australian
littoral, to insinuate itself into the mouths of immigrant children.

—That's the go, Jacko, she was always saying in
public.

This did not seem too strenuous, reforming or
disapproving to me. But to hear Jacko speak sometimes, you would have thought she spent all her time
trying to reconstitute him.

Jacko's mother, Chloe, loved Mrs Jacko, Lucy

(short for Luciana), and sometimes called her on the radio telephone from Burren Waters and asked her when was she going to leave that pisspot of a son of hers.

Sometimes at dawn Lucy went out with Jacko and the camera crew, and stood around in the snow, or else in the harshness of a summer's sunrise, as he performed his stunts. I had an image of her dancing away from the camera but not succeeding in escaping it one Christmas morning, when Jacko delivered snow to a hapless and perhaps over-decorated household in Queens. She seemed to know that a sylph had no place in Jacko's act. Occasionally she made what seemed to me lightly mocking remarks about Dannie, upon whose 'a' she laid a particular weight of nasal mockery. She seemed easy, however, with the idea that the sort of sharp-edged, pretty young women who came ravening up out of communications courses in Syracuse and Brown and Ann Arbor would be enchanted by Jacko's loud good cheer and by his widespread stardom in the matter of hard-talking entry.

I admit that none of these perceptions of mine necessarily counted for much: in private she may have outlaid fearsome energies on amending Jacko. It was simply that her public demeanour in bars and in restaurants, or when you visited their own home as she cooked with Jacko, or as she emerged ill-rested from their bedroom to greet you for breakfast on a Sunday morning after one of Jacko's all night Soho adventures, never showed the faintest trace of bitterness.

There might, at such a time, be small blue triangles under her clear eyes. Too many cigarettes had put them there — she came of a generation of Australian schoolgirls who nearly all smoked, even though only a fragment of the boys did. Sometimes we'd discussed what that fact meant about Australia and boys and girls. I had for example been writing something for the *New York Times Color Magazine* on the question of whether Australia's reputation as a South Africa for women was well founded. I tried to encompass anecdotal material from my own daughter's history and from Lucy Emptor's related experience. And I thought of other Australian women, of the great barefooted matriarch of Burren Waters, Chloe Emptor, dam of Jacko whose sire was Stammer Jack. It was an invidious situation, of course, writing such a piece: I was like a German trying to prove I liked Jews; an Israeli trying to prove that Palestinians were often treated with every courtesy.

But that's another story.

Mrs Jacko — Lucy Emptor — was rarely seen to have had enough sleep or enough oxygen, but she was of an age where it didn't make a dent in her splendour. This wife who — according to Jacko's confiding word — harried him in secret, smiled girlishly in bars at midnight and said, A cherrypicker. That's the go.

In a way that made the heart turn over.

I couldn't see any of it as wifely tyranny, but was always assured by Jacko that it was.

*   *   *

Jacko and the despised cameraman helped themselves to more of Bob Sondquist's coffee. After the cold ordeal of their rise to the fourteenth floor, it was very sweet. They took the coffee back to the living room, for Jacko wanted more gesturing room for when they went live again. Bob Sondquist followed them indirectly, having gone away to collect the framed picture he now carried in his right hand. He made as if to show the picture to Jacko, but Jacko was *cinema verité* incarnate and told him to hang onto it until they were *on*.

—Jesus, mate, this is ripper coffee.

Jacko noticed Bob Sondquist turned his daughter's framed picture in his hands, as if any given inch of the frame were too hot to touch for more than an instant.

When — at Fartfeatures' command and at Durkin's voice in his ear — Jacko was back on, he said, Okay Mr Sondquist, show us all this face of your daughter's which is beneath the attention of more reputable networks.

The photograph Bob Sondquist displayed to the camera that morning was of an oval-faced, athletic looking girl of eighteen years or so. Her status as a lost woman caused the photograph to make its own demands on Jacko at the spot and on me at the Broadway corner of East Fourth. The fact she was long gone meant she couldn't be written off as an average visage.

In part her father's daughter, she carried her father's face but in a different form. It seemed full of an edgy goodwill. You could not imagine her at any age greeting the dawn cherrypicker with the composure her father had shown at his window. She looked competent somehow, like a child who ironed her own clothes. Jacko thought of that face as good at softball, which he had, in the past, gingered up his viewers by calling *a neutered version of cricket*. All in all, if you didn't have honest Bob Sondquist's word, you wouldn't have thought it the credible face of a lost woman.

Bob Sondquist said in his monotone, straight into the lens, Has anybody seen my daughter?

* * *

Hearing this simple, electronically burred appeal, what Jacko thought of as a strange rash of compassion prickled his flesh and caused him to shiver inside his overcoat. For there was a lingering reflex, a frontier side to his nature, the side he exploited for the sake of hooking an audience yet which he believed falsely he had grown out of. His body *was* taken now, at the sight of Sunny Sondquist, by a biochemical impulse to send out horsemen searching, to use the mustering helicopter flown by Stammer Jack's mad friend, the American named Boomer, who had once flown with Air America and who could fly for miles at barely ten feet of altitude above Burren Waters' pasturage. A brief image of Sunny Sondquist lost out amongst the grey sand, grevillea, rubberbush, perishing for water, seized the screens at the forefront of his brain, his own rebel television.

He expunged this useless impulse though, the desire to call on stockmen and Wodjiri tribespeople to go searching. The canyons where this face had lost itself were not readable in the same way as the water courses west of Burren Waters.

Jacko said, She's a lovely girl, Bob.

—Went missing about five years ago. Then she turns up with some guy at her elbow while I'm in

Veterans Hospital. That was six weeks ago. On my back and without a voice. She just said, Hello and that this was her fiance and she was happy and that she had to go. She looked scrawny and I wanted an address. So I got a note pad and pushed it at her. Even threw it after her when she started to go. But she just went.

There was as much of a glitter of tears in Bob Sondquist's eye as Dannie, and Durkin back at Vixen Six, could have desired of a tough confused old man.

—She wasn't under any threat from this man? asked Jacko softly, and Durkin said in his ear, Lovely mate.

—She seemed a bit far off, and she wouldn't say anything much when the nurses came along. Thinner. A lot thinner than this picture. But the same face.

Bob Sondquist buffed the glass so that millions of viewers would more clearly see the face. Jacko did him one better, taking the framed photograph from him and putting it close up against the camera.

—Let's get this focused, he told the cameraman in a sort of genial vengeance. Come on, we got that focused? You have to excuse the cameraman, ladies and gentlemen. A New Zealander. His mind's on the ewes.

This was a running joke he had with his audience. But he did not enjoy it. He was still full of what he thought of as a rootless concern. Sunny Sondquist's homely face put all his morning clowning out of key.

At Durkin's instruction he went into the if-anyone-recognizes-this-girl sequence . . . call us at . . .

Fartfeatures was signalling him Dannie's windup, and Durkin was saying, Studio cross, Jacko. Throw to Maloney. See you in the Perugia.

—Well, it's goodbye for now to Bob Sondquist our host, solid citizen and good maker of coffee. Everyone hopes you see your daughter again soon, Bob.

The astringent desire to find her had passed now from Jacko's imagination.

—Yes, Bob interrupted in his quacking, electronic voice. It's been good to see you Jacko. A real upper.

—Okay, boomed Jacko. And if you're out there, Sunny, contact your old man eh love? Well, I don't think me and the New Zealand cameraman want to try the cherrypicker again. I think we'll take the lift, which you blokes cunningly call the *elevator*. But listen one and all. Let this be a lesson eh. Just because you live above the tenth floor, it doesn't mean you're beyond the reach of Jackoman.

Then, with a flourish, he said, Back to you in the studio, Phil.

As much as he could manage it, Jacko Emptor stayed away from the studios and offices of Vixen Six. The air Maloney the anchorman exuded, of being a refugee from a better class of broadcasting, ran counter to the energy and peculiar vision of *Morning Manhattan*'s executive producer, Ed Durkin; counter too to the serious foolery of talking one's way into people's homes, and bringing a camera crew with you to document the encounter.

In Jacko's eyes, by affecting the gravitas of a serious commentator, Maloney managed only to make himself look silly, like some failed viceroy who wears a bicorne hat and braid, missing the point in a mad colony whose rhythms and colours he cannot see. But one of Basil Sutherland's executives had given him a big three-year contract, and so Durkin had to use him.

In Jacko's persistent absence from the studios, a secretary answered mail and telephone enquiries from Jacko's admirers, and if he needed to see Durkin, they met at the Perugia Bar, Durkin's office-away-from-the-office where he spent most of the day, across the road from Vixen Six headquarters. Durkin organized his evening show, *Live Wire*, from a bank of telephones at the Perugia Bar. Segment producers and research assistants kept in touch with him by these means, or else ran material to him from across the street.

After producing *Morning Manhattan* at what Jacko called sparrow's fart, Durkin was usually in the Perugia by nine-thirty, smoking and taking his first beer of the day. Imported: Becks or Dos Equis or Swan Lager. American beer, he said, was like making love in a canoe: fucking close to water.

Here Jacko would meet him at about a quarter to ten to discuss the tasks Jacko would perform for *Live Wire* over the weekend. For although Jacko had escaped the cattle station, he had not escaped cattlemen's hours.

Today, though, Jacko did not visit the Perugia first. He surprised the office staff of Vixen Six by appearing amongst them. The young researchers and production people, brisk, dark, pretty women with glittering eyes, cried out in genial mockery.

—Grab him before he vanishes, ladies and gentlemen! The first sighting of the Great White Australian Marsupial! Who let in the Australian Pope? Et cetera.

Jacko's routine fan mail was, some of it, surpassing strange. Jacko once showed me a letter which began, *My name is Delores and I am a beautiful, loving and free of drug woman from Bensonhurst, NY. I would like to meet you because I think you are boyish and free, and I am girlish and free with two lovely children . . .*

The secretary herself was a single mother who came in every day on the train from Brewster. She felt — despite all the evidence of Jacko's leniency — that she could not risk calling Jacko *Jacko* for fear it might take bread and milk from her children's mouths.

—Mr Emptor, she cried as he walked in. The

switchboard has taken nearly four hundred calls about that girl . . .

He had long since given up the battle to get her to call him by his first name.

—Call me Jacko, he had frequently cried. I'm not a bloody lawyer, love, eh. Well I was, but I recovered.

For Jacko had gone straight from law school into radio. Not serious radio, he insisted, but mayhem radio.

Or else he'd yell at her, Can you see ghosts, love? Mr Emptor was my grandfather. He died in Dun Rootin' in Alice Springs eight years ago.

Four hundred calls. Four hundred people who wanted Jacko's approval, who would see phantoms for him and try to please him — if they lacked any truth to utter — with lies.

The single-mother secretary said that she had put his calls into two piles, little sheaves of paper. A big one was of calls that seemed to lack substance. A very small one gave concrete information. He surprised her by taking both wedges of messages into his hands and taking them through into the cubicle he rarely used, and sitting at the desk he sat at for perhaps thirty-seven minutes per annum.

She had done a ripper job of sorting out the messages, he told her.

In the big pile, he encountered *For enlightenment see John VII, 5, 6–7.* Then, *Ms Horowitz, 203-456-1757, wants help tracing her niece.* Or *Francoise Lachapelle: saw Mr Sondquist's daughter in a dream, Called out to her: the name of Pixley Falls State Forest, Upstate New York.* Yes, Francoise in the forest with a camera crew: a whole morning-show of fame as Francoise frowned and farted round and said that the aura was strong in one place and dimmer in another, but the girl was definitely here somewhere amongst the trees. Mind you, it showed Francoise gave the medium of television its proper weight. Australians took television casually, as a recreation. Americans knew it was life itself, that it defined reality, it was the generating light of God's countenance turned to you. Without its smile, its nod, its sanctifying grace, its infinite mercy for the obscure and the unlovable, there was no existence.

Mr Chester Blaze, 11723 Avenue B, Apt 822 says tell you on camera location of Sondquist girl. From Bridgeport, Connecticut, to Baltimore, Maryland, such squalid offers had arrived by the dozen. All of them desired Jacko to turn up on their doorstep with a cameraman and a truck with a microwave dish. Australians would tell you these things if you promised *not* to invade their hearths! Australians simply weren't serious subscribers to Andy Warhol's dictum about fifteen-minute fame.

Jacko would not be human, however, if he had not somehow been flattered by the demented love these messages represented. Chloe Emptor herself would never have sent him messages of quite such seamless adoration.

However, they were useless for poor, squawking, possibly moribund Bob Sondquist's quest for his daughter.

There were three messages the single mother had graded as of any value. One was from a woman in New Haven who said that her son had gone out for a year with the Sondquist girl, and that she and her son were willing to help in any way. There was simply a chaste number attached, no demand for morning glory.

A second message was from the secretary of an organization called PAW — Protect Abducted Women. Thousands of women were disappearing, she said. The statistics exceeded by far the numbers for breast cancer. PAW could provide figures and case histories.

The third was from a man in Montcalm, New Jersey. He said that he had recently spent time in California with his daughter, who lived in a trailer park off the Riverside Freeway near San Bernardino. He had seen what he was sure was the Sondquist girl jogging around the caravan park at regular hours. The tail of the message gave it a kind of authenticity. *Tell her father she looks a lot thinner than in photograph.*

Jacko went into the outer office, put the wedge of her discards down on the desk in front of the secretary, boomed out some further praise at her — in which adjectives like *bonzer* and *ripper* recurred to a degree some Australians thought strained — and put the three messages she had winnowed out into his breast pocket.

* * *

Durkin was a dark-complexioned, wiry man. He claimed to be the descendant of Irish tinkers who came to Australia with a circus. It was very likely the truth.

Jacko found him, as expected, at the Perugia, a two-thirds expended glass of beer streaked with froth at his right hand. Durkin talked on one of the bar telephones and wrote notes to himself on a page of a little yellow pad. When he hung up, he ripped the note he had just written off the pad and stuck it to the surface of the bar. Sometimes these little squares of yellow adhesive paper patterned the bar all through the lunch hour. Beer, cocktails and wine were served amongst them, and lunchers who worked in less frenetic businesses than Durkin's were foolish enough to accept them as part of the Perugia's colour.

—Jesus, mate, Durkin cried. The cherrypicker! Great bloody idea.

Durkin was always too busy with the overall production of *Morning Manhattan* to enquire beforehand into the tactics to be used in any particular instance of what they both chastely called, like a couple of Mormon missionaries or like pollsters, *doorknocks.* Jacko liked to surprise him.

—Got to be honest, said Jacko. I put up the idea of some alternative form of getting into places. I was thinking more of rappelling by rope down from the roof, and I thought I might call the Marines and get them to teach me eh. Dannie came up with the cherrypicker on the ground that she didn't want to see me as the world's biggest dollop of strawberry bloody jam. So we're putting off the rappelling till later. Although, in the event, we might make it a bloody big sturdy bosun's chair instead of just a rope.

Even that of course would be terrifying, though we, his public and friends, had been reassured a little by the ease, very nearly the grace, with which he had been able to move out of the cherrypicker and into Bob Sondquist's living room. There would not, however, always be a muscular cancer sufferer to lift him in over the window sill.

—Fucking fantastic idea anyhow, said Durkin.

He was dialling again. In between talking with a *Live Wire* segment producer, he kept an ear pitched to Jacko's plans for the coming weekend's filming.

Jacko said, That poor old bugger with the squawk box . . . It'd be great to make him happy. Look, you and I have both had problems getting along with women . . . .

Durkin was in fact contemplating a third marriage.

—Now maybe Sunny ran away but I don't believe it. I reckon you can bet this kid Sunny's been abducted. She might've visited Bob in hospital, but she had a bloke with her — in my opinion, a captor. All right. The argument is that taking a woman off the street and using her and keeping her a prisoner and maybe killing her is just the acting-out of the way all us bloody old patriarchs really feel . . . You know, that the fellers who make women disappear are just acting out the usual male figures of speech . . . .

—Yeah, said Durkin. But that's all bulldust.

—Exactly. *We* are not the killers. We're not saints, but not killers. Some of the people who hide behind respectable language, maybe they're the killers.

—What are you talking about? asked Durkin.

—There are women, young women, going missing all over the country. Why don't we concentrate on one of them eh? This bloke Sondquist's daughter. I've got this crowd called PAW who're fighting the battle. We could talk to them. Then I've got a kid who dated her. And I've got a bloke who claims to have seen her. No, I've got half a thousand buggers who claim to have seen her. But I've got a feller who rings true. So what if we took this one missing

woman? Dying father, regretful boyfriend, last sighter. And we try to find out what in the name of God
happened to her eh? Something we could get passionate about, mate, and the passion would shine out.
We can tell people we're going to shake the tree over
this one. We're going to find out what in the hell
happened to *one* woman.

—Jesus, Jacko. You're sounding a bit like a
missionary.

—No. Not at all. Listen, I'm not saying I'm doing
this because I'm noble, and television is such a noble,
stick-up-the-arse sort of medium. I'm doing this
because I can. And because, honest to God, I found
old Sondquist very poignant. With his Donald-bloody-
Duck voice.

Durkin finished his beer. The barman who'd been
employed mainly to look after the *Live Wire* crowd
in the mornings was along with another bottle and
refilled Durkin's glass.

—What if you find her and all that's happening is
she's hiding from her old man?

At this stage Jacko stood back from the bar — or
at least I presume he did — with his customary hold-
things-till-I've-spoken gesture, his enormous palm out
towards Durkin.

—Worst case, mate, worst case, I admit. But then,
it'd seem that if she's just hiding from him, how come
people like PAW and the police can't find her? And
besides, I reckon she's not hiding from him. He's a
straight shooter. A battler.

A battler. Ultimate Australian praise. A battler is
one who is buffeted by life and left with a squawk
for a voice, but still has energy to greet camera crews
at dawn.

The way Durkin and Emptor spoke to each other, the frank confession of opportunistic sentiment, even of pride in venal motives, was in a sense part of Basil Sutherland's policy. Or at least it was what Sutherland's organization had employed them for. No nonsense about the First Amendment and the holiness of information. The Trinity spoke nobly and delivered sludge. Vixen Six delivered sludge and exulted in it, confessing to it on and off screen. That was why Vixen was occasionally sombrely referred to as a new voice, a new style. Television was the most disreputable, unworthy, sluttish muse of anyone's national soul, and only Vixen came clean about that fact.

Being Australian and being, therefore, able to imagine a time before television — Jacko's first billion heartbeats had occurred thousands of miles from its lurid eye — Durkin and Jacko knew that it was a non-essential, frivolous and captious. Not history, but a parasite on history's arse. Basil Sutherland villainously, some said, seemed to wish to undermine the magisterial poses which characterized the major networks. The mission of *Morning Oz* had been, as now the mission of *Morning Manhattan* and *Live Wire* was: to demonstrate the crooked, gap-toothed, unbuttoned, leering fatuity of the medium.

And Durkin and Emptor . . . never happier than here at the Perugia planning the gipsy antics. The world of women which allured and bemused them in that peculiar Australian way safely relegated to the other end of the telephone. Lucy at home in Thomas Street, her Norman splendour frowsed and smudged by sleep. And they with tricks up their sleeves, viewers to be beguiled and caused to scratch themselves absently in sudden conviction of the world's stunning ghastliness.

So, for the sake of casual mischief and fraternity with Bob Sondquist, and in the belief that certain things shouldn't befall women — although perhaps it was good for Vixen Six that occasionally they did — Jacko got permission from Durkin to put on hold a segment about a talcum powder heiress's decision to endow an institute which researched the paranormal in pets, particularly the capacity of cats to see ghosts. Instead, he would spend Saturday interviewing the callers. He would fly to California with Dannie and a camera crew early Sunday morning and, with the aged sighter in tow, hit the caravan park off the Riverside Freeway later that day.

The world was his circus.

Even before the Sondquist business, a pattern had
been set between Jacko and me. It seemed to be one
lacking in potential danger. We would meet at mid-
to-late afternoon in a bar in West Broadway called
the Odeon. The Odeon was a fashionable restaurant
for young people, but at mid-afternoon it was nearly
empty. The bar itself, the actual altar of wood and
chrome, had been bought at auction from some older,
harder establishment and re-assembled here. It was
less hard-edged and shining-white than the rest of the
place, and I was comfortable with it. We sat there
facing the bottles — not at a table — like two old
Sydney proles: wharfies or truck drivers.

Here we exchanged our unlikely confidences, and
I would hear much of the thorns and exaltations of
Jacko's life. Jacko delivered his secrets readily to me,
on the old and perhaps tired grounds that we were
mates and could rely on each other.

Here I heard for example how he had fallen for
the younger of two exquisite sister-astrologers called
the Logans, who did the stars together on his morning show in Australia. She had responded to him
because, she told him, he was in her stars, and her
sister had found him there too, so that confirmed his
suitability. For a time he was enchanted by the way
the elder sister lunched and dined with the younger

and himself, attended galas, travelled — a senior white witch authorizing his passion for the junior.

But the stars which bless can also burn. Some nights the younger Logan, authorized by astral signs, would avoid him, the two sisters sitting indoors together, not answering his ringing, his calls. Then, all at once, he no longer appeared in what they saw of the heavens.

An extraordinary tale of sister love or malice.

—I'll write a book about it one day, he told me, giving up his attempt to explain the complexities.

By the time I heard these things in the Odeon, the Logan sisters, against whom Chloe used to rail, were married and leading sober lives amongst the eucalyptus trees in Sydney's northern suburbs. Between them they ran a public relations company which took no account — in its advice to clients — of the position of the constellations.

After the sisters had locked him out of their apartment, leaving him weeping in the street for the younger sister, after (to use Jacko's unlikely term) a period of purgation in which the sisters continued to enter the set and effervescently reduce the unknowable to a few flippant items, and after a period in which he did not drink or eat red meat or go to parties, he encountered Lucy, who was promoting an art show on his morning program — tall, pleasant, intelligent and full of good will. Of course he had found since marriage what he sometimes tentatively described as ill will. But no one in New York had any sympathy for his claims. He had pursued her, sensing salvation in her equability and sensuality. He had gone to tremendous trouble to soothe her just suspicions of him, and had made a set of exuberant gestures: a limo so full of roses that they tumbled out on the footpath when the back door was opened; a plane which towed her name across the sky in the day's last light above an open air performance of *Così Fan Tutte* at the Sydney Domain.

—LUCYLUCYLUCYLUCY, said the banner, but, sensible girl that she is, she resisted the apparent imperative of her name scrawled upon the dusk. Until, after every assurance he could think to utter, at last she consented.

* * *

For the sake of making more sense of our conversations in the Odeon, I began to watch *Morning Manhattan* as often as I could. I had noticed that the public are often more interested in anecdotes behind the novel than they are in the finished work itself. In the same spirit I watched *Morning Manhattan* for the tales behind those segments Durkin and Jacko called *doorknocks*, and I listened too for anecdotes about the notorious *Live Wire*.

In this way I came to hear of the significant weekend, the one after Jacko invaded Bob Sondquist's apartment and publicly devoted himself to finding the girl, or else to finding out what befell her.

Jacko had first revisited the scene of the revelation for *Live Wire*'s purposes, doing another interview with Bob Sondquist. The reminiscences of a banal parenthood spent on sundry dismal military bases from California to Utah to Florida, where Bob had done his service for the nation and raised Sunny. In the end Durkin told Jacko all this would have to be edited down, since people could only put up with so much of that squawking; you could more or less hear the surgical knife in it.

Then, for hours throughout the Saturday morning of that weekend, Dannie worked with Bob and an identikit man. Dannie, said Jacko, was remarkable to watch at these moments. Normally frantic for the world to fall into her lap, Dannie worked on Bob and the picture with a weird patience, easing forth a line here and there, like a long-suffering nurse. A thin, be-spectacled but unremarkable face emerged as that of the man who had come with Sunny to Bob's mute bedside.

But at least, said Dannie, who knew how to use a visual resource, it was something graphic to top and tail the interview with.

A little after noon, Dannie, the cameraman Clayton and Jacko travelled by car to New Haven to see Sunny Sondquist's former boyfriend. They spent a dismal late afternoon in a poor white suburb in New Haven, far from the graces of Yale, interviewing the young man. On television he appeared to be a cock-sure stocky boy, a student of accountancy who lived with an anxious mother. A good talker, he knew the sort of mixture of small talk and particularity the medium favoured. He explained that he had met Sunny in New York when she was sixteen. She had lived there with her parents — Mr Sondquist had taken a job with a security company. Sunny disliked New York, since it was so hugely different from most of the other places where she had lived. She wanted to go to one of the University of California campuses. He had asked her how she would pay for it, especially the first, expensive year when she would not be a California resident and would need to pay out-of-state tuition fees. She said that her father had put aside money for that. She spoke glowingly of her father.

The young man (perhaps to please his mother) repeatedly said what a nice girl she was. But far too shy for him, he said with a false Jacko-esque confidence, as if since he had last seen Sunny he had concentrated purely on robust, rowdy women.

Yet at last a softness entered his face and he said, She used to spell all the time.

—Spell? asked Jacko.

—Yes. We'd be waiting for the train to New York, and you know how conversation dies out between people. Well, she'd start spelling. It was a nervous habit, like biting her nails.

—What would she spell?

—Any difficult word that came into her head. *Mischievous* and *aggregation* and *ligature* — any word like that. It was a habit of hers.

—*Aggregation*. Her father didn't tell us that, said Jacko.

—I think her father saw it as a bad habit.

The *Live Wire* crew did not finish until early evening. Dannie had arranged that they would stay in a hotel in New Haven overnight. Then at dawn they would fly in a small chartered plane to Newark, collect the elderly man who claimed to have sighted the Sondquist woman, fly with him to Los Angeles, and drive him south-west on the dreary freeways to the mobile-home park near San Bernardino where he could give his version of his sighting of Bob Sondquist's daughter.

My wife Maureen always presumed — perhaps on the basis of suspicions Lucy confessed to her — that Jacko had probably already been unfaithful to Lucy.

His infamous record with the astral sisters fed that idea. But during an Odeon meeting in the week following the San Bernardino expedition, Jacko unburdened himself to me about Dannie in the manner of a man marginally holding to his line.

Dannie had a drink with him that night in New Haven, that most un-erotic of cities, and told him that she felt an emotional and professional attachment to him, a rugged devotion of the profoundest nature. She told him she intended to have him. She intended to continue to be his producer in both the morning and the *Live Wire* segments, and he would be her lover. She would wait until he had come to terms with the idea, but he should know that everywhere they went to film a *Live Wire* segment, she would wait after dinner for two hours in her room. After that, to hell with him! She would sleep. He wasn't to think she couldn't sleep under those circumstances. She damn-well could. She wasn't a trembling child any more, said twenty-five-year-old Dannie.

Jacko did not come from a tradition where women proposed the terms so directly or applied the leverage so vigorously. In the Odeon he drank his vodka and blinked.

—I said I've got this wife Lucy, and I want to be loyal. And she said, You won't last with Lucy. You and I are television people. And then she said something that really scared me. She said that she was going to write a journal of our relationship, and that when it was finished, she would give it to me, and I could learn about myself from it. That's what these American women are like. It's not enough just to go for a mindless bloody tumble. You have to *learn* something from it. But she's a great little woman though eh. And smart as buggery.

That Saturday night, by his own account, Jacko had not slept till perhaps three in the morning.

—I locked myself in my room with my bloody channel-changer. Even after the two hours had gone, I couldn't sleep for thinking. I'm sure she was asleep right enough. She would have looked at her watch and said, Okay, he isn't showing. Time to get some brain sleep. She's like that. People like her run the Israeli Air Force.

He had risen haggard, meeting bright-eyed Dannie in the lobby. She behaved not a whit like a rejected woman. She did not seem to read his non-compliance as rejection. It was morning now, and they were to go about their jobs.

—Then we picked up this old bloke at Newark, and he was so excited about going out to see his daughter again — we'd given him this open return-ticket — and he was so well-mannered and grateful to Dannie. And I thought, you don't know what sort of fire-eater you're talking to, mate.

—The image of her sitting up with her watch hurt, said Jacko, like a stone bruise. And the old man was a distraction. He said something which made them certain he was genuine. He said this girl he'd seen jogging had muttered as she ran. She'd run past him and he'd heard her.

—When I asked him what she had been muttering, he said it was something like the alphabet.

Once they landed in California, Jacko put on a golf shirt and they all climbed into a helicopter and swung inland, the stained bowl of air between the Pacific coast and the San Bernardino Mountains crowded with skittering machines like their own.

—In Southern California, said Jacko, even the bloody dentists own helicopters. *Especially* the bloody dentists!

They stood in the sun on the outskirts of San Bernardino, within sound of the thunder of the freeway, and introduced on camera the old man from New Jersey, who stood in the entry way of the trailer park. And the old man, so transparently honest and so pleased with his place in history, said that he had seen the girl jogging, and that he'd been aware that she was muttering to herself. Like praying aloud, he told the camera.

—Such a lovely old bloke, Jacko told me in the Odeon. And it's bloody ridiculous, but my brain was full of images of Dannie waiting, and let me tell you, *déshabillé* played its bloody part.

By noon, Jacko had a sense that the search was well-launched, and he confirmed that sense by making doorknocks among the trailer homes.

—The trailer-home park! he expatiated in the Odeon. The world's successful answer to the cost of conventional housing, but thank Christ I don't live in one eh.

As he went on his way down the avenues and laneways, Clayton filmed him from a distance, so that trailer householders would have few grounds for shyness or complaint. A number of people were very pleased to say they hadn't seen Sunny, except at last one middle-aged man spoke with something like the same sort of certainty as the old man.

—She runs here sometimes, he told Jacko, but she doesn't live here.

When Jacko asked him how did he know, he said he saw a man drop her off and wait for her. A nondescript vehicle, a nondescript man. No particular colour, the car. Dust-coloured.

—I'm colour-blind anyhow, the man confessed. She wore a tanktop too. Was skinny. Had a birthmark on her shoulder.

So sweetly did the universe seem to direct Jacko to Sunny Sondquist, such pleasant and self-validating witnesses emerging from the masses of the demented, that Jacko forgot Dannie's tormenting proposition and surrendered himself to the exaltation of his trade. To be in California, with the smutty sun on your face, and making such discoveries on one's own behalf and on behalf of the squawking battler Bob Sondquist.

—Last time I saw her, the middle-aged man had told Jacko, she was jogging along saying, A-N-O-D-Y-N-E.

Anodyne.

—Will we find the Anodyne Kid? Jacko asked his audience.

He was confident in his own brotherly intentions and in assured success. *Live Wire* was seen in San Bernardino. Witnesses, some of them truthful, would emerge.

And he would not be made a fool of by anyone other than Dannie.

— But do you *really* care whether you find her or not? I asked Jacko over a post-Odeon dinner at the Grand Ticino, a cellar restaurant, closer to my place than Jacko's, and one of our favourites. Fettucine Alfredo and Pinot Grigio were succulent in the Ticino's little cellar, with stills from a movie it had starred in displayed on its walls.

—Jesus mate, Jacko breathed to me there. I'm
going to deliver her in triumph eh. To old Bob
Sondquist's window. By cherrypicker.

* * *

Vixen Six always let him fly back Sunday night on
Metro Grand, on a plane which was a cross between
a hotel and a piano bar. In the stern of the aircraft
there were two bedrooms. Jacko always booked one
of these.

Dannie stayed on in Los Angeles to research the
Anodyne Kid story and others she was working on at
Durkin's orders.

From a phone on board the plane, Jacko called
Bob Sondquist.

—Listen, Bob mate, why didn't you tell us your
daughter spelled things?

Sondquist squawked in his pained monotone.

—I didn't know she still did that. I thought she'd
grown out of it.

—But a feller not much younger than you told me
he saw someone like her spelling while she ran.

Sondquist became so excited that Jacko could hear
him struggling to achieve intonation.

—Proves she's still the same kid! The same exact
poor little tyke.

Now Jacko could hear Bob sobbing. Jacko wondered what was the freight of those tears? The weight
of what remembered events had started them? On
the cellular phone at great altitude, the tears sounded
to Jacko like an exclusion, the turning of a shoulder.

—Where is she then? said Bob's robotic voice,

under threat from further unutterable anguish. If she's still spelling . . .

Jacko did not either answer or press him, and said goodnight. Then he sat, ready for sleep, drinking malt whisky in the bar of the plane. At first sip, he was approached by a woman in a yellow suit, who identified herself as some sort of executive from CBS. She had, said Jacko, that ageless look: her mysteriously maintained face, a self-made and perhaps even prosthetically-manufactured body.

She said, Hello, you're Jacko Emptor. I'm so-and-so. You've booked the bedroom, and I have a favour. I'm utterly exhausted. I simply have to sleep.

Jacko said that he was sorry, he was exhausted too. He'd been up all night last night, and tomorrow morning had to go straight from the plane to talk his way into someone's door in New Jersey.

—Well, she said, couldn't we share? You know what I'm saying. I'm saying share. Would you permit that?

Jacko thought of those papers that sell in supermarkets: *I conceived Jacko Emptor's child at 37,000 feet*.

But what was more likely, Jacko quickly saw — for it was in her tone, her briskness even when tired — was that they would lie chastely side by side as a matter of course. It was an idea not customarily encountered in the Northern Territory.

—If I had made the smallest suggestion, said Jacko, she would have called it molestation. Maybe she's right eh. I don't know any more.

Bewildered Jacko told her please to take the room. He found the sofas in the bar very comfortable, and there weren't a lot of people aboard. No, please. I'll sleep like a log in a rocking chair! Please . . .

I was sad that I could not tell Maureen the details of Jacko's confusion so confidentially passed on to me, and, above all, of his survival that weekend as loyal spouse of Lucy. Since I couldn't, the question of Jacko's virtue continued to be a debate in our family.

* * *

In the end, Jacko drank himself to sleep and slept till the last moment of his approach to La Guardia, to a different air, the grit of the day in part absorbed by dirty washcloths of cloud and a dawn of sorts.

A car took Jacko to Paterson, New Jersey, picking up on the way through Manhattan the sommelier of the Rainbow Room. They managed to find the microwave truck and the young producer who substituted for the bewildering Dannie. As expected of him, Jacko chose a house at random and made friends with its occupant — a fifty-year-old retrenched foundry worker, a man frank about his afflictions. His wife had left him. He'd just had open-heart surgery and five of his toes amputated because of diabetes.

—Job, Jacko told the audience. A man of sorrows.

Jacko thought twice about giving him the option. The sommelier had brought seven champagnes, French and Californian, for tasting, but perhaps they should find a householder in better health.

—To hell with it! said Job. I wouldn't be able to afford this stuff if I lived to be a hundred.

And so, his bloody gauze-wrapped stump of a foot

rested on his coffee table, the man drank Dom Perignon, Veuve Clicquot Grand Dame, Heidsieck, Roederer, Krug, and said, Ay, I can see why they go for this stuff! And laughing with the man, Jacko felt safe for the moment from the weekend's complicated claims.

My first contact with the Emptors occurred three
years before I went to NYU, and it was not so much
with Jacko as with his mother and with the scene of
his childhood. I was travelling in the winter through
the Northern Territory with a photographer named
Barry Larson, half-Norwegian, half-Jewish, and utterly
Australian, with both a Norseman's and a Hebraic
enthusiasm for desolation. The country either side of
the road from Hector to Burren Waters, part bitumen
and part red soil, is by some standards plain. The
country is graced only by rare hills. There is discon-
solate grey scrub, and clumps of the imported folly
of rubberbush, which someone in the late nineteenth
century had scattered in the belief it was good stock
feed.

In some lights — early in the day and late — the
Burren Waters country is beautiful. But unlike the
full deserts to the south, you could never quite call it
splendid. Even Australian eyes, used to being beguiled
by evaporated landscapes and by what light can do to
them, could find the Emptor country pretty tedious.

On our way through it, I made the mistake of
saying so to Larson. He got the closest to being angry
with me as ever he did in our three-week journey.

—Are you a Pom or something? he asked. Did you
get so buggered up by Wordsworth and Tennyson

and all that stuff at school that you can't even *see* Oz?

I argued no, and I went into praises of the Tanami Desert and of Docker River west of Alice, all of which I'd loved and written about and closely remembered.

But Larson said, waving a hand to the right and then the left of the car, There isn't one yard of it that's the same as another!

At that stage, as we would both discover to our separate griefs, his more furious than mine, he had only some fifteen or sixteen days still to live. He was entitled to all his frantic loves.

* * *

It is hard to over-exaggerate the isolation in which the Emptors lived, in which Chloe and Stammer Jack had their marriage and begot their family. If you imagined the African veldt without villages, then you would come close to it. Before the coming of Stammer Jack's father, the Wodjiri people, whose country it was, had moved across it in small family groups, setting fire to it to flush out game, celebrating and obeying its scattered resources of food and water by keeping on the ancestral track, and cherishing it in luscious song as if it were a place of bounty.

But in a sense it was a vacancy even then, before the rubberbush, though you couldn't tell Larson that. It certainly came close to being a vacancy in these days of the Emptors. In Grandfather Emptor's day, you needed a Wodjiri tracker, a compass and a sextant to get you here. In Stammer Jack's adolescence the two hundred and more miles had been dirt. And now, the last ninety miles were red-grey dirt.

All this was part of Grandfather Emptor's twelve-thousand square mile leasehold, shrunk now through bad seasons and cyclical drought to the best fifteen-hundred square miles!

On the road into Burren Waters homestead, even the occasional white road post was coated in red dust. As for *signs* of the Emptors, a dirt airstrip came first, then a few cattle grids, and then at last the Emptor homestead and encampment. It was a genuine village. The red dust widened to become a square. One side of the square was taken up entirely by the mustering yards and a sales ring where — we would be told — Stammer Jack exhibited his horses to people who came in from all over the Commonwealth, camped and bedded down here in the Emptor piazza for three days, and then drove out, hung-over, towing their chosen yearling.

An aircraft hangar and offices and Boomer's helipad also sat on this side of the red dust square.

On the south side of the piazza were, first, the black or Wodjiri stockmen's married quarters, a series of corrugated iron huts, then a huge cookhouse and kitchen, built in brick — perhaps to defeat the termites of the area. Next a schoolhouse, single white stockmen's quarters, and a set of offices. For bookkeepers were needed in the cattle and quarter-horse business as in any other.

Chez Emptor itself, the homestead, lay in a highly watered patch of green. Palms, ferns, rhododendrons and other shrubs had been encouraged by a heavy outlay of water to grow there. The homestead structure was an enormous bungalow of red brick, the kind fashionable in the '60s in outer suburbs of Sydney and Melbourne. Suitable to the place, however, it had wide, deep verandahs all around.

Larson and I felt like newly arrived troubadours at some minor medieval court. We did not go at once to the big house with its emerald garden, its pyramid of bottles out the back, monument to the Emptor thirst and its television satellite dish, which had come to Burren Waters late in Jacko Emptor's adolescence, taken his soul and transformed him into Manhattan's Jester of Trespass.

We went instead to the offices near the cookhouse. Beyond a screen door we found a large flaccid man with a boozer's pallor, working at an Apple Mac. He had a Celtic complexion, and sun sores on his lips, and his sleeves were buttoned, as sleeves were in sun-blasted Burren Waters, to the wrists.

—Oh yes, said this man, the bookkeeper. Mrs Emptor knows you're coming. She's up at the house.

When we traversed the garden and reached the huge open verandahs of the Emptors' red-brick pal-azzo, we found that long, ceiling-high bookshelves flanked the front door, and after they finished, a herd of beds, packed together, disappeared around the corner. It proved that this was where friends of her largely vanished children slept on visits to the great outback, or perhaps where favoured clients were put up during the yearling sales. The beds gave the Emp-tor homestead the look of a country hospital.

—They shouldn't bother with this green bloody lawn they've got, Larson whispered. No use pretend-ing it's bloody Toorak and fighting against the re-alities of evaporation. They ought to plant xerophytes.

Xerophytes were Larson's favourite plants. He tried to keep a little cactus garden healthy in moist, sub-tropical North Sydney. At the Emptors' front door, his brave eyes glittered with the concept of a garden of desert plants.

The middle-aged woman who answered the door could only be the chatelaine, Mrs Emptor. She was slightly more than medium height. She had a broad, frank, worried, slightly fleshy face, sun-leathered but not wrinkled. She wore a mumu. The flesh of her shoulders was brown and smooth — she took the sun well, unlike her bookkeeper. She displayed the upper third of the breasts which had suckled young Jacko (whom I barely knew at that stage) and his three siblings, the one predictable brother, and the mad other two, girl and boy. She was not at first view a big enough woman to have produced such a thumping lad as Jacko, but then she had mated with an earlier thumping lad, Stammer Jack.

—Oh Jesus, she told us. Culture's arrived in this bloody place at last!

I would find later how she knew and vaguely liked a few of my books, and knew and despised a few others. She knew Larson had a reputation in the film industry too, as a cinematographer as well as a stills man. A stills photographer of such stature that Chloe Emptor had seen his work on the Sunday afternoon arts program on the ABC, the only channel Chloe Emptor's satellite dish allowed her to get.

—Got to get you blokes tea, said Chloe. Think we'd better sit out here on the verandah with the books. That'd be bloody well appropriate eh.

She had the Northern Territory way of making her questions statements. Perhaps this was because there were far fewer than two hundred thousand people, Aboriginal and white, in the Territory's half million square miles. Questions went out into a vacancy, were absorbed by space and had the inquiring tone leached out of them.

She led us to the shadier end of the verandah, and the floor to ceiling books were here, by the cane furniture, more or less *al fresco*. There was a high proportion of hard covers and as honourable a list as you'd see in any academic library. The Dickens, Thackeray, Twain, Melville, Tolstoy, Hugo had — she later told me — been poshly bound by a firm in Melbourne, and needed to be regularly wiped, and inspected for mildew and ants. Grandfather Emptor had brought these in by dray. I noticed plenty of Thomas Mann also, including *Death in Venice*. Jacko himself, angry at his homosexual brother Frank for reasons which will be canvassed in this tale, once described *Death in Venice* to me as an endless bloody rigmarole about a poofter who dies of cholera. But Chloe got more out of some things than Jacko did.

She sat us down beneath Marquez and Joyce and William Golding and the Australian Nobel Laureate Michael Bickham, and then wandered further down the verandah to where the bookshelves ended and there was a window which gave into the interior of the house.

—Sharon! she yelled. Would you mind making my guests some tea love? We're out here by the literature.

Having got the answer she wanted, but one we couldn't hear, she came back towards us. I'd presumed that she'd been wearing sandals, but I saw now that she was barefoot.

She sat down sighing.

—My son Petie's new girlfriend, she explained. He's had a succession. He meets them at some bar in Sydney, brings them up here and they last about three months. You know, the isolation and the boredom eh. Nice girls. But none of them bloody readers you know, and the other stuff only lasts fifteen minutes at a time eh. So there you go! But he's a deep one, my eldest son. Though he's had the decency to stick around, unlike the other ungrateful little buggers. The one most like the mongrel bastard just the same. You've got to be like the mongrel bastard if you want to enjoy staying here eh.

She gave no explanation of the identity of the mongrel bastard. You quickly got used to the term though, and found that the person she meant was Stammer Jack. Like a lot of Australian insults, the words were also a form of perverse endearment.

She leaned forward, Might as well tell you, you're not going to meet him this time, the boss feller, Mr Emptor. He's in his room with a bottle of rum. He's such a bloody hypochondriac. Men are children eh. He had this accident with his ankle, and it's painful but it's not the fall of the bloody Roman Empire. Had a bit of an accident with a helicopter. With this dead-beat American we've got up here. Just a little twist of the ankle. If it gets worse, I might call the Flying Doctor. In his book, this gives him the right to be totally bloody unsociable. Anyhow, let me tell you, you're not missing much.

—Then son Peter's out in a mustering camp about eight miles out. He'll be bringing some three thousand cattle into the yards here this afternoon. I could take you out to meet them, but I'd rather not. The romance of cattle is over-bloody-done eh.

She turned to Larson.

—You'll be able to get plenty of good shots when they come in here. There'll be dust and black stockmen and helicopters and cowshit and everything you bloody want. You can even go up in Boomer's bloody helicopter, if that's your fancy.

Larson looked at me and shook his head.

I should say that all the ironies operated in Larson's case. He kept saying to me that as much as he liked the words-and-pictures book we were doing together, he didn't want to go in any cattle mustering helicopters.

—Zero height, zero brains, zero chance, he said.

It was bad enough, he said, flying in helicopters for cinematic purposes, hanging by a strap for the sake of live pictures.

The sad and worthy story, which is not really part of the grotesque tale of the Emptors, but which I must relay so that we can get on with Chloe, was that he had an appointment in seventeen days to shoot some footage from a helicopter for a tourism commercial. This in the high alpine meadows west of Canberra, the national capital Territorians like the Emptors despised for its alien bureaucracies. Larson was to film a man and woman riding horses on a great green plateau.

When he took off he would be strapped in with his young assistant cameraman, Bo, a Tasmanian, and a director Larson frequently worked with. As could only happen in reality, just before that seventeen-day-distant take off, Larson would leave a letter tape for his father in which he would say, Here comes the bloody chopper. God, I hate those things.

There was a power line, not marked on the pilot's map. Larson and Bo and the director would all be killed in the crash.

But at the Emptors' place with me he knew he had

a choice about getting into the things, and he was exercising it.

Chloe Emptor leaned towards me.

—Listen, my television idiot of a son said he'd met you. In the studio. He and the blond drongo do that morning program. You know, big Jacko Emptor?

I knew but found it hard to believe that she was associated with hulking Jacko Emptor of *Morning Oz*. The frantic three-and-a-half-minute interviews authors got on *Morning Oz* (if you were trans-sexual or a cabinet minister resigning under a cloud, you could get as much as five) seemed eons removed from the geologic quietude of Burren Waters.

—He's not a bad boy in fact, said mother Emptor. But he ought to leave those astrological sisters alone eh. They don't have a concept between them.

Chloe meant the two Logan sisters who, between them, wearing long, primary-coloured gowns, did the astrology on *Morning Oz*. The Logan girls arrived by the same limo as Jacko at the opening of new malls and cinemas in Sydney. And never losing their breath, they took part in fun runs Jacko was invited to but did not choose to expend himself on. That, in fact, was how I had first met Jacko, one drizzling morning in Darling Harbour, where I was trying to finish a ten kilometre loop on the strength of boyhood fitness and the cut wind of a middle-aged athlete. Hardy, kindly, practical women, the sisters jogged beside me on the spot for a time, attended by Jacko, massive on a trail bike.

Sharon arrived with the tea. She had a pleasant broad face but it was disfigured by some kind of tiredness and by a gloss of sweat. Chloe asked her did she want to drink tea, but she said no in a distracted way. She was not anxious to meet visitors. She went back inside unconsoled.

Chloe said, She won't last long now, poor kid eh. Feel sorry for Petie. He's the pick of the crop. While his dead-beat bloody brother's up to his armpits in sisters in ball-gowns.

She called after Sharon, Might as well go and ask the bloody malingerer if he wants some tea.

* * *

She said she didn't know why anyone with lives as interesting as ours would want to write about some hopeless bloody cattle station on the limits of nowhere. The arse had fallen out of cattle, she said. The European Community had utterly stuffed everything. Now, as we well knew, the Australian cattleman had to look for favours from the Saudis!

Grudgingly, she took us out for a walk around the place. She wore no shoes, relying on the soft, familiar dust. The school was out for a morning break. She introduced us to the teacher, who was a German the Northern Territory Department of Education had somehow managed to sign up. You needed to be a mad German, a sort of Voss of pedagogy, even to think of teaching at Burren Waters. Native born Australians, said Chloe, knew too much to sign on for such a task. You needed to have seen a lot of National Geographic programs in some green place, and you needed to have been as deprived of sunlight and desert places in childhood as Jacko had been of locked doors.

The lean German headmaster wore a pair of board shorts and a green singlet, and during this recess stood basking under the eaves of the school. His class looked fairly evenly split between white and black, and Chloe pointed to a rangy boy seven or eight years old, towheaded as young desert Aboriginals often are. The boy was about to hoist himself up onto Roman rings which hung from a steel bar in the playground. He spat freely on the palms of both hands so that the hot steel wouldn't burn him, and then he jumped and grasped and performed a complete double-jointed somersault of the kind which causes the onlooker to flinch. There was lots of quicksilver athleticism there.

—See that kid there. That's my husband's step-nephew. Want to know how? Ask the mongrel bastard's father, she paused. My daughter Helen went off to study anthropology just so's she could understand her bloody relatives. Then she fell for a bloody anthropologist in Perth and really got to despise her father and me. Mind you, that little bastard there'll probably turn out better than my crowd. Not much of a scholar. Too much Emptor blood for that. Jacko's a qualified lawyer of course, but you'd never bloody know it. A solicitor. He certainly solicited that grinning little astrological sister.

Whether we were looking at the sales ring or the mustering yards or the kitchens where Larson might photograph the early morning steak and eggs of stockmen, Chloe was never far away from the subject of the ironies of her motherhood, the betrayals a woman's progeny were sure to commit, the question of who and where her grandchildren would be. She always spoke as if we had some familiarity with her vanished bairns. Not only Jacko, but Frank and Helen as well.

Reconnoitring the homestead area in the dazzling forenoon, we saw a pillar of dust approaching and heard the sound of aircraft. The smooth whine of a fixed-wing and the lumpy racket of a helicopter.

—There you are, said Chloe. You'll get your pictures now.

Again, they weren't pictures she wanted anything to do with, and Larson's keenness for what was about to happen seemed to her to be a lapse of taste.

And yet it was all wonderful for Larson, and for me. To funnel the cattle into the mustering yards, two great walls of orange-brown hessian, running out some three quarters of a mile in length, had been erected by stockmen to serve as an avenue for the arriving mob of cattle. We had not sighted these walls on our way in earlier that day, so they must have been the quick work of the last few hours. But a genuine work of art. A breeze arrived with the cattle, and the walls of hessian began to vibrate and bellow and flap as sweetly as if Christo had put them there for pure abstract effect. The horsemen, who included Jacko's bulky brother Peter, turned on sixpences in clouds of saffron dust. Whips cracked, men whistled like whips, the herd protested in full voice. Angular Aboriginal stockmen wheeled their horses amongst nests of cattle horns. Larson would get such a picture for the book: a skinny, big-hatted Wodjiri man, the head of his horse awash in a sea of Brahma horns.

As the mob drew up to the mustering yard, freshly dismounted stockmen sat on the tubular iron railings and swung gates open and shut, admitting so many cattle to each compartment, often — by whistling and the nifty use of the gate — separating one beast from its neighbour in line. It all had a purpose. Some of the animals were cleanskins, Chloe would later tell us without showing much interest, and needed to be branded. They had never till this muster seen a horseman.

The mustering airplane which had driven the herd into the hessian funnel now performed one mad victory roll fifty feet above the horsemen and went climbing away to look for the landing strip. The helicopter stayed.

We saw a startling thing. At the tail of the herd was a young recalcitrant bull, as evilly horned as any of his species. He was tossing his head, and wanted to go back to the unbranded hills to the west. But the madness of the helicopter lay between the beast and its line of freedom. The propeller was cutting the young bull's vision to ribbons, just as it cut ours. But this was a brave beast and willing to try to fit itself amongst the tatters of air. It rounded on the machine. A reasonable helicopter pilot with a sense of the limits of his machine would have simply hung in the air and looked down on the bull. But Boomer Webb, Stammer Jack's Vietnam veteran helicopter pilot, wanted to harry it more intimately.

This was great news for Larson, and not bad news for me either. I had already secretly made my mind up that remote and vacant places favoured oddity, and Boomer was proving it for me.

He brought his helicopter down until the skids were nearly at the bull's forehead. It took that to make the young beast turn. After it *had* turned, Boomer descended further, sitting in the air at an inadvisable angle and seeming to prod the beast's rump with the skids. The young bull gave it up and ran off to face the brand and the iron enclosures.

Poor Larson would win some posthumous award for that shot, and you still see it widely reproduced in posters and magazines.

* * *

All this before I really knew Jacko. Jacko would later tell me in New York that Boomer was still flying, although he had had a dozen or so crashes if you included the forced landings. The Department of Civil Aviation had been apprised of only one of these incidents.

When the dust had settled a little, Chloe came out and introduced us to Peter and some of the other stockmen who had dismounted by the mustering yards and were smoking before beginning the branding.

Peter said, You know my citified brother eh?

I said I'd met him doing a television interview.

—Can you tell me why anyone wouldn't want to live up here?

—No. Though he seems happy down there.

—Yeah, well, horses for bloody courses.

And then he said, You blokes'll have a beer later eh?

His mother said, Course they will. Even if they haven't done any real work.

Petie was not easy with us, but you could tell he was a happy man. He and the stockmen had been out for a week, erecting the great funnel of hessian every day to move and contain the herd, using the light aircraft and Boomer's helicopter and the flash horsemen to flush new cattle out of the scrub, and to compact them into a herd which they could then move on in the afternoon. Corralling the mob at night behind those fabric walls, and then, next morning, driving more cattle in again to join the herd and send the numbers up.

It became clear that Petie had not been in the bush solidly for a week. He was, after all, the boss, or at least the young boss, and he could get the pilot to fly him in to the homestead to see Sharon on most evenings. So Petie's wasn't quite the lonely drover scenario favoured by balladists.

Larson of course wished he could have been out in the mustering camp, to see the white and black stockmen socializing together around the night fire, sleeping in the same camp. Whereas back at Burren Waters headquarters, they occupied separate quarters of the Emptors' little city of cattle. Larson would have liked to have exploited, in his gentle way, the ironies of these arrangements.

—What do you reckon next time we're up here we go on a muster? he asked me.

—Maybe for a few days anyhow, I conceded.

Petie and the stockmen spent the rest of the afternoon letting cattle through some gates and not through others, and then laying the terrible iron to them. We saw a lot of enthusiastic bull-dusting — jumping off fences and wrestling cleanskins to the earth by their horns for branding. Best of all, this seemed to be the specialty of certain skinny Wodjiri stockmen.

A half dozen of the shots Larson took that afternoon would honour the book which would be published eighteen months after his death.

*   *   *

Late in the day I looked across through the dust haze and saw Mum Chloe watching from the homestead verandah, amongst all the beds and all the Thomas Mann. Further along the verandah railing stood a hulking, ample-gutted man who wore only a shirt and had no pants. This was my first sight of Stammer Jack. He had nothing to say to Chloe. If by some chance of destiny I'd been hired to paint the cattle nabob Stammer Jack Emptor and his wife, this is the picture I would have painted. It said, as pictures should, everything about the casual power, the lasting hostilities, the persistence of marriage. Everything too about Burren Waters ennui. It answered, unposed, all questions.

After a time he was gone from the railing: the suspected hypochondriac Stammer Jack Emptor.

Evening light came in like a tide and turned the earth of Burren Waters' main pasturage lavender. We went off with the stockmen to the red-brick dining room and ate a thumping meal of steak. In the middle of it Chloe Emptor — who had apparently dined at the homestead — appeared in the room. Working her way towards us, she spoke to various stockmen and then straddled a bench to sit opposite us.

—I was thinking, I hope you blokes aren't going to coat all this in bloody sugar. If it wasn't for the quarter horses we wouldn't make a decent living eh. As for the Aboriginal stockmen everyone considers too bloody cute for words, they've been useless since they unionized. You can't work with the buggers any more eh. I mean, there're still a few good ones ... Anyhow, you won't get any points for sentimentalizing us. That's what's been on my mind all afternoon, and I thought I'd better out with it.

She took a drag from the can of Carlton Draught she'd picked up in the kitchen and carried in her hand. It was the Territory's favourite beer, and half a dozen cans had been issued to all hands along with the steak. She turned her can in her hands.

—Anyway, she told me, no reason for someone like you to be writing about us at all eh. There's got to be a lot that's more interesting going on in your life.

I explained that the Brits and plenty of Australians wanted to hear about her kind of existence. At least there was a British book packager who thought so, and had put up money for such a book.

Chloe bent forward.

—Yeah, but you'd rather be writing about something else. You'd never find someone like Michael Bickham wasting his time writing about people like us. And you're not interested in cleanskin bloody cattle eh. Don't try to tell me that.

—I'm sorry, Mrs Emptor, but I am interested.

—Jesus, I've got a verandah full of books, and all the ones I like are by blokes who just write about their own world. About what they know.

—Okay, I don't have a private income like Michael Bickham. I can't afford not to do this book. And I *am* fascinated just the same. I never knew that people lived like this.

—You didn't eh. Well, it's quickly discovered. I think you're wasting your poor bloody talent.

There are always people who say that to a writer, but one doesn't expect to hear the voice of God, the appeal to higher integrity, in Burren Waters.

—You know your book on Abos? she said. A lot of city liberals liked it eh. But you know bugger-all about Abos. You'd be better writing about when you were a kid or something, or your first love affair.

A few of the white stockmen were sipping from their cans and listening intently. I found that unnerving.

—I'm not trying to be rude or anything, she pursued. But something must have happened to you that you could write about.

—I'm not the sort of writer who writes about himself, I told her. I'd rather visit Burren Waters and that Chloe Emptor.

—No, she said frowning. Take me seriously for Christ's sake.

Though she was the living judgement that ultimately embarrassed most or all writers, she didn't have any malice. This gave her even more the air of one who might have been right. Meanwhile, Larson was embarrassed to silence for my sake, and that at last seemed to produce confusion in Chloe.

She stood suddenly.

—God, a woman's probably said too much eh. Listen, no question you're welcome. That's not what I'm saying. Anyhow, I've got to get back to the homestead to make a poultice for the mongrel. See you boys later.

She went, looking a little lost, as if she weren't proprietor of the place. As she passed them, various stockmen asked her how the boss was, and she said, Whingeing bastard.

—That's a bad ankle he's got though, a senior stockman named Merv told her. We'd met him that afternoon. He was a wiry little man with a skew-whiff thatch of grey-black hair.

—Don't give me bad ankle. You're all a pack of malingering bastards.

—Sit down, Chloe, Merv invited her.

But she wouldn't. She wandered up and down the trestle tables. At last she stood behind Merv. He could not see her. She pointed downwards at the bald crown of his head. Then she bent her arm and raised a fist, grasping the biceps of that arm with the fingers of her other hand.

In case we didn't understand this meant Merv was virile, she added to the impersonation a plunging motion of the thighs. And then she winked.

It was not a snide wink. The Emptors were totally lacking in snideness, that morbid rump of envy.

* * *

Outside, later, we could hear generators and see the lights shining in the Wodjiri quarter of Emptorville, administrative centre of Burren Waters cattle station.

The universe seemed immensely in evidence as we sat under the open-sided brush shelter by the cook-house with the white stockmen and Petie and Sharon and watched a television set for news of the wider world. By grace of the satellite saucer in Chloe's green backyard, there was not only a set at the homestead for wan Sharon to stare at by day, but also one out here on a counter under the brush shelter; a beast on a long lead from an electric socket in the kitchen, the video mastiff from whose first, rare bite Jacko Emptor had never recovered.

In the spirit of this fact, the studiously motionless stockmen frowned at the screen, as if it needed to have an eye kept on it.

Larson and I were quartered in an empty room in the brick stockmen's quarters. Not only was the door not locked, it was not closed. The outer wire screen was pulled across however. Flies were still active. The night was hot and even humid, as if Burren Waters were being asked to pay in discomfort for the lushness which set in a few hundred miles north and north-west. We lay in the dark and could see more stars through the square of window than are seen in an urban month.

—Why did she tell us that about Merv? I asked Larson.

—Well, he said, surer with bush people than I was. To make up for taking you apart over writing.

—Bit of a contradiction, isn't it?

Larson laughed one of his profound, last laughs.

—That's no contradiction. Same thing viewed from a different end. But the point is, how would she bloody know?

So we fell asleep with an engorged memory of Chloe Emptor whose day it had been. We had our alarm set for four-thirty in the morning, and it was a little before that time that Chloe appeared again, wearing the morning star on her shoulder and rattling our wire.

—I got the cook up early for you boys. You can't travel without a breakfast ch.

We opened the door to her, and we brushed our teeth as she chatted with us. She seemed to be trying to feel out and expiate whatever follies she had been guilty of the night before.

She said to me at last, Look I'm sorry for coming the heavy with you like that. None of my business eh. But Jesus, I do like a good read. I wanted to ask you, do you know Michael Bickham?

Bickham was the now aged novelist who had won the Nobel Prize, culturally validating the nation in the mid-1970s.

—I've met him, I admitted.

—Have you read *The Mother as Aphrodite*?

—Yes, I lied. I had at least begun it, and it was customary for people to lie about how much Bickham they'd read. I had read all his early works and found them a revelation. I'd been defeated by the later ones.

—He really knows women eh. The way he writes about that old lady who's dying in that big bloody house in . . . what's the name of the place? Holloglo. And her weird children. I was wondering, if I was ever in Sydney visiting that useless Jacko, d'you reckon you could . . . ?

—I don't know Bickham that well, I rushed to say. He doesn't mix with a lot of other writers.

Even his name was a kind of reproach. When I was young I'd been compared to him, but I had — by that night in Burren Waters — disappointed those who had first nominated me to be his heir. I had met Bickham a few times at political events. He never had anything to do with the Sydney literary mafia, but invited people he respected to his house. If you were invited, you were proven to be a person either of taste or of talent. If you were not invited — and most writers weren't — you could console yourself that you were in some way a challenge, or maybe not epicene enough to fit Bickham's crowd. Either way, you knew you were telling only half the truth.

Bickham was something of a misanthrope and

a gnostic. In rawly democratic Oz, he believed undemocratically in the salvation of only a few chosen and shone-upon souls, and these were the ones he sought to choose for company. In the land of mateship, he despised the herd. That made it hard for his kinsmen to place him in the national pantheon.

But it had to be done. Because the Nobel Committee had spoken . . . and made him the nation's Nobel Prize winner, and so an institution, like the Monarchy or the Church of England or Anzac Day.

For a start, he seemed to feel ambiguous about me, and the odds were that Chloe Emptor would lie far outside his list of the redeemed.

—You could ask him to lunch, couldn't you? she challenged me. He'd come to your place. And I'd bring Jacko eh, but not the astral bloody sisters. I wouldn't stand for that.

—Listen Chloe, I told her, knowing that I needed to be desperately frank. He wouldn't come to lunch at my place. He doesn't like me. Like you, he thinks I'm a journeyman. Not one of the washed. He thinks I'm shit.

Chloe exhaled.

—Then who's his agent?

—He doesn't have an agent. He transcends agents.

—I suppose he does. He's an absolute genius. And I've got to ask him some questions.

—He's a misogynistic old bastard, I told her. But yes. An absolute genius as well. He wouldn't go on Jacko's show. He wouldn't go on anyone's show, and he wouldn't be interested in lunch at my place. I'm sorry Chloe.

Chloe went to the screen door and looked out at

the same morning star which, on first waking, we'd thought she might bring indoors with her.

—Well, I reckon it's not good enough to write great work and leave your readers hanging for a bloody explanation. Maybe you could look into it for me eh. He might hate women but he knows us to the last atom of our bloody wishbones.

—That's how unfair the distribution of talent is, Chloe. Say you use the crappy old term muses. *They* don't give a damn whether you've got an ounce of human kindness.

Larson said, You're right there.

Chloe kept talking though, saying that she had to see him and she knew I could arrange it all if I wanted to. She half-suspected still that it was her criticisms of the night before which made me deny her access to Michael Bickham, that megalith of the Antipodes.

—Anyhow, she said, we'll be discussing this further eh. Because you say you're coming back. I really need to talk to him. Before he dies.

—Yes, we're coming back, said Larson. We want to talk to your husband. And maybe go out mustering.

—Yairs, she growled. Let's hope he's over his sulks by then.

Larson said, This is a great place. For atmosphere. And for light.

—Christ eh, said Chloe. If you write me up as a quaint bloody bushie, I'm going to be ropable.

Larson said softly, I think you're great. You exceed the sum of our expectations. You ought to trust us, Chloe.

It was a reckless proposition of Larson's. But Chloe stopped arguing with me, and we kissed her goodbye.

I left promising that I would see what I could do with Bickham. But I knew I could do damn-all.

* * *

Three weeks later, I had the honour of giving Larson's eulogy in a chapel at the Northern Suburbs Crematorium. A great crowd came, for, in the world of tricky and crooked images, Larson was considered an honest man. With his intimate eye, he had photographed Australia so extensively that advertising people went to his enormous stills library whenever they were stumped for an image. And so now they too came to his funeral, along with all the people who'd worked with him in live footage — in commercials, documentaries, features.

The crowd spilled out onto the lawn cemetery.

People who work at such visual tasks have a particular look. This made it easier for me — just as I was praising Larson quite accurately for his openness, his generosity, his powers of observation, his lust for Australian light, his vision, and the range of his gifts — to see Mrs Chloe Emptor, in a black dress and a broad-brimmed straw hat, standing by the main door of the chapel, being killed — I was sure about this — by her pair of unlikely, stiletto-heeled black shoes.

She looked, nonetheless, a fully paid up member of this union of grief. Beside her was her great moon-faced son, Jacko Emptor, looking something of an outsider in this serious film congregation.

More so outside afterwards, when everyone was remembering Larson and consoling each other with anecdotes and falling on each other's necks. Jacko approached wearing the sort of shiny, pristine suit only television people and cabinet ministers wear.

—Sorry for your loss, mate, he told me.

The corners of his mouth pulled deep into his cherubic cheeks.

Chloe Emptor said, Boomer — you know Boomer the heli pilot — he had to fly the machine to Mount Isa for maintenance. I came on down to Sydney by commercial jet.

With breaks for re-fuelling, it would have taken them a day in the mustering helicopter to get to Mount Isa. Then another two thousand or so miles to Sydney. A Burren Waters commute.

—I couldn't believe it, Chloe murmured. When I heard the radio news eh. I mean, you blokes were due back to interview that mongrel of a husband . . .

—I'll still come if you'll have me.

—Course.

She turned to her son.

—Our friend here's going to try to arrange for us to have lunch with Michael Bickham.

—Shit, said Jacko. Yeah?

The lips hung part open in the kind of speculation I'd seen in Chloe.

—The only one of our family who's met him is Frank.

—That'd fit, said Jacko, and he turned to me, keen to make things clear.

—Frank's my poofter brother, he told me with a mixture of gaugeable ill will and affection both. Lives in the Eastern Suburbs. The opera. Makes sense Bickham would've met him.

Jacko put his giant arm around my shoulder.

—Listen, maybe you could tell me. What's the connection between Banjo Paterson and Michael

Bickham? You know? What's the line of succession?
Is Bickham Banjo Paterson gone sour? Or does Banjo
not even appear on the same planet as Bickham?

And as if he had his own answer he began to recite
Banjo Paterson's famous mythologizing verse *Clancy
of the Overflow*:

—I am sitting in my dingy little office, where a
　　stingy Ray of sunlight struggles feebly down
　　　　between the houses tall,
　　And the foetid air and gritty of the dusty, dirty
　　　　city,
　　　　Through the open window floating,
　　　　　spreads its foulness over all . . .

And I somehow rather fancy that I'd like to
　　change with Clancy,
　　Like to take a turn at droving where the
　　　seasons come and go,
While he faced the round eternal of the cash
　　book and the journal —
　　But I doubt he'd suit the office, Clancy of
　　　"The Overflow".

I said, Your father's Clancy of The Overflow. Your
brother Peter is. You could have been.

—Oh, I know, mate. I'm pleading guilty right now
to not liking the cattle station life. You meet a very
limited range of people, don't you, Chloe? But you
know, Banjo stated the Australian equation. He said
you can go for A, or you can go for B. With Bickham
there's only Z, and most of us poor bastards don't
get to Z.

He shrugged, made that winking motion of the
head without actually winking (one of his trademark
gestures) and quoted from Banjo the balladist again:

—And an answer came directed in a writing
    unexpected,
  (And I think the same was written with a
    thumbnail dipped in tar);
'Twas his shearing mate who wrote it, and
    verbatim I will quote it:
    "Clancy's gone to Queensland droving, and
    we don't know where he are."
And then, finally, he did wink.

V

Early in our friendship, I found myself questioning Jacko on the basis of what I knew of his abnormal childhood. How, from Burren Waters, did his fervour for the television medium derive? The medium had lain in wait for him in his babyhood, yet let him have his childhood before declaring itself to him.

From these questions, I built something like a history of Jacko's infancy. I am touched to think of little Jacko, yearning already for secrets which the landscape doesn't hold, beginning his education on the radio telephone with School of the Air. The teacher would be sitting in a broadcast booth in Alice Springs, while baby Jacko sat some four hundred miles away in the radio booth of Burren Waters, wearing his headphones, listening to his class, reading aloud for them when the teacher pressed *his* button on her switchboard, competing with other members of the class to answer questions such as: What is four multiplied by two minus one?

The classmates, spread all over the Northern Territory, were involved in competition with children whose faces they could only guess at. Jacko Emptor of Burren Waters, Sharon Tinsley of Apsley Waters, Robert and Timothy Cartwright and Catherine Ryan of Victoria River Downs, Astrid Kravitz of Morgan

Waters, and so on. All their doors and faces locked to him by outrageous distance.

When he was eight there was a boom in cattle prices, and the rainfall was a phenomenal two and a half inches above average. Stammer Jack expanded into the quarter-horse trade, and, at Chloe's insistence, a school was founded at Burren Waters to provide an elementary education to the children of all the new men and women Stammer Jack and Chloe needed to employ.

But there was still the question of high school. Petie had already been sent to the same school which had given Stammer Jack his polishing, a vast boarding school in a leafy suburb of Sydney designed especially for boys from the bush of vaguely Catholic persuasion. St Kevin's was in some ways a factory farm for Rugby internationals, but when Jacko went there in his turn he showed a lack of commitment to the football code whose promoters called it *the game they play in Heaven.* Jacko was accused of poor teamwork. His lack of focus was all the more blameworthy in contrast to his brother Petie, who had been a great line-out specialist and had so much teamwork as to be a notorious inflictor of gashes to the forehead and eyebrows of those who got in his way when the winger threw the ball in.

The adolescent Jacko nonetheless harboured a sense of being a great team-worker. It was simply that he had not yet found his team. He made friends with a boy named David, an extraordinarily delicate beauty, too fine a flower of a boy to be lost amongst the Rugby warriors. I have seen their class photograph: David's delicate stalk of a neck, his chin thrust forward as if he knows that someone who sees the picture will love him, whatever sort of pariah he is among his own herd. The teachers kept an eye on both of them, aware that Jacko's heart, or at least his testosterone, was already at war with the pale and immaculate mysteries of faith.

David's parents lived in the city. They were both doctors, honest technicians who did not know where their heavenly son had come from. Jacko used to go home with David on weekends out of school. They would be left alone on Saturday evenings, when the doctoral spouses had dinners to go to. It was on these Saturday evenings with David that Jacko first saw Fred Gudgeon, a television comic. His impact on the young Jacko was all the more marked by the fact that Jacko had been eccentrically protected by distance from an earlier sighting of television clownery. Jacko was stunned and captivated and converted at a stroke, or more accurately, at the appearance of that one angelic creature of light named Gudgeon. Yet to some people all Gudgeon did was stick pieces of toilet paper on his face as if he had given himself frequent cuts shaving and then, with tape recorder and mike, gatecrash the Sydney airport press conferences of arriving stars and cabinet ministers. With ingenuous questions, he made the wise seem fools.

Jacko understood that taking-the-piss idiom of Gudgeon utterly. It was the idiom of Burren Waters.

When Gudgeon did not gatecrash press conferences, he intruded into homes and interviewed bemused people. Even in the cities of Australia the doors were sometimes double-locked, barred and heavily panelled. But Gudgeon got mysterious access. It was delicious even when he didn't.

One Saturday night while David and Jacko watched,

a gate-keeper at the Royal Australian Golf Club asked Gudgeon where his authority to enter was, and Gudgeon faced his own camera, the other side of the tube and mirror at which David and Jacko gazed, and tapped what seemed to Jacko to be the inside of the television he and David were watching, and said, This is my authority.

The idea of such kingship filled Jacko with ecstasy. Nor could he stop choking with laughter. He and David mutually choked for Gudgeon's sake. Their supply of love for Gudgeon united them, for a time, in a sort of love of their own.

Until one weekend Greggie Emptor, a cousin from Port Macquarie, a twenty-year-old who had gone straight from school into horse breeding, came and took Jacko to dinner at the Cross, and then to a massage parlour where a Chinese girl functionally demonstrated how Jacko's affairs might be arranged more to his liking. And the next time David asked, Jacko said, Mate, you should be growing out of that by now!

As well, Chloe had written to Jacko to tell him that a satellite dish had been installed at Burren Waters. He would be able to watch Gudgeon in the holidays. His spiritual dependence on David had been lessened.

Jacko wrote the script for the annual revue at St Kevin's, and a former New South Wales breakaway called Matt Henessey, who taught mathematics, toned it down so that parents wouldn't be affronted. Six-foot-two, fifteen and with the beginnings of a moustache, Jacko now talked himself into work around radio stations, and sometimes read news or filled in for late-night announcers who had flu. Gudgeon came

to the station where Jacko was working in his six-
teenth year. They drank coffee together and Gudgeon sombrely told him how it was done. Act
innocent, said Gudgeon, flashing sad eyes, and don't
take a backwards step.

Jacko studied law at Sydney University. Chloe and
Stammer Jack wanted it, and Jacko did not fight too
hard. He believed the law gave him an extra dimension, women liked that, and being liked by women
had taken on the importance it would thereafter
retain. He was, in any case, interested in the consti-
tution, and the laws of trespass and privacy. But he
was also hosting television variety shows by the time
he was eighteen.

Meanwhile, and at last, Gudgeon's device wore
thin with all of the public except Jacko. Gudgeon's
creator, the man who had advised Jacko in such
cogent terms, went away to try to make comedy
films.

In his young manhood Jacko was looking for a
chance to reinstitute the genre of comic trespass, the
whole Gudgeon act, but the Australians weren't
interested.

—Done to death! the television executives told
him.

Introducing the Logan sisters on morning television, under the direction of Ed Durkin, Jacko knew
in his blood that the Gudgeon day would dawn at
some time, and in some perhaps unimaginable place.

Then, as we know, Basil Sutherland called Durkin
and brought him to New York to plan assaults on
public taste. Durkin missed Jacko and called him

from Australia. It was the most liberating call of
Jacko's life. He knew now there was a chance to cut
loose in fresh fields with the rites of intrusion.

*   *   *

Now, in his days as a transplanted Gudgeon, Jacko
lived with Lucy in a loft in Thomas Street, Tribeca.
Tribeca ran more bars per square mile, said Jacko,
than Burren Waters ran cattle. There was one downstairs from Jacko — Mary O'Reilly's — a sentimental
Irish pub where you could leave letters and packages
for collection by Jacko. Across the road was a more
hard-edged, Belfast and Derry pub, Coghlan's, which
took up collections for the families of men in the
Maze in Belfast, and where Irish-named cops from
the First Precinct could sign letters of support for
hunger strikers. The cops who drank at Coghlan's
felt paternal towards Jacko. The times that I waited
in Coghlan's for Jacko or Lucy to come home, they
would say, Oh yeah, the big Australian guy, Jacko!
All in a way which implied that the world needed
more of Jacko's kind of innocence and cheek.

And then they would recount their versions of the
morning Jacko talked his way in through the door of
a racketeer's house in New Jersey. This had occurred
some six months before Jacko began his search for
Sunny Sondquist, the Anodyne kid. The microwave
truck had gone out, followed by Jacko and Dannie,
and picked up the signal from Manhattan on a street
of unwalled mansions in Bergenfield.

I was watching that morning, in our sweet little
apartment — what I insisted on calling a *flat* as a
token of Australian nationalism — in the narrow

Cotton Building on the corner of East Fourth and Broadway. From the window of our bedroom we could see the World Trade Towers to the south. From the window of our living room we could look north up Lower Broadway, a thoroughfare of astounding liveliness.

Every morning a saxophonist who would have been hired by one of the better hotels in any other city than this one used to play for three hours on the corner by the Bottom Line, the famed cabaret where the young queued two blocks on Friday nights for the right performer. Under the violet flags of NYU, an Ecuadorian band played high Andean music full of images of big-hatted, coca-leaf-chewing mountain folk and of llamas and condors.

And I watched Jacko acting the goat in Bergenfield.

*   *   *

Jacko is therefore in the street of unwalled mansions. He walks up a pathway through the snow, past a freshly delivered copy of the Jersey edition of the *New York Times* wrapped in blue plastic. It is an encouragement to Jacko since it promises occupancy, and he knocks on the broad, double-leafed door panelled in an Italianate manner, looking somehow reinforced like the door of a bank.

When there is no reply, Jacko tells us he suspects someone is hiding within.

—As is of course their right, he assures us, making a face which implies otherwise. And then in vengeance, or perhaps because his producer Dannie is urging him to, he tells the cameraman, who is in this case his friend Clayton, to put the muzzle of the

camera up against the glass side panelling of the door.
Hence we see, through Clayton's lens and the further
lens of armour glass, someone's dream of opulence:
a floor of creamy marble, a broad swathe of stair
arising with gilt banisters and a lit chandelier fit for a
casino.

—Let the people enter, roars Jacko, rapping on
the window of this Jersey version of Versailles.

—Okay, Clayton, says Jacko, no sport this side of
the road.

Clayton's camera swings and takes in the rest of
the street. There is a glimpse of Dannie skittering
away from the frame.

—Identical place across the road, roars Jacko. We'll
give that one a burl next.

And then he returns us to the studio, where snide
Maloney, the anchorman, says he was sure all viewers
wished Jacko better luck on the far side.

*   *   *

When at last, after a lot of video persiflage, we were
returned to Jacko, he was positioned by a door identical to the one he'd tried across the street. This time
we got a sense from his face that his knock was
almost immediately about to be answered.

—Somebody coming, somebody coming, he told
us with his great oafish grimace.

The door was opened by a young man, barefooted,
dark-haired, a little overweight, but wearing a track
suit as if he intended to do something about his
obesity.

—Mornin', he told Jacko, a thorough greeting.

Jacko went into his spiel. He was Jacko Emptor,

boy from the bush, somehow associated with a microwave dish truck and a camera crew, wanting a little succour and warmth at a New Jersey hearth.

The young man could hardly wait for Jacko to be finished. He yelled, Come in! I know you.

He had a jerky joviality which may have derived from something he had ingested with his morning coffee.

So now Jacko was transmitting from the morning's second floor of cream marble, beneath a chandelier identical to the one across the road. Many a small town would not have eaten as much electricity as that one crystal beast.

—Goll-ee, said Jacko to camera. I've known cattle stations smaller than this place.

He asked the young man the normal questions. Was he married? Were there a wife and children somewhere in the wings of this suburban palazzo?

—No-oo, said the young man stringing out the negative! My father's given me another year of freedom before I have to find a good wife.

—So you live here alone? Jacko boomed.

—Not always alone, the young man boasted rolling his eyes for the sake of remembered lusts.

—What do you fill this place with? asked Jacko. You've got sheep, angoras, llamas?

The young man thought Jacko was a hoot. Jacko said, winking at the camera, This place is big enough to be a drug rehabilitation centre.

So that confirmed my innocent view that the boy was sniffing something. Seriously, Jacko asked, what did the young man do in this great house all on his own?

—Ah! said the boy. I have friends over. My life's full.

As a demonstration of this, he indicated a table on which three telephones stood. Now he led Jacko and Clayton up the stairs, followed — I imagined — by Dannie and by cable handlers, and quickly the party were across a landing, wide as Lafayette Street, past a table with more telephones, and into the bathroom. Onyx, marble and glass. On shelves and in cupboards the young man swept open, hundreds of bottles of men's cologne and aftershave lotion were revealed. Some were of blue and green transparent glass; some of white opaque; some like amphoras; some like shards of ice; some like fists and some like phalluses.

—Jacko, the young man casually and loudly boasted, I don't believe that any of your viewers has a bigger collection than mine.

So that was the nature of Jacko's show: some men wanted from it to trace their lost daughters; others wanted their after-shave sovereignty confirmed.

Jacko himself was genuinely stimulated by such a collection. He picked up this and that bottle and exclaimed over its shape and inhaled its fumes.

—You don't realise, he told the boy. The quantity of design talent that's gone into making these things.

—Really excellent! said the young enthusiast at his elbow.

—I mean, what is it? Jacko asked. A little bit of rubbing alcohol, a little astringent spirit, ladies and gentlemen. And yet these bottles give it special significance. Aftershave is the rhinoceros-tusk powder of the modern world. And again, folks, like our and other shows, the triumph of design over substance!

Jacko's great virtue was that he meant these enthusiasms. The western world was still full of wonders
to him, since he had been sheltered from it in childhood. Stammer Jack and his head stockman had nineteenth century habits and would never have used
such fripperies as aftershave. As I would discover,
Stammer Jack did not even use such authentic mid-
twentieth century amenities as antibiotics.

So this boy's massive array of astringent nonsense
enlivened and astounded Jacko. Other media people
would have had to pretend to be enlivened and
astounded.

—My god, said Jacko. All this marble, all this glass,
all this aftershave . . . and how old are you?

—Twenty-two, confessed the boy. He spread his
arms. I'm here, girls!

—A house like this! said Jacko. At twenty-two!

—My father built me this, said the boy, his eyes
insanely coruscating. My father built a pigeon pair
either side of the street.

Jacko confessed that he and Clayton had just been
trying to break into the identical house across the
street.

—That's it! the boy said. My father and mom live
there.

Jacko stamped his big foot.

—No! This is the kiddies' wing? No! Can I join
your family?

—Big brother, said the young man, embracing
Jacko.

—I'm going to ask the main question, said Jacko.
But first I want to see your most exotic shave lotions,
young man.

The boy was quick to oblige. He showed a bottle

of South Korean lotion in the shape of a ginseng root. A Chinese version: a Chou En Lai-like rebel, fist raised, the sickle-shaped lid fitting into the fist. An Italian bottle in the shape of a forearm, a Colombian bottle in the shape of a bird.

—This isn't the only stuff you've got here from Colombia, is it? said Jacko, winking at the camera. I thought I heard someone out-of-shot, perhaps Dannie, cough sharply. A warning.

—Now big question! All this marble and shaving lotion doesn't come cheap eh? What does this wonderful father of yours — I love the feller already — what does he do for a crust?

Regular viewers of Jacko knew by now that *for a crust* meant *for a living*. Reverse bloody imperialism, mate, Jacko would tell you proudly. Bringing the tongue of Burren Waters to the unwashed.

—He works in sanitation in New York. He's a servant of the public.

—Geez, does he own his own truck yet?

The young man rolled his eyes.

—He's got friends who own plenty of trucks.

More questioning, and the boy, blinking in the manic after-glow of whatever he had taken into his body, admitted that he too was an employee of the Department of Sanitation, but the family were honoured to number among their closest friends, Sanitation Commissioner Giacomelli, a maligned but very Christian man.

—D'you mean, asked Jacko, turning arch in a way he did not do in the homes of humbler folks, these places are built on garbage?

Viewing all this, diminished by half-processed booze

and aching for a trigger of easy sentences and crystal-line insight, I was not aware that lovely, darting little Dannie and Ed Durkin in the studio began crying commands into the little mikes in both Clayton's and Jacko's earholes. Jacko and the crew were to apologize and leave at once. Dannie was mouthing the advice she was hearing from the studio. Giacomelli was under a grand jury investigation. This kid's name was probably Pilsano, and his father Rudy Pilsano was a target of the FBI, etc., etc., and was known as the King of Trash. Two witnesses the FBI and the NYPD had marshalled against Giacomelli were believed to have disappeared into the maw of an industrial strength incinerator. Dead at the time, of course. Nonetheless it was enough to give Dannie a panic attack over the future security of Jacko's huge combustible body.

Jacko therefore had Durkin yelling omens in one ear, and Clayton and Dannie making throat-cutting signals with their free hands. The sniff of danger, however, inflamed Jacko's boyishness glands.

—Oops, they want us out of here. We've violated the advertising regulations of the Sutherland Vixen network, which has an ordinance against the advertising of ginseng shaving lotion. Sorry, my young man.

And Jacko reached out and shook young Pilsano's hand.

—It's been a bracing experience.

—Okay, okay, said the boy Pilsano, holding his hands out in front of his shoulders. Listen, I'm doing a big acquisitions trip to Asia at the end of the summer . . .

In his addled brain he might have thought — at least he gave me this impression — his collection did not measure up to the world of wonders Jacko Emptor was accustomed to. I could not see Dannie's mute cries of terror or hear Durkin issuing his orders from the studio, but I understood, despite my inexact knowledge of the politics of the Rome of the modern world, that something was endangered, that some line of peril had been crossed. Clayton's camera was racing downstairs and out the door, where it dared turn once more to show that Jacko was the last to leave the marble hallway. His hand on the bewildered young Pilsano's shoulder, he helped him close the door.

—Listen, my boy, Jacko roared through the aperture, if we're breathing, we'll be back. You reckon you can look after the breathing part eh?

Within the house, the young man's phones could be heard raging. As Jacko would later say, you didn't have to be Sherlock Holmes to work out that it was the kid's father and half of New York's racketeers who were enraged.

As it was not quite time yet for the cross back to the studio, Dannie and Clayton were now making *continue-talking* gestures to Jacko. Walking down the garden path of young Pilsano, Jacko intoned:

—When they reached the mountain's summit,
    even Clancy took a pull,
  It well might make the boldest hold their
    breath,
  The wild hop scrub grew thickly, and the
    hidden ground was full
  Of wombat holes, and any slip was death.
  But the man from Snowy River let the pony
    have his head,

And he swung his stockwhip round and gave a
   cheer,
And he raced him down the mountain like a
   torrent down its bed,
While the others stood and watched in very
   fear.

*   *   *

According to Jacko, when they all went back to the
microwave truck and the limo and packed up for the
morning, young Dannie came up to him, fragrant
with barely assuaged fear, kissed him full on the lips,
began to weep, and said, Jacko, I love you!

And later in the morning, when Jacko got back to
Thomas Street, he met a First Precinct cop emerging
from Coghlan's Fenian bar.

—Hey, Jacko! Caught your show this morning.
The boys are making book on which day you're
gonna be hit!

Jacko confessed to me that he stopped then and
took the man by the shoulder. They were of approxi-
mately equal height and so Jacko could stare into the
cop's eyes.

—Are you fellers serious? I've got a young wife.

—As evidence, the cop explained, what you got
this morning is kind of graphic in regard to opulence.
I can imagine prosecutors getting mileage from it.
And I'll tell you what for free. That jerk-off shaving
lotion kid is definitely for detox and drug rehab now.
The Mob will lock him away in there and he won't
get out till he's cleaner than Mother Teresa.

Jacko was worried enough to go over to Coghlan's
and drink with the First Precinct boys, just so that

any ambushers would know that he was a friend of detectives.

—Well look, a cop told him. You've got an interesting statement about assets there, in your interview with the kid. The houses belonged to his father, so he said. I wouldn't mind guessing the records *don't* disclose that. So we've got that on tape now. And then the thing about being very close friends with Giacomelli. You've been a helluva inconvenience to the Pilsanos, Jacko. But they're not stupid enough to take on the media.

—Is that what I am? asked Jacko.

Jacko even called my wife and asked her could Lucy share our second bedroom with our visiting journalist daughter? But divine Lucy heard of the plan and baulked, laughing at Jacko and bringing her clenched hand down emphatically upon his muscular forearm.

—The one you should be worried about, she said, is *Dann-ie*! She put emphasis on both syllables and uttered the name with a New York breathiness, part Italian, part Ashkenazi Jewish.

Dannie was so enamoured of Jacko that she did not hide it even on the mornings Lucy went out in the limo with Jacko to meet the microwave-dish truck. Or maybe it was partly Dannie's strategy not to hide it, since New York girls were tough that way, scarily forthright.

I watched Lucy teasing Jacko and wondered if she could be so wise so young, or whether it was naiveté, whether she was still in the playground of James Ruse High in the west of Sydney, kidding about love as they say. Her high school was named after a convict, James Ruse, a sheep thief who had nonetheless learned farming in the west of England and who became, on a ticket of leave land grant, the continent's first private agriculturalist. A man no doubt less serpentine and less full of cunning than *Dann-ie*.

VI

On the evening of my writing classes at NYU, I would allow myself an hour of television, Judge Wapner or *Superior Court* or *Jeopardy*. During this indulgence and at the height of Jacko's search for Sunny Sondquist, I would see Vixen Six promos every half hour. *Is Sonny Sondquist the Anodyne Kid? Have you seen her? Join Jacko Emptor in his quest . . .*

Despite all the noise, I had already heard from Jacko that in some sense the quest had reached a halt. There was, to use Jacko's terminology, *viewer excitement*, but no more credible sightings.

At a loss, Jacko had interviewed Bob Sondquist again. Returning from this interview, he called me and asked could I meet him at the usual place, the Odeon on West Broadway.

As always, I should have been pleased that Jacko was filial enough to consider me a fit client of the place. But I needed to teach that night and was not in the frame of mind for a bar where everyone drank Finlandia vodka and spritzers and boutique water. The old problem: there were few ugly or aged Odeon clients, and my taste today was for the ugly and aged.

—Come on, he begged me in a tone I had never heard before, however familiar the idiom was. Be a sport. I've had a shit of a day eh. Depressing as hell.

I need to wash my damn mouth out with some honest vodka.

And so I ran down to the corner of Lafayette and found a disgruntled cab driver headed uptown, who didn't want to go around the block and who was even more outraged when I told him, No, not Broadway itself. *West* Broadway.

As I arrived, I was pleased to see that the young, rich, immortal and fragrant had not yet turned up in pernicious numbers at the Odeon. Jacko sat alone at the bar, and he half turned and watched me come in. He had little more than a grimace for me, and his greeting was mumbled.

—I might get some sleep tonight, he told me then. It was such a rare proposition to hear from Jacko's mouth!

His mannerisms were abnormal. He put first his chin and then his brow in his big hands. Then he raised his head, blinked, took up his vodka, and sipped briskly and medicinally.

—Well, I asked. What's the matter?

—What's the matter, he repeated. And he drank again and told me.

Dannie, he said, had put a research assistant onto scanning microfilm of regional newspapers for the period of Sunny Sondquist's childhood. During Bob's military career the Sondquists had lived in Florida, in Page, Utah, and in Connecticut, and Dannie had got from the military records the dates of all these postings. She had done it because she just didn't feel that four-square Bob with his competent use of his new throat box was the good citizen he affected to be.

—That's Jewish, you see, Jacko told me. If you present them with a good WASP, trim-bellied and square-bloody-shouldered, they just won't take him on face value eh. They've been slaughtered by that sort of bugger since the crack of history. They know there's got to be something wrong.

Another sip.

—Why do people have kids? he asked me, without expecting me to respond, even though I had a child of my own. He certainly didn't wait for an answer.

—So Dannie found it there. These awful bloody stories in the Salt Lake papers fourteen years back. Bob was in the quartermaster corps. And he was cooking the books some way. He had deals going with contractors *and* the sort of people who supply arms in quantity to paramilitary idiots of various bloody stripes. And his company commander knew all about it, for years, but took no action. And the question all the investigators asked was why he took no action eh. Was he in it? You know. Was the bugger in it? He *did* receive sweeteners from Bob, in part monetary. But you couldn't guess what the main sweetener turned out to be?

—No Jacko. I couldn't.

Though I did repent of my brusqueness when I saw no smile from him, saw him simply pinch his left eyebrow with his forefinger and thumb. Such serious fastidiousness of gesture had its own weight.

—The main sweetener, said Jacko in his resonating murmur, was that Bob gave his company commander his own beloved daughter, Sunny. Honest to Christ! She must have been eight or nine years old.

I was struck to silence. I listened to the riot of innocent traffic beyond the Odeon's glass walls.

—Can you imagine that scene? asked Jacko. Can you imagine it? I'm such a bloody innocent, I think that Dannie promising to dress up as an SS woman and screw my ears off is the big bad world. But *this stuff* is the really big bad world. Christ's blood, mate . . . Christ's blood hasn't reached some of these bastards. Nor has poor bloody Sunny Sondquist ever been out of the big bad world eh. Can you imagine what he said to her while he drove her round to the captain's place? All the normal fatherly advice turned on its head eh — like *Be a good girl*.

Jacko shuddered and, of course, drank again. He dropped his voice lower still.

—Why did Bob approach you like this? I asked. Well, not you . . . the other people at CBS or NBC or whatever? When he had this in his background?

—He thought we wouldn't research him. And let me tell you, others wouldn't have. That's Dannie for you eh. Dannie's work. I tell you there's such bloody evil in this country. No way I'd raise kids here. I just wouldn't. There are zones of bloody, bloody evil in this place. They believe the founders were the Pilgrim bloody Fathers. I think the founders might've been fucking Satanists. Why here, mate? Why the Bermuda bloody Triangle of malice?

If his sadness hadn't had such authority, I would have raised — not for the first time — the old, tired, always valid argument about whether *Live Wire*, and television as a whole for that matter, didn't feed into the unspeakable triangle he was speaking of. Was television the tree from the old garden, here as nowhere else? Did television make evil by daily raising the possibility of evil? Did it provide an up-till-now unthought-of option? Did it say, Lock up your women. Above all, guard your children! Even, and particularly, from yourself!

of BEE.

Or then again — a defence Jacko but, above all, the networks put up — did it act as a crucial valve on the pressures within the soul? Did it burn up the accumulations of methane which people like Jacko believed to rise in mad clouds off the swamps of the nation's Calvinist and obsessed-with-destiny spirit?

—So, Jacko breathed, Dannie and Durkin want me to hang on to this nifty little bit of info and save it for later on in the search. For now, they've made me go up there and talk to Bob about what sort of kid she was, and how she got her flare for bloody spelling bees. Well, I can tell you now how she got it. I can imagine the poor little bugger spelling for all she was worth on the way *to* and on the way *from* that bloody captain in the quartermaster corps. Northern Utah? It's right there, right in a big zone of bloody malice. No wonder she only visited that old bastard Bob Sondquist when he was flat on the recovery table and couldn't speak.

His dejection had an unaccustomed weight of its own, and I respected it. I reached my hand to his arm and caressed it. This was a gesture of extraordinary warmth for an Australian male. Beyond my own shock, I even looked forward to telling my wife about Jacko's, given that, on sound evidence, she doubted Jacko's humane qualities.

* * *

At last I needed to go. The graduate writers would already be gathering, sipping their coffees, opening the two bottles of wine they took turns to bring. I apologized about leaving, but Jacko rose and came with me anyhow. Why didn't he talk about these matters with Lucy? I wondered. Why was I the confidant?

It's just about the truth to say I had to lead him to the corner of Thomas Street and direct him home to his loft. But he delayed me on the corner of West Broadway by the big Korean grocery.

—What am I going to do, mate, about this mad Jewish sheila?

I said, You know what I think.

—Yeah.

He closed his eyes.

—Just go over that stuff about television again.

—It sounds so bloody pious.

—That's okay. I'm used to it from you. You know what I mean . . .

—Well, you know . . . I think television demands great saintliness of its practitioners. The medium, since it deifies men and women . . . it forces the necessity on them to live calmly or else destroy themselves.

—Live bloody calmly? With little Dannie after a bloke's kidney fat?

—I think I'd go home to Lucy, Jacko. You're not saying, are you, that you don't know how to tell a young producer to get lost? Well, you've got the force of character to tell Dannie to get lost.

—How do you know?

—Because it seems to me you've got enough character to be appalled by the Sondquist story. Not just as television material. Appalled by the history.

—Oh mate, he said in a near whisper. That's different. The poor bloody Anodyne Kid eh.

He opened his eyes again and considered me.

—You're like everyone. You're in love with Lucy.

I didn't feel any threat in this accusation.

—Not the way you are with Dannie.

—Come on, mate. No fantasies?

—Jesus, I protested. I suppose I was being punished for my advice. If you want to know, she's off limits in my mind. Forbidden degrees of relationship.

—Okay. You're a mad bastard. You're not telling me you were always ridgey-didge with Maureen. Loyal in all bloody circumstances, mate.

—I wish I could. We're so happy now, and if you can't see that . . . Well, if my work was better, I'd be globally happy. And drink less with yobbos like you.

—Okay, okay. No more challenges to you tonight. Look, I've got to go, and you've certainly got to go. Back to your happy home. Why does good old Maureen put up with you?

—I wake up at night with a nearly crippling regret for some of the pain I've inflicted in the past. That's what's ahead of you if you don't watch out.

—Thanks for the fucking cheery forecast.

He lumbered past the plastic and deal-encased annexe where a Korean with an axe cut kindling for sale and trimmed the flowers his family sold. What a weapon in a hold-up that tool might become.

Even now there was the chance that Jacko would seek a final comfort with the First Precinct cops at Coghlan's or with the sentimental Irish in Mary O'Reilly's.

* * *

The mystery of Jacko's not being happy with Lucy continued to exercise Maureen and me. My wife told me Lucy's version of why she did not travel with him on his *Live Wire* weekends. They fought when she did. In the end she offered to stay home, hoping he wouldn't take her up on it. He said that was probably wise. He gave her the usual promises about his behaviour — this still my wife's version of Lucy's version! Lucy spent the weekends going to galleries and concerts, more often than not with Maureen. Maureen and I were becoming the parents of these two dislocated children.

Maureen argued that it was Jacko's culpable choice *not* to be content. He had, she said, the air of a man who hadn't yet come to rest. I defended him of course. I argued that he was as bemused about it all as any of us.

And whatever the women (if they'd known) might have made of Dannie's stated desire, it seemed to me to have little meaning to Jacko one way or another. It delayed him not a second longer on the corner of Thomas Street or sent him home not a second earlier.

The following night I watched in cringing fascination as old Bob Sondquist squawked away to Jacko on *Live Wire* about Sunny and spelling bees, about how, in the pattern of her childhood habits, when she disappeared she had been studying linguistics at the University of California, Santa Cruz. His enthusiasm for the vanished girl seemed, in the light of what Jacko had told me, so fraudulently poignant. The unjust father redesigning his own daughter's childhood, working up into some sort of effigy the ashes of the burned years. All this to accord with the culture's lust for that wholesomeness, that sheen of redemptive niceness, which habitually — at least in Jacko's zones of malice — covered monstrous sins.

It was ghastly viewing, but I viewed it just the same.

VII

Some time after my first visit to Burren Waters, I made accidental contact in Sydney with Jacko's younger brother, Francis Emptor, through a friend of mine, Oscar Mulcahy. Oscar was an operamane, a member of the Board of the Australian Opera, headquartered as it was beneath Joern Utzon's great white ceramic sails on Bennelong Point.

Oscar was a big-boned, beefy, generous and polemical sort of man, deriving perhaps from the same hulking Scots-Irish-farmer gene pool as the Emptors. People often said his shoe manufacturing business was the largest in the country, but Oscar would tell you it was the only and the last. Imports from Asia, he robustly declared, were killing him.

With an elegantly thin wife he had nicknamed Hefty, Oscar lived on the upper floor of a beautiful art deco apartment block above Elizabeth Bay. The Mulcahys' was one of my favourite places for a party. From its windows you could see the beautiful mid-Harbour, the Heads and, close in, the little green island on which vegetables had been grown by a lovesick lieutenant of Marines called Ralph Clarke during Sydney's first few starved years as a British gulag.

There was also the excitement inherent in the fact that next door to the Mulcahys lived the greatest

Australian diva since Nellie Melba, Dame Roberta Murdoch. A large-boned, pleasant woman, widowed some years past, as iconic as Michael Bickham but more open. Less terrifying to the beholder, she was occasionally found at Mulcahy parties. A great part of the year she lived in Switzerland, from which she had access to the great opera houses of Europe and where — according to sniping opinion — she found a more congenial tax regime than she might enjoy in Britain or Australia.

Some Sydney operamanes, participants in the brother- and sisterhood of those great white wings of the Sydney Opera House, fashionably believed — at least on the days she did not come to Oscar's parties — that Dame Roberta was past her best. They even showed a common anger that the mass of the Australian public did not participate in their belief in Dame Roberta's decline and remained devoted to her and were excited by her as by no other singer. They were somehow annoyed by the well of love and respect the public harboured for her. It seemed, too, that the managements of La Scala or the New York Met, bereft of the sophisticated tastes of some of Mulcahy's guests, went on ignorantly renewing her performance contracts, and Philips records went on reissuing new editions of her recent work.

The proposition that Dame Roberta suffered from diminished timbre was not one on which Oscar and his sylph wife Hefty laid particular stress. Their fixed idea had more to do with what they called the *gay clique* amongst the devotees of the opera. They would fulminate about it in front of their thin, middle-aged housekeeper, René Fabre, a former ballet dancer from

London. René, French by birth, would frequently agree with the Mulcahys, camping it up and telling the assembly at cocktail parties, These young queers are not as responsible as we older women.

But whatever René and the Mulcahys said never seemed to cast doubt on the standing of young Francis Emptor, Jacko's brother and a notable member, if not a focus, of the clique. Without question, the Mulcahys loved Francis, and René admired him.

—Very wealthy, my dear, said René, explaining young Emptor to me as Hefty took tall Francis's cloak of ermine off his shoulders and hung it in the hall cupboard with the coats of less flamboyant opera buffs. Works all week, just like a wage slave, even though he's so wealthy, don't you know.

René had learned to speak his English in the corps of Sadler's Wells, so that his conversation was full of these *don't you knows* and *my dears*.

—Independent wealth, said René. But he labours away as an airfreight agent during the week, my dear. Says he wouldn't be able to fill in his time without work.

I had heard nothing about Francis's wealth from Chloe, and very little about his friendships with the renowned. But at the Mulcahys' or at the opera, you could find Francis speaking with Sydney's wealthiest and most cultivated people, although, as Oscar would readily tell you, the two categories did not always coincide.

Francis Emptor had the enormous, plate-faced look of Stammer Jack and of his brother Jacko, but of course somehow different and refined down by the input of Chloe. The truth was — and I hesitate to say it since it is such a cliché, though even clichés recur with a biological frequency — that Francis Emptor resembled the young Oscar Wilde. The similarity existed in the enormous brow and long jawline, and was heightened by Emptor's taste for Wildean dress. He had that same celestial quality too. None of the houndlike sexual avidity which sat frankly beaming on Jacko's features.

Francis lived with a houseful of boyfriends in Woollahra, but that did not draw any sort of comment, nor did it make him look one iota less ethereal, less pre-Raphaelite, less like a visitant angel with significant tidings to impart.

—Life isn't fair to heterosexuals, said Oscar — who had also seen the resemblance to a Renaissance saint. Or maybe it's too fair. Women put up with a lot of grossness in men. But those buggers root all night and still look like the Angel bloody Gabriel.

One evening in Sydney's bright Opera House, I found myself sitting beside Francis Emptor at a performance of *Il Trovatore*, a neutral performance not involving Dame Roberta. I'd never been an opera lover, and Mulcahy frequently invited me out of a kindly perversity. I argued that the form was a kind of largely nineteenth century folk opera, which had become gratuitously sanctified to the point where people who wanted to be seen as respectable attended as at best a sort of necessary religious observance. A religious observance which then had to be subsidized out of consolidated revenue. I half believed this rhetoric, though I was always captivated by Dame Roberta Murdoch, who transcended all the rules.

* * *

The night I sat beside Frank, however, *did* suggest the limits of opera by featuring a fine English soprano who was nonetheless some fourteen-stone in weight. Her voice was as slim, piercing and angelic as Francis Emptor himself, but over her body — we were led to believe — the tenor and the baritone were willing to enter a death struggle with each other, or take into their hands the means of their own destruction.

The set designs that night were magnificent, the work of a man who shared a house with René, an older and soberer gay than Francis Emptor.

At the end of Act I, my wife Maureen and I left our seats briskly, keeping up with Francis who, as it proved, showed an unapologetic urgency to reach his preening station near the champagne bar. We talked with him about the designs. I said they were the only things I liked about the whole rampant excess of the thing, and he asked nicely whether I didn't think the design was totally out of character with everything else.

—Rococo and the surreal just don't fit, he threw over his shoulder.

We were separated. I saw him from a distance, laughing by the bar, a flute of Moët in his hand, amidst a flock of young, seamless-faced men. He was a young man so frankly enraptured by the elements of his life that I, a so-called *straight* boy from the west of Sydney, could imagine embracing him more or less as a kind of aesthetic congratulation. I was taken by the look of him, the same transcendent appetite I would come to see in different circumstances and in a different tone on his brother Jacko's face.

Maureen and I went back to our seats. We were

close enough to the curtains to hear the urgent thump of stage hands. Francis returned too and settled himself.

—I met your mother at Burren Waters, I told Francis.

—My God, he said. You didn't meet my father the stammerer?

—He was sick.

—Tell me about it, said Francis, arching his epicene eyebrows. The man is so full of hate. I wish I could do something for him. Above all, for my mother.

—She's a rare woman.

—Oh yes. Lost up there amongst the cattle. Her only salvation: the arts program on ABC television! Don't worry, I've asked her to come down here and live at my place. I mean, all this . . . she'd love this.

In one sense it was true. But I imagined Chloe amidst the sybaritic pack giving off the same air of discontent as she did amongst Stammer Jack's dusty herds.

—She might simply love your father, I suggested, the result of an odd impulse to challenge him.

—Well, he said indulgently, she likes he-men. That's a weakness. She would like your friend Mulcahy. Oscar's the muscle man of the Australian Opera.

So we had another act, in which the English soprano delivered herself of the gravity of her size and achieved the weightlessness of her top register. I saw that beautiful Francis Emptor dozed for a time, his faintly tanned cheek leaning towards the shoulder of his cape under the weight of his own perfection.

I was more fascinated by him now than by the action on stage, the relentless coloratura of Verdi.

When he woke up in the near dark, he seemed embarrassed. I looked fixedly at the stage to convince him I hadn't noticed. Just in case I had, he yawned at the end of the applause.

—It's the San Francisco Opera season, he said as people rose around us for the interval. I've gone over there the last two weekends out of three. Sometimes I feel my brain is located halfway across the Pacific. Neither at one opera house nor the other.

He rose wearily, but was soon sparkling in the company of others, this time in the Opera Board's enclosure, where drinks were served to business folk like the Mulcahys and to the stars of the opera audience. It became impossible to get near Francis — a woman parliamentarian from Macquarie Street was hogging his attention.

When we were back in our seats, I had time to ask him, How often do you go to San Francisco for the opera?

—I believe it's twenty-one times in the past nine months, he told me, certain of the authority of these facts.

—That's two weekends a month, I said, doing my awe-struck sums.

—Sometimes three a month, he told me softly.

He was readier than I would have expected to give me the logistical details.

He always ended work half an hour early on Fridays, since a limousine arrived then to take him from his office block in the city to the airport in time for the evening flight to San Francisco. He lay back in his bed-like seat in first class, took champagne and a sleeping pill, and slept all night. He knew all the stewards on Qantas, he said, and they were very kind to him. It was like spending a night in a good hotel where the staff respected you and did all they could for your comfort.

Due to the mercies of the dateline, he arrived in San Francisco on Friday morning, at an hour earlier than he'd left Sydney. He had lunch with friends, took a nap, attended the San Francisco Opera, where he said he felt just as much at home as he did at the Australian Opera. He had made friends with Delva Costa, the great American contralto, and he was frequently invited to attend her levees after the performance. He told me in confidence and without braggadocio that he was very well known in San Francisco — a radio station had interviewed him about his passion for crossing the Pacific just to hear Delva Costa on Friday nights.

—They think it's a long way, of course. We Australians are the only ones who know the secrets of the size of the world. We *know* it's not such a long way.

Then he would catch the noon plane from San Francisco for Sydney, shedding Sunday as again he crossed the dateline, stopping in Honolulu, and arriving in Sydney around six in the morning, just in time to have breakfast and to go to his desk.

—That sounds really punishing.

—I love it. I absolutely love it. I've got this weekend off, but I go again the following weekend. I get high on Delva's great amber voice, and on champagne and jet lag. I mean, other people are terrified at not knowing what the time is. I'm stimulated by it. Sometimes though, midnight *does* hit me on the head in the middle of the morning.

—You land at dawn and work at your desk all morning?

—Oh yes. I know the air cargo business backwards. The whole operation would fall apart if I weren't there to tell them what to do. That's why I stay on. What would I do with my days anyhow?

I imagined him on humid Sydney Monday mornings, returned from Delva Costa and capeless at his computer.

It was only when the applause had died and Francis Emptor was turning to me to say goodbye that I remembered Mother Emptor's large objective.

—You know your mother wants to meet Michael Bickham?

—Yes, I know.

He made a tushing noise with his lips.

—I'm sorry, he told me. There's nothing I can do now. We fell out. I'm not really Michael Bickham's kind of queer, though his friend Khalil likes me. But with Michael — *persona non grata*.

His mouth set in a fierce line. There had been some savage exchange between Francis Emptor, clerk-operamane, and brother Bickham, modernist god.

VIII

At last, soon after my first meeting with Francis Emptor, I went back to Burren Waters with my wife and a second photographer, poor Larson's successor in the book project. My desire to lay eyes on the mongrel bastard Stammer Jack was dampened. I had nothing of any promise to report to Chloe in the matter of organizing a meeting between the great modernist and Nobel Prize winner, Michael Bickham, and herself.

Even though someone had once given me Bickham's number, I hadn't wanted to call him directly and perhaps delay his work. So I called a young poet I knew to be his friend and asked him would he kindly call Bickham's place and give my number to Khalil, Bickham's companion and — as some would say — housekeeper.

Nearly half a century before, Khalil had been a pleasant Levantine agent of British Intelligence whom the young Lieutenant Bickham of the Second AIF had met when the Australians captured Syria from the Vichy French in 1941. The gossip about their present domestic arrangements was that Bickham was a bit of a house devil and that Khalil was gentle and genial.

Khalil did call me at last. I told him that there was a woman from the Northern Territory who was desperate to discuss motherhood with the great writer. I said that at first sight she was not the sort of woman Bickham might like meeting, that she was loud and, in the terms of Woollahra, a bit primitive, but she had sensibility and passionate admiration. My shameful internal excuse for explaining Chloe away was that I was anticipating Bickham's snobbery by giving voice to my own.

Khalil said, Michael's having a bad time with his emphysema at the moment. He's only seeing people he knows well. He'd love to see this woman, but he's not in good enough health for adventures of that nature.

I was half relieved to hear it — I had fulfilled my duty. But then I asked him if I bought a copy of the book Chloe loved and dropped it in to Bickham's place, could Mr Bickham find the time to sign it?

Even at my level of accomplishment, people asked such questions tentatively of my wife Maureen, who was my protector and mediator with the world the way Khalil was for Bickham. Khalil said grudgingly, but without rancour, that would be fine. I could understand why he would be reluctant. He was the one who would have to answer Bickham's questions: Who? Him. Why didn't you tell him . . .?

To write a major work and then have to put more verbiage into signing copies of it than you did into the work itself!

So I bought a hardcover copy of *The Mother as Aphrodite* and brought it to Bickham's fine two-storey colonial mansion in Woollahra. The house sat behind a grey sandstone wall. Its sandy garden was full of roses and its wide verandahs ornamented with the sort of wrought iron which had come to Australia in the nineteenth century as ships' ballast. Used then for building fences and grille work, it had been taken for granted by Sydney-siders until John Betjeman, poet laureate to the Court of St James, had so praised it in the '60s.

I pressed the button on the gateway, and the gate buzzed itself open. As I walked up the path amongst the roses, the gentle-eyed Khalil appeared on the verandah to greet and intercept me. He said that Michael again sent his regrets, but he was having a very bad patch at the moment and couldn't face people. I was very flattered that the great man found it necessary to offer me such excuses. I'd put a slip of paper in asking Bickham to sign it, *To Chloe Emptor, a mother*. Khalil brought it back at last in his soft, cautious hands, the hands of the young man Bickham had fallen for in a campaign which even Australians no longer remembered.

—Michael doesn't usually do personal inscriptions, or should I say personalized ones.

The misogynistic old bugger — as I thought of him in that second — had written only *Michael Bickham*. Chloe would have to be content with that. I had spent three hours of what could possibly have been writing time on fetching the signature for Chloe, and it would get me — in her eyes — barely a pass.

That afternoon I made a complicated radio telephone call to Burren Waters. Stammer Jack answered the phone. I wanted him to know we were coming.

—We've b-b-been expecting you.

—Could you tell Mrs Emptor I'm bringing my wife too? Over.

—Okay. That's fine with C-Chloe. I'll t-t-t . . . I'll let her know. Over and out.

Like Michael Bickham, Stammer Jack was pleased to be finished with me.

It took a day of flying from Sydney and the better part of a day of driving to get to Burren Waters. When we presented ourselves at the homestead on the afternoon of the second day, my wife, myself, the skinny English photographer who was taking over from Larson, Chloe clearly didn't know that we were coming. She did not even know that my wife was my wife.

—And what are you? Chloe challenged Maureen. Some sort of production assistant or something?

I gave Chloe Bickham's book and told her that explicit arrangements to visit Burren Waters had been made through Stammer Jack.

—That mongrel bastard! she said. He didn't say a bloody word. He does it deliberately you know.

She stood on the verandah by the bookshelves and whistled. A young thin-faced Aboriginal stockman, who must have happened to be in the bookkeeper's office, came jogging across the Emptor red dust station square.

—Mrs Emptor? he said.

—Go and tell that mongrel bastard Jack Emptor that I said thanks for not letting me know these people were coming.

The boy said Okay and Chloe, turning to us and adjusting her sarong around her brown breasts, said, Just as long as he knows I'm keeping a bloody score eh.

I was in sweet with her now. She liked Maureen and I had given her the Bickham book as well. She turned the hardcover of *The Mother as Aphrodite* over in her hands, considering and reconsidering it.

—Gotta thank you for this, she said.

Meanwhile the young stockman carrying her message of conjugal chagrin sauntered off towards the enormous hangar near the quarter-horse sale ring. In the hangar, apparently, Stammer Jack kept office hours when he wasn't being a hypochondriac.

—You met my son Frank at the opera, murmured Chloe, pensively stroking the gloss of Michael Bickham's dust cover with her thumb.

I said we had.

—What did you think he looked like?

My wife said that he had looked pretty splendid in his cloak.

Chloe stayed reflective. In a small voice she asked the vacant, blazing air above Burren Waters where she'd got her damn kids from.

—Anyhow, I said, he uses his inheritance pretty stylishly.

—Inheritance? asked Chloe, clamping on the word like a hawk.

—Everyone in Sydney thinks he's had some lucky inheritance. I think he might even say so himself.

—What inheritance would he have that Jacko and Helen and Petie don't? she challenged us. What he tells me is that some Australian tycoon who's secretly a queen keeps him in style. Like a mistress, you know.

She thought about this for a while, balancing her huge passion for talk against her pygmy one for discretion, and then she said, The little ponce has even implied that it's Basil Sutherland, you know, the press baron. He even reckons that's why that hoon Jacko got the job with the blonde on morning television eh. But I don't know if it's the truth, see. Frank's always had these fantasies about all of us being beholden to him. He wanted me to go and live with him, can you imagine that? Surrounded by mincing bloody popinjays eh. But he'd love to have me totally dependent on him, you know. Instead of being totally dependent on that mongrel bastard over there in the shed!

I asked how Petie and Sharon were. She told me Sharon had shot through. She missed her family and the soapies on the commercial channels.

—She just wasn't right for here eh.

I didn't tell her Frank Emptor felt the same about her, Chloe. That Chloe wasn't made for it either.

—So . . . Petie'll be off to Sydney on another shopping expedition soon, and we'll end up playing host to another little twat who doesn't know what in Christ's name she's letting herself in for.

*   *   *

We drank tea amongst the books and then towards mid-afternoon an enormous man in an Akubra, overalls and stockman's boots came lumbering through the continuum of bright light and red earth towards the verandah. Chloe gathered herself as if she had an invisible handbag clutched in her lap. Giant Stammer Jack, whom I'd only got a glimpse of on my last trip, came through the gate, into Chloe's bore-watered, hectically green garden of succulents. Wearily he mounted the steps.

—Gidday, he said. The word of greeting caused him no stammer problems, since it involved the tongue very little and was as guttural as a throat clearing.

—Listen, Jack. Thanks a million for telling me these people were coming.

—Oh yeah. That's right eh.

He said it in a tone of revelatory memory.

—I t-t-talked to you two d-days ago. Didn't I eh?

His eyes were neutral and a little glazed. According to what Jacko would tell me later, from breakfast onwards he steadily drank Bundaberg Rum shipped inland from the Queensland coast. A riverine map of purple lay on either side of his nose. Tan did not hide it — in fact he was not very tanned at all. He came from a place and generation which saw no kudos in being blistered by the sun. For his sun was a different creature from the sun of the Gold Coast, Australia's version of Florida, two thousand miles away on the Pacific coast.

Chloe said, Bloody hell!

Stammer Jack told us he'd see us later eh, show us some of the quarter horses if we liked.

—Most of *them* can communicate better than you, you old bastard! Chloe called after him in a way which made the words sound well-worn, habitual as a wedding ring.

* * *

Later in the afternoon, Stammer Jack fetched us from our rooms in the stockmen's quarters and took us as promised to see some of his horses, who were being exercised on a long rein by his chief black stockman, Nugget. Nugget waved with an anthracite hand, for the Wodjiri were intensely black and, unlike the blacks of Manhattan, not even their palms had a pinkness. Nugget was a superb, ageless, skinny figure. He was both a Wodjiri elder and a distant in-law of the Emptors. At the time of course I did not understand this connection.

As we watched quarter horses do their circuits, I reminded Stammer Jack that last time we had been up here in Burren Waters he had been in bed with his damaged ankle. I asked how was it now.

After a number of assaults on the words, he said it wasn't bad these days.

—What happened? I asked him.

I'll relay what he then said without the stammers which punctuated it.

—I was out mustering with Boomer in the helicopter. Bloody thing lost aerodynamics. Crashed right in the middle of a herd of cattle eh. Must've killed a hundred of the buggers.

I said it was lucky it was just his ankle he hurt.

—Well, see, I had my ankle out the bloody door and the whole bloody contraption came down on it.

—On your ankle?

—Yeah. Bit painful eh.

He seemed to take thought and then decide that perhaps I wasn't too bad a poor bastard. Perhaps Chloe had complained about me to him, how I was wilfully neglecting my real work to write a travel book about the banal, bloody Territory. Being complained about by Chloe gave us a fraternal bond. In any case he hoicked the leg of his overalls so that I could see his ankle in its cut-away cowboy boot.

I beheld above the excised leather something which resembled a purple tree trunk: scaly, the white of dead flesh hanging loose.

—Gave me a hell of a bruise, see. Sometimes it just

swells up so hard I've got to let it all out with a knife and rub some meths in eh.

Since he clearly didn't want me to, I didn't exclaim and make undue noises of horror. I thought of Florey synthesizing antibiotics more than half a century ago for the sake of injuries like Stammer Jack's. But in the Emptor world the knife and methylated spirits were men's medicine. And Stammer Jack, hesitating perhaps before plunging the knife into his own ankle, became a hypochondriac in the eyes of his spouse Chloe Emptor.

*   *   *

The English photographer, seeing the little grandstand at the quarter horse sale ring, decided that he would get the entire population of Burren Waters — Aboriginals, stockmen, their wives and daughters, white stockmen, accountant, cook, school teacher, Petie, Stammer Jack and Chloe — to sit in there. It would be a kind of team photograph, a portrait of a medieval village in remote Australia.

He spoke of this to Stammer Jack.

—That'll be fine. Just speak to Chloe eh. She'll g-get it all together.

So we went and saw Chloe, and she called various stockmen over from the stockmen's quarters and sent them off with messages, and at about four thirty in the afternoon, when the light was crystalline, everyone gathered at the sale ring for their picture. The children from the school were in holiday mood.

Chloe, team captain, sat in the middle of the front row. But Stammer Jack did not appear.

The English photographer enquired, Should we wait for Mr Emptor?

Chloe sniffed and said, The bastard isn't coming.

I had known Mark Torlucci for twenty years and had written a little screenplay for a quartet of short films he made in the early '70s. I liked him and admired him for his proletarian and — dare I say — *matey* style and for his enormous talents. He was one of the rugged, founding directors of the new Australian cinema, about which people were starting to ask during the late '80s, *Where had it gone?*

The truth was that, having revivified their film industry, the Australians then turned it into a mandarin bureaucracy, and for a time provided investors with tax breaks which made the completion of films more important than their quality. Little by little, control of the making of films fell into the hands of plausible, talentless people, pursuing and approving their own limited ideologies of film-making. By the mid-'80s the directors who had emerged in the '70s, particularly Torlucci, Weaver and Brotherton, began to work in America. They would even seek a great deal of the finance for their Australian films in America.

Though by his fiftieth year Torlucci had worked with a number of esteemed screen writers and actors, and had shot films in Moscow and Prague and Mexico as well as in Australia, he retained the same Melbourne larrikin accent, the same antipodean loudness, the same business of masking his percipience in apparent callowness which had characterized him in his twenties.

I am sure that, thereby, he confused Americans not a little; they were used to people of sensibility speaking in delicate and careful sentences. They were not used to clever people — and Torlucci was certainly more than a clever director — parodying their own gifts in rough argot.

Torlucci did not speak so much differently from Jacko Emptor. His idiom, like Jacko's, was in some ways a device, but it was bred in the bone too.

One braw afternoon as we sat in the Odeon, I told Jacko I was going to Torlucci's birthday party. It was a very informal business at Torlucci's flat up on the East Side in the Eighties. I should have remembered the experience I had with Chloe, for the intrusive gene rose in Jacko and he immediately asked, D'you reckon I could string along with you? I always wanted to meet Torlucci.

My friendship with Torlucci was long-standing enough, and Jacko's renown or notoriety large enough, for me to ask the Torluccis, Could I bring Jacko and Lucy with me?

So Maureen and I went down to Thomas Street to pick up Jacko and Lucy, and travel in the one cab. Jacko was delighted. Torlucci's door was one which he wanted to have conventional entrée to.

Torlucci's apartment turned out to be a relatively plain one and not on the same scale as the Victorian mansion he owned back home. The functional nature of the apartment was explained in part by the fact he had begotten a large and expensive Australian family before meeting up with his present wife, a Los Angeles-bred woman of Russian-Jewish ancestry called Rachel. A woman who — everyone said — could not only control reckless Torlucci but also make him happy about it. I was aware that the feverish quality Torlucci had in the early days, as if he were worried he'd never get enough life, meet enough women, was gone now, and that was due to either age or Rachel or both. I suspected it was chiefly Rachel. Unlike Torlucci's former Australian wives, Rachel spoke quietly in public and had a restrained laugh, a minute titter. But it was obvious my racy friend Torlucci — who had always said he liked loud women — was, just the same, calmly devoted to her in a way that hadn't prevailed in his earlier loves.

Torlucci's living room was decorated with the very fine Central Australian paintings of Rachel Torlucci. Rachel had painted them during a location shoot near Ayers Rock, and they gave the living room a certain spaciousness. Mark showed them to all arriving guests.

Around the living room I could see a number of the actors from Torlucci's last film, which had been shot in the two new glamour locations for making films: Czechoslovakia for the architecture and the melancholy; Jackson Hole, Wyoming for the alpine clarity. As I looked into the room, I felt the electric excitement of spotting a star in the flesh; it is like seeing a ghost and it generates as many anecdotes.

Holding Lucy by one hand, Jacko dug me in the ribs with the other.

—Shit eh! he told me.

Jacko performed an intense version of the *mate* ritual with Torlucci.

—Good of you to invite me, mate. Always wanted to meet you, mate, really have.

We were all introduced to everybody else. Rachel's mother and sister, various publicists, Torlucci's agent, a renowned man named Abe Levi who, leaning on a bench in the Torluccis' kitchen, was reading a *New Yorker* review of Torlucci's new film.

* * *

We tried to be composed when introduced to the lead actors, the man and the woman.

—Oh hello!

As if we'd been trying to put a name to their stellar faces and Torlucci — through his introductions — had now resolved our bewilderment.

Both stars were sober people, drinking nothing but water, not even Perrier and orange juice, and painstakingly trim.

The slim leverage I had over them was that I had known Torlucci since the days when he made commercials in Melbourne. I had even played small parts in his two earliest films, one of which was based on a novel of mine.

Given that everyone expected Australians to be crass, I had my crass line: I'd known Mark when he was unhappily married for the *second* time.

Torlucci's reply: That's all right you bastard, I've known you since Maureen and I were lovers.

The male star told us, When I met Mark Torlucci for the first time, I went back to our apartment and said to my wife, Torlucci is the most vulgar man I have ever met. Four days later, I went home and said, Torlucci is the most brilliant man I've ever met.

He appealed to Jacko.

—Why do you guys send mixed signals like this?

Jacko had the most pleasant way of not yielding, when he chose not to yield.

—Wouldn't you say though, old mate, that you blokes send mixed signals too. Mean to say, we talk uncivilized and we've got some secret class. A lot of you, yourself excepted of course, talk civilized, but . . . well, Jesus Christ, you don't need me to finish the sentence. An example. On the campuses of the universities you've got all this political correctness, calling women and blacks and Hispanics by their right names. All very well and good. But in the big world of the corporations and the government, the *graduates* of the universities treat women and blacks and Mexicans like turds eh. And on the street, mate, on the street . . . women are just cannon fodder.

Jacko and I exchanged glances, mine a warning in part. For a second a kind of pungency, a sort of smoky vacancy, flavoured the Torlucci living room. I remembered the picture of the Sondquist girl offered in the hands of muscular Bob.

It was interesting, too, to ask why Jacko had spoken out like this. It might have been nationalism of a kind. It might have been a case of Jacko getting a few blows in on a movie star, though it didn't sound like that. It sounded in fact a little like that rare Emptor beast: a surge of authentic outrage.

The film star politely agreed with Jacko on the question of American hypocrisy. There was nothing there which he could disagree with. He had made many liberal films about America's sins.

* * *

Amongst the other guests was a small, bouncy woman in a black cocktail dress who came from the same west-Russian gene pool as Rachel Torlucci. For that reason, I suspected at first that she was Rachel's relative. It turned out that she was the wife of the tall, slim Southerner across the room, the man who spoke with that easy lilt foreigners love and Yankees despise. There was a sort of Thespian polish to this man, and I thought he must be an actor. He was as tidily made as that. It had been established that his name was Dart, short for D'Artagnan he told me, his father having been an Alexander Dumas reader.

Lucy Emptor and my wife and I got talking to him, and Lucy asked him with a James Ruse High sort of smile, copious and utterly lacking in malice, if he was in the film business.

He said he wasn't, not directly. He was in politics.

Lucy Emptor said, Politics eh. What sort of politics, Dart?

—I'm Governor of Tennessee, said Dart. That's how I met Mark Torlucci. You remember his film before last. It was shot in Tennessee. We've got this State Film Commission down there. We're a number one location: farmland, forest, plains, mountains. We can even mock up a passable ocean some place like Douglas Lake.

The divine Lucy said, Astounding!

I forget which one of us asked him whether his wife was in politics too.

—Oh no, he said. My wife is conductor of the Knoxville Symphony. We're in good shape with the symphony. Recruiting from all over the nation. Throwing out a challenge to the Scottsdale Symphony. You know? From Arizona.

He held his hands out in front of him making —
with a very handsome half-smile — a disclaimer.

—Now I didn't appoint her. She was appointed by
my predecessor in office. It's on the record. But I was
always a patron of the symphony. That little woman
right there has a very adventurous repertoire. I'd
argue she's extended the tastes of audiences in the
state of Tennessee by a factor of two or three. The
conductor before her tried to cosset folks with the
Barcarole and Ravel's *Bolero* and Gilbert and Sullivan
and even rock and roll and country music. But you
can't beat Nashville with a symphony no matter how
you try. You shouldn't try in the first place. Amy
there does audiences the great honour of taking them
seriously, and giving them the serious article.

Gradually everyone in the room was learning, as
we had, that the mannerly Dart was the Democratic
Governor of Tennessee. They were aided in their
efforts by Torlucci's jovial cry, Have you met my
governor yet? I would have guessed that Jacko was
by now a party to that open secret.

Towards eleven o'clock my wife and Lucy wanted
to go home. Jacko asked Lucy if he could stay on. As
an act of submission, it somehow rang untrue and
made people who heard it laugh. Lucy herself, my
wife, even me.

—Okay, Jacko, said Lucy, with her apparently limitless good will. Let me stamp your leave pass eh.

* * *

By the time Jacko and I saw them off in a cab and
came back upstairs, there were not many guests left.
Dart the governor and Amy the conductor were still

there. Amy stood in the kitchen talking with Rachel Torlucci and her mother and sisters. From across the living room, I saw Jacko sit down on the sofa beside Dart, slap him familiarly on the leg and say, Okay, Dart, you old bugger. What do you do for a crust eh?

—A crust?

—Line of work, explained Jacko.

—No, said Dart with a quiet smile, not totally lacking in intent. I'd rather hear first what you do, Jack . . . Jacko?

Jacko explained that he was a television journalist with Vixen Six, you know, Sutherland's crowd. I was struck with both the humility and pretensions of respectability which were attached to that description. *Television journalist*. Video trespasser might have been more accurate.

Dart asked subtly, And do you work sometimes with a program called *Live Wire*?

—Yeah. I do a bit of work for *Live Wire*. But listen, I'm bored with that shit. You look to me like a feller who's got a real life. Tell me what you do, Dart mate!

—I thought you knew already, Jacko. I'm Governor of Tennessee.

—Gee eh, said Jacko in echo of Lucy Emptor.

But then, as if he was short-sighted and needed to focus better on Dart, he pushed himself back dramatically into the corner of the sofa.

—Oh, Jesus, you're not *that* governor, are you?

Dart said, smiling still, Exactly right, Jacko. I'm *that* governor.

I saw now that Jacko was utterly shaken. He was beyond artifice, beyond the normal cunning of his trade.

—Oh mate, what can I say?

—You might remember, Jacko, said Dart, seeming even to enjoy himself, you might remember the day last fall you talked your way past our guards and we eye-balled each other in the lobby of the gubernatorial mansion. You might remember that.

—Oh shit mate, I remember.

Dart said, It sort of stuck in my memory too, Jacko.

—Oh Jesus, mate, what can I say? I can plead professional duty eh, or I can come clean and confess to you it was my idea to hit the mansion.

—That doesn't surprise me for some reason, Dart murmured.

—All right, fair play! Can I do something to make up? I mean, totally without malice, mate. Totally without malice! Can I do something eh?

Naturally I did not know what any of this meant, but I noticed that Dart's wife, Amy, in the middle of her conversation with Torlucci's wife, had been distracted by Jacko's histrionics in the living room. She came stamping into the living room to enquire. She leaned forward to look closely at Jacko, and recognition swept thunderously across her face.

—Jesus, she asked her husband. Why didn't I recognize him?

Dart still twinkled with irony rather than ill will, but his wife the conductor looked murderous.

—I think we should go now, Dart, she told her husband.

—Just let me finish causing discomfort to Mr Emptor here, honey, said the governor.

—Oh Jesus, mate! Jacko kept saying, raising his hands to his face. Like a literary critic, he had thought till now that he could live on free of any riposte from a victim. His concept of a victim had always been something more akin to Sunny Sondquist than to Dart the governor.

The conductor said, I'll wait for you in the kitchen, Dart.

She pounded out on brisk, firm legs.

Jacko rocked and threw his arms wide.

—Dart, he said, let me assure you of something! That first wife of yours did herself a disservice coming on *Live Wire*. I mean, *Live Wire*'s mad as a meat axe to start with, and if mad people go on it, it's all compounded eh. I mean, electorally, she did you a big favour. And then in one sense, you're fair game, aren't you? We only follow the trail of blood, old son! But we don't actually put the knife in.

I was still trying to follow the argument. I could see that in the kitchen, Rachel and Mark Torlucci were listening avidly to a pell-mell explanation from Amy the conductor about why Jacko was an offence to her. Torlucci had his lips parted and was shaking his head, half-amused, half-unbelieving.

In the living room, Jacko repeated his earlier offer.

—Dart, mate, I'd be willing to go down there to Nash- ville at any time and make an upbeat story about your administration.

Dart said equably, I think you've made enough stories, Jacko.

Still attempting to discern what all this meant — Jacko's discomfiture, Dart's whimsy, his smile degenerating, however, into a grimace at the corners of the mouth, and Amy's fury — I looked first at Jacko as he flailed contritely, skewered by Dart's urbanity, and then at the wife in the kitchen further informing my friends the Torluccis. This wife was surely not the same wife Jacko was speaking of to Dart. I was relieved for the sake of my long love of Torlucci to see that indeed he was making polite efforts not to laugh. Rachel Torlucci, however, seemed as grim as Amy. Whatever Jacko had done clearly shocked women more drastically than men.

—Sure, Jacko was saying, I behaved like a circus, but that's the medium, Dart. Because television *is* a circus, and it's only bloody hypocrites who dress it up as if it's Moses receiving the bloody tablets eh. I mean, honest to God, you would have let into your office by appointment video jockeys who had more ill will against you than I had. I just wanted to ask you what you thought of what your mad missus'd said? Sure, I did it in the style of our bloody awful show. But they're all pretty bloody awful shows, Dart mate, all those bloody stick-up-the-arse commentators who are clowns but don't know it.

—I didn't realize, said the Governor of Tennessee, that your approach to the medium was as philosophic as this, Jacko.

And he winked across the room at me.

Watching the impact of that wink on the party in the kitchen, I was aware that Mrs Dart had seen it and — not knowing what a savagely wry gesture it had been — decided that her husband was letting the dreadful Jacko go free. On the minute heels of her fashionable shoes, she came pounding into the living room again. Though a coffee table laden with half-empty plates of food stood between him and Dart's wife, Jacko flinched.

—I've been trying to think, the governor's wife announced, of an act of reprisal vulgar enough to match you, your program, and all that immoral television Basil Sutherland has brought into our lives. If I could I would organize a group of Tennessee ex-cons, even bigger and flabbier than you, to sodomize you. Except it would be bad for my husband's political reputation. As it is, I am reduced to slapstick. I'm sure you understand slapstick. It's the art form which followed Impressionism.

From the table she lifted a two-thirds full jug of orange juice. All the film people, except Mark's agent and the lead actors, had drunk of this orange juice very slowly, cautious of its power to fatten them. She made as if to hurl it by the handle, but then thought of the Torluccis' upholstery. So she reached across the coffee table and directed all the fluid fairly accurately over Jacko's chest and lap.

She placed the jug back on the table and murmured, Ape.

Turning back towards the kitchen, she called over her shoulder, I'd like to go whenever you're ready, Dart.

She kissed Rachel and Torlucci. Torlucci was leaning on the refrigerator, beating the enamel in hilarity. When the governor's wife and then Rachel looked at him, he tried to restrain himself. Rachel had a level, compelling gaze. I could hear the conductor apologizing formally to Rachel and to Mark Torlucci. And then she disappeared down the hall and into a bedroom, searching for her coat.

Jacko had stood up. He flapped his hands, dripping orange juice, and spluttered as if he had been swimming. But he showed no anger.

—Oh mate, he said in a chastened voice. Oh mate!

He seemed to be offering an acknowledgement of the justice of what had been done to him. Like a bystander and witness to an act of God, the barely amused governor fraternally handed Jacko wads of tissues and paper serviettes. I also took a wad of paper serviettes from my end of the table and presented them to Jacko. But he only had eyes for those offered by Dart. Such was the transaction between them.

Torlucci wandered in with a spacious grin on his yokel face. He said to Jacko, I'd offer you some clothes, mate, but I don't think they'd fit you.

—Look, I know, Jacko told him.

Jacko was still in the mode of level acknowledgement.

At last Torlucci was overcome by great shivers and then a throaty gurgle of honestly declared laughter. It tended towards the baritone.

—Christ, when you beat your way into the governor's mansion, you didn't know one day you'd have to face Amy!

I was still there, watching Jacko now become contrite towards Torlucci, saying he was sorry he had destroyed the birthday party. Torlucci, of course, told him that the opposite was true: he had saved it from oblivion, set it in the memory against all the other soon forgotten parties, the ones that blurred.

With a last courtly smile and a shrug, Dart excused himself now and went to get his overcoat. Amy could be heard in the corridor offering to send someone round to see that the sofa wasn't stained. Rachel Torlucci gave one little bark of laughter and told her not to be ridiculous.

We thought they were gone then, but Dart reappeared once, sticking his head round the doorway into the kitchen and living room.

—Jacko, he breathed in his Secesh lilt, I was wondering if you wanted my business card?

Jacko put his head back and he and Torlucci bellowed with hilarity.

—Go to buggery, Dart. And listen. Keep your bloody door locked from now on!

—How can I, Jacko? asked Dart. I'm a servant of the people.

Sporting Rachel Torlucci, who did not talk much but who attended to things, including the thing of keeping Torlucci himself under control, loaned Jacko a bathrobe and dried out his orange-juice-stained shirt and pants in the communal laundry up the corridor. Jacko was fully restored by these kindnesses.

—Christ Rachel, he yelled after her up the hallway, you'd be just about the only Jewish sheila who ever put quarters in that drier eh. Hope it bloody takes them from you.

He meant, of course, that generally Puerto Ricans and Jamaicans came in to do the laundry of the apartment dwellers. Having paid his price to society, he was now entitled to be impudent again.

So he drank some wine and flapped the inadequate bathrobe across his thighs.

—Because, he'd told the Torlucci women, I'd hate you to be affronted by a sight of the old Aussie pork sword.

—I've seen it, I've seen it, murmured Rachel. It's nothing to write home about.

* * *

In the cab we shared on the way home, Jacko, warm in his stained, dried clothes, told me what had happened in Tennessee to make Dart so socially lethal and Amy so furious. A year before, towards the end of the governor's first term in office, his former wife began to campaign for the Republican candidate, claiming that Dart was a homosexual. Jacko had been sent down by Durkin and *Live Wire* to interview her.

—Mad as a cut snake, said Jacko. She would have caused him real harm if she hadn't been so rabid, but she overdid it. She made remarks about the size of his old feller, and said that if he couldn't put a smile on a woman's face how could he put one on Tennessee's? She was so over the top, even the Republican candidate disowned her in the end.

This wife's attack caused Dart to go public about Amy. You couldn't work out America any more — Amy was Jewish and a New Yorker, but they really loved her in Knoxville.

After Jacko interviewed the furious first wife, the idea of gatecrashing the governor's mansion occurred to him. Somehow Jacko and Dannie and Clayton, but above all — you could bet — Jacko, had talked their way in through the guards on the gate, and were in the foyer when Dart had emerged and asked at the yell what was happening. Jacko and the others had been seen off the premises by armed guards, and so on. Lots of *Next time get an appointment!* and *You're lucky you're not locked up!* from the mansion officials. Repartee from Dannie: *I thought the First Amendment still applied, even in Tennessee.*

All shame expiated through the little penance of the orange juice, Jacko jack-knifed with laughter about it all the way home and wanted me to go on drinking with him in the Odeon in honour of the fact that it had become a story about itself. Jacko, to whom legend was more important than history. This had to be said of Jacko: unlike that oafish bumper sticker which said *He with the most toys wins the game*, Jacko believed in *He who made the most myths goes to heaven*.

I begged off the proposed session in the Odeon.

—Not even for a glass of orange juice?

It was curious that all the men who had women waiting for them *did* prefer to drink with other men once the right glands had begun to secrete a fable by which we could sail and fight together. We'd all been mates that night. Torlucci had been a prime mate, and Jacko was very pleased with him. And in a way, Dart, with his gracious, whimsical revenge, had been a mate. It was Amy who'd fallen into the classic woman posture and been sparked by the masculine languor of the party into throwing the orange juice.

The Haitian cab driver flinched as Jacko roared forth his favourite mantra:

—But the man from Snowy River let the pony
    have his head,
  And he swung his stock whip round and gave a
    cheer,
  And he raced him down the mountain like a
    torrent down its bed,
  While the others stood and watched in very
    fear.

The question the cop had raised outside Coghlan's some time before, was waiting to be dealt with at some darker hour. Orange juice was a gentle projectile. There were more severe ones available to the aggrieved.

Sylph-like Hefty Mulcahy, operamane wife of the operamane-in-chief Oscar Mulcahy, loved Jacko's young brother, Francis Emptor. Her horror of queers did not extend to Francis, who really knew his opera and who was so admired by her housekeeper, René. It was the gays who considered Francis Emptor and his ermine coat vulgar that Oscar and Hefty felt most opposed to. To Oscar's Australian soul, the enemy of my enemy is my friend. He approved of the fact that Hefty went to lunch on Mondays with Francis, who had often returned only the same morning from San Francisco and who chivvied an extra hour from his boss. For the lunches, Francis wore Italian suits he had put on at dawn to face the Sydney Monday, but his memory of operatic Friday nights in San Francisco lay unsullied in him and ready for recounting.

He shared his lunch table at Emilia's, a Double Bay restaurant which specialized in seafood, not only with Hefty Mulcahy but with Irma Lauber, wife of a real estate tycoon who served with Oscar on the Opera Board.

There, in the salad days, in the last seasons before the cold rumour of AIDS arose and threw a pall over the epicene Harbour and the sun, Francis Emptor sat unthreatened between these two fine women. The young waiters all knew him, and wanted to favour, emulate and please him. He would tell Irma and Hefty what Delva Costa had said at one o'clock in the morning at the reception in her honour at the St Francis Hotel, San Francisco. The names of film stars and American senators fell from his lips like oyster shells and crumbs. The waiters moved like charged ions in a cloud chamber.

* * *

I visited the Mulcahys one Saturday afternoon and found Hefty sitting with a glass of gin by the big Mulcahy windows, looking up-harbour to the Heads. Her eyes were misted and her chin shuddered.

—Oh, she said, sit down here.

I obeyed her, and the sun cut across my lap, making my knees hotter than the rest of my body.

She sopped up her tears with a tissue.

—Poor Francis, you know, that divine boy. He has cancer.

When I stared at her she said, nodding for emphasis, I've seen the letter the doctor wrote him. Lymphatic cancer. Or is it lymphoma? He had pain in his chest, you see.

I did not realize that doctors broke the news by letter. The only experience I'd had of the phenomenon was from breaking-the-hard-news scenes in films or on the stage. I hadn't imagined warnings of death coming in buff envelopes with the doctor's letterhead.

I noticed now that rosary beads were entwined like ivy in Hefty's long fingers.

—He has to have radiotherapy. I can't believe it. So beautiful. René and I went to see him at home, and that terrible mother of his was there, down from some burned mulga tree in the bush. Oh she's a virago, that one!

—Not really. She's an honest woman. You and she would have a lot in common, Hefty. I mean, you're both great readers. She likes Thomas Mann and she's crazy about Michael Bickham.

—That old queen! said Hefty.

Michael Bickham lay on the dark side of Hefty's map of Gaydom.

—Is it really the truth? I asked, remembering the large, sensual-ethereal mouth of glorious Francis Emptor at the Opera House.

—Give him a call anyhow, Hefty urged me. He likes you a lot. He was telling me.

I gave way to the temptation of saying, Will I go round there when that terrible woman isn't in?

—If you like her so much, I suppose you could go any time you want. I think you ought to take him a really good bottle of champagne. It's against the rules, but he can still get a glass or two of that down.

—How long has he got? I asked.

—Six months, tops, said Hefty, full of generous tears again.

I delayed telephoning him. If Chloe happened to answer the phone, the only way I could console her at all would be with news of a possible meeting with Michael Bickham, and I didn't have the capacity to offer her that.

In all I delayed for two days. The night after Hefty broke the news to me, I drove into Sydney again from the beach an hour north of the city where I lived. I was used to making that car trip, and it was a pleasant enough drive unless the Bridge was clogged, as it was more and more. Nothing is like Sydney;

nothing is like the arms of the Harbour on which our low-grade immigrant forebears stumbled. The regular regimen of that drive would add to my later delight in finding that in New York you were rarely more than twenty blocks' walk from the dinner or the event to which you were travelling.

The cultural event I was driving to that Sydney night was the opening of an exhibition of photographs of Australian writers. Bickham would not attend of course, even though he was the one of all of us who was internationally known as *The Australian Writer*. There were, of course, other internationally known Australian writers: Morris West, Colleen McCullough, Nevile Shute. But they would not be found represented here. They had broken the rules by writing about subjects other than the *Australian* subjects approved by the Aussie culture police, the critics whose purpose in life was to convince themselves there *was* indeed an Australian literature — as indeed there was, independent of their huffing and puffing and however indifferent the large world might be to it — and who confirmed their faith by generously sponsoring calendars with Australian writers' faces on them, and by holding exhibitions like this.

I was very flattered to have been included in this exhibition, and yet uneasy. Because of occasional commercial success perhaps, and because I'd written about Europe and Asia and Africa as well as Australia, I was placed on the cusp between a certain international renown and the perceived duty to write continuously about Australia and enrich the national cultural well-springs.

I had been photographed at the beach, others in leafy back yards in Woollahra, or against dour factory walls in Richmond. Melbourne writers in particular clung to the dour. It was a sign of their seriousness and their melancholy.

And then, Michael Bickham pictured walking in Centennial Park, an ageing, long-faced man with great bravery, great melancholy, and some annoyance in his face.

—What do you think of Michael? said a heavy Germanic voice tinged with Australian vowels at my side.

It was Erich Tallemann, a poet who was always sombrely present at these events. He had been an Austrian emigrant in his youth and had learned early to graze the fringes of the Literature Board, the both beloved and inveighed-against chief endower of Australian writers. No tradition in Australia of private patronage for writers! Either you lived off your royalties or you got help from the good old Board or you gave up your desire to write.

—I think Michael looks like he should. The prophet Elijah.

—Very good, said Erich, giving me a B minus.

He was the heaviest of the cultural SS, the sort of critic who measured up, in every Australian novel, the quantity of it located in Australia, and brought down his axe accordingly. I had once written a novel set in a jet crossing the Pacific. It had been a novel full of Australians, of Australian perceptions. But introducing me at a reading, he commented that once again I had not set my book in Australia. To him Australia was not a continent of the mind, but a continent of postcodes. I could have been philosophic about that if he had not also gratuitously told his audience that the Australian reviews had been bad, when they had in fact been adequate enough to please both myself (a damn hard task) and the publisher. He had probably not been consciously lying though. He had probably run his Aussie-meter over the book and it had begun to beep.

I was quite willing to pick a fight with him. But I was careful enough these days to wonder what it would benefit me. Would it benefit me anywhere near as much as my association with the Emptors?

—This is a superb exhibition, I told Erich.

—I saw yours too, on the beach, said Erich with a vulpine smile, as if that too were a crime against culture.

—Listen, I've got to go and congratulate the photographer. Nice to see you, Erich. Look forward to your next book of verse.

I found the photographer, and waited for him to be finished with interviewers. When he was free, I asked him how it was that he had taken the picture in Centennial Park instead of in Bickham's own beloved home?

—I didn't have to force him at all, said the photographer. Bickham goes there every day, after lunch, no later than three.

—Centennial Park?

It was a superb picture. It didn't look like Centennial Park in high summer. It looked like a park in Lausanne, against a sky as severe and exacting as modernism. There was a sweet tension between Michael Bickham's winter beanie, which may have even been in the colours of some football club if one didn't already know that Bickham despised that sort of thing, and that stern heaven and wintry parkland. The photographer must have gone to the spot on one of Sydney's occasional, full-blown winter days.

—He walks every afternoon? I asked. Even in bad weather?

—Well, his emphysema's not so hot. But he trundles around. He loves it.

I felt delivered of a weight. I could now approach the gorgeous boy Emptor with my intense, astounded sympathies, and I would have something to tell his mother to distract her from her bruised flower of a boy.

I was so pleased with the new knowledge that I called Frank Emptor the next morning. He was in, and I told him how grief-stricken I was for his sake and Chloe's. He was restrained and very calm, and asked me if I would come up for afternoon tea with himself and his mother the following day. He put Chloe on then, and I commiserated with her and then told her I had some good news about Bickham. I could hear that she was for a moment delighted. It was a comfort to her. So I felt bound to say that it was sort of indirect news. Even so, she was cheered.

She said, I still want to see Bickham and quiz him irrespective of what's happened. It all has a bearing you know. I thought my bloody children would live forever in their perverse ways, and now my mad flower of a son has the mark of death on his forehead eh. Good of you to call. Francis likes and admires you. You had that good talk at the opera.

Though liking or admiration could not be based on such a fragile foundation, I wanted to be counted in, a partner to the tragedy. I shrank from contemplating the damage presently being done to Francis's triumphantly sybaritic cells.

I went up to town the next day, crossed the bridge

and found the sweet little streets of Woollahra. Abnormal, all this coming and going between the primeval beach and the racy city, and beyond it to Francis Emptor's fashionable terrace. When I rang the bell, Chloe came to the door. She wore a business suit but was barefooted, just as in Burren Waters. She hung around my neck.

—Oh Christ, she told me, holding on to me by the neck, a fierce, demanding embrace. I didn't know that this would happen. I thought the mad little bugger would go on being a mad little bugger for good. Let's go inside.

In the living room, looking out at the Japanese garden he had installed, Francis sat in a large arm-chair. Though he was dressed stylishly (white slacks, white cricketing sweater, rope-soled shoes), the way he looked filled me with a mortal shock. The full cheeks were shrunken, the skin of his wrist looked dry and was scaled with dead flesh. The skeletal condition suited him even less than it might have most people, given that there had been so many broad planes in his face to cave in and atrophy. His wide-set eyes flashed out at me a sort of grateful welcome. In what I saw as his thirst for life, he needed to renew himself and take nutriment even from casually known faces.

When I asked him the usual trite question, he said, I'm fine now. It's only for a day or so after radio-therapy that I feel appalling. I don't want to know anyone immediately before, during or after it. I don't even let Chloe come to hospital with me. I just get the old reliable limo service to collect me, take me, bring me home. At that stage, I'd rather be helped up and down stairs by a near-stranger.

According to Hefty's demand that I bring Frank some nice wine, I had with me a bottle of vintage Perrier-Jouet.

—For when you're feeling better, I told him.

—Oh no, he said, I'm fit enough to choke down half a glass.

Chloe was already fetching from the cocktail cabinet behind Frank the little silver clasping device designed to withdraw recalcitrant champagne corks. So I opened the bottle and Chloe held the glasses for us, and Frank choked down, in fact, nearly two glasses, urging me to drink the rest. Chloe would not help me. She had got a can of her habitual Carlton Draught from the kitchen. On her way back to join us, she picked up two letters from Francis Emptor's sideboard. She stood behind him, just as once she had stood behind the stockman called Merv. She pushed both of the letters down over my shoulder, in a manner which meant I should consider them. I couldn't see them in detail, but I could see that they carried, embossed at the top of each, the names of physicians — crops of letters followed the names. I thought I saw a San Francisco address on one of them. They were both addressed to Frank's GP in Woollahra. My eye grazed over such words as, *topical lymphoma, pleuritic chest pain, dyspnoea*. A number of technical tests were mentioned, and radiotherapy and eventual chemotherapy invoked. Displaying the frightful news like this, Chloe went on dolorously shaking her head. At last she gave it up, withdrew the letters, returned them to the dresser, and came and sat with us.

I asked after Jacko. I did not know him then the

way I would get to know him in New York a year or so later, but I had read that Basil Sutherland, or maybe more correctly Basil Sutherland's chief initiator of tabloid television, Durkin, had taken him away to America to work on the morning and current affairs programs of Vixen Six.

Jacko, said Chloe, was working hard in New York. At least she hoped he was. If she found out that he was only chiacking around there, she'd be bloody cranky with the little bugger. Jacko claimed he'd get home next month to see his brother.

—Anyhow, she said, delicately patting Francis's shoulder, you're with the old girl now. Better than all those bloody nancies you used to surround yourself with eh. And Jacko says he's coming home. Christ knows when your sister will see you. Far as she's concerned, we're all limbs of bloody Satan.

Francis wet his lips with the champagne and laid his head back against his chair and smiled sideways at me. The fading Keats couldn't have smiled more seraphically. I had an obscene suspicion, which I sat on at once, that Francis may have been getting some pleasure from the more operatic aspects of his dissolution.

After we had finished our drinking and our talk, I got ready to leave. Promising further visits, I shook hands gently with Francis, and Chloe followed me to the door.

—Well, she said softly. Well. Poor little bugger went to see a doctor in San Francisco while he was there for the opera. Human hope, you know. But it's all bloody futile. The San Francisco people came up with the same diagnosis.

Tears were spilling down her brown cheeks. It was

terrible to see her possessed by such mourning.

—I can't stand thinking of that, the poor little bugger, going to a second doctor in another country. Hoping eh. Or wanting just to get out of the death bloody sentence.

I took her in my arms and kissed her on the forehead. It felt sun-roughened and salty.

—Listen, I told her. When Francis's having the radiotherapy, why don't you go up to Centennial Park for a walk. I've got it on good authority that Michael Bickham goes walking in Centennial Park every day after lunch. Around three o'clock, my source says. And it's a free country. You can confront him. The miserable old sod would have to talk to you.

She stared at me, becoming lively again. I had an impression that, inside her cocoon of grief, she was pulling her bones together.

—You'd come with me?

I shook my head. I did not want to seem to ambush the Nobel Laureate in alliance with a cattle station matron.

—Listen, Chloe, I don't mind coming in from the beach to see Francis, but I'm a writer and I need to write every day. It's just not easy for me to break up my day and come up to Sydney at lunch-time and walk in Centennial Park.

—Oh yeah. But it's okay for you to go two thousand bloody miles to Burren Waters, isn't it? Taking two days to get there eh. You've got enough time to go all that bloody way and interrupt *our* bloody pattern!

I shook my head. There was a stinging justice to

her argument. Her hard, bunched face was aimed at me. She would not let me off the hook.

So we made the arrangement. Next time tragic Francis Emptor went off in his limo for his radiotherapy, Chloe and I would go walking in Centennial Park.

—I'll ring you with the details then, said Chloe, appeased for the moment.

* * *

Not only did Francis Emptor have radiotherapy to attend to, he kept up his Monday lunches with Hefty Mulcahy and Irma Lauber, patron wives of the Opera. Hefty Mulcahy told me it was touching to see the way the waiters were now affected by Francis Emptor's signs of mortality. The increasing loss of hair, the thinness and the pallor.

Francis managed lunch bravely, though his appetite — said Hefty — was shot.

Chloe herself never got invited to these events. She was as contemptuous of those *opera tarts* as Hefty Mulcahy was of her. It was on one such Monday, a glittering Sydney winter day, clear and dry and barely cold, that Chloe called me and told me that this was her day for trying to meet the great modernist Michael Bickham. I pleaded and sought excuses. But Chloe insisted. She knew her day and her hour.

Again I drove in from the northern beaches of Sydney into the centre of the city, over the Harbour Bridge. Later, in Jacko's and my absence, they would build a tunnel, but for the moment that arched bridge had to carry all the Sydney-bound traffic. Off to the left, the immensity of the Harbour and the white-sailed Opera House were a case of art and nature cajoling each other. That Monday, however, I crossed into Sydney like a man going towards public humiliation. I feared being no more than a joke at Bickham's table and even in his inevitable biography.

The traffic conspired against me by being light, and within fifty minutes of leaving the beach I was collecting Chloe from Francis's terrace house. For the possible encounter with Bickham, she was wearing an emerald green business suit, which didn't go well with her high tan and her ample but sun-kippered look. The suit, just the same, signified serious planning and the taking of thought.

—You look bloody lugubrious in the service, she told me.

It was a short drive to the park. We found a place to put the car, in the park itself, down near the Showgrounds and the Sydney Cricket Ground. The earth of Centennial Park, as we entered it, was green and heavy from recent rain, and had that heavy plum jam smell which reminded me of the sodden Rugby League fields of my childhood.

—This is where he'd walk? asked Chloe closing one eye to focus on me.

—It's the end of the park closest to his home.

—Well, that's not exactly what I asked you eh.

—I'm not trying to cheat you, Chloe. If he walks, it will be around here. Now listen, I don't want any accusations if he doesn't turn up. I'm doing my best.

—Jesus, you bloody Sydney people have such thin hides.

We strolled up a path which fringed the bridle track, and then out onto the pleasant greensward, designed in the British manner with lots of imported trees. The park was founded on the hundredth anniversary of European settlement, 1888, by a colonial government which had a nostalgia for the centre of Empire, for England and its flora. It was this fact which had made it possible for the photographer to get that undifferentiated European look into the portrait of Bickham.

Chloe kicked the park's heavy sod with the toe of her shoes.

—Jesus, if all Australia was like this, we could run four cattle to the acre.

Hooded for a severer sun than this, her eyes squinted out over the parkland — open ground screened by trees at the Randwick end, pleasant hillocks at the Paddington. Those two poles had been honoured in test matches at the Sydney Cricket Ground, where bowlers, pace or spin, operated from either the Paddington or the Randwick end. We were bowling up from the Randwick end, trying to take the wicket of the sublimest novelist of the age.

He was nowhere in sight at the moment, and I reassured Chloe that we were a little early. I filled in time by asking how Stammer Jack was.

Chloe said, About as good as he's entitled to be. I've got to go back for the Brahma Breeders Ball, you know. He might have a stammer, but there are other parts of the bugger that act more directly eh. There're a couple of tarts in Hector got their eye on him. He's a very attractive man in a dinner suit, Jack Emptor.

I wondered what any seducing woman would think, if she got Stammer Jack alone, of his purple, demi-gangrenous ankle.

—You notice I don't have any Wodjiri women

working in the house? He's got too much of a weakness for the bloody Wodjiri women. He and his father before him.

She looked behind her and grabbed my arm.

—Jesus, is that him?

I turned and was sorry to see that it was. No one else in Australia wore quite the same knitted cap of the kind Michael Bickham had worn in the photograph in the exhibition. And then there was Khalil's chunky form beside him in windcheater and suede cap. They were making slow progress, but seemed to be enjoying the day. Moving in from the Randwick end. Bowling for the Immortals XI.

—Let's not turn around straight away, I pleaded. It'll look as if we've been lying in wait. Let's walk up to the monument there, and then turn around.

—He might turn around too and bugger off.

—No, no, I said, hoping she was right in her fears however.

I steered her towards the modest stone gazebo where in 1901 the Commonwealth of Australia, whose citizens Bickham so despised and glorified, had been promulgated.

—Even if he does, I told her, we can come back another time.

—I'll be bloody ropable if you're wrong, she warned me.

She stumped along at my side, grimacing as if her shoes hurt her, as they probably did.

We reached the little monument, with its modest circle of columns.

—Any other nation would have built a pantheon, I said, being philosophic to delay things.

—Oh yeah, she said, but she was impatient with

my reflections on Australia's modest nationalism.

—Michael Bickham doesn't give us much credit for building sensible monuments, I said. He doesn't give us much credit for anything.

—Why bloody-well should he? Chloe asked.

We rounded the monument, reading the names of the states carved on its brows.

—Bloody Territory doesn't get a mention, Chloe complained, but more for form's sake. If Sydney people could omit the name of the Territory from this ceremonial plinth, they could certainly sabotage her chances of meeting Bickham. I decided to distract her with a bit of harmless information.

—The Territory wasn't federal then. It was part of the State of South Australia in those days.

—It'll be part of the state of madness if I don't get back there soon.

When we'd finished our circuit of the plain stone pergola, I was disappointed to see gaunt Bickham and his four-square lover still trundling along, making calm but steady time from the direction of the Sydney Cricket Ground, that venue of oafish enthusiasms so despised by the continent's Prophet Elijah, Michael Bickham.

Chloe advised me, Keep your bloody nerve, son.

We strolled along, counterfeiting ease, on a compass bearing which assured an encounter. I saw Bickham and Khalil pause, but even if they turned back, we would overtake them at our current pace. They did not turn back, however. We were close enough now to pick out the great asthmatic writer's shoulders raised in that involuntary and poignant hunch which characterizes a man who cannot get enough air. Yet he came on, intrepid as his devout readers would want him to be.

We were fifteen yards apart when Khalil noticed us. I saw his eyes flutter in a way which said, Michael won't like this. But next they grew genial and he smiled. By then I could hear Bickham's painful breathing. It shamed me. I knew that this unilaterally planned meeting was not right. But Khalil had already begun murmuring at Michael Bickham's shoulder, and the great writer, propping and putting undue weight on his stick, glowered down under his lids at us. He looked gaunt and blue-grey enough to have been dying, though somewhat more slowly than Francis Emptor. His eyes were clear and dreadful in their severity.

—Hello, he groaned very loudly. He greeted me by name. I felt berserkly flattered.

—Hello, I said with the rushed gratitude of some-one much younger. Knowing the kindness wasn't deserved, I burned with an adolescent confusion.

I said, This is Chloe Emptor, Michael. You might remember I once asked you to sign a copy of *The Mother as Aphrodite* for her.

—I sign so many, he panted.

In his rigorous honesty, he was a consistent bastard.

—Of course, I said like a neophyte, like someone who didn't himself frequently have books of his own thrust on him for signing. But we were all neophytes beside Bickham.

Now the vocal and normally bullying Chloe Emp-tor had been struck silent.

—This is a lucky surprise, I said, feeling idiotic and sending more blood still to my face to back up the lie.

—I must sit down, said Michael Bickham to Khalil, and indicated a park bench.

I hoped that this was his dismissal of us. I would never be able to read him again without feeling a blazing remorse.

As he turned towards the bench, Michael Bickham's breathing sounded more and more alarming. As great a writer as he should have been entitled to take an afternoon's tortured walk without being intruded upon by a fan and a lesser writer, bonded together in conspiracy.

But Chloe felt no disgrace and followed him to the bench. She must have chosen to think that somehow he was inviting her to sit down with him for a spell. Of course, it was a very Northern Territory sort of assumption: that he was going to sit down the better to chat with us, not the better to dismiss us.

Soon the three of them were settled together on the park seat. I remained standing on the flank, a sentry who might flee at any shock. Chloe smiled up at me briefly, winsomely, yet with what I could see was an intense form of thanks. I noticed pockets of oxygen-starved blue under Bickham's eyes. In an habitual yet anxious way, Khalil himself inspected the novelist's face. Then he too looked up at me, as one spouse will look up at an acquaintance to appeal against the foibles of his partner in life.

—He always comes too far, Khalil complained.

—Don't talk about me in the third damned person, the Nobel Laureate gasped. Give me my inhaler please.

Khalil produced the thing from the pocket of his windcheater, a little grey tube with a mouth piece. To think of such a fantastic life dependent on a little

tube of vasodilator! Bickham exhaled the scant air he
had to work with, and put the spout of the inhaler in
his mouth and depressed the tube. He seemed to be
panting more at the end of the process, but perhaps
that was because he had drawn in the medicine so
strenuously. Now, however, he turned to Chloe with
a sort of strangulated courtliness.

—Is your name the same as the Latin word?

—Yes, Mr Bickham, said Chloe.

Her voice too was so gagged that for a moment I
thought she was locked in a reverent mimicry of poor
Bickham's condition.

—*Caveat Emptor*, gasped Bickham. And you're
from the Territory?

From the flank, I said, Chloe's got a remarkable
library up there on Burren Waters.

—Are you all right, Bickie? asked Khalil, still
inspecting Bickham's clear-eyed but ravaged face.
Would you like another dose from the inhaler?

Bickham cocked his head and focused for a while
upon his breathing, gauging its volume.

—Things aren't too bright in that department, he
admitted. Yet I feel no panic.

Khalil warned him, Doctor Ho told you not to
assess yourself by subjective standards.

—I *will* take the inhaler again.

Again we all watched him exhale, inhale, hold his
breath. If his breath did not return, every news service in the world would take note of it, and of our
disgrace as well.

Khalil said, Michael and I have met a young man
named Emptor at the opera.

Breathless Bickham cast his eyes up and smiled not
totally pleasantly at the memory.

Chloe said, That's my son. But I don't know where he got that ermine cape stuff from eh. Mean to say, he grew up a few hundred miles west of Hector. You don't get too many ermine capes up there.

—Not with the climate, Michael Bickham managed to say with his first returning breath.

—That's the thing, Mr Bickham. I'm like the old lady in *The Mother as Aphrodite*. Helena of Hologlo, you know. How she decides when she's dying that it's her children who've killed her. That they've been killing her since conception. That hit me like lightning. And I always wanted to meet you so I could ask: how did you know that eh? I wanted to ask you, are you talking about some sort of universal law, or are you just talking about *that* character? I've been thinking for years: in what way did he know it? That feller Bickham.

Bickham laughed. He laughed at her calling him *that feller Bickham*. The most patrician mind in the antipodes had surrendered in part to rough but willing Chloe Emptor. As Jacko would later open remarkable doors in America, she had penetrated, at least a little way, Bickham's remarkable door.

—That's an old book, he said, dismissing his novel. But I think I knew it both ways. As a figure of speech and a law.

He paused, but you could tell he intended to keep on talking.

—It applied to Helena, it applies to all women. Their children exist to assail them with chronic confusion. To murder them by bewilderment. Mind you, it is what you could call the reciprocal service. As the humorist has it:

They screw you up, your mum and dad.

They don't intend to, but they do.
They give you all the faults they had,
And add some new ones just for you . . .

To hear Bickham reciting this ironic doggerel filled me with a kind of vertigo, and a sort of delight too.

He turned painfully to me, Don't tell the Australian Culture Police that I recite low rhymes.

He seemed to have enjoyed delivering these sentences, and had rushed them out, but his breathing seemed somehow worse than when we first met him. Weariness rose in his eyes. His face was grey, and the cruel triangles of blue had deepened under each eye.

—Walk with us, Mrs Emptor, Bickham was able to say. I believe I must go home to my oxygen cylinder.

Even rising from the bench caused him to gag and rasp and cough. He began to move off, and behind his back Khalil confided in Chloe and me.

—Sometimes the lack of breath makes him euphoric. Could you help me get him home?

Chloe fell in on Bickham's left side and reverently took his elbow. I told Khalil I had a car nearby if he needed it, but Bickham overheard and said, All that . . . fussing around . . . with seats . . . and seat belts . . . I'm better . . . as I am. Mrs Emptor . . . what were we discussing?

—There's no need for you to say more than yes or no, Mr Bickham, Chloe told him, tears in her eyes now. But I really wanted to know and I'm not clear about it yet. When you had Helena in the novel realize that her children were what she was dying of . . . do you think *I'll* feel like that by the end? A bushie like me? Do you think *my* children feel that way eh?

Bickham paused a second, pointing his awful face to the sky in what I saw as a speculative way, as if Chloe had raised a possibility he might exploit one morning at his desk.

Chloe said, You see, I've had the feeling for quite a time that my children are really killing me, and one of the poor little buggers is killing himself in the process!

—Killing himself? asked Khalil in alarm, as if self-destruction might be contagious.

—Frank. Cancer, Chloe murmured to Khalil, though not wanting the great modernist to hear or be burdened.

Khalil, wide-eyed, absorbed the news and reached behind Bickham to touch Chloe's elbow. Even then I was astounded. I had thought Chloe would terrify Bickham and Khalil, but within the limits of Bickham's emergency, she was somehow a success with them.

Given his problems with breath, Bickham had to keep his chin up and so he did not see Chloe weeping at his shoulder.

—If it were so . . . Mrs Emptor . . . there's nothing you can do . . . Nothing the child can do either . . . We can't re-institute the process . . . *A man cannot . . . enter the womb again* . . .

Chloe was wavering and stumbling with sorrow and bewilderment. I therefore came up to her left elbow to keep her upright so that she could perform the same service for the Nobel Laureate.

—Let me say . . . I am not . . . a sociologist, Mrs Emptor. It *could* . . . be just a metaphor . . . for all I know.

Chloe got her sorrow back under rein.

—I don't think I've been the same woman since I read that passage. I've been what you could call creatively insane eh? That's what books are for.

—Definitely ... to make ... us utterly ... bonkers. Oh ... dear.

Even at our minute, sub-processional pace, Bickham had run out of impetus. He stopped by an evergreen and put his forehead against the bark. He seemed to be in a bad way but, as Khalil had suggested earlier with all that talk about euphoria, to be unaware of it.

—Oh Jesus, oh Jesus, cried Khalil. Why do you put me through this, Michael?

Michael Bickham was beyond answering. We heard his breath dwindle. His knees yielded. Soon he was kneeling, his cheek now against the trunk of the tree, his eyes closed, his respiration sawing frantically. Khalil had also gone to his knees, embracing Bickham, trying to tear him back from his crisis of air. Appealing to the novelist of the age, Khalil spoke the banal, suburban pleas which any spouse would utter to an almost wilfully ill partner.

—Michael, Michael, for Christ's sake, what can I do? Stay awake, darling boy! Stay awake!

Chloe was addressing herself more effectually to the fallen novelist. She too was on her knees, but feeling for his pulse. Reasonably enough, I believed that this tragedy was my fault and that I could not expiate my culpability; but I felt also that it showed a perversity of Bickham's. On some stupid level, I believed he was trying to prove my fatuousness as a writer by perishing at my hand. He was trying to reduce me to an assassin, locate me eternally and merely as a comic-disreputable figure in his last few seconds.

—I'll run and call the ambulance, I offered.

Studying Bickham's face, Khalil cried over his shoulder, The nearest phone box is right down there near the Showground.

I saw that this was a long, long sprint. Was I capable? Yet I must be. I must be the Pheidippides of the age, bringing the news from Marathon; not joyful though, heinous news. Perishing if necessary after giving the message.

—The house is closer, I said. Do you have the key to the gate and the house?

I was trying to make the decisions that counted. But it was Chloe who had the manner of command.

—How close to the house? she asked.

Khalil gestured, panic-stricken, behind him.

—Over there, over there.

—Oxygen eh, stated Chloe.

Khalil raised his face to the sky. He was pleading with the Maronite God to bring the cylinder closer to hand. Chloe jostled his elbow.

—Come on, Khalil, point the bloody place out eh.

Khalil turned on his knees and aimed his hand at the big Victorian house behind its wall and in its garden.

—There! There!

He found the keys from his windcheater and passed them to me. I pocketed them and moved to raise Bickham. Chloe forestalled me though. She stood up and kicked both shoes off.

—Carry those, she told me.

I took them, too stupefied to see at once that accepting them disqualified me as a rescuer. In the instant of my accepting the shoes, she had bent again. Now the barely gasping and comatose Bickham, a remote deity of hers an hour ago, was over her shoulder in a fireman's carry, and under the burden she was half-jogging towards Bickham's house directly across the turf of Centennial Park. Khalil and I ran behind her, offering to help. She told us to go to buggery eh.

I overtook her at last, and opened the garden gate and then scurried up the steps to get the door open for Chloe and Bickham.

Behind me, poor Khalil gasped, Ground floor. Ground floor.

I had always imagined Bickham's bedroom as high in his house, above the park, above the ground level spying of vulgar devotees. But of course a loving Khalil had moved Bickham's bedroom down to the ground floor, so that the Nobel Laureate did not need to exhaust himself on the stairs.

Chloe jogged down the hallway, the novelist slung familiarly now on her shoulder. She found the room and heaved Bickham onto the bed and, by the time Khalil had rounded the door into the room, had the oxygen mask on Bickham's face and was turning the succouring knob on the cylinder. Above the mask, Bickham's forehead showed purple. Still applying the mask two-handed, Chloe looked across at us both.

—Well, you're not far from a phone now are you?

Khalil went and rang. I could hear him weeping into the receiver as he described Michael Bickham's symptoms.

* * *

So we had saved Michael Bickham from a threat to his life, from his own clenched air passages. Chloe had, by not being effete, by not wavering. Bickham's own forebears had been sheep and cattle people. In fact he had a brother who still worked a massive property in the region of New South Wales called New England. His cattleman brother tried to pretend that Michael didn't exist, and Michael tried to ignore that such a cliché of Australian balladry as his squatter brother occupied the same continent as himself.

But perhaps something of his own background, of the rough kindnesses of his childhood, recurred to comatose Bickham as Chloe put the fireman's-carry on him and toted him home to the oxygen.

While Dr Ho the asthma specialist attended to him, I waited in Bickham's living room. This home visit by a prominent physician was something rarely seen in Australia, where most emergencies were taken to casualty wards. But even the society Bickham wrote off as philistine and damned and brutish cared for him this much.

With the end for the time being of Bickham's pulmonary crisis (a crisis of world letters also ended), I would soon have to drive Chloe back to poor Francis's terrace house, and I would go with Khalil's gratitude instead of the potential accusation, disgrace and dread I probably deserved.

Chloe and Khalil had left the living room at the front of the house where I sat pretending to look at pictures in an art book. Easing the book precisely and soundlessly back into its stack, as if I wanted to show unseen witnesses how little I wanted to intrude upon the fabric of Bickham's life, I went looking for my two companions. As I passed up the hallway,

I noticed through the door of Bickham's bedroom that Ho and his nurse had a drip set up.

Chloe was making tea for Khalil in the kitchen, while Khalil himself sat disoriented at the table. It was she who pulled out canisters and found milk and sugar as if she were a familiar of this hearth.

—Thank God he's got a strong heart, Khalil told me as soon as I came in. He can stand all that strong stuff they have to give him to bring him round.

I asked what the strong stuff was.

—Adrenalin, phenergin, you know. Stimulants. He has a stout Scots heart. His people are really very tough people.

Khalil and I drank our tea slowly, but Chloe took it at the gulp. She was searching drawers in the refrigerator.

—So pasta eh? I'd rather cook you a great whacking steak, Mr Khalil. It's good shock food.

But he said that pasta was normal. Michael liked it. I saw a piteous gratitude on Khalil's face as Chloe found the right pot, began boiling water, slung in an unfashionable bush-handful of salt — but Khalil wouldn't complain — and began to sing an Aboriginal Land Rights song.

—Poor bugger me, poor bugger me,
  Got no place in me own count-ree . . . .

I knew it was purely the tune she was interested in. The content was, to her and most other Northern cattlefolk, city liberal bullshit. Through song and clattering, she was making a place for herself in the great modernist's kitchen. I wondered what would happen between her and Bickham if she established herself here. And what if future conversation came round to

the Wodjiri and other tribes, and what equities should
be applied to them?

Later in the night, when we left Bickham's house,
asking Khalil to say goodbye for us since Michael
Bickham was sleeping, I drove her back to Francis
Emptor's place. It was clear to me she was delighted
with herself.

—Well, she said, you came good for me, didn't
you eh? After a fair bit of squirming.

And whether or not she had ambitions to become
a familiar in Bickham's household, it would soon
enough become obvious to many in Sydney that she
had succeeded. The two old gentlemen were pleased
to be supplied with regular pasta, and serving the
failing Bickham distracted her from Francis's state.

So Bickham, the rarest and most patrician presence
in the Southern Hemisphere, took Chloe as a friend.
Since I was not a friend I did not witness the process.
But perhaps it worked because, unlike everyone else
in Sydney, it didn't occur to her to try too hard.

Though Bickham's crisis in Centennial Park was an
omen of the way his life might end, he was — to
quote Chloe — *full of rum and bacon* by the following morning. Chloe no longer talked of Burren
Waters, of getting north for the Brahma Breeders Ball
in Hector. The women of the Northern Territory
were welcome to Stammer Jack, for he meant little
now beside the two high destinies which had befallen
Chloe: to make Francis Emptor beloved in his last
days, or better still to relieve him of the need to kill
himself as a means of killing her; and to be maid and
companion to Michael Bickham.

I heard someone say at a party at the Mulcahys'
place that maybe Chloe reminded Bickham of the

rough generous Hunter Valley women his grandee
parents had hired to bathe him, feed him and put
him to bed in his childhood. And when I thought of
it, Bickham's novels would sometimes exalt someone
unlikely, someone other than the sort of people he
liked to invite to his table. Some creature of unde-
signed wisdom like Chloe. In *Travelling with Elijah*
there was a figure called Mrs Karnak who was dismissed by both the formally godly and the intelligent
as an uncontrolled and stupid woman, but who was
in fact a *knower*, one of the chosen, one who found
justification by taking events madly into her own
hands. A ham-fisted transcendentalist of the bush. It's
obvious to me that Bickham later transmuted Chloe
into a character called Mrs Cowley, a frank, battling
saint, a genius of honesty, in his last novel, *The City
of the Sisters*.

Hefty Mulcahy called me.

—Oscar and I saw Bickham and Khalil at *Godunov*.

She had the opera buff's habit of dropping part of the names of operas.

—They were there with Francis Emptor and his mother.

I noticed at once: *mother*, not *horrible mother* as Hefty's normal estimation of Chloe ran.

—And do you know, I've revised my estimation. She's quite a pleasant woman in some ways. Oscar and she were thick as thieves. And a tragedy about Francis. We have to do something. If we had a final lunch for him at the beach, would you come?

The Mulcahys also had a wonderful house above one of the northern beaches of Sydney. They'd bought an enamelled plaque in Paris which said *Place de l'Opéra*. They stuck it on their outside wall facing the Tasman Sea, and so they entitled the house.

In Place de l'Opéra, Oscar produced superb and very robust weekend meals for his guests. He was no respecter of angel-hair pasta. He had, from his Irish working class origins, a generous respect for red meat and the complex carbohydrates of potatoes.

—Of course, Hefty told me, I'll invite Bickham too. You like Bickham all right?

* * *

When we arrived at Place de l'Opéra for the lunch which had been prepared to succour and farewell Francis Emptor, I found some friends already seated under Oscar's prodigiously big white and blue sun umbrella, nearly marquee-sized and tethered in place against the southerly by a heavy base filled with water. Amongst those already sitting in the shade was Dick Evans, a tall, boyish-looking and acutely thin playwright I was friends with. Dick was folded up angularly in a beach chair, and his smaller wife Renate was beside him in an upright. She had sharper features than Evans and always looked the more worldly. They both had untouched glasses of champagne in their hands, held in a way which made it look like they did not want to start drinking till the other guests turned up.

Earlier in her life, Renate had been a rigorous journalist and had been feared. But she had given that up to do writing of her own. The change had made her a genial soul. I loved the company of both of them. It held none of the menaces that the company of Bickham might. When I'd first known them, their marriage — very public because of Evans's fame — had been turbulent, the stuff of feature articles. But now it was obviously successful, and so was subject to even more snide comment.

Immediately I saw the two of them I felt more at ease about Bickham's threatened arrival. Dick Evans and Renate utterly lacked rancour. Maureen, who had quite a nose for people and could sniff out pretension, liked Renate and soon got into an energetic conversation with her. Dick had written some of the screenplays of the best Australian Revival films, and had — virtually on his own — created the modern Sydney and Melbourne theatre. Now, of course, he was flayed by critics for entertaining people and for not having given experts exactly the theatre they knew to be best for them and, above all, for the public. He was as beloved of the public as Dame Roberta Murdoch, had the rewards to show for it, and so was a largely content man. Still fresh-faced in middle-age, he uttered an occasional anxious thought about the waspishness of his enemies. I knew by the sort of thing he said about my work that he had a generosity of spirit, and was bewildered by the lack of it in others.

The other guests were as hulking as Oscar: Norris Chambers and his wife Marie, enormous, robust people with resonant opinions and a fine line in whimsy. Chambers and Marie were getting older now — they would have been at least in their mid-60s. Yet their faces were somehow fixed in the minds of the populace as ageless. Or at least you beheld them and age was not something you thought of. Like Evans, they were characteristic of the lustrous Australians Oscar was willing to serve up to the cancer-threatened Francis Emptor.

Norris Chambers had been Prime Minister of Australia until sacked one unhappy morning by the Governor-General, the Viceroy of the British Monarch, for not adhering to the Viceroy's desire for a new election to break a deadlock in the Federal Parliament. Thereby, Norris had become something of an icon of Australian nationalism. His fall had en-fabled him, like Ned Kelly. The Australians like their mythic creatures either dead or neutered. They had never been comfortable with him when he ruled them, but their love for him had increased yearly since the Governor-General took away his power.

To suit the size of his myth, he and Marie would come close to filling the Mulcahys' swimming pool when later they went for a pre-lunch swim.

We all had time to shake ourselves into place before the car driven by Khalil and carrying Bickham and Chloe and her tragic son Frank arrived and imposed a special nervousness on us. Coming up the stairs toward the big beach umbrella, Bickham seemed in good wind, but Frank moved fragilely. On the landing, he brushed the women's cheeks with dry, dry lips.

We made functional conversation with Bickham, who seemed genial under a big straw hat. He sat down happily and accepted some wine.

—Not the bubbly stuff, he said.

—It gives him an allergy, Khalil explained.

When the Chambers went for their swim in the Mulcahys' pool, Francis trailed behind them, refusing offers of help to get down the stairs. Brave and thin, he sat on the pool apron in a beach chair, and took his shirt off. He wore nothing but board shorts now, and his chest and middle body were marked off with some indelible pen for radiation therapy purposes. The Mulcahys were serving Dom Perignon and Francis held a barely sipped flute of it languidly in his hand. Looking down at him from the verandah of Place de l'Opéra, I wondered if his strength to keep the glass upright would last the lunch hour. Hefty had told me that when she and Irma Lauber took him to lunch at Emilia's on Mondays, he ate a third of an entrée and nothing more. The waiters fussed around him, trying to make him taste this or that new dish the chef had devised. But he took only token nibbles.

Hefty told me, He'll perish of malnutrition, you know, even before the cancer gets him.

I could see the big-boned and not particularly obese Chambers swimming in the pool, Norris's masses of pale flesh, Marie contained in a large one-piece. We could hear them too, calling to Francis as they swam.

—And are you still working, comrade? he cried out to Francis. He had got the habit of calling everyone *comrade* from his early years in the Labor Party.

—I go in now and then.

—You're a brave chap then, said Norris in his huge, aspirated voice. But I suppose it helps one's mental attitude.

—It does, Mr Chambers. To see friends.

—Oh bugger this Mr Chambers stuff, Francis. Call me Norris, please!

Marie had left the pool and picked a long-stemmed carnation from a flowerbed near Francis's chair. She dived into the pool again, holding it above the water in one hand.

—Look! called Marie. Esther Williams.

She put the stem of the flower between her teeth, and swam backstroke up the pool. Francis's laughter could be heard, and Norris's. And Bickham looked down on them and began to chuckle and applaud.

It took Marie about four strokes to travel the length of the pool. Her arms looked as strong as a robust girl's.

Chloe had put down her Dom Perignon for a can

of Carlton Draught, the beer whose white cans you found strewn all over the landscape of the Northern Territory. *Outback confetti* they called it.

With her free hand, she pulled me aside.

—You jokers get together a lot, you and Bickham and Evans and the Chambers eh?

—No. This is a red letter day.

—But I mean, what goes on eh? Do you get together and decide what's best for the poor bloody country. All you socialist buggers! Because Bickham's a great man, and okay he's short of breath, but he's also a socialist bastard . . .

—Chloe, I don't know what you're getting at.

—You never invite any cattlemen or women, that's for bloody certain.

—You're invited, Chloe.

—Yeah. But that's a bloody accident eh.

I could by now guess what was gnawing at her. After all, she had shown in Centennial Park that in her world picture, all things were planned and nothing was contingent, even the folly and treachery of children. And so also city liberals like the Chambers and the Evans and the Mulcahys met over Sunday lunch, and orchestrated dismal outcomes and government intrusions for cattlemen and their families far, far in the interior. Nothing happened by accident. Everything was specific intent.

So it had been more than literary inquisitiveness which made her anxious to check with Bickham and discover whether he had framed a law in *The Mother as Aphrodite*. For some reason, in her mind, her children and the people at the Mulcahys' lunch had the power to hammer out effectual statutes.

Such was the perceived might of the Chambers,

those two big-boned people, splashing about in the Mulcahys' pool, making it look pint-sized.

When Oscar Mulcahy had his famous roast potatoes to a nicety, he came and asked me if Maureen and I would go down to the pool with him to help Francis up and into the house.

—I hope the bloody Chambers haven't splashed the poor bugger too much, he told me.

The Chambers had left the water and were towelling their great bearlike shoulders and talking with wan Francis. Oscar Mulcahy called to Francis that it was lunch-time, and Francis set his flute of champagne down on the concrete of the pool. Then, elbows on the plastic mounting of the chair arms, he tried to lever himself up. He seemed to lack adequate strength for it. I got on one side and Oscar on the other, but it was Maureen, a nurse in her earlier years, who was able to heave him efficiently upright while the Chambers watched, compassion on their big faces. I could see Hefty and Chloe watching from the verandah, Hefty caressing Chloe like a sister.

We helped him up the steps onto the verandah, where he got his shirt on, manoeuvring his bony elbows. Then we walked on either side of him to the door which led to the Mulcahys' long dinner table. Because of its massive cliff-side window, the room seemed to hang above the pristine blue sea. The Evans, the Chambers, Maureen and Bickham and Khalil stood back solemnly from the table and watched us steer Francis to it. We were a procession rendered holy by the young man's skeletal valour. At last we got Francis seated at the head of the table. Light as a wafer, he sank down with a sigh.

—There you are, *mon ami*, Chambers said in his

hooting intonation. He laid a tentative hand on Francis's shoulder, massive enough, you would have thought, to put a strain on Francis Emptor's stick-like framework. Chambers himself must have got the same impression and took it away again after a second.

We began the meal with Balmain bugs, and — orchestrated by Oscar — the males (why is it always so?) told their best stories in turn for Francis's sake. Chambers told one about UNESCO and a relic. When he had been Australian Ambassador to UNESCO, living in Paris a block from the Eiffel Tower in Rue Jean Rey, he had been appalled by how, for weeks on end, the French press attacked UNESCO; all at a time when the United States was abandoning the organization, allegedly because of its cost, in reality because it sometimes opposed American policy.

—So, said Chambers in the cavernous, aspirated voice with which he had once dominated debate in the House of Representatives. So each day in *France Soir* there was the accusation that UNESCO was wilfully impotent and that its officers lived off caviare and Moët — all at the price of the world's poor and of those who lay in darkness. When I would get home in the evenings, I wouldn't be able to face the paper until I had a solid Scotch, so used was I to abysmal UNESCO-bashing.

—You can read French, can you Norris? asked Mulcahy, winking at the rest of us. And, though it seemed to pain him, Francis Emptor managed a laugh, knowing Norris fancied himself as a Francophone.

Chambers persisted.

—I was so accustomed to the nightly trauma that I leave you to imagine my pleasure when I shook the paper out and found that one particular night the institution which had come in for attack was not UNESCO but the Church. It seemed that in a parish church in the Umbrian Hills there existed a shred of tissue — suitably displayed in a reliquary — which purported to be the foreskin of Jesus, the prepuce of the Saviour. The relic was, it seems, a centre of local pilgrimage and devotion. It had developed that not only had the Vatican refused to recognize this curious cult, but some blackguard had stolen the thing. Thus I had the pleasure of sending a cable to Foreign Affairs in Canberra, and informing my Minister that at last we'd been driven off the front page by a foreskin!

Laughter. People looking secretly to Francis to gauge the impact of the story on him.

In turn, lanky Evans and his wife told of a bungled drama prize giving they had attended in London a little after Evans had his first play bought by a West End theatre. Evans was full of the excitement of bringing his raw new voice to the dwindling but still estimable centre of empire. Their cab driver said to them, Come over here for a bit of culture, have we?

And then, at the reception, one of the Dames of the British theatre beat her way across the floor to say, I always wanted to know, why do you Australians (which, as Evans told us, the super-Brits always pronounced *Awe-strel-yines*) need an Oprah Hice?

Renate — it turned out — was a better social storyteller than her husband. He was fair enough at it but lacked the waspishness for it in ordinary life. And yet all the characters said scathing things in his plays. He was an example of the way art liberated people to be their *Other*. But Oscar's dining table wasn't art, so the anecdote depended on Renate for some of its better connecting lines.

Mulcahy told us how a massive Italian tenor in the Vienna Opera House, gesturing with a sword in *Rigoletto* had it fly from his hand into the orchestra pit, where it caused a wound among the string section. With scarcely a glimpse in the direction in which his sword had vanished, he had continued with the aria, but at its close he had stepped forward, laid a hand on his stomach, bent down over the orchestra and said, *Scusi!*

Francis Emptor touchingly spent more hilarity on that one than seemed medically wise.

Asked to follow, I told the story of a CIA man I'd met in Sichuan, and the trouble he had with pit toilets. Funny how at a feast, lavatorial jokes always work.

The democracy of this tale-telling had, at least in my mind, reduced Bickham to an ordinary citizen at the table. He seemed to be having an ordinary, not an Olympian, day out, and he confirmed it by telling, with an almost hectic relish, how he had met and become friends with Chloe.

—A cowgirl with whom I have learned to discuss my work, as I never have with any other woman. Especially not with any academic.

Chloe radiated a flush of good blood and a kind of watchful contentment. And she, who could have told us stories to curl our hair, told none.

Francis ate a fragment of one of Mulcahy's magnificent spuds, one or two shreds of the beef, and a third of a forkful of peas. He chewed slowly, then after swallowing his fragments of food, took minute sips of his Cabernet Sauvignon. He refused the dessert and the cheese. Chloe watched him all the while, I noticed.

We were still eating dessert and Oscar Mulcahy had opened a second bottle of Château d'Yquem when Francis said, Would you all excuse me for a second?

Most of us half-stood. We looked at each other wondering what gallantry the moment required of us.

—Please, he said, putting out a hand to stop us.

He made hard progress out of the dining room and across the living room and disappeared into the back of the house.

Bickham said in a hushed, uncharacteristic voice, You should take great comfort, Chloe, from the fact that he has so much fight in him.

Francis was gone some time and we half forgot him. I was sitting at the wrong end of the table to see his return, but I heard his light, painful tread on the polished jarrah floor of the living room. I heard too the noise of a minor fall, as if a jacket had been taken off and dropped on a chair, and saw on the faces of those who *were* placed to see — including Hefty and Oscar and Khalil — a sudden appalled look. In the next instant we all heard something sharper, an awful thud, somehow metallic, somehow to do with glass, and Chloe and Hefty screamed together, at this pitch of distress indistinguishable from each other.

Everyone rose from the table and rushed into the living room. Francis had fallen against the glass corner of Hefty's enormous coffee table. The glass had cut his forehead deeply. Blood had sprayed a coffee table book of Hefty's on Magritte, and began to clot in the fibres of a Berber rug.

Former Prime Minister Chambers had a bad back, and of course, Bickham had emphysema, and this and horror caused those two men to pause. No-nonsense Maureen was already on her knees, trying to ease the fallen, bleeding boy onto his back.

With her own child gushing blood, Chloe seemed too stricken to apply the fireman's carry which had saved Bickham's life. Khalil, Oscar and I rushed in and helped turn Francis over and flinched at the damage he'd done to his eyebrow and forehead. We lifted him, Maureen telling us to be sure to support his spine, and carried him into Hefty's bedroom. Blood poured down his face onto the light blue pillow, but Hefty did not complain and went to get a towel to mop it up. While she was gone, Francis opened his eyes.

—Did Chambers see it? he asked us.

Oscar and I blinked at each other, not knowing what he meant.

—Did Norris see it? Did Norris?

—I did, *comrade*, said Norris, massively frowning.

—Course he did darling, Chloe assured Francis.

—It's delirium, Bickham pronounced.

XII

It was during my last bright Australian December, the year before I went to New York, that I got a further urgent call from Chloe. The damage to Francis's brow had long since healed, but his health had declined further. So I was pleased to hear Chloe sounding excited. Her son Jacko, she said, was coming home from America to see his brother, Francis. He only had a week. Could my wife and I come around to Francis's terrace house in Woollahra for drinks with Jacko?

I asked her if Bickham and Khalil would be there, but she said in a chastizing voice that I must know that Tuesday and Thursday were her days at Bickham's. That was the usual limit of what Bickham and Chloe saw of each other.

But even then, before I had my New York acquaintanceship with Jacko, I relished the idea that patrician Bickham might need to meet up with that video stockman, Jacko Emptor.

Maureen and I were surprised by the Chloe who answered the door of Francis's terrace house. In caring for Francis and Bickham, and in bearing the pre-loss of both men, she had taken on a suburban pallor and had achieved a thinness which had come to her too late in life and left her not slim but pouchy.

The shock of seeing this reduced Chloe was followed by that of meeting Francis. At the Mulcahys' he had seemed as pared down as a human could be, but, crouched in one corner of a large easy chair in the living room, he had achieved a new and terrible incorporeality. The bookshelf behind him featured a complete set of Bickham's works. With that as his background, Francis squinted out at the sub-tropical colour of his little December garden. He was done with the world of lushness. His hair, thin at the back of his scalp, had nearly disappeared from the front. His nose and cheekbones were sharp as gems behind the dry flesh. The acceptance in his eyes was of a kind I wasn't used to seeing in Western faces. I had seen it however in the faces of Ethiopian women and children from minorities not usually favoured by the aid funnelled through the Ethiopian Government of Mengistu. And the way the teeth thrust forward, prognathous, but without expecting any nourishment! He had exactly reproduced it.

Maureen and I looked at each other, as if to work out the best way to commiserate with Francis over his condition.

He wore a crisp white shirt, in which — as in the chair — he seemed lost. White slacks, too, and his bony, pale feet lay bare on the Berber carpet like claims for mercy.

From the hallway big Jacko Emptor appeared and came towards me grimacing and with his hand out. It seemed as large as a small horse's head.

—Gidday mate, he told me sepulchrally. You pulled it off eh? You got to Bickham. You made the old girl very happy. You know Francis, don't you? Would you introduce me to your missus.

I did. I could tell Maureen wasn't much impressed.

Francis flashed us a smile brief as a blink. Carrying a cup of jasmine tea which she put down beside Francis, who fluttered his eyes in appreciation, Chloe joined us.

—Jesus, said Jacko, let's get into the Scotch eh.

He and Chloe went to fetch the whisky from the sideboard. We all drank hungrily, even my wife, a modest drinker. The sight of pitiable Francis drove us to anaesthetize ourselves.

Chloe said, Jacko wants to take Francis to America for treatment.

—To Mexico, amended Jacko.

—No, he isn't going to, said Francis, in a voice thin but wiry.

Jacko closed one eye, ignoring this.

He said, They sent me down to Tijuana to do a story on a cancer clinic this bloke runs down there. Southern California is full of cancer-sufferers who swear by this feller. He injects some serum he makes up from the saguaro cactus. He reckons the saguaro cactus has an astounding immune system.

Francis said, It also doesn't have a brain or a nervous system.

—Oh Jesus, Francis, said Jacko. Where's your famous open bloody mind gone to?

He turned to Maureen and me.

—The results are astounding, he told us. I don't care if they're based on auto-suggestion or hypnosis or psychosomatic fakery. As far as I'm concerned, what works works. And this guy has absolutely amazing figures for remissions.

Maureen turned to Chloe.

—What do you think, Chloe?

She shook her head. In the bright afternoon light, her withered jowls hung like old fruit.

—Oh Jesus, I don't know. But I wouldn't mind it if Francis wanted to go. I wish to Christ he did. Nothing to lose eh.

—Listen, said Francis, panting and, I felt, using up a resource of strength he'd never get back. Listen! We know this is all bullshit! Witch doctory only works if you believe in witchery in the first place. Of course the Californians *believe* in cactus juice. They think John Wayne *really* fought the Apaches.

Pausing, he closed his eyes. He looked so spiritual, in a way uncharacteristic of our callow harbour city. Only the filament of his flesh separated him from the eternal.

—I don't believe in any of that, and I won't waste my last strength going to fucking Mexico.

—But your brother means the best, said Chloe. Bugger it all, Frank.

Clearly, there was no expedition she would fail to undertake herself, or even look to Francis to undertake, as long as Francis might be saved even by sleight of hand.

—I'll tell you one thing for bloody free, said Jacko. Saguaro cactus live for nearly three hundred bloody years.

—Oh for God's sake, so do our cells. Our individual cells. There are cells in mummies that are three thousand years old. If that's life, the mummy knows fuck-all about it. Do you know what I think? I think you'd like to get me freeze-dried, and a recorded message put up my arse.

Chloe wailed and looked to Maureen and me. Sure enough, her children were killing her.

—I'm dying in the most beautiful city on earth, said Francis. The only one I want to die in. I'm dying in the city of the Bickhams and the Evans, the Chambers and the Mulcahys and the . . .

He had the generosity to include my wife and me in the distinguished roll-call.

—They've all seen me, he said. They aren't fooled. They know how sick I am. The Chambers know. Ask them. They saw me bloody fall!

Jacko began to mutter about what that had to do with any bloody thing. Chloe seemed awfully appeasing, though somehow I could imagine her carrying Francis onto the plane to Los Angeles, Bickham style, over the shoulder.

—I'm not going to Tijuana to suffer among strangers. I'm going out next Monday. To lunch with my favourite women, other than Chloe. I mean Hefty Mulcahy and Irma Lauber. I'm going to do that every Monday until it's impossible to continue to go. I'm not going to Tijuana to be injected with cactus juice.

Absorbing this, Jacko looked away across the room. He could not show anger in the normal way of course. Maureen and I began to move the conversation on. Jacko's answers when we asked him about New York and the show were clipped, a mere token of the volumes I would later learn from him at the Odeon. He would have liked to have gone on shouting it out with his brother, but you can't scream insults at the dying.

When we were leaving, it was Jacko who followed us down the hallway and out to our car.

—Listen, he told me, I always really admired you . . .

It looked to me like an unlikely claim.

—You don't have to, I'm just a friend of Chloe's.

—No, I mean as a writer. You're bloody readable, mate. Give me you any day over bloody Bickham eh. And you did that good job there. Fixing that meeting for Chloe.

—I was just a witness to that adventure. Chloe made her own way.

—Yeah, she does that. Listen, would you give Francis a call at some stage? Try to talk him round?

My wife said, Those Mexican clinics were all discredited, Jacko.

—But in his condition, what does it bloody matter eh? Ask him to do it for Chloe's sake.

The plea had some force with me. I suppose I had expected Francis to look something like a ghost. I'd prepared myself for that. But I didn't expect the old Chloe to be reduced down like that. She needed something done for her.

—You know, I told Jacko, smiling. You operate on me exactly the same way your mother does.

—Well, said Jacko, I'm her darling little bugger, aren't I eh? I inherited all her moves.

My wife shook her head at me. She was a trained nurse. Broadminded — she had once studied acupuncture — but she didn't believe in cactus serum.

—Well, you ought to think about it, he said, seeing that he couldn't get past Maureen.

*　*　*

My wife and I argued about the question for three days. She had worked with the dying, the *terminally ill* as they are known now. She had seen all the false death-bed hopes and understood how cruel they were. Everyone knew there was indeed no salvation in cactus juice.

On the third day I had a call from Bickham himself. I was just back from a swim in the surf, and brine stuck to my bare legs in that gluey, itchy way peculiar to humid days when you've been swimming. This was a banal condition to be in for a significant call like this, one that I might want some day to put into an autobiography — always allowing a publisher could be found. Bickham's voice on the line creaked with breathlessness. I could tell he was suffering another bad day.

—I'm lying here waiting for the doctor, he told me. I may need to go to hospital . . . And I've been thinking about the poor Emptor boy. You probably know the ill don't have much strength. Strength is the relevant dimension for them . . . Not time . . . In fact the ill don't think of time at all . . . Only, as I said, of strength. They think of wasting strength . . . They don't want to.

—Well, I said alarmed at the length of this speech, you shouldn't waste yours either, Michael.

—I began gasping as a child on that damn spacious great sheep station my family owned. I've tried everything . . . Asthma papers as a child, and asthma fucking cigarettes as a young man. I've been to herbalists and naturopaths . . . acupuncturists and shamans. And if someone came in here now . . . and told me there was a village in Anatolia where an old man possessed a substance . . . which would make it easy for me to breathe on a long term basis . . . then I'd have to say I'd want to go and get it. Even though I'd know in my water there was little chance of recovery. But at the same time as wanting to go, I would beg not to be taken . . . Because my mind would quake for lack of strength . . .

—You think Francis should be persuaded to go?

There was a silence as Bickham re-gathered that very strength he'd been extolling and regretting the loss of.

—For his own sake and his mother's, Bickham answered at last. I wanted to say that he's right to mistrust his strength . . . Because that's his business. Whereas, let the well worry about time . . . And about travel arrangements too.

I scratched my leg and said, This question's been with me for days, Michael.

It felt very strange to call him Michael. I had heard of him that he destroyed friends at the dinner table. No one had the Nobelist's gift for vituperation. Khalil was cast back upon Arab stoicism. Men gagged and women fled weeping, savaged despite their sisterly warmth. Against that background, against such a reputation, Bickham's kind advice regarding Francis took on a perverse poignancy.

—What do you suggest I do?

—Chloe has certain plans, he gasped. Mind you, it's a pity she's got to work with that other son . . . Such an oaf.

Jacko represented everything which Bickham had most actively and brilliantly despised at six hundred pages a time in his sundry, grand books.

—I think you . . . should do what you can for Chloe, the great modernist croaked, and then said goodbye and hung up.

I hadn't had a chance to wash the crystallizing brine off when our door bell rang. Jacko was there, very New York pallid in a sport shirt and slacks.

—Come in, mate? he asked.

He went lolloping down the stairs and into the living room and saw that wonderful azure and foam which is the surf off the coast of New South Wales.

—Why would anyone ever leave a place like this? he asked, and then answered it himself, Fame and bloody riches I suppose, that's why.

I got him a beer and we sat out on the deck. The cries of children, the surf hitting their waists, rose to us. The same primal sounds whenever children were struck by mother brine. I'd always listened to and marvelled at and been soothed by the rising fragments of that sound.

—I still remember, he told me, not finishing the sentence.

He still remembered making the long journey in Stammer Jack's tank of a car, through the rubberbush and the mauve desolation to Hector, then north to Darwin. And the Arafura there, the stickiest, most humid sea, full of sea wasps, brimming with fascination. That was what he remembered and was too wise to express.

—We're going to take Francis, he told me.

—He's agreed? I asked hopefully, wanting to be off Bickham's hook.

—Chloe and I are going to sedate him. Then we're just going to bloody take him.

I looked confused. I couldn't see how this could happen.

—We've got his passport, said Jacko. We'll take him on the plane. We'll tell customs and immigration that he's under sedation.

I would later get more used to the casual lawlessness of Jacko's tone.

—Chloe and I are going to take him Sunday night. If he goes to his normal Monday meeting with Madames Mulcahy and Lauber, they'll just reinforce his resistance. Mind you, the little bugger will engineer them to do that eh. From their point of view it will seem the right thing to do. He'll get 'em so bamboozled they'll beg him not to give in to his yobbo brother eh. Cunning's the last thing to die in a human being, you know. Frank's got bags of it left.

I took a breath.

—Bickham called me, I told Jacko. He says Francis should go.

—What? He said that? I'll never say another bad thing about the old bugger.

Indeed, Jacko's eyes had softened into a pitiable gratitude. He turned them towards the eastern horizon, where the waves were white-horsing out in the Tasman Sea.

—Chloe and I wondered if you could come out with us, you know, to see us through immigration and everything. You're a respected figure here. You can say he's travelling to California for treatment and the buggers at the desk will believe you eh. We've already arranged to do his check-in in the first class lounge, but if you're there with us at immigration it'll stop them thinking his brother's trying to abduct him.

—But you are abducting him.

—Noooh! said Jacko.

But neither Bickham's persuasion nor Jacko's and Chloe's desire had yet quite convinced me this wasn't abduction.

—Come on, mate. You're a bloody wordsmith,

aren't you? You know the definition of kidnap. We're not holding him to ransom. He's been holding us. The little bugger.

—Does this request come from Chloe too?

—Mate, he said, reaching into his breast pocket. She wrote you a letter.

When I saw the pink envelope, and the hopeful large loops of Chloe's handwriting, I knew I was embroiled.

*   *   *

I avoided any further argument by the dishonest but not abnormal marital means of telling only part of the truth. I implied that Francis himself had consented under the influence of his mother's good friend, the Nobelist, to go to Tijuana. The flight across the Pacific was hardly one he was unfamiliar with.

I was vaguely grateful just the same that, on principle, Maureen did not want to come to the airport with me to see the Emptors off.

After lunch on Sunday, a limousine ordered by Jacko arrived to collect me from the beach. As I was dragged away in its front seat — Australians like to signify mateship with the driver they don't even know by sitting in the front rather than in the back of limos — I saw Maureen frowning up at me from the bottom of the drive. I was sure she suspected I'd misled her. I know it sounds thin now, even to me, but at the time, I have to plead, I believed what that sick man, Bickham, had said. And believed, too, under the pressure of Chloe's misery that there was no harm in hope and in placebos.

Fifty minutes later, we stopped in front of Francis's

terrace, and Jacko appeared through the front door at the trot. He and the driver and I quickly packed the Emptors' extensive luggage into the boot of the car, and I went into the house to help Jacko manage Francis out the door and into the limousine, all under the supervision of Chloe. I was appalled at how limp and glazed Francis looked. His eyebrows flicked, trying to focus. We simply lifted him by either elbow, and I heard his feet scrape along the pavement. Chloe got in ahead of us, and when we eased Francis in beside her, she received his head on her shoulder. At the sight of this Burren Waters *Pietà*, I found myself swallowing tears. In that second, I was irrationally pleased with myself for doing something to allow Francis to meet the cactus doctor.

That afternoon there was a tight test match between Australia and India in progress at the Cricket Ground, and people were on their way there for the afternoon session. Chloe looked at the cars, the drivers avid for the sight of cover drives and square cuts. She sighed.

—Michael Bickham despises cricket, she told me in her smallest voice, but as if she agreed utterly with Bickham. People cluttering the roads for the sake of a mere game!

I mentioned that Bickham's biography claimed his father had adored the game. I don't know what made me challenge her quoting of Bickham. She was after all in an innocent enough state of impatience, this woman whose son was dying. I was pleased anyhow that we so quickly got past the Cricket Ground crowd and were able to turn south for the airport.

Jacko had called ahead from the limo, and a young man in an airline uniform was waiting on the pavement outside the glass doors for our arrival. There were too many of us being too solicitous, but between us we got Francis safely into the wheel-chair, where he slumped, his head lolling. The young man in the airline uniform leaned forward to his ear.

—Francis, it's Arnaldo. I met you at the Friends of the Opera party last year. I really hope this trip works well for you, Francis.

—Okay, okay, Jacko announced. They're going to check us through in the Captain's Club.

—I've been told, said the young man, beginning to push Francis's wheel-chair.

Chloe raised her eyes at me. Francis, Michael Bickham and Khalil were the only homosexuals she had room for in her world view.

Sydney's growing Asian, Arab and Turkish population seemed to fill the airport. Transits and reunions turned these latest immigrants into airport habitués. A provincial-sized airport that was required somehow to service a big city full of perhaps the most wandering people on earth!

Strolling past queues of passengers, Jacko put his arm around my shoulder.

—Okay, mate, here we go. Me for fucking lustre and you for renown.

The combination seemed to work well enough in the lounge to which we were led. It was the sort of place which was used for ministers of state and film stars, visiting and departing.

Especially for Francis, a sofa had been set up with pillows. Jacko and the young airline official lifted comatose Francis onto it. Chloe pulled up a chair and held Francis's diaphanous hand.

The young airline official asked, What can I get you from the cocktail bar?

We all ordered Scotch. And even though we knew
Francis could not possibly drink it, the accustomed
flute of champagne was votively placed for him on
the coffee table by the sofa. The young airline official
took all the Emptors' passports and tickets and immigration forms and went away to deal with them. It
was an hour before boarding, he told us.

—Do you mind waiting here with us, mate? Jacko
bleakly asked me.

I said that of course I didn't. I wanted to see the
Emptors get away safely.

Chloe murmured, You're really a kind old bugger,
aren't you? Compared to Bickham eh. Do you think
you have to be an utter prick to be a genius?

—Let me tell you one thing, Jacko breathed. You
don't have to be a genius to be a prick.

—Bickham let me know he wanted Frank to go, I
confessed to Chloe. That was one of the deciding
things with me.

—Yeah, said Chloe, her eyes clouding again. I
didn't really mean to imply he wasn't kind. But tell
your missus we appreciate her lending you to the
bloody cause.

Waiting through the next hour, we drank a lot.
Francis's Heidsieck went flat on his coffee table, but
none of *our* drinks stood long enough to go off or
alter their states. Jacko found time to reiterate his
belief that saguaro serum, administered by the healer
of Tijuana, could very well work by one means or
another, and there was a lot of talk about how complex the chemistry of fatal illness was, and the role of
the mind, etc., etc.

Jacko said, It's funny — Australians think Californians are gullible. True enough in a sense. They've

got a capacity for belief. But they're hard-headed too. More hard-headed than we are eh. Stuff that we'd just let go, they'll sue over. But down in Tijuana the cactus doctor injects Californian architects, lawyers, movie producers. Let me tell you, these are the toughest bastards on earth. They don't lightly declare themselves fixed up, remitted, cured. They don't lightly give up the idea of lawsuits. And there are hordes of these tough old American bastards who swear by the cactus doctor. So who gives a bugger whether it's magic or not? Those bloody opera friends of Frank's think that even dying has to be in good taste.

The young man who had met Francis at the Friends of the Opera affair returned with a youngish but motherly colleague, who helped us pass the time by fussing over us. Jacko put his arm on my elbow and asked her, Can my friend get a clearance to come with us into the immigration hall?

The young woman said yes and uttered my name as if it were all the argument that was needed for such a concession. In my liquid condition, I felt wonderful about this, as if I had stolen some glory from gods, perhaps even from Michael Bickham.

In these genial circumstances, boarding time came quickly. At last Francis was lifted into his wheelchair, and we caught a lift and emerged amidst the Turks and Arabs to roll Francis down towards the large yellow immigration hall door. The young yet motherly airline official tapped my shoulder to convey to the security guard that I needn't be delayed by enquiries as to whether or not I had a boarding pass. She then asked a number of passengers whether they minded if Francis went straight to the head of the line. None of them did. Asian, Hamitic, Caucasian, they stared at the ravaged fragment of golden boy who occupied the wheelchair Jacko now fraternally pushed.

A bald and sun-tanned immigration official looked at me and half-nodded.

—Not on Sunday television today? he asked.

For one season I had been a regular on an arts program on television, and everyone still thought I was. Such is the power of television, even in Australia, to fix you in people's constellations.

And to prove that it was so he also breathed the name of Jacko's old program, *Morning Oz*. Then, This is your brother?

—My son, said Chloe. We're taking him to America for treatment.

It seemed to me that two men in business suits were growing impatient with our queue-jumping and were pressing round either flank of our party. One of them opened his wallet and showed a card to the immigration official. He said, We have a court order to seize Mr Emptor's passport.

Jacko, taller even than this policeman, reared back and looked down his vast cheeks at the man.

—Which Mr Emptor's passport?

—You're free to go, Jacko. Mrs Emptor, too, if she wants. We have an ambulance waiting for your brother.

Jacko, Chloe and I found, by comparing notes afterwards, that at that stage we had all believed someone had brought an injunction against Francis's leaving Australia for quack treatment in Tijuana. Yet who knew and disapproved? Only Maureen.

Jacko bellowed at me, Who is this man?

I was not able to answer that.

The policeman who had made the speech about the passport turned with studied patience and showed Jacko the same card he had already shown the immigration official. Jacko read it and seemed flummoxed all the more. He and Chloe exchanged looks. I had been expecting her to speak but she was hard of breath, her chest heaving. Suddenly, like Bickham, a sufferer in matters of respiration.

—What . . . What in the hell? she kept muttering, and turned her eyes to me.

Jacko told the suited cops, I'll have Tom Hughes QC down your bloody throats within half an hour.

He was invoking the name of a lawyer he admired.

The senior cop could see that Chloe was beside herself and leaned down towards her, looking her straight in the face.

—Mrs Emptor, we have intravenous set up in the ambulance. We'll bring him round for you. You're not to blame in any way, Mrs Emptor. He'll be back to full health in no time.

Chloe swung both hands against his upper ribs, trying to do him damage, but Woollahra and her long grieving had debilitated her.

—No, no, the policeman advised her softly, more like a counsellor than a cop.

I saw the crooked plaint in Chloe's mouth. Jacko's pallor also drove me to do something for the Emptors.

—I'm calling the press straight away, I assured Jacko.

The senior policeman quietly informed me that the press were already outside in large numbers in any case.

Meanwhile the immigration hall seemed to have

emptied of travellers and to be full now of uniformed police and ambulance men. Chloe wailed as Francis was lifted from the chair and put onto an elegant, wheeled stretcher and pushed away. Chloe and Jacko kept pace with it, and two uniformed policemen had to restrain Jacko, who made a dash from the flank as if to rescue Frank.

—Come on, come on! Jacko yelled. I hope you know what you're doing! My brother's dying.

In the stretcher's wake, I saw the chief, suited policeman collect the Emptors' passports and tickets, which they had left behind at the desk. I said that I would swear in court that I saw him take receipt of them.

Calmly he said, That's okay, sir.

I had no choice but to move in Jacko and Chloe's wake. The trolley carrying Francis was loaded into a lift, and the rest of us were told to use the stairwell. We raced down, Jacko and I supporting Chloe on either side.

Outside the glass arrival doors downstairs, police were restraining journalists and radio and television crews. One of the television people called out a question to me about whether I'd been helping Francis Emptor escape? I said I was helping him go to America for treatment for lymphatic cancer. Or lymphoma. Cancer anyhow. Whereabouts in America? they asked, but I would not answer. Vanity and discretion stopped me now from saying the name of quackery's capital: Tijuana.

Amidst the surf of people around the ambulance, I saw Chloe turn her pink gash of a mouth to me.

—Call Bickham! she yelled. They reckon it's all a put-up job.

Waiters at Emilia's in Double Bay, who thought the Fraud Squad's claims outrageous, left the table normally occupied by Francis and Hefty Mulcahy and Irma Lauber free that Monday. On its plain white cloth, they sat a thin vase charged with one white rose. If you had seen the ghastly Francis of past weeks, it was possible to read everything that had happened as police barbarity.

In fact Francis was revived under guard in hospital, charged with fraud, fed intravenously, and then given a meal. Relieved of the burden of creating his own fiction, he was reported to have eaten parts of the food, and to have got more voracious still over the next few days as he ate. He would in fact put on fourteen pounds in the first week.

But Chloe and Jacko and I were not to know this that first Sunday afternoon at the hospital, as we all sat in a lounge drinking coffee. Chloe looked appalling, and Jacko swore at officials. Then they got a hospital psychiatrist to come and speak to us.

—This miming of the symptoms of cancer might be a result of Munchausen's Syndrome, a desire to attract attention, or else an attempt to deceive the authorities which became a pathological game. Apart from starving himself, he rubbed depilatory cream into his hair to simulate the effects of radiotherapy. In any case, you have to come to terms with your anger at him . . .

This might have been a struggle for all but Chloe. For Chloe, I could see very plainly, was ecstatic. She turned to me a face ravaged with tears of relief.

Frank had made everyone look very silly, except perhaps Jacko and Chloe who had blood ties to explain their behaviour. Jacko would never forgive him for his deception. Chloe herself would tell me years later, The little bugger's an actor. He got into his bloody act and he couldn't pull out. Jacko should know all about *acts*. He's got a bloody beauty of his own.

Ten weeks after the drugged Francis was stopped from leaving Australia, he stood trial. Chloe asked us all to write references which could be put before the court's attention, but I don't think anybody did.

When Chloe asked me, I said, But how can I write a reference for someone who duped *you*? And as cruelly as that?

—I'm the mother, said Chloe. And I'm bloody asking.

Bickham must have refused too, because as far as I could ever tell, she forgave me. No doubt the Chambers, the Mulcahys, the Evans and perhaps even Dame Roberta Murdoch, the great diva, were also asked. Full both of loathing and pity, Maureen and I and all of us followed the trial. I even saw footage of Chloe and Stammer Jack, hand in hand, entering court together. Chloe did not look as drawn as the day on which we had attempted to kidnap Francis for saguaro juice therapy. Her son had been restored to her. She did not need any more answers from Michael Bickham.

It was alleged in the trial that Francis had plundered an amount of two million dollars from the international freight company he worked for. Somehow he had been able to over-enter into a computer the cost of air cargo shipments, so that the computer itself instructed him to issue credits. He directed these credits to certain bank account numbers, which in fact were accounts run by Francis himself. He had once told his mother that money had been left him by an older, grateful lover. He had told Jacko the same, and also that he had profited from some antiques deals. He had always known that some central airline freight computer in Europe would catch him out in the end. So that when it did, and the first enquiries began to be made by company officials, and the Fraud Squad was brought in, Francis had acquired some letterhead from a cancer surgeon recently deceased. He did some research and then wrote himself the letter breaking the news of lymphatic cancer.

He had then somehow found the will to starve himself, to make himself a tragic being, to launch himself against the corner of the Mulcahys' glasstopped coffee table at Place de l'Opéra by the sea.

After I had the inevitable row with Maureen, all the worse because now my behaviour looked ridiculous, she said, It's a wonder no one ever looked for lymph swellings under his arms. But I suppose he never went near doctors, and it's bad taste to ask a dying man if you can see his lumps.

Chloe was right to be impressed by the heroic scale of Francis's mortality play. He had hoped, said the prosecution, that the freight company and the police would back away from his mortal, cadaverous act. What sense and decency was there in prosecuting a ghost? Except that a little investigation showed that Francis took no treatment at the cancer centres and hospitals where the limo dropped him. Instead, he walked through the halls, out into the laneways, and was picked up there by a sole friend and confidant, a young painter who had shared a number of his trips to the San Francisco Opera in the salad days.

He would often spend the night at the painter's

flat, returning to the hospital the next day or the day after that to be picked up by the limo.

For Chloe's sake, I went to court on the last day and was surprised to see Bickham there, shoulders hunched, face long and sallow, in need of air. Sacrificing so much of his remaining breath for Chloe. Led by Khalil, he would make the arduous escape from the television crews afterwards.

Francis got eight years and a good talking to. Some misguided commentators, the judge told him, had thought this a stylish crime. But it took no style to exploit computers, at least temporarily. Thousands had done it, and thousands were in jail for it. And where was the stylishness in fraudulently evoking the pity of others, and the grief of the Emptor family?

As I left, I heard one loose-tied journalist say to another, He won't mind jail. He'll be in root heaven.

XIII

There was a particular New York lunch Jacko invited us to. This was at the Grand Ticino, and Lucy and Jacko, Maureen and I (Our favourite older couple, said Jacko) were celebrating the second anniversary of a marriage ceremony they had gone through in New York, having earlier been married in Sydney. Francis was at that stage perhaps near the end of his second year of serving time in medium security, learning to paint, and teaching a class in music appreciation. He was not mentioned at the lunch, nor even our attempted abduction of him, which was, after all, a wonderful lunch reminiscence. Jacko, Lucy said, had written Francis off so thoroughly he didn't even tell me.

There was a less than charged ardour to this long lunch. I did not know exactly what to think of the anniversary. Lucy had confided to my wife that Jacko did not really want her to chase after any excellence in her own right, to develop her cello and join music schools, in which New York abounded, or to seek out a music teacher. She was thinking of art classes, since she painted sometimes and people who should know liked her work.

Jacko, in turn, was still complaining to me that despite her even and casual public demeanour, Lucy depended on him utterly for her validity, was not driven to take the city on and to find for herself a name other than that of spouse of the Great Trespasser.

One or both of them were badly and earnestly mistaken, and I felt that a murderous little smog of incomprehension hung over the anniversary feast. The balance of judgement had surely to favour Lucy, since there was nothing we could publicly see to contradict her general stance of tolerance and casual good sense towards Jacko. Besides, one night recently, leaving a dinner table we'd shared at an Italian restaurant in Tribeca, I'd met Lucy in the corridor on my way to the lavatory. Lucy stood, her face blurred with tears, by the telephone. She looked as if she'd forgotten her way back to our table.

—Lucy, I said.

She turned her eyes to me.

—I hate this city, she told me. It makes me powerless. I'm a different woman in Australia. I can do anything. Start anything, you know. Here I can't get started.

I held her for a moment.

—Have you ever written? I asked.

The bright idea being that I could take her into my class at NYU. Bloody Jacko could afford it.

—That's kind, she said. But no. Music and a bit of painting. That's all I've got. Just manual stuff.

—Pretty good manual stuff!

She smiled and wept then, and I uttered flat reassurances. She dried her eyes, went off to the women's lavatory, and returned to the dining room ten minutes later, glimmering, smiling. Wearing the James Ruse High smile, saying *whacko!* and *that's the go.*

Now, at the anniversary lunch, we had barely finished the main course when a waiter came and said that there was a call for Jacko.

—Good, said Jacko, as if he'd been expecting it.

I thought it might be some act he had planned for her — say three or four Renaissance players in drag to play bagpipes and flutes and do some juggling at the table. Lucy, her long lips still fixed in a smile, cast her eyes up though. She expected nothing very startling.

At this slack stage of the search for the Anodyne Kid, Jacko had interviewed a professor of psychology at Columbia for *Live Wire*, which, having devoted itself at Jacko's urging to the search, now needed to find a result. The psychologist said that even on the slim evidence so far presented, there was a likelihood that the Anodyne Kid might very well coincide with Sunny Sondquist. A number of possibilities therefore existed. One was of course that Sunny had been taken by someone who had disoriented her in some way, had *turned her mind*. Like Patty Hearst, he said.

And Maureen said to me, What would they do for an analogy if they didn't have Patty Hearst?

The other idea was that she was wilfully staying away from Bob Sondquist. It was not possible to guess what motivation, said the psychologist to Jacko, what perceived wrong any child might have for staying away from someone as genial and ill as Mr Sondquist seemed to be. Swallowing his news of what motivation that was, Jacko had bravely gone on asking the prosaic questions.

Then in Baker, California, in what was called the High Desert, a bright little, middle-aged block of a woman who on videotape reminded me somewhat of

Chloe, said she was sure she had worked in the past in a motel with Sunny, except that she called herself Ess. Ess lived with some family or other outside Baker. Occasionally, in the early mornings, a man in a station wagon brought her to work, but most of the time Ess ran to the motel and ran home, even at the height of summer. The habit of spelling under her breath? Everyone had noticed that about Ess. She spelt words as she jogged, and if you turned the vacuum off while you were cleaning a room, you heard her spelling as she washed the bath out. But if she was a victim of some sort, why didn't she just tell someone? the woman asked. Why did she jog back home of her own free will?

Ess was very private about the family she lived with. When she said they were moving and she was going with them, she gave away no details at all.

The psychologist, consulted yet again, said, Well, someone might be keeping her under very steady mental and physical control.

I presumed now that the telephone call Jacko got at Grand Ticino had something to do with all this; some other direction for the search for the pitiable Anodyne Kid.

In Jacko's absence, the waiter came, flirted casually and stylishly with Lucy, and took our orders for dessert and coffee. As the young man balletically withdrew, Jacko himself returned. He did not sit down. Instead he clenched both fists against his chest, like a child who could not contain his delight.

—You won't believe this, boys and girls, he announced.

—Sunny? I asked.

—Not Sunny. Something really big. Durkin's just

called me from the Perugia. Something's happened in Berlin. People are walking through the Bornholmer Strasse checkpoint. It's wide open. Durkin says they've just opened another five gates. People are milling in front of the Brandenburg Gate, right up to the Berlin Wall, and the Vopos are grinning down at them.

Jacko raised his hands in the air.

—This looks like the end of East and West. This is the end of bloody, bloody Stalinism, brothers and sisters.

He bent to Lucy and kissed her on the top of her head.

—Darls, listen. We've already missed the start because we don't have any bureau people there in Berlin.

—Only got bureau people in cherrypickers in New York eh? Lucy remarked.

—*Touché*, love. Sutherland's authorized a flight of us anyhow. They're assembling everyone up at the Perugia. All the *Live Wire* crew. Some rented useless bastards of technicians, including my old mate from the cherrypicker days. They've chartered a plane for us, leaving New Jersey as soon as we get ourselves together.

Again he kissed the part in her blond hair.

—Sutherland's really insisting. You'll let your old Jacko go, won't you? History, love. Eh?

Lucy looked forlorn for a second, but then revived. Although she did not answer him directly, she did not seem chagrined. She raised questions to do with shirts and toiletries. Not to worry, he said. He'd just duck round the corner and grab a few clean things and be off. He was sorry to run out on her.

Then he turned to my wife.

—I wonder, could I borrow your husband eh, Maureen?

—You're joking, said Maureen.

He turned to me.

—You don't have any classes till next Tuesday, do you?

Accustomed to my compliance, he didn't wait for me to answer. He appealed again to Maureen.

—He's got some sense of the history of it all, and no one else at *Live Wire* does. He wrote that piece on Poland for the *New York Times*, so he understands the Eastern bloc. And I bet he'd be a good interviewee, you know, right in front of the Wall. Spunky little Aussie, you know. Right there in front of sky-high falling bloody tyranny. Eh? Eh? What do you reckon?

Maureen cast her eyes up, then turned them to me.

—It's up to you. You know you have those pretty heavy revisions to do.

Lucy said, Jacko, you just want to include your friends in the big events!

—Got it in one, hooted big Jacko. Mateship rules OK.

—So, were you going to ask me to go too?

Jacko grinned, choosing to treat this as a jest. Then he spoke to Maureen again.

—Can he come? We can scare him up a fee — maybe as much as $10,000. But I mean, I'm not in the business of wrecking marriages . . .

—Except your own, said Lucy with her broad James Ruse High smile.

I was, of course, in a fever to go with Jacko to the huge moment. But I had to go through the normal Australian inter-male ritual of declaring myself not up to scratch. Indeed, I was only barely up to scratch.

—The *New York Times* piece was a bloody long time ago. Three or four years ago.

Martial law, dismal Soviet apartment blocks, and the electrician Walesa in retreat.

—Look, doesn't matter. The *New York Times* is all we'll have to say, and people will trust us.

My demurrer so quickly dealt with by Jacko, he and I rushed shamelessly through the last courtesies of getting marital permissions, and left our two handsome women behind in the waning light. We deserved to be traduced, for, rushing to pack our bags and go raging uptown to the Perugia, we barely looked back.

Jacko fetched his gear from Thomas Street first. When he returned from the loft to the cab on the corner of West Broadway, he was panting with cold and exertion.

—Thank Christ, he told me. I can get away from that bloody old hypocrite with the squawking voice. But did you notice? Lucy's not like Maureen. Lucy didn't put up any sort of a fight, even though she was more against it than Maureen.

—Do you really want a fight?

—Better than nothing. She's so scared of quarrelling though.

—Jacko, I think it's bloody ungracious of you . . . The girl kissed you goodbye. You're an awful bloody man.

—Oh yeah. No question about that eh . . . I don't express myself well.

While he waited in the cab, I fetched my things from our apartment high above the Ecuadorian singers and other gifted performers at Broadway and Fourth. I was by now so stimulated by the idea of the

end of a great human phase that I did not stop to
seek any chemical stimulus from the bottle of rare
Irish malt someone had given me one Christmas.

We found that the Perugia was, for all purposes,
closed to the public. What Manhattanite would want
to spend the cocktail hour at a bar where Durkin was
answering seven telephones, performing a media
triage? Dannie was already there and greeted Jacko
with a distracted yet somehow promising kiss.

—Listen, you're the Wall.

—What do you mean the Wall?

—Al Bunker's taking East Germany itself. They're
hunting up an East German in one of the bars uptown
to take back for a reunion with his relatives. We
haven't found him yet. Whereas you're right on the
Brandenburg Gate.

—Sounds bloody marvellous.

—So you're the Wall and Bunker's the East.

—But aren't you coming with us? Jacko asked her.

—Durkin's running it from here, said Dannie
brusquely yet with her dark, casual, sumptuous manner. I *might* be producing your segments on the
ground — if they can fit me in the plane.

She gave us some papers, printouts which had
come in on the wire.

I heard Jacko ask Dannie, What're you going to be
wearing, love eh? If you come with us? What'll you
wear?

—When? Dannie asked.

—In Berlin, I mean.

Behind her teeth she made the faintest tut and
walked away. It wasn't possible to know what any of
it meant, but I felt that I was being made privy to

something, some existing arrangement between Dannie and Jacko. And Jacko must know I could overhear. I might be being told perhaps, Don't make a fuss.

At one stage I went out to buy some toothpaste and beheld a fleet of limos backing and edging in the last of the wintry light outside the Perugia, emitting soft clouds of exhaust. The plan was to drive to Teterboro Airfield in New Jersey where the meter of the jet was already running against Basil Sutherland and Vixen Six. But we couldn't leave yet. Durkin had us waiting for the arrival of the East German. One of the young production assistants had been sent to find him.

Soon the girl was back, coming in aglow and leading the man she had found in a bar in Yorktown, a solid man with a red face and a boozy manner who may have been drinking all afternoon. She said his name was Gunter. He said *Good evening* but the effort of it seemed for a moment to deprive him of the ability to focus.

He looked around and came to the presumption that Jacko was boss, and came up to Jacko and me as we read the latest printouts from Berlin.

— God bless freedom! he told us.

— No worries, *Kamerad* eh.

— Do they serve Beck's here? asked Gunter, speaking in such a measured way that it sounded like a question from an English phrasebook.

Jacko asked one of the assistant producers to get Gunter a beer.

— He looks like rent-a-Kraut, Jacko complained to me.

Yet he was a good representative, I thought, of

people's imaginings of Eastern bloc man: somewhat
high-cheek-boned and alien-looking. He had twisted
teeth which I thought of as somehow connected with
too much cabbage and not enough oranges. As Jacko
and I watched him drink a Beck's, in Durkin's mind
the last thing we would attend to before leaving for
Teterboro, the young producer named Marian asked
Gunter for his passport. It was discovered he didn't
have it with him.

—My uncle's house, he said. Over in Queens. Give
me the goddam shiny car and I get it.

Durkin covered his eyes with a hand and said, No
mate, stay here, maybe have a sleep. We'll send someone. Is it in your drawer? Top? Middle? Top! Okay,
we'll send Denise. Give us your uncle's telephone
number and we'll tell him strange people are coming.
Bugger it!

While Denise fetched the passport in Queens, first
one and then another of Basil Sutherland's energetic
employees tried to find out from Gunter where his
relatives were and who they were and what they had
done for a living under Honecker's fatal regime.

His brother was a chemical plant supervisor in
Bitterfeld, he told Durkin. One of the girls began
looking at a map of East Germany and was relieved
to find that Bitterfeld was perhaps as little as seventy-
five miles south-west of Berlin.

—How long since you saw your brother? Durkin
wanted to know. Durkin was interested in a loving
reunion long delayed by tyranny.

Gunter said, I see the sonnerbitch three months
ago. His daughter's wedding. In Leipzig.

—But you told Denise you hadn't spoken to him
for fifteen years.

—I don't speak to him. He's a big sonnerbitch party asshole. Fifteen years ago he come into the factory I work in and toss his weight here and there. Bigtime party asshole!

Like a small prayer, Durkin's breath escaped him and he laid his forehead on his hands on the bar of the Perugia.

—Oh dear, oh dear, he said. He seemed to sleep for a time before opening his eyes and gazing up at Gunter again.

—You were back in East Germany three months ago?

—Right, said Gunter.

—Do you go back often?

—Three, four times in the last year.

Durkin looked around the room to see if everyone else had heard this debilitating information. Marian and the American journalist Bunker wanly received the news.

—Gunter, I have to ask you, said Durkin. Are you a spy or a bloody drug-runner or both?

—I am a traveller. I go back to Bitterfeld so I have the joy of shoulder-colding my asshole brother.

Durkin noticed Al Bunker dolorously watching Gunter.

—Sorry, Bunker, said Durkin.

—Make them reunite anyhow, Jacko suggested. Gunter, if we're going to fly you across the Atlantic, in a you-beaut airplane, the least you can bloody do for us is to put your arm around your miserable, Stalinist brother for thirty seconds.

—All relationships soured by Marxist dialectics, said Bunker, more vigorously than I would have expected. Brother torn from brother. I think that'll fly . . .

—We don't have a bloody choice, Durkin told him. It's the small hours in Berlin now. The networks are drinking their first coffee and getting ready to start poncing up and down in front of the Wall. *As dawn breaks over the no-man's land around the Brandenburg Gate, etcetera.* God bloody help us.

—Take him some luxuries from the good old West, Jacko suggested. Corrupt the bastard eh!

Durkin thought this a good idea and asked Gunter what Gunter's brother was partial to.

—Tangerines. And Calvados. That sonnerbitch, Gunter told him.

—Are you serious?

For Durkin feared Gunter might be stating his own preferences. Indeed, did this brother exist to have preferences in the first place?

—I tell you, tangerines. And *verdammt* Calvados. Communism has rot his brain. But his belly and his liver are all stinking capitalists.

And so I saw bright girls from the best communication schools in America sent to the Korean stores on nearby corners to buy up tangerines by the crate, or else to liquor stores up on Lexington or Third who might stock Calvados by the crate. Bird-boned Jewish and Italian girls of the finest Westchester families lugged wooden boxes of fruit and liquor into the Perugia, to be told by Durkin that they should deposit them in the limos outside. Vixen Six would export tangerines across the Atlantic! For one could not be sure that they could be procured in Berlin.

Jacko and I helped in this loading process.

—Hereya love, Jacko would boom, taking the crates

out of delicate, stretched hands. Your parents didn't send you to Vassar so you could be a wharfie.

At last Denise arrived back with Gunter's passport, but was treated coldly by Durkin, as by Dannie and the other producers. She came to Jacko for an explanation.

—Well love, you picked the wrong bloody Kraut, didn't you? Don't let it worry you. You weren't to know.

His mood had grown more elevated still now that it was clear that Dannie was certainly coming to Berlin with us.

* * *

A few minutes later we pulled away from the curb, leaving Denise in the doorway of the Perugia with a scowling Durkin. The poor child carried on her forehead that smudge of failure, the peculiar and damaging failure of one whose best is not thought good enough.

In our fleet of limousines, which swung down beneath the river, taking the Holland Tunnel to New Jersey, we carried the latest printouts. Honecker, spiritual son of Joseph the fearsome Georgian, was still under detention by his own police.

—The muncher has been munched, Gunter told us.

I think he meant the biter had been bitten, the oppressor oppressed.

On visits to Africa — Poland first for the *New York Times Color Magazine*, then starving East Africa — I had seen Honecker's security forces running the intelligence systems of tyrants like the Ethiopian Mengistu. I also knew the East Germans had given plenty of free advice to the Polish secret police too — they had written the manual on how to interrogate. So I was as gratified as Gunter that the muncher had been munched.

Before we were out of the Tunnel, and in what passed for the open air again, Gunter had fallen asleep on Jacko's shoulder. His breathing was the busy, industrial breathing of the deep drinker.

—Thank Christ I'm the Wall and not the sodding reunion, Jacko told me.

We emerged out into the cold swamplands of trans-Hudson: Jersey as despised by Manhattanites. Rendered piquant by our destination, the moist, migrainously yellow and red lights of the commuting traffic seemed less dismal tonight, more jubilant. The headlights behind, the taillights in front, softened by mist, glowered with abnormal promise, lights from the re-made world, a sweeter realm. We rolled at last through a gate where a customs officer waved us through and straight out onto the airfield! No immigration officials, no security search, no squinting at departure information. The jet waited for us all with its stairs laid down for our ascent! A telex machine was fitted aboard with — we were sure — further news that distant tyrants had been locked away, had been hoisted on their own weapons of state. Was the century declaring itself at last a fable, a tale for hopeful children, the casting out of dark knights?

A steward in black tie welcomed us at the top of the stairs, relieving us of the boxes of tangerines and Calvados, promising to stow them. He ushered us all into a cabin designed as a saloon — a bar, banquettes, sofas. Dannie was already collecting more telexes, and I could see Jacko and Gunter prowling amongst the upholstery.

The American Al Bunker told the steward, I'm charged with getting this damn thing off the ground immediately.

The steward reassured him. We had clearance. But he wondered would Jacko and Gunter kindly strap themselves into one of the banquettes for take-off, instead of sitting on stools at the bar.

Dannie briskly distributed more sheets of paper, and everyone but Gunter hungrily read them. Krenz, the new leader of East Germany, was nervously saying that the stability of Europe depended upon the existence of two Germanies. But the drift and the comradely symbolism of events was already against him. Early morning crowds were parading the Ku'damm, embracing Easterners who were coming over through the opened checkpoints. Krenz was calling for an equitable Marxism, a new human-faced socialism. Until tonight, Krenz's plan had been a sentimental dream even to Westerners. I myself had always imagined it as the only possible happy result: Marxism turning kinder, more like the societies that old Jewish Yahweh buried in Highgate Cemetery had had in mind when he took the trouble to craft *Das Kapital*. But the Berliners had lost all confidence in dialectics. They wanted to go shopping. Communism had waited too long to turn humane. Its credit had at least been postponed, and perhaps utterly cancelled.

* * *

During take-off, I sat soberly in my banquette, relishing the hour's joy. I had a sense that the work of East

Germany's interrogators in the dungeons of Africa may have somehow spurred the dawn now breaking in Berlin; may have fed first the great weariness, the Eastern accidie, and now this day's primal humanity, this great European corroboree.

A new telex Dannie gave me said that every East Berliner who danced across the border was given a hundred marks for shopping.

Although the Wall had been opened, it seemed it was meant to stand. One printout said that when a panel of the wall was attacked by enthusiastic Berliners at dawn, the border guards of the East had driven them off with fire hoses. Again, this appeared to me a realistic limit to what could be permitted in a flawed world. After all the Cold War's occasional flying lead, after the misery and inimical air of that cleft city of Berlin, water seemed almost a kindly riposte to the over-enthusiasm of the Berliners. We were so glibly used to the Wall, so accustomed to looking on it as a perpetual device, that we could almost feel brotherhood with the East Germans with the hoses.

Dannie approached me now with a sort of frown. It showed that maybe Jacko's idea of interviewing his favourite and — according to him — clever mate in front of the Brandenburg Gate didn't generate much zeal in her.

—You've really written for the *New York Times Color Magazine*?

I said I had. I told her of Poland. And the Horn of Africa.

—Well, that's the sort of thing we want. Maybe a bit more specific. A sense of the human event. Nothing highly political. Observations. Humorous if you can manage it. A bit of history. You worn makeup before?

She seemed to imply I might need it if I were to come near exciting any of Vixen Six's thirty million viewers.

Al Bunker was trying to get a not quite coherent Gunter away from the bar and to shoot an interview with him in mid-air. Bunker hoped people might think Gunter's mumblings arose from the despair of exile, and from the disabling hope which had now been released upon the earth, in particular upon Germans who lived in Queens.

Three enormous sofas lined the walls at the rear of the plane, and people were going there to sleep now, leaving Bunker with a silent plane in which he could try to make something out of shifty, unfocused Gunter. Dannie had sprawled herself in the corner where two sofas met: her feet still on the floor, her shoes kicked off. Along the rear bulkhead lay Jacko, his head on her lap. She patted the sofa on her left, against the side wall.

—There's room for you here if you want, she told me.

I felt somehow sundered in two by exhaustion. It seemed to me that my brain was bouncing against the ceiling and my feet were ten yards away, the two connected by one thin wire. I took to the sofa gratefully. There was no room to lie full length, but plenty of room to recline, as Dannie had. Only kings like Jacko, entitled to six and a half feet of upholstery, lay full length.

I saw that Dannie stroked his head, and was talking softly, though loudly enough so that I could make out what she said. In this context, history's most joyful and clamorous night, the words didn't quite make sense. Gradually it became apparent she was talking about something our wild preparation and departure had already wiped from my mind: Sunny Sondquist's case.

Slavery, was the word which recurred in Dannie's mouth. She was listing a sub-bibliography of slave magazines I never knew about.

—Basically they tell you how to capture, secure and then wreck the mind of your slave. They're extraordinary publications. This is our glorious system of freedoms we're about to bring to the East Germans!

—Who put you onto this stuff? Jacko groaned on the edge of sleep.

—This psychologist, that new one I found. Young, Jewish, sexy. A damned good talker.

—Ah, murmured Jacko. Fancy him, do we? It'd make your mother very happy.

While the rest of us grew somnolent, Dannie still brimmed with information.

—Jesus, Jacko, he told me stuff that would make even Durkin take a long pull on his beer. *Great* material as a matter of fact. Did you know, for instance, there exists something called NAMBLA? North American Man Boy Love Association. Its members share information in their published magazine and through their computer network. These apparently respectable men punch up the program, direct some computer mail to someone they've met, or someone they've talked to before by computer mail, and say, Let's go out and take some adolescent boy prisoner.

—Holy Christ, murmured Jacko. Suddenly it's great to be out of America eh.

By now we were over the Atlantic, and America's perverse computer mail lay behind us.

—There are cases, Dannie continued, where they call up each other and propose enslavement followed by murder. An FBI man punched himself into the network and caught two of them. They asked him to join them in a kidnapping.

—But what about Sunny? Jacko urged her, anxious to get to that and then sleep. What about women?

Dannie continued in that soft, forthright way.

—This psychiatrist agrees with the other guy we had: this is a case of enslavement too. Sunny's so circumspect at work. She goes obediently home. She *runs* home in fact, spelling all the way. The only time she turns up to speak to her father, he can't speak back and she's with a man, a minder.

Dannie's hand on Jacko's head at last became languid.

—He lets her go jogging here and there, but then he reclaims her. Classic slave-master stuff. The magazines publish a slave-master contract! How's that for the land of the free?

—Bloody appalling, said Jacko drowsily.

There was something so conjugal about the way they sat trading horrors on the edge of sleep. Was she still offering to wait for him, functionally, and for an exact slice of the night? With a view to improving him, was she still writing her memoir of their friendship? A missionary woman murmuring of slave magazines, she was proving Jacko's theories of her nation. The pressure of evil, remitting at the Brandenburg Gate, was still building in America's computer traffic.

* * *

On one of those determined grey mornings characteristic of England, we landed at Stansted near London. Every one of us who rose to disembark carried a refugee greyness in·the face. Dannie gathered up our passports and went off to a shed to do business with British immigration and customs about our transit.

No official intruded on our activities as we heaved equipment and supplies across the tarmac to two smaller chartered aircraft. I remember a crate of Gunter's brother's tangerines cutting into my shoulder. Jacko carried a silver case of camera gear in each hand, and had more cylinders and cases clamped in his armpits.

Halfway across the concrete, on our passage between the newly provided aircraft and the one in which we had flown across the Atlantic, I saw the American journalist Al Bunker arguing with Gunter. Gunter seemed a much better, ruder colour than the American. He gestured with a well-rested man's vigour. Bunker appealed to us.

—Says he's not coming to Berlin.

—Makes sense, yelled Gunter. Bring my sonnerbitch brother out here to the West. Regent Street, Piccadilly, Soho . . .

Al Bunker said, Durkin's already got the promos running for tonight: *The Great German Reunion.* You'll just damn-well have to come, Gunter.

A dark-eyed little fury, Dannie had just returned with our passports. She tore her way into our group with her elbows, and temporarily put the wad of our documents into her purse.

—Listen, Gunter, we've had enough of this fucking nonsense. Are you wanted by the East German police or something? House-breaking? Black market? Drug-pushing? What? What is it?

Gunter turned his eyes to her.

—This is sickness with Americans. First thing you think of is guilt, guilt, guilt!

—Listen to me. Listen. Don't talk to these men. Don't talk to Bunker or Jacko. They're too goddam kindly. Talk to me, fuck you, Gunter!

—This is not the way I speak to women, said Gunter, making a pious tuck in his mouth. American poor sonnerbitches put up with woman Hitler. Not me. I don't speak to women like this.

—You're talking to this fucking woman that way, you bloody Kraut prevaricator!

Of course she had picked that *bloody* up from Jacko. The Australian version of goddam. Bloody. Said to be ancient English By-Our-Lady. The imprecation to the Virgin found now on the lips of another, dangerous woman.

—You can put me in a hotel in West End, said Gunter. You bring my brother. Sweetness and light is all guaranteed! I take him to Harrod's and buy him beer.

It was touching that he believed Dannie might, by this sort of speech, be quietened and forced into retreat. She reached up and grabbed him by the collar of the shirt and shook him with a virulent little fist.

—Gunter, try to understand this. The fucking Berlin Wall is coming down in Berlin. It's not coming down in the West End of London. Do you catch the difference? You'll come to Berlin or I'll murder you here, right on this runway!

Then, smoothly, she had produced a little black revolver from her shoulder bag. Her protection against New York assaulters and intruders, brought without hindrance across the Atlantic.

I was transfixed by the sight of this weapon, and so I think was Al Bunker. But Gunter was not easily terrorized. Jacko could be heard chuckling, of course.

Gunter asked, Do I have a contract with you? Am I being paid? Does the land of freedom and home of the brave not allow liberty of movement to men named Gunter? Shit in your pistol, lady!

Jacko put down a camera tripod he was carrying. Hanging from it was one of those rolls of thick silver gaffer-tape which cameramen seemed to use for everything — marking clapper boards, sealing cartridges, providing a point on pavements or floors to show commentators where they were to walk to and stick each foot. Jacko unhooked this tape with one hand and with the other gave one of those deft, economic punches of the type he probably learned to deliver in his boyhood on Burren Waters. A perfect punch, say, to deliver to troublemakers at the Brahma Breeders Ball. Despite the breadth of my writing, I had led a fairly protected life. I'd rarely seen a pistol produced or a punch like this one thrown. I had very little experience of the way the legs gave way under a blow of this kind or how the interruption of the brain current produced so instant a collapse in so massive a frame.

Gunter fell sideways, a fall so dead that I feared he would crack his skull against the runway.

Jacko himself was now a man utterly undelayed by doubt. He bent and ran strands of the silver gaffer-tape around Gunter's legs. If Al Bunker and I seemed a little abashed at this fast action, Dannie didn't at all. She attended Jacko, a helpmeet.

—Get him upright, get him up, get him upright, she exhorted us.

Mumbling and stupefied, Gunter was hoisted and dragged towards one of the Berlin charters. I wondered about the British officials in the hut across the tarmac. But they must have been reading their *Daily Mails*. We all helped in the process of toting Gunter. His legs pinioned together and scraping monopedally on the tarmac, he must have looked, if there was anyone to see him, like television talent who had celebrated the historical rarity of this night too well. No one, not even Bunker and Dannie, both of whom came from such a litigious nation, seemed worried about legal action. But just in case, Jacko reassured them.

—Who's going to worry about him? He looks so bloody unreliable.

XIV

When, very soon after, our charter was rolling down
Stansted's runway, Jacko ignored the *Fasten Seatbelt*
sign and knelt at Gunter's feet, unwrapping the silver
tape from around them. Gunter's head jerked backwards against his seat, and he looked down his sallow
cheeks, trying to achieve a clear image of Jacko's
moonface gazing up at him. He gagged, and Jacko
held a sickbag for him.

—Feeling better, mate? asked Jacko, folding up the
bag functionally when the spasm had passed. I think
you had a little cerebral episode there. Bit of a black-
out. Ought to watch your consumption of brandy!

—We are where?

—Going home, son. The big B. Berlin the bloody
free, son. Whacko!

The chances of my saying anything passably clever
on camera seemed to grow less as we sat sleepless
above Europe's grey morning. The weak sun and the
dun clouds below us did not look epochal. Punished
for our late arrival, we were put to circling above the
city. By the time we taxied up to the terminal, it was
mid-morning, and Al Bunker was anxious about how
he could hope to get Gunter south, reconciled with
his brother, and edited and ready for transmission in
time for that night's *Live Wire*.

The one hopeful aspect was that Gunter seemed

reconciled to completing his journey. He landed docilely. We waited with him as Dannie concluded her negotiations with the few over-worked customs and immigration officers who guarded Germany from marauders from the West. It was like 1945 in that regard I suppose — most of the forces of civil Germany turned to greet the Easterners.

Jacko and I saw Gunter and Bunker and Bunker's crew, and all the cases of Calvados and tangerines, into a hired Mercedes. Its driver was helpfully telling Bunker how impossible it was to get south towards Leipzig today. But it was clear that Al Bunker would get Gunter there somehow, perhaps not quite as fast as two genuine pirates like Dannie and Jacko, but with dispatch just the same. The driver's unwillingness had no chance of matching Bunker's frenzy. If he did not get the filmed reconciliation of Gunter and Gunter's brother back to Berlin and transmitted to New York by midnight, he would suffer video death. He would become a newsroom anecdote, a dark memory.

In that event, the question might be asked, What is he doing now?

—Selling imported cars, the last I heard.

Or engaged in some other form of nullity.

In our car, Dannie announced that she had managed to bully some rooms for us out of the Kempinski Hotel. How astounded would Hitler be to discover that so late in the twentieth century Polish Jewish girls like Dannie were gouging Berlin's best hotel rooms out of Aryan management? However, said Dannie, we had to double up. All the other news organizations were doing that. She'd share a room with Jacko.

* * *

Our driver's name was Raoul. He was a worldly
young Alsatian who wore a bomber jacket and
confessed to a French mother. He, Jacko, Dannie and
— to do him justice — Fartfeatures, filling in for
Clayton once again, seemed on first-name terms
within seconds. Fartfeatures had been inoffensive and
without complaint in the Perugia and on both planes.
Now, however, he seemed less enthusiastic.

All of us discussed the traffic, how surprisingly
light it was.

—Lots of people at home, just watching it all on
TV said Raoul. If it's on TV, it means more than if
they see it being there.

—Yeah, said Jacko, taking Raoul's reflection as
praise for his chosen medium. Isn't that bloody great?

In such a little time, we were bowling up the
Ku'damm, which, as a bewildered and fairly
unworldly tourist, I had visited with my wife twenty
years past. These flashy shops had seemed to me not
glamorous, but a mean outcome to all that Nazi
triumphalism, all that bombing. A cosmetic form of
amnesia for the past, and a flippant condolence, not
always in good taste, to all the German and other
corpses.

Here today, people bundled in shabby overcoats
were window shopping.

—'Ayseeds from the East, said Raoul.

And they did look like pasty-complexioned extras
in a propaganda film about the inhumanity of Stalinism. Senator McCarthy and his descendants would
have been pleased to see their enchantment and
bewilderment in the face of the hydra-headed wonders of Western consumerism. I had a sense that the

West might take some fairly glib messages from phenomena like this. As we drew up, Marx's grey children were also round the door of the Kempinski, which looked like the sort of grand hotel I had seen in the films of my childhood in which German generals entertained beautiful double-agents. The last time I had been here with Maureen, we hadn't been able to afford the Kempinski, but had had a cocktail there.

On the pavement not far from the front door, a young man dressed like Raoul was passing out something to the East German visitors, accepting bank notes from them — part of their reunion bonus — and handing out change in return.

—They're buying *Do Not Disturb* signs from that guy there, Raoul told us. They're like children.

—Jesus, said Jacko to Dannie and Fartfeatures. We've got to get some footage of that.

Fartfeatures nodded grudgingly and stared out at other facades across the street.

We filed into the big rococo lobby designed it seemed, like the outside, by some sly film designer for intense assignations and the loitering of spies. Dannie signed in for all of us with a few competent swipes of the pen. She turned from the reception desk talking.

—We've got to get over to the Brandenburg Gate for a direct transmission. Vixen Six's suspending normal programming and we're it. There's a satellite truck waiting out there for us, ordered by Durkin. Raoul's ready with the car. Fancy stuff like the *Do Not Disturb* signs later. You've just got time for a slash before we move out.

Again, it was strange to hear that item of Jacko-idiom, *slash*, rolled casually around Dannie's mouth so familiarly, like a wad of chewing gum. There was an aspect of claim to it too. It was a sign she meant to have Jacko. As she'd taken over his idiom, she meant to take him over.

* * *

Upstairs, Fartfeatures and I chose beds. I was relieved to find it a very big room because Fartfeatures' air of disengagement gave me the sense that somehow he would be a sloppy and noisy sleeper.

Soon we had refreshed ourselves and cleaned our teeth, and then we travelled with Raoul up the Ku'damm past the ritzy shops and their fringe of gaping Easterners, past the ruins of the Kaiser Wilhelm Church and the Tiergarten and Zoological Gardens. We turned then onto the broad Street of the 17th of June. Here, crowds of people, most of them young, many of them on the roadway, were pressing in one direction — towards the Wall and the Brandenburg Gate. They did not care if Raoul or other motorists honked them or threatened to run them over. They were under the influence of an ecstatic magnetism. Moving, if you like, in the always preferred German direction: eastwards. Dannie was so taken by a sense of this primal drift that she sat up straight and grabbed Jacko's wrist to incorporate him in her sense of celebration. Jacko half-smiled and patted her bird-boned forearm with the enormous fist he'd inherited from Stammer Jack.

We could see ahead, above the hats of young Germans, the renowned Goddess of Peace and her four horses surmounting the Gate. I was moved to consider including her in my commentary.

Something like: When the Brandenburg Gate was first built, it was dedicated to the Goddess of Peace. She became, however, a symbol of racism, tyranny, and division. Only today does she enter into her full estate . . .

Beyond this great Gate, which I had first seen in childhood cinemas in the Western suburbs of Sydney as a symbol of Hitler's power, the bleak swathe of concrete fence had been thrown up to provide the ideologues of East and West with fields of fire or of observation. This prohibited area behind the Gate was now full of people. Many young men had climbed and straddled the Wall, uniting Germany as it were with their loins, with their honest arses. The watchtowers beyond the Wall were unguarded. No fire hoses from the East assaulted the Wall-sitters.

Raoul showed our pass to a West Berlin cop who told us where to park. We could see roofs and dishes of satellite trucks ahead, and went looking for ours and, after only a minor search, found it. Its German crew seemed languid with waiting, but were enlivened now by the contact. They listened to Dannie's instructions and said, Sure, sure. Fartfeatures hooked his camera up to the cable it carried, and Dannie told Fartfeatures where to set up and where to stand.

Someone put a plug in my ear and a mike on my tie. I could hear Durkin in New York issuing weary yet somehow crisp orders to unseen people, and then he began talking to me.

—Get any sleep on the plane? he asked me, and without waiting for me to reply, told me and Dannie and Jacko we were on in two minutes.

—Does it feel historic? I heard him asking us all.

It was significant above utterance, but I didn't get to say so.

—Bloody historic, mate, Jacko told him in a voice aerated with the awe of it all.

When the time came, Jacko spoke to camera as passing Berliners cheered us as if they were flattered we'd taken an interest. Jacko passed to me and my vocal cords turned for a moment to little balls of marble. Then I spoke, Dannie kindly nodding approval from behind the camera. I said that I had rejoiced in the fall of the awful Erich Honecker. What we were seeing was the result of the lifting of his dead hand. Yet, I said, I knew that we could not convey through flat videotape the peculiar three-D character, the intoxication, of this leaping and singing and milling crowd.

This was true enough, but I said there was also something unresolved about it all, something which was more expectation than fulfilment. I drew the attention of Fartfeatures' camera to the youths pecking at the wall with little masonry hammers. Something more drastic would seem to be needed to bring it finally down, I said.

* * *

When we paused for an extended commercial break, Jacko clapped me on the shoulder and said, You're right about that, you know. It's like a crowd waiting for the kick-off of a football game. And no bugger's blowing the whistle eh.

—That's good, Dannie told us commending our work. We've got something to start things off. And even in replay, that'll go well with Gunter's reunion. Now we can get creative.

—So you're actually satisfied with *that*, love? Jacko asked her, a fairly gentle challenge.

At the question, we all looked — for whatever reason — a little to the south, where on top of a truck Harris Morgan of CBS stood with mike in hand and spoke sombrely (you really could tell this) to camera about the new age: making it by saying it.

—It's not much better than what that bastard's feeding up to the punters, said Jacko.

Consulting her clipboard, Dannie said, Let's get a walk along the wall out of you next, Jacko. Then some *vox pop* and a bit more commentary from your friend. Then we'll grab a quick meal and run through any ideas you've got.

With Raoul acting as interpreter, Jacko strolled amongst the Berliners. Dannie and I following behind Fartfeatures and his cable handler. Jacko questioned members of the crowd below the Wall. As Jacko and Raoul yelled to the young men atop the great concrete barrier I, like many other people in the crowd, laid my hand on the cement-rendered surface. For a wall in the November air of Europe, it felt as warm as if the enthusiasm had penetrated it, or as if it were thawing from within. From this point I could see Harris Morgan and his truck edging in for the same purpose as ours.

At last I did a further little piece to camera myself, reading some of the graffiti which had appeared that day. I spoke of one slogan which read *Eine Deutschland und Freiheit!* Would there really be one Germany? Would the West want it? Would the great, comfortable middle classes of the Western sector want to pay for their poor brothers and sisters in the East?

Hours had — to my lay astonishment — been used up by our blather. Dannie harried us back to Raoul's limo. We needed to be back by early evening to transmit the super-long version to *Live Wire* which Vixen Six and Durkin were making this startling night. Somewhere to the south one hoped Gunter was embracing his familiarly despised brother for the same purpose.

* * *

Back at the Kempinski, Dannie and I went up in the lift together, since Jacko was changing a lot of Basil Sutherland's money at the cashier's cage and Fartfeatures had gone off on some errand of his own. Inside the ascending lift with me, little Dannie, pretty and tired, leaned back against its brass grillework, her shoulders tucked into the frame of the glittering mirror in the centre of one of the side walls.

—Notice that? she asked me. He's not satisfied yet. Jacko. He's funny. Just doing a competent job depresses the shit out of him. He has to do something crazy to make himself content.

The lift sighed upwards, graciously imperceptible in its advance.

She said, I know that you're a friend of Lucy's. I want you to understand something. I'm not just fooling around.

—I see.

—I think Jacko's a genius, and he's got this edginess Lucy just doesn't understand or relate to. Jacko's empowered by me. I can give him direction. We're going to be a great television couple.

Then she simply stared at me, sealing the point, the certainty of her video-aristocracy sharp as a blade in those dark eyes.

—Jacko doesn't believe in great television couples, I warned her. It's too pretentious an idea, Dannie.

—He believes at base. He believes in the artform.

—Do you think so? He's always telling me how television is the domain of clowns. Maybe he'll let you clown with him.

—Well, he's only half right. Clowns, maybe, but we put the spin on the direction history goes. We're putting the spin on it this afternoon. We make up out of our own heads the way people feel about this!

I felt anxious, as if I had still not adequately stated my fealty to Lucy.

—I don't know what you and he have against his wife. She's the most tolerant woman I've ever met.

—Do you think that's what Jacko needs? *Tolerance?*

She laughed a tight, managerial laugh. At the same time it was very sumptuous.

—What he needs is encouragement and a lot of discipline. Dear old Lucy can't give him that, can she? She doesn't understand the medium.

The lift had stopped at our floor, and the brilliant, brazen grillework of the door concertinaed back to let us step out. In the corridor, I was still left discontented about the poor job I had done for Lucy.

—Listen, I said. With the greatest respect, you've got no chance of fitting yourself and Jacko into the one household. You're both monsters.

—Jacko will be flattered to hear you said that.

—I mean it in the most admiring sense. But it's the truth.

—Say it was, murmured Dannie, already at the

door of the room she was sharing with Jacko. He needs someone to *lock in* with him. The snow maiden won't last. I'm barely hastening events. Let's all get quick room service, and then back out to the Gate.

* * *

Somehow, in a city which this afternoon was open to the bidding of a thousand news corporations, Dannie had managed to get a small Kempinski suite for herself and Jacko. This meant that it was palatial by comparison with the space any modern hotel chain would give you for an equivalent amount of Basil Sutherland's money. Dannie also managed to get us food within a quarter of an hour of her placing the order. The kitchen too could tell she was a monster. The five of us, including Raoul, ate hungrily — chicken, dumplings, red cabbage. Slices of torte. Jacko rose licking his fingers. He explained his urgency to Dannie by putting his hand on my shoulder.

—I've just got to see my clever mate in the corridor.

I got up, half guilty, half flushed with a potential anger. Perhaps Dannie had complained to him about the monster remark and now I would have to defend or apologize for it.

Outside, however, he did not pause to debate. He made one spacious gesture with his hand and led me down the gilt-panelled corridor. He stopped by a metal and glass box in which sat a fire axe, its sharper end steely, reflecting light from the Kempinski's chandeliers. The fire axe's blunt end was red. It had a very long handle.

—I just want to get at that Wall with something

better than a bloody hammer and maul. Keep nit for me, will you eh?

He pointed to a place where the corridor took a right-angled turn. Without saying anything, I went back to that corner and took up my station. Meanwhile Jacko wrenched off his shoe and hit the glass with its heel. It did not shatter. He put more force into it. I heard the glass crack and the clatter of its fall to the carpet. Somewhere, distantly, a bell began pealing. Surely the bell had not been started by the breaking of the glass!

I focused my gaze on the grille doors of the lift shaft, but it was, in fact, the door of the fire stairs nearest to Jacko that jerked open. A large Slavic-looking man with sweat on his face came pounding through it. I noticed that he wore a good suit. Jacko already had the axe in his hands, however, which may have been what made the man pause.

—Are you a guest of the Kempinski, sir? he asked.

Jacko said, D'you think I'd steal one of the hotel's fire axes if I weren't?

A younger man in the uniform of a security company emerged from the lift now and moved past me and behind Jacko. Since Jacko had been discovered in the middle of his theft, I did not attempt to delay this guard.

—I am the Kempinski Hotel security director, the man in the suit told Jacko. Is there a fire anywhere, sir?

I was pleased to hear that Jacko spoke in his calm, level way, not at all like a parodist or a smart alec.

—The fires of liberty are ablaze up the road from here, and people are chipping away at it with little hammers. I want to hack off a great bloody chunk.

I felt sorry just the same for the house detective faced with this manic, mixed metaphor.

—If there is no fire at the Kempinski, sir, you must put the axe back.

Jacko leaned the axe against the wall. He took out deutschmarks from his wallet.

—Okay, I'm willing to pay the hotel for the use of the axe and make a great donation to the security staff welfare fund. I'll give you the equivalent of five hundred dollars for the axe.

—It isn't possible, sir. If we had a fire tonight . . .

—Oh mate. Have you honestly ever met anyone who was ever saved in a fire by a fire axe?

The detective stood still and gave no sign of being tempted. Raoul had come out of Dannie's room by now and had begun arguing with the man in German. But it did seem that the entire security of this grand hotel depended upon that single implement.

—Bugger it, said Jacko, and heaved the thing savagely back into its bracket. He was angry now and turned on the house detective.

—Don't think I'm paying for the fucking glass eh. You bastards are totally lacking in imagination. There would have been someone just like you counting the bloody eggcups in the Chancellery the day Hitler suicided!

Raoul stretched his arm up around Jacko's shoulder.

—Never mind, I know a fire station . . . We'll get you an axe there, my friend.

Jacko turned away and the rest of us followed him. We collected our overcoats, and found Fartfeatures and Dannie ready to go. The detective and the man in uniform were still waiting for us in the corridor as we emerged. They followed us apologetically to the lift.

—Who says Stalinism is bloody dead eh? Jacko asked me loudly.

The security man, perhaps on orders, attempted to follow us into the grillework contraption when it arrived. Jacko could be heard growling, and Dannie told the detective that we wanted to travel down alone. The detective ordered his uniformed man away, and we descended towards the bonfire of freedom and the quest for an axe for Jacko.

* * *

Raoul drove us only a few blocks and stopped by a corner fire station. It was an old building, either a restored one or one which had survived the bombing hecatomb of World War II — the Imperial Eagles of Kaiser Wilhelm were still on the stone facade. Raoul said he should talk to them himself, and was about to wander in amongst the red engines, when Jacko, growing reflective, grabbed me by the upper arm.

—A jackhammer eh, he told me. A bloody jackhammer and a compressor.

Dannie had begun snorting and looking at her watch.

—We've got to get out there, Jacko.

Jacko turned to Raoul.

—Ask the firemen where we can hire a compressor? A frigging compressor and a jackhammer. You know, a compressor. You know, jackhammer. Dur-dur-dur-dur!

And Jacko did a mime to illustrate these new instruments he sought. Raoul went in, and a few firemen appeared in half-uniform and old-fashioned voluminous boots. There was a discussion and Raoul came running out and threw himself into the car.

—Right, he said.

We surged away, Raoul driving frantically. Jacko comforted Dannie.

—Give us half an hour eh love.

*　　*　　*

We drove south through residential streets — old pre-war houses in their own gardens, Bauhaus apartment blocks, a platz with a statue of Goethe and another with a statue of Bach. Beyond the metal fence of a new building site we found at last a yard devoted to excavation equipment hire. Yellow compressors stood around in muddy ground in the moist afternoon. Lights already shone in a prefabricated office.

Again Raoul made the approaches, the heavy man behind the counter speaking leadenly, in a way that gave us little hope.

—He wants to know what you need it for, said Raoul.

—Tell him we're renovating a house, Jacko suggested. In Tiergarten or somewhere flash. We want to knock a wall out.

There were problems about our not having an account with the hire company, and pages of documentation to be filled out.

—Time's wasting, guys! Dannie kept crying out. Seventy minutes to air time.

—It's going to be worth it, Jacko reassured her.

The man laughed and shook his head when Jacko

gave his address as the Kempinski Hotel. Neither were any of Dannie's credit cards acceptable. But Jacko was, of course, in a position to make large deposits of cash.

In the end, the paperwork was done and the hire company man telephoned for one of the staff truck-drivers to drive the thing to the site Jacko proposed. As we all stood in the cold yard, Raoul had to make the truck-driver more accurately aware of the location. And at last, in this man, he found someone who would take a few rolls of Basil Sutherland's deutsch-marks, pocket them and haul a compressor off behind us towards the Brandenburg Gate.

I remember the divine berserkness growing in Raoul's limousine. Dannie, Jacko and Raoul were hooting at the stratagem by which they would subvert not simply the Wall but the harbinger-of-history gravity of the chief commentators. Even Fartfeatures was caught up, animated, ready to shoot. He and Jacko and Dannie discussed camera angles and I was surprised to hear him agree to mount the Wall with Jacko. The truck and compressor rumbled behind.

Jacko said, I used a jackhammer when I had a road job as a student.

I didn't know whether that was the truth, since he seemed to have worked in radio and television since his childhood. Perhaps he was just trying to reassure Fartfeatures.

—I won't knock off such a big chunk, Jacko promised, that you'll go with it . . .

But Fartfeatures, suddenly a risk-taker for his craft, seemed willing to countenance even that.

Police still formed a loose cordon at the rear of the great Brandenburg Gate enthusiasm, keeping vehicles

— except for the media — away from the mêlée.

—Tell them, said Jacko, the compressor's needed for power generation.

Raoul got out, attended by a very serious Jacko with a straightened tie and a wallet full of currency in his breast pocket in case that was needed. The professional-looking, authoritative Dannie also strung along, and only Fartfeatures and myself were left in the vehicle. I saw Raoul explaining and persuading as a policeman frowned, and Jacko remained sombre while Dannie displayed the press cards she had collected for us at the airport.

At one stage, the policeman obviously asked who was in the car, because I heard Dannie trill, Our commentator and our cameraman.

And to my amazement, the policeman nodded and let them return to the car. We were allowed to roll through with the truck and compressor in our wake. The reasons that machine itself was let in are still a mystery for me. I know what Raoul told the cop, but I couldn't see why the cop would accept it. I'd always believed the World War II propaganda which said that the Germans were creatures of manic efficiency and a sense of good order. How did Raoul persuade them to admit a lord of chaos with a compressor in tow into the heart of the great Germanic ferment, the magic acreage by the Gate?

The crowd likewise stepped aside in what looked like wilful agreement with Jacko's intent. Snug in under the Wall, we found our satellite truck.

Dannie had me rigged up, the earphone in place, the mike on my tie, and she and I discussed what I could say.

—Latest news is, she briefed me, they're saying Krenz will resign during the night.

Jacko had no time for me. He was talking to the compressor man through Raoul and muttering to Fartfeatures and pointing up to the Wall.

Dannie said, Tell them to expect something amazing.

Durkin asked in my ear, You fine to run, mate?

—Yes.

—You first, minute and a half. Then a commercial break, and Jacko on the Wall. Okay?

—Okay.

I wondered how I could say anything coherent even for a modest ninety seconds. The energy of this chaotic event weighed on all our senses, obviously even on the cops' senses, and had somehow to be defused.

—Sixty seconds to go, Dannie told me.

In front of me, Fartfeatures raised his camera, and I saw the cable handler lassoing coils of cable at his feet ready for the assault on the Wall itself.

I don't know exactly what I told the viewers, but I could hear Durkin and Dannie applauding me in my ear. I *did* tell them to expect amazing gestures from people at the Wall, perhaps even from Jacko, who having trespassed over every American barrier was now about to take on the ultimate one. My segment now ended, I was briskly thanked and reduced to what I most wished to be: a spectator.

By the compressor, the truckdriver stood smiling, ready to press all its rowdy buttons once Jacko and Fartfeatures were positioned. Like all the Berliners, I yowled rabidly as Jacko, wired for sound and having got the signal from Durkin and Dannie, walked up to the wall, the inert jackhammer cradled in his arms, the slash of a larrikin grin beneath his porkpie hat, his tie awry from the violence of events.

As Jacko handed the implement to Raoul and myself to hold, it seemed that these waves of enthusiasm lifted him onto the Wall, hands reaching down from where a number of other young Germans were standing, other hands pushing his great arse and thighs from below.

Soon he was seated on top, and then stood tentative but massive, arms out for balance, and found with a smile that there was enough room up there to support him in an upright position. He embraced a red-haired German youth, and their mutual breath went up in the one cold cloud.

Raoul and I and the truck driver hoisted the jackhammer, which seemed coated with an amalgam of oil and mud, to others up there, who delivered it into Jacko's hands. Receiving its weight, Jacko seemed to over-balance, and I wondered whether we should be concerned about how he would keep his footing up there. But he steadied himself, and then, with legs carefully spread, raised the jackhammer in both arms towards the crowd, whose frenzy was thereby, if possible, increased. Like the Berliners, Dannie and I too screamed our applause as, theatrically, he tested the point of the drill with a thumb, and seemed to conclude that he had brought the right tool. Then he lowered it point-first and ceremonially to the top of the Wall. In the posture of a road worker, he yelled, Boys and girls, we're going to improve your view to the East!

Dannie and I could hear these words. God knows

how many of the crowd heard or needed to hear them.

With both thumbs on the buttons, he called to the compressor man.

—Start her up, Fred!

The compressor's mechanical rage began. Yet the cheering seemed in no way suppressed by the racket of the machine. Somehow, despite the vibrations, he remained in place and in command.

Fartfeatures first filmed Jacko from below, hammering away, and then was himself hoisted onto the wall, and his camera lifted behind him, still running as in the tradition of *Morning Manhattan*, the lock on its shooting button. I remember my hand upon its metal. Topside, Fartfeatures accepted it in one movement and aimed it at Jacko.

Young Germans atop the Wall, who did not want to fall along with the masonry Jacko hoped to bring down, were keeping their distance from him, clapping and whistling. Fartfeatures, however, edged bravely close, and I revised my view of him.

It is a truism to say there is no narcotic like the ecstasy of a crowd, and of all crowds, the political crowd, the crowd that thinks it is on the edge of the answer, is the most exhilarated. Though the very word *exhilarated* is a pale term for the primal joy, for the frantic sense of liberation of a crowd which has the same true north, whose brains from the lizardy cortex to the angelic reaches of the cerebrum are all magnetized in the one direction.

And then the happiness with which the crowd greets the man or woman who owns the right gesture, the gesture which is the model or niftiest metaphor for their frenzy! The man tonight was Jacko and the metaphor was the jackhammer.

Below, Dannie and Raoul and I and all the witnesses made a semicircle leaving a space into which debris was free to fall. A slab of brick and cement soon did so. Jacko himself, a giant holding his suddenly quietened jackhammer one-handed, picked up, with the other hand, a section of the wall which had come loose but had been small enough to stay up there. Jacko raised this, an executioner raising the head of the devourer.

—Look, he yelled, the bloody Wall's hollow.

I could see him collect himself, remember that he was on television and that he must foreswear the normal profanities. But it was unnecessary for him to restrain himself. He was such a figure now, such a focus of all our ecstasy, that he had transcended the proprieties others practised in this po-faced medium.

—This symbol of tyranny and division, he said for the camera's sake, is hollow at the core. Its contents nothing but air.

Just to demonstrate, he dropped the jackhammer into the hollow of the wall to its handles. The agility of this in particular was a delight and derived more from Stammer Jack's province than from the normal endowments of Vixen Six employees. And of course the crowd bayed. Jacko had come all the way from Burren Waters to be, for half an hour, the nub of the new Germany. I yelled for him, too, beside a howling Dannie. His primal imagination had made votaries of us. I had my arm around tough Dannie. I must admit that Lucy was forgotten. But then, so was everything else.

Jacko went on applying himself. More masonry

fell. Fartfeatures backed up the Wall, not once seeming to look behind him. You could tell he was saying to himself, I've found something worth the trouble. He was no longer the freelance cameraman on casual rates. He was taking the footage all the others would have most wanted to take; the footage the networks would at first avoid showing because they hadn't shot it themselves; the footage which, paying Basil Sutherland, they would have at last to buy rights to use in every current affairs program ever likely to be made on this exultant night.

The gap hectic Jacko made was first three feet, then five, then seven across. It had not achieved a depth of more than a few feet however. Until now. Jacko, in his porkpie hat and overcoat and cradling the jackhammer in his arms, descended into the gap itself and, with one foot on the eastern casing, another just about beside it on the western, began further subversion there. God, how we cheered now, more like a howl of acclaim. Dannie was weeping in my arms, and Raoul was bleary with delight at these passengers he had been fortunate enough to pick up in his limo.

In the end a young German, hoisted up there by colleagues, approached Jacko from behind. He nudged Jacko's shoulder. He was claiming the jackhammer. The justice of the boy's demand was apparent to all of us. Jacko took his thumbs off the buttons and spaciously, without hesitation, reached the thing behind him to the young man. As he did, I could see the gloss of a huge sweat on Jacko's face.

The young German took the jackhammer and applied his thumbs to its rubber buttons, laughing as his shoulders jolted. Jacko sat, jumped off the Wall and landed heavily amongst our upraised hands.

There had been some press photographers in the crowd who had shot Jacko at work, but now everyone there recognized this German boy with the jackhammer as the sublimest image of the late century, and the night crackled with the spiky intensity of their flashlights.

The media would not give any credit to one of their own for the best and most anarchic picture of the end of the Wall. The *New York Times* would say that young Germans had brought the compressor up there. The same mistake was gratefully repeated by the television networks.

That night was Jacko's apotheosis, his transfiguration. No one of us would forget it, and of course everyone who saw it would forever after use it as an adjustment to anything snide that might be said of him.

We made other television later that night and at mid-morning the next day, but nothing touched what Jacko had done with the jackhammer.

If he wasn't already, I suppose that night he was Dannie's lover. For going home to the Kempinski, we all clapped his shoulders and caressed him, and in our hysteric condition it might have just about seemed the right thing. Fartfeatures bought him cognac at his own expense, I ordered for him a ninety-eight-dollar Riesling from room service. God knows what actually went on in his room, in that prevailing air of nothing being too good for him.

I noticed as we all sat drinking on a commercial jet on the way home, and as new editions of magazines with the picture of the young German with the jackhammer accumulated around us, that Jacko never seemed to find any inequity in all this.

—We make up the news, he told me one afternoon. So we can't be part of it, can we eh?

It seemed that to him the doing of it, being seen by citizens and peers to do it, was more important than to be credited with it. He took a paternal pride in the quickly enough famous picture of the young man on the Wall.

—What I don't understand, he told me, is how I stayed up there so long. I mean, there *was* room, but just enough eh. Add in the jackhammer and I should have fallen. Except I knew I bloody wouldn't. I bloody knew it.

There was a kind of bush gallantry in this. It was a better story, more stylish in his own terms, if, at the end of everything, his place in it went unrecorded and frankly declared as being beyond his normal powers or pretensions.

Full of wine, I rose in my seat on the plane and recited in Jacko's honour the words which generally were found on Jacko's lips.

—And down by Kosciusko, where the pine-clad
    ridges raise
   Their torn and rugged battlements on high,
   Where the air is clear as crystal, and the white
    stars fairly blaze
   At midnight in the cold and frosty sky,
   And where around The Overflow the reed beds
    sweep and sway
   To the breezes, and the rolling plains are wide,
   The man from Snowy River is a household
    word today,
   And the stockmen tell the story of his ride.

A steward interrupted me.

—Excuse me, sir. The fasten seatbelt sign is illuminated.

From the transcendence of Jacko on the wall, I returned to New York and my Wednesday night graduate writing class. Fourteen writers, nearly all of them capable of publishing fiction if they could stand the ignominy and disappointment of it all. They were two-thirds women, and they wrote about the intimate and the domestic: post-AIDS love in New York; the business of finding a good man in a poisoned city; the raising of children; marital ennui. Their heroes were Grace Paley, Alice Munro, Raymond Carver, and someone had got hold of them at a young age and told them that they must all write like a *New Yorker* short story. Considering the difference in our taste, we got on well. I liked to tell them that if I had one virtue as a fiction teacher it was that I gave all genres equal credit. I urged them to do the same. You never knew when a genre would come ravening out of the bush and claim you for its own.

They didn't believe it though. Their range was very nearly the awful things mother and father had done, and then the perfidy of lovers. Of Dickens's trilogy of terrors, hunger and want had been largely taken care of, and love remained, unappeasable under any political regime.

In one of the students' stories, a woman betrayed by men of average fallibility meets a Persian-American in a Soho bar. He is a gentle soul, but he wants to suspend her in an apparatus designed for men who like to see women swinging powerless from the ceiling. He is embarrassed to ask, but would she consider it? More conventional males have adequately traduced her; she consents. In mid-suspension though, as she gyrates in her captive state, he's overwhelmed by the shame of his perversion and goes off and reads *American Track and Field*. Suspended between his desire and self-loathing, she swings in an empty room. It's a poisonously accurate image, a wonderful New York tale.

If such stories have a fault, it is that they do not carry a sense of the wider world, the world of China, the world of Africa, in which the apparatus of suspension is even more savage and the yearnings of women even more radically thwarted. But I suppose that is America, ruler and ignorer of the earth!

Despite the admirable revolution of Washington and Jefferson, agonies remained. The pursuit of happiness was both guaranteed and elusive. In a self-absorbed city, the graduate fiction students got their stories published all over the place, and one of them became a legend by cracking the *New Yorker*. Another had her book accepted by Knopf. At the following class I provided two bottles of Moët, so much cheaper in New York than in the antipodes that I couldn't work out why Manhattanites didn't drink it all the time.

I would come home exhilarated from these workshop sessions, walking down University Place, past curfew-quiet Washington Square, by the University Gallery and the faculty eating house named the Violet, notorious for salmonella. There is a plaque on the wall somewhere along that stretch which honours the first Dutch teachers of New Amsterdam-New York. After a good session I might sometimes pause at it and — even as a novelist, a teacher-manqué — feel part of a long, decent tradition.

Next I usually swung past the complex of apartments named Washington Square Village. It had been home for Maureen and me when we first came to New York, and I visited it both for nostalgia's sake and to congratulate myself on my escape from it. Good, if poorly plumbed, brownstone buildings had been torn down a quarter of a century past to make this poor imitation of Le Corbusier's *Île des Hommes*, and its rent-free or rent-cheap apartments made it possible for NYU to attract faculty to the dangerous and expensive city.

I knew that retired staff stayed on in the building long after their teaching years ended. On our floor, for example, was a formerly dazzling cancer researcher who wandered the normally empty corridor asking whoever stepped out of the lift what time it was. He held a clock in his hand, with the intention of immediately correcting it once you answered him. The man's still-blazing cerebrum knew that memory was largely a sense of time, and so he tried to get evidence of the day and the hour from all the tenants on that floor as a means of validating his own vanished memory.

Widows and widowers of staff also stayed on in that cold imitation of Le Corbusier's work. One day, when I was rising to the eighth floor in the lift, the door slid back on the fifth floor and an elderly woman with a bottle of seltzer water, that highly effervescent New York speciality, presented herself. She passed the bottle in to me and said, Would you mind opening that for me? I obliged her, opened it without spraying the interior of the lift, and passed the bottle out again. She thanked me. And so the doors closed.

I wondered what sort of expert she or her husband or both of them had been. For the floors were full of experts from all over the world, as well as prime-of-life stars from Harvard and Yale, Cambridge or Trinity College Dublin, to whom NYU offered research fellowships and double professorships and attractive deals.

Once I hit Washington Square Village on my way home, I would swing eastwards, thereby evading the sad cancer professor who waited there on the eighth floor with his clock, palely maintaining his nexus with time. And so I would negotiate the two cold blocks to the Cotton Building.

Returning there after the first post-Wall Wednesday workshop, I found my wife sitting up, drinking a bottle of Australian chardonnay with Lucy. As ready as I was to settle to a quiet glass of wine with my wife, I was still stimulated enough to be pleased to see Lucy. Apart from the affection both of us felt for her as a forthright, sensible woman, she represented yet one more instance of that continuum of the young and talented for which New York is the holy city and of which my group of writers was a fair sample.

Accepting a seat and a glass, I asked her what she thought of her husband's Wall renown? This was a silly question, as good as rhetorical. Something to say. When she didn't answer, I saw her eyes were misted and her cheeks pink from tears. I remembered Dannie's ferocious speech in the lift at the Kempinski. It was such an assertive slash at Lucy, the fabric of her marriage, that it might have woken Lucy from her sleep in New York. She might have been weeping for days and only now delivered herself tearful into my wife's company.

By silent accord we swung the subject to a Dmitris Sgouros concert she had been to at Carnegie Hall, all in the period when Jacko and Dannie and Fartfeatures and myself were returning from Berlin. After that she was ready to tell us new stories she'd heard from Jacko. She recounted what had happened to Al Bunker when he went south of Berlin to Bitterfeld in a limo stacked with cases of Calvados and tangerines to find the drunken Gunter's brother and force a reunion upon the two of them. They had needed to make their way past Vopo checkpoints and security police with uncertain orders by giving away bottles of the brandy. But there was still an ocean of it by the time they found Gunter's brother's slightly superior, middling-official residence in the south side of the town. Gunter's sister-in-law had answered the door, and the brother had refused to come out. Curtains were drawn, a siege was in progress and night was deepening on the only great fraternal reunion available to Vixen Six to film. At last the brother came out to prevent Bunker from knocking desperately on the windows, and the camera ran. Then Bunker rushed the tape back to Berlin with Gunter, who was not welcome to remain in that squalid town with his brother. The Vixen Six people in New York received it and edited it up so that the brother's anger looked almost like a grateful smile!

Cheered by her own re-telling of Jacko's version of this and with her mood nearly recovered, she rose to go home. I went down to Houston Street with her to help her find a cab.

—I'll be fine, she said. You know, I miss Oz. You and Maureen don't seem to.

—Maureen loves it here, despite her dead-beat bloody husband.

—Too much weird stuff here for me.

A cab found us and Lucy got in. I bent to its window to wave her goodbye, and saw her sadness resettle itself darkly, like a crow on either shoulder.

When I got back to the apartment, Maureen first told me simply that Lucy had got a more or less anonymous telephone call about Jacko and Dannie. I wasn't to mention it to Jacko, even though we were friends. On the other hand, had *I* seen any signs of a problem in Berlin?

Yes, I said. Between Maureen and me, and taking it no further, there *could* be some basis for the idea. I told her that Dannie was in aggressive pursuit, and Jacko . . . well, she knew Jacko. I began to say that Lucy had no concrete reason to think Dannie and Jacko were . . . But then I thought of the shared room, and so let the sentence trail away. And she wasn't to tell Lucy any of this, I added, even though she and Lucy were friends.

—And you and Lucy aren't? Maureen asked.

—Jacko talks to me, I argued, and Lucy to you. It's the best arrangement.

—What a load of rubbish, said Maureen.

—Jacko doesn't have my uncritical support.

—Yes, but you always obey his instructions. Because he's picturesque. By obeying him, you'll earn the privilege of writing about him in the end.

She had me, as the Brits say, to rights.

We went to bed, and when I woke at three o'clock in the morning I found that Maureen was awake too. I wandered off to the bathroom, still unsure whether I was by the Pacific in Sydney or located above Lower Broadway in populous Manhattan. I had the impression, as I left on the outward, dazed journey, that my wife was clear-eyed and insomniac. When I got back she had the bedside light on and was sitting upright. It was unlike her to put the light on this late unless she was reading.

She said, Lucy got a call. As I told you. I didn't tell you who called. It was from a particular woman . . . one who claims to be married to the Sondquist girl's kidnapper. She'd read about Lucy and Jacko in a television magazine. She told Lucy that she'd watched Jacko and his producer — what's that girl's name again? — filming somewhere in California. San Bernardino or Baker. She knew where her husband took the girl to work or to jog, so she took to ducking away from home and visiting those places on weekends . . . Sitting there for hours. An obsessive thing. And according to her she just happened to see Jacko's camera crew. And Dannie. She said she knew by looking at the two of them, by the way they behaved, by the way Jacko kissed Dannie, by all the body language . . . that they were having an affair. She said she knows the signs, because she'd watched her husband fall in love with the Sondquist girl. She could tell by the way Jacko conducted himself. And she hunted Lucy down through directory assistance — I've been warning Lucy to get a silent number — and called to tip her off. And to confide in her.

—Then she said she'd like to meet Lucy at some

stage, so they could discuss what they had in common. She said this just like a normal, pleasant, wronged woman. She said she'd let her husband kidnap the Sondquist woman and now she knew he'd fallen in love with her! The ingratitude of men! That was the theme.

Having told me all this, my wife looked at me.

—The wife calls the girl prisoner Ess, exactly the same thing as that motel woman in Baker called her. Of course she, the wife, could have got that from the interview Jacko did with the motel woman. Anyhow, Lucy doesn't know what to do. She's wondering whether to tell the police about the phone call. And she's frightened that if she tells Jacko what the woman said, she'll look ridiculous and get the usual denials, or a quick apology. And then he'd be off like a terrier again, after Dannie, after Sunny. And she's scared, too, it might make a contribution of some kind to the euphoria Jacko and Dannie feel working together, and draw them closer still . . .

—Besides that, said Maureen, if Lucy and the woman had a meeting, Jacko and the others would want to use Lucy to film the encounter. Even if it's a hoax, they could use it to make another segment of the Sunny Sondquist quest.

The search for Sunny needed to be referred to and pursued at least twice a week on *Live Wire*.

The other option was that Lucy could ignore the call, but she worried that she could contribute thereby, perhaps, to the continuance of Sunny's enslavement.

My wife said, The woman's called her three times, long distance, and Lucy's in agony.

* * *

In the following week, on the basis that I did not betray any of this news to Jacko, I received further confidences from my wife, who was receiving them in turn from Lucy Emptor. The woman continued to call Lucy, but they were brief calls. The woman said, I don't want anyone to be able to put a fix on where I'm calling from.

In one call she confided that she had children. In another she told that she had given birth to a child in the same room in which Sunny Sondquist's, or Ess's place of detention was located.

Lucy told Maureen that each call was more circumstantial than the last. In one call, Lucy was told that the woman's husband was building *another pit*. The wife saw this as a frank declaration that the man intended to take yet another woman.

The pit-digger's wife would also express some sisterly feeling — Lucy noticed it wasn't straight-out jealousy of Ess which possessed her. She and Ess, said the wife, had suffered so much at his hands that they didn't want another girl to go through it.

What unnerved Lucy was that throughout her calls the woman spoke so averagely, so suburbanly, and seemed so convinced of her confidante's, Lucy's, ordinary sympathy. As if, out in the Sydney suburbs where Lucy was bred, husbands commonly signified marital discontent by digging dungeons.

—She must tell Jacko, I said. And then the police.

—Give her a little time, said Maureen. She will. She doesn't have to act on calls that might have hoax written all over them, like Frank Emptor's stunt.

Just the same, during that week I felt my own and my wife's dread, guilt and bemusement grow as a shadow of Lucy Emptor's. Even New York had not prepared us for the idea of these frightful confidences.

Jacko got back on Monday at dawn from a week-end of Los Angeles interviews, and Lucy at last broke down and gave him the information about the dungeon master's wife. Lucy had struck on a median course for saving her own dignity and delivering Sunny Sondquist.

—Now, she said, we can tell the police.

Jacko argued against it. What had the police done so far? They'd found nothing, pursued nothing. Meet the woman, Jacko told Lucy, and we'll film it. And then the police.

She told him that she would not meet this woman, real or hoax as she might be. Since Dannie wished to be Mrs Emptor, here was her big chance. Let her have breakfast or lunch in some dismal corner of Southern California with the wife of the pit-digger, and trade mutual fears of betrayal with her.

At that time I suffered my own minor confusions regarding loyalty. Jacko asked me to another afternoon's drinking session with him at the Odeon. At last New Year's Eve celebrations, Lucy had worn her party-piece black miniskirt with tassels. She looked magnificent in it, and, for what I hope were avuncular teasing purposes, I called it her 'waistband'. At our table, Jacko had had us all inhale helium and sing the Australian national anthem. The Odeon always carried that redolence for me — Lucy with her long lipped, vivid smile singing in the voice of Minnie Mouse:

—In history's page, let every stage
Advance Australia Fair.

Today when I arrived at the Odeon, Jacko's big Burren Waters backside spilled defeatedly over either side of a bar stool. Seeing me, he spoke with a throaty mournfulness. That morning — as I knew from my viewing — he had taken the Harvard Glee Club to a house uptown and had them perform in some Bulgarian refugee's kitchen.

—Lovely, lovely boys with so sweet voice, the Bulgarian woman had cooed.

All the electronic enthusiasm of that encounter had, however, vanished from Jacko now.

So I had to hear again, as if for the first time, how a woman who claimed to be the enslaver's wife was talking to Lucy on the telephone, and that Lucy was pretty pissed off with him at the moment. She had made it clear she was passing on this news only for the vanished girl's sake. Jacko too — even as one who had seen everything, who had met racketeers' children with aftershave collections, who had watched men with freshly lopped digits sipping Veuve Clicquot in Paterson, New Jersey — expressed amazement. He too was astounded by a woman who called another woman and, in the most normal tones, sought compassion and understanding on the grounds that her man was digging further holes of detention, as men will, not being monogamous that way!

Lucy, he told me, refused to meet with the woman and be filmed from a distance by a *Live Wire* crew. She said that she was not part of the circus. Dannie was part of the circus. Dannie would not look silly if the woman turned out to be a hoax. If Dannie were worried about looking silly, Lucy had told Jacko with rare acerbity, she wouldn't work for Vixen Six.

Lucy wanted to call the police, but *did* seem to accept the idea they would mess things up. Maybe better to have the woman filmed, and then get in the police!

Jacko complained to me that the woman's tale about Dannie and himself hung on the question of whether the woman herself was authentic or not. Jacko felt cheated somehow that Lucy was willing to consider the idea that the woman was a hoax, yet not willing to believe the tale of Dannie and himself could also be false. This, he kept telling me, was the usual irrational stuff he'd got used to from the astral Logan sisters.

Then, said Jacko, Lucy reversed her principles, the stylish, casual attitudes which had marked her till now, and struck a deal that if she travelled to California and did the meeting with the woman, then she wanted thereafter to travel with Jacko all the time!

—You'll have nothing to do though, protested Jacko (according to his own account).

She said she'd knit or read. Or write a book, as I had suggested to her.

—You should let her do it, I advised Jacko. Let her travel with you everywhere.

—I'd feel too crowded, he pleaded. It's the truth. I'm not designed for closeness.

—Then you ought to stay away from Dannie. She intends to strangle you pretty comprehensively.

—The two things have nothing to do with each other, Jacko complained. Dannie and whether Lucy comes with me on bloody weekends. Nothing in common.

I'd got weary of Jacko's wrongheadedness, his wilfulness in marriage. On the other hand, Lucy's presence might leave Jacko fewer occasions with Dannie in the short term, but might encourage them in the long.

—I just don't want to see her demean herself like that, he told me sombrely. Keeping an eye on me. Being a watchdog. It isn't her nature and it'll turn her sour.

As we drank, it was hard to tell which of Lucy's two present aspects most grieved him: that she now had an idea of Dannie's plans; or that she would not consent to play the *Live Wire* game. I felt an obligation to bring him back to the essentials.

—Can't you reassure her, Jacko? I asked him. Can't you offer anything? She's genuinely distressed.

—How do you know? Did she say anything to you?

—Not her. Dannie said something though. She warned me off. In the lift in Berlin.

—Oh Jesus, I feel like a bloody football field, and both teams are tearing me up. I suppose you're barracking for Lucy eh.

—Listen, melodrama doesn't become you, Jacko. What's wrong with Dannie doing the meeting? You implied before we flew to Berlin that she likes dressing up and acting parts . . .

I could see that he was stung. He took two sips of his drink to still the anger.

He said, It wouldn't be the same eh. If Dannie put on a blonde wig and did it. There wouldn't be the same amount at stake. It'd be fantastic television with Lucy.

—Are you willing to film the part where the woman tells Lucy about Dannie and you?

—That's not germane to the question, mate. We'll edit that out because it's not exactly of public interest.

—I suppose you would edit it out.

—Go easy. Dannie and I aren't news. Lucy and I aren't news. *I'm* not keeping anyone in a bloody dungeon.

There was an angry silence in which I thought, To hell with you, Jacko! Until at last he could trust himself to look at me.

—Lucy's not the right woman for me. I need a dangerous, bossy little sheila like Dannie. I realize these things too late, like every other dumb bugger.

I said, If you talk Lucy into doing it, it could be the end of things, Jacko.

He conducted an invisible chorus with his left hand, a chorus whose voices were an echo of my voice. Conducted it in one sense; dismissed it in another.

—I know what everyone says. I give more of a bugger about a girl whose picture is all I've seen than I do about dear Lucy, the prize cellist of James Ruse High, whom I've got at home and everybody loves. Guilty, cobber. Guilty, guilty, guilty. But we still come back to the main question. I just hope Lucy does it. That's all.

* * *

There were further visits by Lucy to my wife. Jacko was still pressing her, but the dungeon master's wife had not rung back. Lucy hoped she wouldn't, that the question of a meeting would now pass. But both Jacko and Dannie, who had a nose for these things, knew that the pause was brief and that Lucy should hold herself ready to meet the woman and speak persuasively.

In the interval, without telling Jacko she was doing it, Dannie herself went to visit and reason with Lucy about a meeting with the woman.

Judging by what Lucy told my wife, the conversation hadn't been a happy or even friendly one. Though it was no surprise to me, Lucy thought it an outrage that Dannie could begin so strongly, taking the moral advantage, speaking of Lucy's obligation to Sunny Sondquist. It was of course clear that Jacko had been complaining to Dannie about Lucy's reluctance.

Dannie proposed it to Lucy in these flat terms: any mistrust Lucy felt shouldn't be an excuse for her failing her duty to the lost girl and to *Live Wire*. Let's all be professional and responsible about this whole thing, said Dannie.

I could see, just by watching Lucy's face when she came in our door, that Dannie had succeeded in turning her into a new kind of woman, the sort of aggrieved territorial woman you saw wearing an embittered mouth on any Manhattan bus.

For the second time in a few days I went to the Odeon, to hear from Jacko — again as if it were fresh news — that he and Lucy were quarrelling. The trouble was, he argued, she was using marriage, as well as her uncertain American visa situation which didn't let her get a job, as an excuse for sinking all she had into him, Jacko. Also, she deliberately avoided answering the phone. He found it hard to understand or overlook this evasion. Okay, it was all right to be ambiguous about tabloid television ... but Jesus, Sunny was a *real* girl, *really* vanished ...

He told me he was losing his respect for his wife.

Firmly, I put her case as I knew it at second hand from my wife. I argued that first he took away her self-respect, and now blamed her for having none. A pretty low trick, I told him.

Jacko weighed this and again dismissed it.

—No, he said, unreally certain. We've all got to keep self-respect no matter what other buggers do to us.

—Come on, Jacko, I said. This is Manhattan, not Burren Waters. Lucy hasn't fallen off a horse. Or if she has, Dannie pushed her.

But Jacko had the magisterial sadness of a man who has found both his professional and personal justification.

—For God's sake, I appealed to him. It's not like you to be so bloody pompous. You're talking like one of those CBS anchormen you say you despise. It isn't right to make Lucy feel that refusing to be televised makes her an accomplice to kidnapping and enslavement. She didn't kidnap her. And before that it's good Bob Sondquist who set a pattern of enslavement, and the kidnapper brought it to fullness. But it sounds as if you'd rather blame Lucy for the whole bloody mess.

He looked away, as he did frequently now, and punched the zinc top of the bar.

—What's bloody got into you tonight? Listen, I admit it'll be a circus when we find her. What do you think it would be if the cops found her eh? And anyhow, it isn't a question of a circus. It's a matter of cosmic bloody forces . . .

And he began to distract me by speaking of his old theory of zonal cockpits of evil.

*　*　*

At this stage, when Jacko and Lucy and Dannie were arguing over the pit-digger's wife, I was distracted from the question by a call from upstate New York. An institute in Albany, who had money from the MacArthur Foundation, asked if I could get in contact with Michael Bickham for them. The man who made the call, a celebrated American novelist in his own right, said the institute was willing to fly Bickham and a companion first class from Australia and pay him $10,000 for a lecture and a reading. They realized he was a reclusive man, the novelist told me, but Bickham had always felt he got better reviews in the United States than in Australia, and his visit would be highly publicized and put him back in contact with his American readership.

I advised the man that there was very little chance that Bickham would come. There was first his emphysema, but perhaps more important than that, his temperament, his terror of and contempt for audiences.

—That's why we thought we should contact him through a fellow Australian, the novelist told me. Through someone he trusted.

To refuse would have required me to spend a long time explaining myself to a man whose intentions were full of kindness and regard. It struck me halfway through that perhaps I could take a middle course and sound out his confidante, Chloe Emptor, first.

Early evening in New York is morning in Australia, and so, after the evening edition of *Live Wire*, I called the number I had for Frank Emptor's terrace house in Woollahra.

The phone rang a long time, and I could feel the

emptiness which surrounded the pealing. Frank was in jail, but where was Chloe?

At last the phone was picked up and I heard a thin voice say hello.

—Oh, I said, I must have a wrong number. Is that the Emptors'?

—Chloe here, said the voice, and I could hear now that it *was* a thinned-down version of Chloe.

—It's me, I yelled at her with forced joy.

—Good to hear, she said.

I asked the normal questions and told her I'd seen plenty of Jacko and Lucy. Then I asked her how Frank was.

—Plump as a bloody fart, she said. He's in medium security already, the little bugger, and he runs a class in music appreciation. He's all set up eh. I'm the one in bloody disarray. On my way back to Burren Waters. The mongrel bastard's playing up, as you'd expect, and that's nothing compared to my bloody daughter and her boyfriend.

I seemed to remember the daughter's name was Helen, and that she had left the Emptors in Burren Waters and was now living with an anthropologist in Perth. The sublime to the ridiculous, if you ever heard of it!

—Some of the bloody Wodjiris have a land excision claim on part of Burren Waters. And you know who the counsel for the Wodjiris is? My bloody useless daughter's bloody paramour, the anthropologist. So I'm going back to whip the old bastard into shape, and then make sure the excision thing doesn't go anywhere. But honest, I'm so bloody tired of the whole pack of them. All I'd need now for total bloody disaster would be for useless bloody Jacko to dump the only decent thing on our useless bloody horizon eh. That Lucy.

I deceived and consoled her on that score, and then asked her about approaching Bickham with the offer.

—No use talking to me. He bloody sacked me as a friend and spaghetti cooker.

—Sacked you?

—I didn't say the right things about the bloody Wodjiris. His bloody loss. And mine. I wouldn't mind taking this present mess to him and asking him about it. Mind you, the longer you spend with a writer like that, even a supposed bloody genius, the sooner you find they know sweet bloody nothing about humans eh.

—But you still talk to him don't you Chloe?

—It's him that's not talking. The miserable old bugger. Won't let me in the door. And Khalil says, I can't disturb him Chloe. That's Khalil's version of bugger off eh.

This was no help to me at all, though I had a sudden sense that Chloe was about to be liberated. Her voice and her body would expand again in Burren Waters. As she had confessed to me at Place de l'Opéra, she wasn't up to the weight of urban conspiracies.

We said goodbye fondly, and I wished her well and hung up. I now was faced with calling Bickham direct.

I would not call him that day. I waited until well into the following evening.

I dialled in dread and to my horror it was Bickham himself who picked up the phone. I heard his sepulchral Yes?

—Oh Michael I didn't expect to get you, I said.

—Khalil is out doing some shopping.

—Well, I hope I'm not intruding on your writing.

—I've just finished. I start at four in the morning these days. Are you calling from New York?

As always, I felt absurdly flattered that he knew any details of my life. I passed on the invitation to him, reddening as I did so, feeling foolish, knowing that I sounded over-anxious. Now I felt passionately aggrieved at the institute and the smooth novelist in upstate New York for landing me with this job. I told Bickham I'd tried to contact Chloe Emptor to arrange that the message be passed on casually through a friend at some convenient time.

He said, Mrs Emptor. She's not my friend, I'm afraid.

—No. She told me that.

—The woman is a throwback to the age of Paterson and Lawson. She's a monster.

—Well, I can't make any judgement on that, Michael. But I did think this proposal was of sufficient weight to pass on to you.

—Since I wouldn't go to Stockholm to receive fifteen times as much, did you think I'd really come to New York?

But I was pleased to hear that he sounded more amused than chagrined.

—What can they do, for example, about the climatic variation? he asked. Because that always puts me in hospital.

—Of course. I'm sorry I didn't think of that.

—No one does. I get misjudged for it. People think I'm being anti-social, don't they? Whereas, I just want to keep on breathing.

—I think it's of paramount importance that you do.

—Thank you, he said. Perhaps after my death you could remind people that my respiratory ailments played a large part in my behaviour.

—I will do that on every occasion I can, I promised. Always assuming I don't go first.

—Thank you. Tell the New York people that I decline with regrets.

He hung up at once. I stood pole-axed by my telephone. I had been given a mission. I had become his champion. How many people had he similarly recruited? I found myself hard-headedly and fondly asking myself.

No one would be more faithful a defender than I.

* * *

And then the worst thing happened for Lucy. The woman, the dungeon master's wife, called again.

She told Lucy that she was recklessly using a telephone credit card. Her husband would be angry when the bill came in.

How that must have horrified Lucy. The burden of information to be passed to Dannie.

XVI

Through an electrical accident, I found myself taking a demented part in the argument, a part which would prove to be something very close to the part Michael Bickham had taken in the question as to whether Francis should be taken to Tijuana for saguaro juice serum or not.

I had never had a very accurate understanding of the American electrical system. I had never understood why some plugs were marked *Shavers Only*, and why power points in American bathrooms had little yellow and red reset buttons. If pushed for time I would use any power point for my shaver and shaver power points for other appliances, since in Australia all power points were equal, and equally accommodating to the electric shaver.

I had now become more careful with the act of shaving itself. Age is the condition in which your bristles begin to look not like the product of testosterone, but like a curtain of ashes on the jaws. Nature was casting me forth, kindly supplying me with the first of the dramatic props I would need — if I were lucky — for my ultimate nursing home role. My stubble, which had once been reasonable and even a little too masculine to take out to dinner, now stood on the jowls like dust on a church pew. Hence, my late afternoon trim-ups.

One afternoon, whether in the wrong power point or for whatever reason, my electric razor turned into a brilliant yellow ball in my hand. My brain instantly turned to stone. I felt myself dragged backwards across the room by the shoulders and tipped brutally against the step which led up to the spa pool which served us instead of an old-fashioned bath. The air felt full of what I thought of as sizzled ions, and I could smell the metal stench of the razor's demise. The flesh of three of my fingers and the pads of my hand were burned, and some of the skin was already sloughing away. I ran cold water over it all, and with my left hand safely jerked the shaver plug out of its socket.

I felt angry and insanely wary. The electrical systems of Manhattan had taught me too harsh a lesson. The power surge had carried into my hand a sharp little measure of paranoia.

My wife came back with some jackets from the Korean dry cleaner and was immediately competent, making soothing noises and applying burn cream gently to my scalding hand. Then she led me downstairs, as I carried my hand in front of me, and we got a cab in Lafayette Street to take us over to St Vincent's Hospital in the West Village.

Until now I had thought of St Vincent's in terms of its distinguished reputation and literary repute. Everyone knew it had served such figures as Dylan Thomas, Brendan Behan and Delmore Schwartz *in extremis*. Now I brought it my humbler talent and small but screaming injury.

A young Chinese doctor injected my hand with

anaesthetic, cut away the dead flesh, and had me put to bed in a pleasant enough public ward. It was too early to dress the wound, and a burn specialist would need to look at it to decide on treatment and the necessity of a skin graft. The hand worried me barely at all, but the feeling of constriction and panic in my head was harder to negotiate with.

It was, in the spirit of the city, a loud but not very sociable ward. Though there was certainly space for me amidst the other patients and the trays and tables and bed pans, I felt somehow enclosed. I put my earphones on and listened to PBS, but even that gave me a sense of being confined. In the middle of some engrossing view on Mozambique or Azerbaijan, I would tear the phones off and reach my mouth upwards for free air I did not, objectively, need.

When I slept it was feverish. In some of my dreams I found myself to be a woman. I did not like the transmogrification — not because the change itself worried me, but more because of the relentless way the idea of being a woman frantically weevilled into my brain. It was a misrepresentation; that was what upset me. It was, I have to confess, associated in my jangled mind with being flung across the bathroom, with being a token of electric savagery.

I knew I would not rest properly, or get over the wild electricity of it all, until I fretted that all out, until my dreams became random again.

My recurrent dream was that I was a young woman, even a girl. I was afraid, but anxious to please. I stood by what you could call a rural freeway in clearly perceived country, not New England or New York, somewhere of lower rainfall, alfalfa and onions and orange trees. Perceived down to the last branch, this place. The average rainfall in the dream was perhaps eight to twelve inches. Traffic I was anxious to appease raged past me, indifferent to my good intentions.

From the direction of a carpark, a young man walked up the verge of the freeway. He carried a very large book in his hands, and, as he approached, opened it to one of the middle pages. His manner of carrying it was a little like an altar server with missal: the spine of the book and its clapboards held against his chest, its open pages faced towards me, his fellow ritualist. If it is not too melodramatic to say, the glare of this landscape had no impact on the face of the pages. The pages were darkness itself. He raised the dark book to my lips. Confused, but on the basis of a childhood church-going memory, I kissed it. It tasted of fur, like a pelt. Before I could withdraw, he — as I knew he would — closed the dark book on my head. I became an iota in the darkness. I was damned in the hairy black world of that book.

So I would wake gagging, and my little yelps, my cries for the compassion of passing motorists on that busy Californian-style highway, were lost in the rowdiness of the ward and the echoing joviality of nurses about to go off duty in New York.

Having suffered that dream three times one afternoon, before *Jeopardy* had even come on the ward TV, I found a quarter and went down the hallway, carrying my hand like a separate and delicate artefact in front of me. I dialled one-handed and found that both Emptors were out.

But it turned out that they were on their way to visit me. Before *Final Jeopardy*, they appeared in the ward, hulking Jacko and the sylph Lucy. They both wore conjugal kinds of faces which would have better fitted people whose marriage was older and more static.

When they arrived my burned hand was resting in a supportive mitt of cotton wool, the injury itself bared to the ceiling.

I tried to behave myself, but the book of darkness was too close to the surface of my brain. The confinement could easily be tasted, again like cat hair on the tongue.

I said straight away, I'm sorry Lucy, but I've got something important to tell you. Saving the Sondquist girl is more important than your dignity. I'm sorry.

My lips were bubbling with the words and I was weeping. Only later would I think that this had given me more authority.

—This girl is in darkness, Lucy. The woman who called you knows where in the darkness Sunny is . . .

I remember tacking on sundry *pleases* and *sorries* and *I can't help myselfs*.

Jacko had the grace to keep quiet while I compelled Lucy with my prophetic voice. Naturally I was ashamed, but not as much as I was afraid. The heat in my face was not from blushes. It was the purest fear. The *McNeill-Lehrer News Hour* wasn't even on, and I had had the dream so often already, and the limitless night remained.

—I'm not saying Jacko's not a prick, I told her in his presence, and then wept over that.

Jacko looked so sage and sad as I said it. There was no anger there, and I thought that, though he acted the fool, this proved he wasn't one really. Lucy began to look wan, just because of the pressure I was putting on her. Though the truth was the pressure was already there, and I confirmed it in my mad high pitch.

At last Jacko attempted to mention normal things. He asked me was my wife coming to the hospital. I began to weep again, because even that cherished face couldn't save me from the dark book.

—Jesus, mate, he told me, putting a hand on one of my knees, we've got to get you some sedation stuff. You've had a bloody great whacking shock eh!

I saw him go out of the ward. Old men with oxygen hoses up their nose called after him in voices aspirated with emphysema:

—Hey, Jacko, catch your show. When ya coming to my place?

From my bed I could see the hallway, where Jacko talked to a young Indian doctor. He confided in the man, touching the white-coated shoulder, cajoling, frowning. He came lolloping back, and I felt a child-like gratitude, an ineradicable devotion. Such enormous, paternal shoes, I noticed, on the hospital floor. He had to get them made up out of haunches of leather by a bespoke bootmaker in Queens.

—He'll have you fixed, mate.

Lucy took hold of my undamaged hand.

—Stay a while, I pleaded.

* * *

The hand healed faster than the appalled soul. It took only a day or two of medication — and my wife, who knew from her earlier career in nursing how to talk to doctors, firmly kept on reinforcing Jacko's demand for sedatives — before the dream became less specific as to landscape, grew to be as confused as dreams should be and carried only an average freight of night fear.

When poor Lucy got a call from the woman, she dutifully passed it on to my wife so that I in turn could be reassured. The woman wanted to know if Lucy ever came to San Bernardino. She let Lucy know that, because of recent storms, Ess had at least been taken out of the lined and furnished pit in which she had been living — the first pit, that is. Not the new one he was digging. Her husband had tried everything with that first pit, said the woman, talking, according to Lucy, like a typical handyman's wife. He had put in an electric pump. He had laid a new drain. The second pit he was digging for his future infidelities had also flooded, even worse. Expansion plans were, for the time being, cancelled.

There was a Ramada Inn in San Bernadino where she would willingly meet Lucy. She had been thinking of all this for a long time, she said. A woman in her position needed a confidante, but having another woman on the premises, sometimes hidden, sometimes frankly acknowledged as the family babysitter, made things very difficult. When Ess was allowed to be visible, people wanted to know why she had come back. The effort of explaining that detracted from the friendship the wife sometimes felt for Ess. For while she was locked in the box for all that time, the woman and her husband had been able to put around the easier story that Ess had gone home to her family.

All this, recounted by Lucy, cheered Jacko. The subtlety and growing length of the woman's story, and her tone, full of the right sort of madness, the tone of one utterly unmotivated by some conscious dream of publicity, was convincing. For, she told Lucy, she did not want to be interviewed by Jacko, no, never . . .

One afternoon at the hospital Jacko said to me, Tell you what. We're going to get just one of the poor bitches back from darkness eh.

I felt my brain clench.

—Darkness?

He said, for he was ignorant of my dream, We're going to bring her up from the pit that bugger dug for her.

—And I suppose then you'll interview her, I said harshly, though he was used to that. He tolerated my recent greater acerbity, writing it off to the burn.

—No, no, mate, he told me, shaking his head. We're going to win one back in this sod-awful, hypocritical vacuum.

—So, I said, you'll take both of them with you, eh? Lucy and Dannie on the Metro Grand flight to LA. Hi-bloody-ho!

—It won't be easy, he told me. So best not to make a joke out of it eh.

* * *

Able to wear a white linen glove, I came home from hospital the Friday they left in the belly of the Metro Grand jet. The tenderness I felt in the palm of my hand seemed to me an image of the stricture Jacko had made for himself, as with Dannie to one side and Lucy to the other, he was borne high above an America made of human energy and God's hand. So pristine a country: the huge blank blue of the Great

Lakes, and Minnesota's snowed-upon pastures; corn-fields and feed lots along the North Platte; the pro-found red of the Colorado's august pit, primped up with snow, its old geology delineated in ochre and white. To the right, the tangle of canyons where Mormon polygamists once hid; to the left, the Painted Desert muted under cloud. How could such villainy as the book of darkness be contained in that land-scape? How could time be wasted on malice and slavery when there were so many glorious National Parks?

I waited in New York, sure that Lucy would tell my wife the whole of it, and the residue I would have from Jacko.

It would not be welcome news to me to discover everything they could do now. Now they could film and hear conversations from four hundred yards away. Video snipers.

They wired Lucy and put her in the bar early, and then they filmed from the street every woman who arrived on her own and parked her car in the hotel's lot. They had Lucy seated in a window seat. The lighting was good, though sadly at seven o'clock, the appointed hour for the rendezvous, the bar pianist turned up and the lights were dimmed. A table candle cast some light on Lucy's lower jaw and long lips, and you could tell it was her on the film.

The woman who ultimately approached Lucy turned out to be a small red-haired woman with thin shoulders and full hips. She had left an old yellow Dodge station wagon outside. She carried her hand-bag retentively under one armpit and her mouth looked embittered and narrow. She wore torn pants and an orange blouse in a brave but fated attempt to dress up to the standards of the Ramada Inn cocktail lounge.

I heard and saw it all on the tape. They said hello to each other and sat down and ordered drinks.

—I hope you don't mind me calling you. I mean, you must have had your suspicions.

—That's right, murmured Lucy. But don't worry about me. I have my plans. Your situation, it seems so serious.

—It's been serious a long time, said the redhead. And in more than one way.

—This woman, Ess. She's been there . . .?

—Years. It's hard to excuse . . .

—No, breathed Lucy.

—It was all so normal for so long. He'd take her out to suspend her. But nothing sexual. That was our arrangement. He honoured it for a damn long time. Until they fell in love.

—*She* fell in love with him? asked Lucy.

—It's a long story, the woman told her, again like any normally wronged woman. I see now that he used both of us. Ess and I got pretty close. Sometimes we were like sisters, and then sometimes we were like rivals. He jerked us around. Not deliberately maybe. But he decided which we'd be.

Lucy surmised aloud that this means the girl wasn't always in the box or in the pit.

The redhead said, No.

Though for one period Ess had been in a box, this was after they changed houses, for two years, and she and her husband told their neighbours Ess had gone back to her family. The husband would take Ess out only at night, to give her a meal, and suspend her and so on. Sometimes he'd give her a bath.

—Baths are a mixed blessing in our house, said the woman in a normal tone.

Of course Lucy asks why.

—Well, he holds your head under. He can't help himself. It's an experiment with him. He sees how far he can go. That's why I let him have Ess in the first place. I was sick of the baths.

*   *   *

They had both moved on to a second glass of wine by now. Some men came over and asked them if they wanted a drink, and the red-haired woman and Lucy both said with a touching flatness, Thank you. Maybe later. Thank you.

The woman said, You see, I'd be held under so long I'd pass out.

As I watched the tape, I felt the flat, banal terror of this news. I wanted to succour this plain woman, take her out through the minefield to a sort of refugee camp of the kind which I know doesn't exist in a flawed world. A refugee camp which is a refuge.

Her testimony was made more affecting for the matter of fact manner of utterance! Even with the bad lighting you could see Lucy shake her head, and then shake it again. She could not address herself for the moment to asking more questions.

The woman said, I've been guilty of a big lie. You see, I *know* a man can turn a person right around by keeping them in the dark for years. By keeping a padded box on their head. And he told her that all of this was *sanctioned*, and that he had paid for it: he had a licence to keep her. He said there was a Corporation, and he produced a contract, a very fancy legal document. He did it on the joinery works type-writer when he was working back. He put all sorts of embellishments on it and it looked highly legal and official. And he got her to sign it which she did without argument, because she knew he could use a whip or electricity on her. Or else she signed it because she'd just lost hope of a different kind of life. And at one time he took her to a building in Riverside which he said was the Corporation's building, and told her the Corporation was everywhere: half the cops, his own father, neighbours of ours, all the judges in the United States. He showed her stills from movies where painful things are done to people — stills of folk who'd died in torment — and he told her that this was the work of the Corporation. That what she was seeing were runaways who'd paid the final penalty. It was all a long damn rigmarole! No man loves rigmarole more than him.

Lucy says, You don't sound as if you hate her at all. You don't sound very jealous.

—I try to be a good woman. It's not her fault.

—So you want to give her her freedom?

—I keep meaning to tell her there's no Corporation. Yet I keep putting it off too. I mean, he spent two weeks wages taking her to New York, just to see her father. So I thought, Damn her! I felt like that for a while. It was a lot of groceries he spent.

Lucy asked how the woman's husband had known old Bob was in the hospital. He hadn't, she said. He got the idea that that would be the big test, to be able to take her home to see her people. He didn't even know her mother had died. He found out when he called the father's place. A talkative neighbour was minding things for the father.

And did the husband tell Ess her mother had died?

—Oh yes. She took it pretty well. And then they went to see her father. I mean . . .

The wife clearly thought this journey could be read as rank marital disloyalty, even though she herself might be a tolerant woman.

Lucy said, You know full well you'll have to tell her eh.

—Yes, said the redhead. But everything will come unglued, and I kind of fear that. I've got children . . .

Lucy said, I know how you feel. But do you expect me to keep totally silent about all this? You're not swearing me to secrecy are you? I mean, it strikes me you're telling me this because I don't have to keep secrets even if you do.

—Oh God, said the pit-digger's wife, beginning again to weep, I don't know what I want to do. Things can't go on though . . .

—You're right about that, said Lucy.

By candlelight Lucy's tears showed up as a gloss on her face.

—You ought to realise that everything you tell me is horrifying to me. It's been your normal life all right! But to me it's utterly bloody shocking. I can't keep it a secret.

The woman began thrashing her head about.

—But don't tell him we met like this.

—Who? My husband?

—No. My husband.

Watching the tape, you see Lucy reach her hand out.

—He might find out not from me but from what others say to him.

Watching the film, I thought this was desperate

bush casuistry of a high order, saving her own soul from the taint of outright deceit, but preserving *Live Wire*'s filming rights. And maintaining the fiction too that they were sisters in grief, if it was a fiction.

—You've told the police you're meeting me, said the woman, standing up and staring around her.

Finally she hung her head from her shoulders in a frightful way. It was the posture of bellowing and awful to see.

—We are being filmed, Lucy can be heard to say on the tape. You had to expect that.

And she held and soothed the demented red-haired young woman. Lucy looked out of the window for the answer, but knew it was only the clowns of *Live Wire* out there.

Dannie asked Jacko, Why did she say that? She didn't have to say that.

The woman tore herself away from Lucy and ran out of the bar. The camera crew filmed her getting into her old yellow station wagon.

* * *

After the unconsoled woman ran away, Jacko left Lucy in the Ramada Inn to wait long hours until he had finished his purposes. Jacko had broadly interpreted Lucy's earlier stated condition that he contact the police at once. Dannie and Clayton and Durkin would all have considered it simple-minded of him to meet that condition straight away in any case.

Abandoning Lucy therefore to wait for them in that awful hotel, where a room had been booked for her, they followed the redhead for fifteen miles into the hills, into an area of scrubby five-acre lots at the top of the cactus belt, before the conifers set in. Clayton drove: he was trained for that sort of pursuit.

They watched her get out of the car and stand for a while, composing herself. Jacko and Dannie debated whether she would tell her husband. If so, the husband would run around destroying evidence.

Without any urgency, she walked up to a mobile home set up on cinder bricks and entered it. The camera crew could see in the moonlight, on the far side of the mobile home, a water pump, half-covered with plastic, lying on the ground. The device with which the industrious husband had attempted to empty Sunny's pit of its flood water. There was a garden shed, too, screened by a few scrawny eucalypts.

Jacko described later how strange all that seemed to him: Could such Satanic ambitions of enslavement, ambitions of the order which the woman had described to Lucy, be accommodated in the modest dimensions of this little trailer home?

Clayton held the mobile telephone. If they saw lights go on, the pit-digger emerge to look around or fill in his dungeon, the police would need to be called. But they saw the redhead pensively drinking water in the kitchen, and then there was darkness.

Outside, Dannie appealed to Jacko. Why couldn't they, the *Live Wire* team, break in anyhow, crack the case, expose the pits this man had been digging for women? What was his name? Jacko crept out of the car and inspected the letter box. *Kremmerling*.

—So are we going in or not? asked Dannie.

Jacko might have been enthusiastic to do it too, if this Jacko were the same Jacko who had taken a jackhammer to the Wall.

—We'll go back to town and see the police, he said. They have to be involved now.

—What's this lack of daring? Dannie asked, laughing acidly in the night air.

So Dannie called Durkin on the cellular telephone, getting him just as he arrived at the *Morning Manhattan* studios, at an hour New York was not yet awake.

—No, he said, don't do that. Don't barge in. That's too much anarchy, and it could be dangerous.

—Come on, urged Dannie, nothing's too dangerous. We're *here* and no one else is.

—What will you do? Arrest him? At best, he'll run around wrecking evidence. At worst he'll fire buckshot at you.

Jesus, said Dannie. They're limp-dick reasons. Just to be there when the cops break in? It isn't enough! Not for this case.

Jacko had begun to get anxious about Lucy. It was nearly midnight now. Was she still waiting in the Ramada Inn bar, expecting someone to come in and tell her sanity was restored to the earth and that she could go to bed?

And he was in trouble with Dannie. Later she would say to Jacko that if he'd supported her then, instead of being distracted, they could have overridden Durkin, and Durkin would have been grateful to be overridden. Except that Jacko hadn't supported her.

So after half an hour they drove back into San Bernardino, to the City of San Bernardino Police, a fortress in the midst of shuttered liquor stores and service stations with barred and enmeshed cashier booths. The sergeant on night duty called his superiors at home and punched the station wagon's numbers into a computer, etc., etc., just as in cop shows, and the banal answer came back fitting the address and the name: Kremmerling, Charles. No fly-by-night, he had lived there four years. His wife: Kremmerling, Joyce. Two children: a boy and a girl. Just as Joyce, the red-haired woman, had told Lucy.

—Not what you'd call an offender's profile, said the sergeant.

—And, Jacko explained to me later, Dannie's saying everything with an edge, as if I'd let her down. So that at one stage by the coffee machine at the cop shop, I pulled her by the elbow and I said, Listen, he's kept a woman locked up in a head box. Just think of that! And she said, Yes, oh yes. Don't you think I'm thinking of that? It's the Olympics of evil, and we're the only ones here. And we're farting around.

He recounted how, throughout that long night, he got more and more depressed, and more and more value went out of finding the poor lank-haired child. The question was: what had she been rescued for?

A number of senior officers had now come from their beds and needed to see Clayton's footage. They were startled by its authority, its circumstantial feel. Next they needed a warrant, and that took an hour or so. Time went very fast in that near-desert city. The policemen complained how cold it was outside, five degrees in the inland night, and Clayton claimed they didn't know what cold was until they'd lived in New York.

A wiry lieutenant, surely close to retirement, argued how it might be best if they put the mobile home under surveillance but — all things being equal — wait till dawn to stop Charles Kremmerling on his way to work. That would be away from the house, and they could be as aggressive as was warranted. Then they would visit the house and start to speak to the women. That would be all the better if it turned out that the red-haired wife was lying about her husband, punishing him maybe for a love triangle.

Dannie, the lieutenant suggested, might want to put two camera crews in place to cover the near-simultaneous events.

Dannie made calls to Vixen's Los Angeles station, and it was all briskly arranged. A second crew was on its way.

Since she also spent a certain amount of time staring at Jacko, Dannie's accusation seemed clear. Invading Kremmerling's home and finding him in mid-enslavement, with Sunny Sondquist hanging from some apparatus, would have required only *one* determined crew, the invincible crew of Dannie and Jacko. But Jacko hadn't been willing to participate. Jacko had chosen, at the supreme hour, to go through channels.

She said to him towards dawn, before both expeditions set out, I might have been utterly wrong about you, Jacko. I thought you had ambitions.

* * *

At the end and beginning of everything, Jacko returned to the Ramada Inn in San Bernardino only long enough to deliver an expiatory breakfast to Lucy. By then he had oodles in the can, even though these days there was no can, video tape being the medium. He had Charles Kremmerling being detained on his way to his regular employment at the joinery works. He had the police entering the mobile home and finding scraggy-haired, skinny Sunny Sondquist — identifiably Sunny despite all the horrors —

preparing breakfast for the children. He had the astounding business of Joyce explaining things to dumbfounded Sunny, the long trick that had been played on her with the aid of dark, sound-proof boxes. And so was uncovered the furnished pit in the yard which contained stagnant water from the last rains, and a second pit half dug, the one Joyce had complained of in her earliest contacts with Lucy.

At that point, Jacko told me, the children were sent out to play in the care of a young production intern from one of Vixen Six's affiliates assigned to child-minding by a prescient Dannie. As the children's cereal went flaccid in its bowls, limp-haired Sunny sat bonily at the kitchen table, suspicious of the strangers who had come tumbling in, wondering about their motives as well as their affiliations.

Jacko, at that moment, suffered his gravest loss of faith.

He simply couldn't find any questions he wanted to ask of this girl. She could not say anything to enlighten anyone. Her case transcended the usual entertainment quotient of horrifying events. As Clayton filmed all that passed in the mobile home kitchen, Jacko envisaged Sunny at her mute father's bedside in New York, imbued with the belief that everyone was in evil alliance, old Bob Sondquist too. Hadn't he traded her to his captain to cover his old crimes?

And so now, as the police sat with this wan girl, she conducted herself subtly within the bounds of the fable Kremmerling had, through his darkness and rites of discipline, imposed on her. His laughable tale of incorporated slavery.

* * *

In what I have just written, my perhaps highfalutin idiom intrudes on Jacko's, as it has many times in this account, but the sentiment is exact. For Jacko harboured now a fatal wish to leave Sunny Sondquist alone. For one thing, as everyone had promised, he could see her lips moving. As she waited to be interviewed, he passed her chair a few times just to be sure.

—P-A-R-S-I-M-O-N-Y, parsimony, she was muttering the first time.

—G-L-O-B-U-L-A-R, globular, the second.

She seemed to repeat each exercise a number of times before moving deeper into the lexicon.

A middle-aged woman who proved to be a police psychologist turned up in case she was needed to reassure either Joyce or Sunny. Against this woman's wishes, but because Dannie was so persuasive, Jacko was allowed to sit beside her. She spoke to the girl, who slowly brought her gaze to bear.

—This is not an interview. I just want you to feel comfortable . . .

—I'm comfortable, said Sunny in a colourless voice.

—Is it painful for you to remember what was done to you?

Sunny shrugged and looked away.

—Why are you asking me? she wanted to know. I remember most things.

But she had made no furious denunciation of Kremmerling.

She said, I always thought that it was better than being in the box. You know.

Then she stared away. The psychologist looked at Jacko as if he might have some ideas.

From Clayton's side, Dannie whispered in the

device in Jacko's ear, confessing to being disappointed and having second thoughts.

—I'm beginning to wonder about all this. He takes her to New York for Christ's sake! And she comes back with him!

Jacko however believed Sunny's muteness somehow proved her case. He would later argue this and other points with Dannie.

Dannie hissed in his ear, What's wrong with you, Jacko? Rally, will you, bugger it all eh? Ask her if he hung her?

So he did, and Sunny's eyes slewed across all the men in the room. And, Jacko suspected, she believed most or all of these men hung and whipped women, and cased them up regularly in darkness. So why would they be interested in Kremmerling's casual behaviour? This, she could be seen fearing, was a trick question, and Jacko perhaps the master of the random torturers.

—Well, she said lowly. Hanging. Yes.

The feel of the questions and answers was of clumsiness, for which Jacko himself was partly to blame.

She answered it all so woodenly.

—First he put a box over your head?

—That's right. It was very hot.

—Didn't you scream?

—For the first few times. But one time he took it off and put it on his own head and showed me how nothing could be heard.

—And during all this, he left you without clothes?

—Yes.

—But for how long?

Not a *mate* or a *love* emerged in Jacko's shocked diction.

—Joyce says a few years the first time. Until he felt I was trustworthy.

—And then he took you out and you went to work for him?

—Yes.

—And then he got scared and told you to stop work, and he dug a pit for you.

—Yes. I spent some more time in the box first. Then out of it again. But he got worried what neighbours would think if I was around the house all the time. He got worried about his kids too. They were getting older . . . So he made the pit.

Dull and wary, she continued to look for signs in Jacko that he was indeed a party in the conspiracy against her.

* * *

Watching the interview a few days later, I felt again — communally with Sunny — the flush of black terror which had overtaken me in hospital. I exulted in her release. But such awful dreams! Cramped naked and prone in her body box. A blanket. A little container for human waste. Swallowing on the furry dark. Her spine wasting, her muscles atrophying. Spelling P-A-R-S-I-M-O-N-Y and G-L-O-B-U-L-A-R.

She got the muscle tone back by jogging during her phases of liberation.

When she finished talking, Jacko thanked her, nodded to Clayton to turn the lights off, and went to the men's, leaving the psychologist to attempt to get more from Sunny. As he went he could hear Dannie complaining desperately to Clayton.

—We'll just have to do that segment again.

But there was a kind of progress in train too. The wiry lieutenant and his detectives had a quiet talk to Joyce in the living room. They put before her the details of an earlier, unsolved crime: an undergraduate from UC Riverside found buried in Waterman Canyon. From the marks of constraint on her body, the surgeons surmised that this was a case of accidental death, at least in the mind of the male who had used her. It was to have been his purpose and his pleasure that she suffer and survive.

Now, of course, the police urged Joyce to work with them as a witness. In return she would not be charged with having concealed this early, fatal experiment by her husband.

With the *Live Wire* crew filming all, the police were able to go calmly about the house retrieving instruments of torment: the head box out of a cupboard; the body box in which Sunny had spent some years of darkness from beneath the bed; the electric shock battery and its wires; and the hanging apparatus from a closet.

—Okay, said Dannie, sure she could rely on Jacko now. Just show and tell with this stuff.

—You mean the box and wires?

—And the rest.

On the kitchen table and floor were piled the box and the wires used for electric shock, Kremmerling's straps, whips and knouts, the head box that opened and closed over a hapless neck.

—Just hold on a tick eh, said Jacko.

He took Dannie aside yet again. It seemed to have been a night and half a day of takings aside and hissed differences.

—What's the problem. You're lying down on this

damn story, Jacko, and it's the best we've ever done. Pick up the bloody torture implements.

—I reckon it's enough to film them, Jacko argued. I don't want to dignify them. There's enough space given to dignifying things like this in this bloody country.

—Oh, Jesus, beat us to death because we're a demented nation. But you won't even look professional if you don't show and tell with those fucking things. Even Walter Cronkite would, for God's sake.

Jacko said, I'm not going to spend any breathless damn excitement on electrical boxes. Not ones used for purposes like that.

—Hell, argued Dannie. Normal people love to hear this stuff. They're entitled, because it confirms them in their normality. It makes them thank God for who they are.

—You can say that all you bloody want, said Jacko.

—And if you don't say, *and* do it, you're in the same camp as Jesse Helms and the moral majority and all those other shit-for-brains.

Jacko said, I've come twelve thousand miles to find this kid with the butchered bloody soul. These instruments are evidence, but beyond that they're sacred to her. I'm not going to paw them over.

—What? yelled Dannie. What did you say?

—It's because this *is* the most important story . . . that's the reason I won't touch them.

Jesus, said Dannie, I can't go on working with somebody like you.

And Jacko realized that within her own terms, which were usually and comprehensively his own terms as well, she was utterly correct, and Durkin would ask him in the Perugia what had bloody-well happened, and advise him not to let it happen again.

But Jacko kept refusing, and at last everyone packed up and went to the police station in town, where Kremmerling was already being held. I would ultimately see him on television: an angular man with no remarkable features. He looked like a man who might ask permission before proceeding with anything, a reliable, unindulgent fellow. These two impressions would serve him well in court, I surmised.

Live Wire turned their attention to him and for some reason, he took to Jacko, the sober Jacko of *this* particular interview, the Jacko who, against his own preaching, seemed to achieve the solemnity required of current affairs programs on other networks. With Jacko, Kremmerling was like a man who had at last found a sympathetic ear. He had picked up this girl on impulse: his wife had persuaded him to do it because she wanted a baby and thought he should be compensated. Then, after he'd picked Ess up, he hadn't known what to do with her. He knew he'd be in trouble if he let her go. So he built restraints. And then he found that the women were forming a conspiracy against him. He shook his head, a victim of unnatural, irrational, alliance-making tendencies of the sisterhood.

When Jacko emerged from that interview, Sunny was sitting in a waiting room refusing coffee, being careful of her caffeine intake, just like the victim of an average tragedy. Durkin had already spoken to Basil Sutherland, and told Dannie by phone that she was authorized to offer Sunny Sondquist $60,000 for her story, exclusive rights to Vixen Six. Sunny too had been on the phone, speaking to her father, and they had wept on either end of the line. Jacko resisted making much of this call, given what he knew of old Bob. Nonetheless Clayton had filmed her making it. Now she wanted to call him again. The lieutenant let her into his office, and she called Bob Sondquist a second time, all with a strange untentativeness. She needed to seek his advice on this matter. She came out after a minute or two saying that Bob Sondquist wanted to speak to Jacko.

Dannie felt she was the only one competent enough to deal with Bob, and followed Jacko into the office.

Jacko, picking up the phone to Bob, found that Bob's electronic monotone sounded authoritative now.

—I have to thank you, Jacko. But I told Sunny she oughtn't sign anything till she's heard from the big networks. You found her. But I've got to advise her like a parent.

—Let me talk to him, Dannie raged at Jacko's elbow. Crazed with sleeplessness and having already taken enough rubbish from Jacko, she was ready to flay Bob Sondquist.

—Bob, said Jacko calmly, and again his tone infuriated Dannie, since this was certainly an hour to fulminate, and all he was doing was chatting.

—Bob, you can certainly get $100,000 from one of the networks. You might get more. But they'd want a share of book and movie rights as well. Does she want all that? Do you want it for her eh? They'd pay her a heap, mate, but use her to death. They'd have her making fucking sneaker commercials eh. But it's not what she needs. We're giving her maybe $60,000 for one long interview, no other rights involved. I'm sure you wish, like me Bob, that she could buy some time back with it. But one long interview, and then she'll never have to mention it again to anyone unless she wants to.

—That isn't what the agreement will say, Dannie whispered.

An agreement transmitted by Durkin was already on its way by fax.

Bob Sondquist said he wanted to talk to an entertainment lawyer.

—What? What is he saying? Dannie asked.

Jacko covered the mouthpiece, told her briefly, but did not wait for a reply before addressing Sunny's father again.

—Bob, he reasoned, by all means speak to an entertainment lawyer, but ignore everything the bugger says. Because when it's all said and done, what are you going to tell him? Are you going to tell him you traded your kid to that captain at Page Air Force Base?

Bob Sondquist uttered an electronic protest down the line from New York.

—See, Jacko persisted, in some terms that would explain what happened to poor bloody little Sunny, wouldn't it? It would show how she was set up to take as normal the sort of rubbish that bastard Kremmerling tried on her. It'd explain — wouldn't it eh? — how she was ready for any old rubbishy story. Because she'd already heard them all from you, Bobby, old son.

After weeping for a few seconds, as so many people had in that night of tears, Bob gathered himself. He began to argue in his unearthly diction that Sunny was entitled precisely because of all that! His affliction did not allow contrition to be audible in his voice, and maybe that was both his punishment and his deliverance. For he might be able to reassure himself secretly that the man with the cruel squawk was not the same man who'd sold his child.

She deserved compensation from him, said Bob, and from others. But television had helped make the world crazy, and they should pay their share.

Jacko found himself laughing, and consumed by a great impatience.

—Listen, listen to me, Bob old mate. You've got the California State Victims' Fund to go to. And we'll give her solid money. You sign on with us, and one interview and she'll become a forgotten woman, as she should be eh. When the trial comes up, of course, it'll be a different matter, poor little bugger. But I'm telling you this straight up, the alternative is, we trump whatever the networks do with this story with one about *you*, about cozy old Bob on the fourteenth floor and what a dead shit he was when his daughter was a kid. I'll do it, mate. I tell you I'll bloody do it.

By these means, it was established quickly enough that Jacko and Vixen Six would reap the ratings inherent in Sunny Sondquist, Charles Kremmerling's hapless slave.

Bob asked again to speak to his daughter.

So Jacko stormed to the fax machine at the police station, seized the agreement from Durkin, and with Dannie looking on and protesting, ran a line through all the subsidiary rights Vixen routinely and hungrily desired a share of — the film, book, comic book, electronic image, television drama and physical representation (T-shirt and coffee mug) rights.

—You've gone fucking psycho! Dannie cried.

Agreement in hand, saying nothing while Dannie raged, Jacko sat outside the lieutenant's office, waiting for Sunny to emerge and sign.

XVII

There was a disturbing news story I saw one night in New York, soon after Kremmerling's arrest, a story in which the San Bernardino County Supervisor questioned whether the county could afford the trial against Charles Kremmerling. It could cost, he said, five hundred thousand dollars, and this could mean some forty or so county workers would need to be retrenched.

—Here we have, he announced, a case which will be long-winded: an alleged victim who was allowed to go jogging and who was taken to New York by the supposed perpetrator, and even held a job for a time, and never took her chance to escape! To make the case stick, the county will need to use expert witnesses and all that's highly expensive . . .

He sternly argued that the District Attorney's office should weigh the chance of a conviction against a possible loss of forty family incomes.

This plea arose in the wake of Jacko's curiously touching two-part interview with Sunny. She spoke in a neutral voice, a voice so drained of feeling that some people thought she was lying, and only those who had had a glimpse of victimhood saw it as the voice fit for her condition and her tale. She mousily confessed to having been kidnapped, enclosed in a head box, then in the body box, then in a pit; to having been suspended by the wrists or else stretched on a cunning table Charles Kremmerling had constructed; to having been forced to perform intimate favours and undergo intimate sufferings for her dominator. And throughout, Jacko seemed stricken. It was as if he felt the terrors as closely as I had during my startling nightmares in St Vincent's.

Then, far beyond the normal mandate of a program like *Live Wire*, Jacko had got her talking about the growth of affection between Kremmerling and herself, and about her times at large, the years she was permitted to baby-sit and to contribute to the Kremmerling family income by working in a motel in Baker and a fast food place in Riverside. She had made Easter and birthday cards for Charles and Joyce. With what I would like to think of as a writer's insight, I believed that this admission was utter proof of the validity of her story. For if, crazy from the dark as I had been after my electric shock (and she had received many such shocks from Kremmerling while hanging from the reinforced beam he had installed in his garden shed), you accepted that the Corporation governed all events of cruelty which befell you — if these were the sanctioned conditions of the planet you inhabited — then of course you would try to live within it, and be genial and send cards, and be an honest player!

Jacko must have agreed with me, otherwise he would not have risked evincing such information from Sunny.

But crasser and more respectable commentators than Jacko wondered if this, instead of validating her tale, disproved it. There was a lot of talk along these lines in the *News* and the *Post*, those arbiters of sensibility.

And now the County Supervisor didn't want the matter prosecuted.

Inevitably, and almost as a means of absorbing the shock of this, Maureen and I began contrasting the American county-based systems of justice with the state-based system at home. If Charles Kremmerling had tortured Sunny Sondquist in New South Wales, the prosecution wouldn't have been charged to the account of one particular hard-up region, but to the entire state.

This was in no way to pretend that there are not manifold problems in our own justice system. An Aboriginal actor we had known in Sydney had hanged himself rather than face trial for car theft. Earlier, in Western Australia, he had been briefly held in prison and had been beaten up by cops. He feared the way black prisoners were treated there prevailed throughout the entire country. He was probably right.

At home there was no uniform system of due process coast to coast, no Bill of Rights; only the patchy common law and a few scattered constitutional and statutory freedoms. But on the positive side, you would never get a situation like this San Bernardino one. You would never find a state treasurer pleading with the Attorney-General on the grounds of expense to ignore a case like the one against Kremmerling.

In the middle of the friendly little comparative law session Maureen and I were sharing, the door bell rang and I went downstairs to answer it.

It was Lucy Emptor. She looked just like a twice-shy New York woman in her navy-blue overcoat. A riotously coloured scarf at her throat seemed to be the only trace of spaciousness about her, the only remnant of the young woman in the Odeon on New Year's Eve singing *Advance Australia Fair* in a helium-squeaky voice.

And, hello, hello, she said, in a weary big-city voice.

I said hello cheerily, as if an inflated greeting could assuage her. She knew I was privy to things heard from Jacko in confidence. I was the friend who had kept harmful things secret from her, whereas Joyce Kremmerling was a stranger who had made them plain.

I took her wrist and said I was sorry she'd had to go to San Bernardino. I did not dare tell her I had seen the film of her meeting with Joyce Kremmerling, not only on blatant Vixen Six, but in a private showing provided by Jacko a few days before.

—Yes, well eh, she murmured in reply to my trite words of condolence.

And even more than usual when faced with the suffering Lucy, I thought with shame of all the casual confidences I had received from Jacko — two of the brethren wryly considering the enigma of female intent.

I took her upstairs but then offered to go down again, and read or watch television in the spare bedroom. Lucy said there was no need.

It was a good New York night. You could hear the jazz saxophonist who graced Lower Broadway performing to the students of NYU who waited at the Bottom Line. Across Fourth Street, the lights from below hit the gargoyles and great empty windows of the proud but ill-kempt building opposite. This structure awaited only the end of a recession to become fashionable condos. The empty windows which showed its empty floors were still eloquent of the ghosts of nineteenth-century seamstresses and warehousemen. Looking downtown through the apartment's southern windows, every commercial floor of the Trade Towers could be seen wastefully glimmering.

My wife and I intended, later in the evening, to hit Chez Jacqueline in MacDougall Street to celebrate the end of the final draft of my book. In China, a young English teacher from the West gets involved in the politics of dissent and falls for a Chinese woman who is under police surveillance, etc., etc. All the adventures, all the ideas, all the assignations now brought to a conclusion, ready for the printer! And the cheque for final delivery being processed in the publisher's accounting department.

Lucy sat down still wearing her overcoat.

—I thought I'd better let you both know, she said, looking at the carpet. I'm going home.

We both exclaimed of course. But we didn't really have to ask why. She supplied reasons just the same.

—I don't like what this place has done to us. I still feel as if I was abused, like Joyce Kremmerling. Pretty mad eh? But I can't get over it. Besides, the old stuff: Jacko believes I don't let him breathe, and I feel like that also, but as if I can't breathe. We had a talk this afternoon. He's moved out to let me pack.

My wife rose and walked to where she was sitting and embraced her.

Lucy said, I'll be all right, I'll be all right. I'll go back and keep studying the cello eh.

—This isn't final, is it? I asked.

—I can show you the air ticket. Tomorrow night's flight to LA, and then the Great South Land.

I could see my wife was particularly stricken. Maureen couldn't imagine New York without Lucy. I went to comfort her.

I remembered Jacko's account of the arguments with Dannie over the way implements of torture should be held, and their arguments over the method of interview to be applied to Sunny Sondquist.

I said, From all I know, Lucy, that Dannie business is well and truly over.

She gave her broad, hectic grin.

—This has nothing to do with *l'affaire Dannie*.

We all stared at each other. What could be said?

—You'll come and see me in Oz, won't you?

—God yes. Yes.

From being so content with this night, I wanted now the bite of that remote sun and the outrageous blue of the Harbour. Here all waterways, even the Atlantic, seemed too relentlessly dun.

We had a last glass of wine together. So hard to believe that New York could lose its hold on this woman! It was like a form of civic negligence. But she was already, perhaps, leaching the city itself out of her system. She said she could not join us at Chez Jacqueline.

—Packing, of course, she said.

My wife and Lucy hugged each other, and I walked her to the lift and took her downstairs and got her a taxi. For our demi-posh building, with its closed-circuit television in both lifts, was besieged by two dozen of New York's most aggressive beggars, and, as justified as their spikiness might be, I believed she shouldn't have to put up with it tonight.

Besides, these lifts were capable of their own surprises. I had been waiting downstairs in the lobby one day when the lift door opened and two cops wheeled out a skeletal, shrouded form on a trolley. A man had died in the very waiting room of the AIDS doctor on the fourth floor.

The lift — the *elevator* as the Americans grandly call it, bold Latinizers as well as bold abbreviators — was empty. While going down I said to her, Look, I think it's just as well *you* spoke to that Kremmerling woman. No one else could have done that, no stand-in. They wouldn't have had your human skills.

—Yeah but, said Lucy, what do you think of a country where you really find out about your husband from someone like dear old Joycey?

I had nothing to say to that, and wondered again if it was an accusation. She looked directly at the television camera in the roof and then closed her eyes for it.

—D'you know, she said, Jacko expects to get marks for not being Charlie Kremmerling. A lot of you fellows are like that eh. *Yeah but at least you can't say I'm an axe murderer.*

She laughed at this tendency, her old laugh, as if at some time in the future such male innocence might again seem charming.

Reaching the lobby we scooted past the pleasantries from the doorman on duty, a fine arts student from City College who must have wondered about our rush. We moved out onto Fourth, and then the mad corner of Lower Broadway, with its hordes of students and children from New Jersey looking for drugs, and its veterans of Vietnam and of psychiatric hospitals waving their white polystyrene begging cups at us.

Lucy said, You should know, he lied like hell to me. I felt very safe with Jacko. I don't mean that he's a liar as such eh. But he lied to me. I'm sure he told the truth to his *good* friends. But I suppose his mother Chloe taught him that it's best to keep women in the dark, they're so wild and out of order.

The normally savage, unloved and sullenly-driven yellow New York cab came along. Soon she'd be back with the cabs of Sydney, where you sat in the front with the conversational driver and all the doors were undented.

The hungry-eyed driver looked out at us — he might have been Pakistani or Bolivian, Haitian or Arab or Azerbaijani. To him and to his cab with its stuck back window, I committed sweet Lucy.

—Will we see you tomorrow?

—There's no point, she said.

The broad smile again and for the last time.

—You won't get any sense out of me until I'm back in Oz. Wait till then eh.

—Forgive me, I said.

—What for?

—I've been too attached to the high colour of the Emptors to give them the hard time I should. Same goes for Chloe. I'd really like to get Jacko now though and sort out his head for him.

—Don't be silly, she said. Nothing to forgive anyhow with you. Sydney, okay?

She was hauled off down cold Broadway to the melancholy plaint of the saxophone.

* * *

The following morning, by all signs the last of his marriage to Lucy Emptor, Jacko called me from the hotel up in the Fifties where he was staying out of sensibility, to allow Lucy a last unfussed, unfraught night and day. He wanted me to come up there for a drink. I was confused about what my demeanour should be, and the chances were that I would futilely lose my temper. So I raised the obvious objections — I had a dread of Lucy hearing somehow that as she was ordering the car to take her out to Kennedy, I, Jacko's *true* friend, had been drinking with him at the city's heart. What a malicious rite that might seem to Lucy!

—Aw, come on! he said. I've got to have a drink with some bastard who's sensible.

There had been much public comment on his long, painful interview with Sunny Sondquist, and the television reviewer in the *Village Voice* had remarked on his unaccustomed sensibility. On that suspect basis, I decided to consent and go and see him.

Jacko was camped in one of the newer midtown hotels. The place had none of the atmospherically dim, lock-yourself-in-with-a-bottle-of-Scotch sort of feel of the Algonquin or the St Regis. It was not a bad place to come to do business, but it certainly was a depressing place to wait until Lucy packed her bags and left your loft in Tribeca vacant.

I could tell by the plastic glitter of the chandeliers in the lobby, by the egregious fountains of dyed water, that Jacko *must* be pretty depressed here.

As soon as I called his room, it was clear he didn't want to come down and head west to Seventh and Eighth Avenues looking for squalid bars.

—Come'n up, matie, he growled at me sepulchrally. He spat out the room number.

I found him in a corner suite forty floors up. Opening the door, he massively occupied the hotel's dainty bathrobe. He left me to close the door. Smoking at a rare rate, he prowled amongst the ice buckets which sat on the occasional table. His mini fridge lay emphatically open, as if he were wilfully mixing his drinks.

Blowing smoke from his meaty lips, he kept saying, I think it's a good thing. I think it's a *really* good thing for both of us. I mean, mate, you must know I've been unhappy for a long time.

I thought of asking just who it was he'd been unhappy with: Dannie or Lucy? But smart-aleckry like that was not my style, and wouldn't do much good today.

—But you could lose her, you know, I told him.

—No, mate, he insisted. I could bloody find her. She could bloody find herself. That'd be a bloody start.

I felt an edge of anger at the fact that he seemed so conventionally sad to see Lucy leave. I couldn't help myself telling him.

—I never quite believed that stuff about her depending too much on you. About her frying her own fish. If you want the truth, that's always sounded like nonsense to me.

He looked dismally at me for a moment.

—Well, mate, as our brethren here say, I can only call it as I see it.

—But you're not so depressed about it . . .

—Of course I'm bloody depressed. I'm depressed and sad. Jesus, it's her decision to go eh. For God's sake, I've been rejected by two women in a week . . .

—Sorry to tell you, Jacko. Not too many people weep for you . . . You seem to be riding pretty high to me.

—Oh, he conceded. Professionally? Professionally things are jake. I agree with you. Dannie's trying to tell people how incompetent I am. But generally eh, I agree. The man on the street won't spend too much time being sorry for me.

—Especially since you pursued Lucy, Jacko. You say that yourself. She kept saying no. Maybe she could see the dangers.

—Oh God, all that's true. Sometimes the greatest bloody reprobate gets a craze to get married. I don't know where it comes from. It's primal eh. And romantic. It's men's tragedy to be romantic about marriage, and women's to be practical. I mean, we're romantic in a seriously dangerous way. I certainly was.

—So, I challenged him, if you're not depressed about Lucy going, what is it?

He sat down and was finishing some Scotch. He leaned forward.

—I don't know what I'm doing. I don't know where to go from here. For one thing, I've got Bob Sondquist and Sunny staying down the hall. Separate rooms.

I asked, Why ever here?

—Bob says being on the fourteenth floor at his

place scared her. Agoraphobia. Opposite of claustro-phobia. Stands to reason eh. Having her here on the fortieth floor isn't necessarily the answer. But the drapes are drawn and we've got a plain clothes psy-chiatric nurse sitting with her.

I wanted to know what had happened? Why didn't they draw the curtains and pull down the blinds in Bob Sondquist's apartment block?

—They did. But they were besieged.

This fact really seemed to oppress Jacko. Lucy saddened him and her going was painful. But did it reach the core? *This*, this siege, just like the entire Sondquist affair, moved him in the spirit. He was pacing the space in front of the plundered refrigerator.

—I mean, at Bob's place there were camera crews in the lobby, and people who wanted to ghost write her book, and feminist defence groups who wanted to succour her and pay her legal costs and take her in. What an item this is for them: woman tortured and raped and locked up in the bloody, bloody dark! I talked Durkin into putting our own security guards in there to manage the flow, but before we could Sunny had a sort of panic attack. Not one that makes you scream eh. The kind that makes you go utterly silent. And her pulse rate was impossible. Then, this morning, she was woken up at four o'clock by a camera crew in a cherrypicker imitating me. So noth-ing for it but to move them in here eh. Anyone getting off the lift at this floor is frisked by security.

—I wasn't.

—I told them you were coming. Mate, you *are* in a contradictory frame of mind today.

—I'm grieving for you, you bastard.

He stopped in mid-stride.

—Okay, let's stop this and go and see the poor bloody Sondquists.

Without allowing for further argument, he opened the door and held it to let me through. In the corridor, a man in a para-police uniform emerged from a room with its doorway permanently open — the base of security operations. When he saw Jacko in his bathrobe, he gave a half-wave of approval and disappeared.

Bob Sondquist answered the door Jacko knocked on.

—Mind if we come in, Bob?

With a body builder's vanity, old Bob still wore the same sort of T-shirt he'd worn the morning Jacko found him on the fourteenth floor.

—Sure, said Bob's miracle voice.

He led us in. His television was busily blathering: Judge Wapner and a Czech emigre arguing over damage a dog had done to somebody's Astrakhan rug. Bob invited us to chairs placed around the little table by the window. The window of Sondquist *père* gave an unabashed view of the Avenue of the Americas and its berserk uptown traffic. One pane was ajar to let dusty, cold air in. Bob had no fear of the open day.

Jacko introduced me to the man.

—He's a writer, Jacko said.

Bob Sondquist cast his eyes up.

—No, no, Bob. Not that sort of writer. He makes his own shit up, he doesn't live off other people's. I wanted to let you know. We're just going in to have a look at the girl.

It was clear that Jacko's tone towards Bob Sondquist had changed. Perhaps what had muted Jacko's

hostility a little was the admission of guilt and fallibility Bob had made on the telephone while negoti-
ating his daughter's fee. The massive betrayal still
stood, but perhaps the primitive in Jacko believed
Bob had paid away his voice in part expiation.

—Okay. You won't wake her?

—No way, Bob.

—Can't get rid of that goddam sleeping bag she
had at Kremmerling's, he complained. You'd think
she was homesick.

—Well, he buggered up her mind, Jacko explained
to Bob.

Sondquist was still looking at me with suspicion,
and so Jacko put his arm on my shoulder.

—Look, Bob, he's my best friend eh. Involved in
this search from the start. He doesn't want anything
from Sunny. Okay?

—I take your word, said Bob, so competent in
speaking that you could not see any preparation of
the diaphragm muscles.

—Mind you, I only *think* he's my bloody friend.
He's pretty cranky with me at the moment about my
wife.

—Okay, said Bob, as if this were another explanation of why I was entitled to get a glimpse of his
sleeping daughter.

On the screen the Czechoslovak emigre said, I
know the judge is doing the best he can according to
his lights. But justice this isn't.

—Yes, said the *People's Court* interviewer. But as
you must know, there are countries where you
wouldn't even be allowed to complain . . .

With Bob's blessing then, Jacko and I went to
Sunny Sondquist's room. Jacko knocked on the door,

and a handsome young woman wearing street clothes softly opened it. Jacko asked if we could come in for a second. This was his friend, he said pointing to me.

The woman said with a broad cautionary smile, You're not trying to make a freak out of her, are you, Jacko?

—No, listen, he's my best friend. He's known about this case all along. I want him to be a witness to the way she is now.

Vixen Six had provided a spacious room for Sunny. There were two double beds, and a little alcove with a settee and coffee table and second television. That television was also playing softly, on the same station as the one Bob Sondquist had been tuned to.

—Don't *any* of you ungrateful buggers watch Vixen Six? Jacko whispered to the nurse.

On the floor, between the second double bed and the window, lay small, scrawny, scraggy-haired Sunny. She wore a track suit and socks on her feet, and lay foetally on a much worn and not very clean, opened sleeping bag. She had no pillow. Obviously, since the room abounded with pillows, this was from choice.

—That's the sleeping bag Joyce gave her. During the time she was working for the fast-food place and minding the kids, she was allowed to sleep in the bathroom on that. But then she had that sodding sleeping bag in the box with her and in the pit with her. How's that for a sequence eh?

Jacko shook his head. The mystery of all Kremmerling's shifts of tyranny would never leave him.

Jacko turned to the nurse.

—Is she still muttering?

—Not a lot. Sedated. She's as well as you'd expect.

But very dependent. I think I'll have to be her friend for life.

—What's your name? Jacko asked, looking down at the nurse from beneath his brows.

—Delia.

—We'll all have to be her friends for life eh, Delia, said Jacko.

This was admirable, of course, and said with great determination. It made me wonder though where Lucy would go for friends.

Jacko put his arm around me.

—So you can tell the bloody beak you saw this.

—Beak? whispered Delia.

—Judge, said Jacko. We can tell the judge we saw this. A lot of silly pricks would have us believe that the way she clings to that sleeping bag is a sign she enjoyed the past. But let's hope the prosecution will have experts by the score to say the obvious.

—Well, we all cling to our chains, Delia said robustly. At the end of the Civil War, there were old slaves who didn't want to leave the plantation.

—Listen, Jacko asked her, why don't we have dinner downstairs tomorrow night? Bob can sit with Sunny for a while.

—Okay, said Delia with an arresting smile. That'd be okay. But let's just be straight about certain things.

—I know what those things are, said Jacko.

She then pushed us out into the corridor, laughing softly. In the hallway, Jacko sighed.

—The trial, you know. I really doubt she'll make it through all that. No way she could stand that particular hurly-burly. But a funny bloody thing: when she wakes up she asks them about the trial, as if she can't wait for it. She won't get off that bloody sleeping bag till then, anyhow. Come and have another drink. Then I've got to get dressed for the airport.

I suppose I looked away, and he said, Yes, I know it's bloody crazy asking that nurse to dinner. I'm not grabbing for excuses, but I'll tell you something.

He paused in the corridor and leaned against one of the walls.

—When I was bringing Sunny home, after the police were done with her, I brought her on Metro Grand. I booked the bedroom so she could rest. I was worried about her eh. She was dazed still and her voice was just as neutral as her old man's. So I took her back to the bedroom, to show her where everything was. I wasn't going to stay. I was going to have a drink and get some sleep in one of the easy chairs. Soon as we were alone, she dropped to her knees. She had her eyes half closed. I don't have to tell you. It was automatic. Not in her control. Jesus, it made my blood creep. That bastard Kremmerling's poisoned everything. He's poisoned everything even for me. And I'm the one who has to go home tomorrow. To the empty loft. I'm not trying to make excuses eh. But I've got no interest in that nurse. Only in Sunny.

I was not willing, yet, to let him off that hook.

—You're not *still* asking me to feel sorry for you, are you?

—Bugger you, he said.

He opened the door to his room. I said I should go, but he reiterated the offer of a drink, and there was enough desolation in his eyes to make me stay. Inside, he looked at his watch and then all around

the room, at the ruins of lunch and the empty Cabernet Sauvignon bottle, at the wrappers of peanuts and
confectionery, all the signs that misery had made him
omnivorous.

— By the way, thanks for coming over, he told me.
You miserable bastard.

* * *

As Maureen and I sat drinking coffee and, of course,
watching the box while the yells of beggars and the
music of the saxophonist outside the Bottom Line
contrasted with the calm murmur of news readers, a
further astonishing item of information appeared on
the evening news. Again, it was hot from San Bernardino, and momentous. Kremmerling had been found
hanging in his cell, and two jail-house deputies had
been charged with fabricating a supposed suicide.
Investigators had concluded that he'd been strangled
before being hanged.

It was about ten days since Lucy had departed.

A psychologist was interviewed, one who'd had a
long conversation with Charles Kremmerling during
the day. He said the prisoner hadn't been at all
depressed or despairing or shameful. Besides, said the
psychologist, people who commit such self-centred
crimes as those Kremmerling was charged with are
not likely candidates for suicide.

During the interview, the psychologist told us,
Charles had said he was so happy at last to be away
from the two women who were tearing him apart.

Maureen and I, like the Sondquists and the fashionable nurse Delia, were guilty of not watching Vixen
Six. This story was network news, the sober-sided

network news Jacko thought was good for nothing. I wondered if Jacko had been told about Kremmerling, and called him just in case. I heard Lucy's sky-wide Australian accent on the answering tape.

—Well, you haven't found us in eh. Jacko and Luce are hitting the town at the moment, but they're anxious you leave a message, coherent as you can make it. Do your worst!

I called the midtown hotel where Sunny Sondquist and her father might still be staying. I said I thought that Jacko had checked out by now. They told me, Yes, he had. I asked for the psychiatric nurse on the fortieth floor, but they told me that no calls were being put through to that room.

I could still so vividly see the sleeping girl, oblivious on her little unzipped square of dirty quilting, a dog on its blanket. She mightn't know yet that two county officials had achieved for her judgement without grief. Two sheriff's deputies taking their primitive industrial action.

I hoped she was asleep still the next day, when — in my new avocation as media ecologist — I heard some of the radio gurus say her story didn't add up, given the opportunities for escape and so on, given too the blameless work and civil record of Charles Kremmerling. They surmised poor Charles was just another honest victim of the sisterhood.

I called Vixen Six and the Perugia, but both Dannie and Durkin said they hadn't seen Jacko.

—I've taken over producing Al Bunker's segments now, Dannie told me. I'm not with Jacko any more.

* * *

I so wanted to find Jacko and discuss it all with him that I decided to go down to Tribeca and wait in Coghlan's bar across from his front door in Thomas Street. Big Irish-American detectives from the First Precinct, into whose hands I would not like to have fallen, drank at the bar, facing a mirror covered with IRA and Sinn Fein posters. *No extradition. The Bobby Sands Memorial March, Falls Road, Sunday August 14, 1990* and *Political Status in the H Blocks Now.*

The barman greeted every newcomer with, Is Belfast free yet? When the cops said, No, Michael, not yet, he'd say, Then you've still got to pay for your drinks until that happy day.

I drank the Ulster drink, Bushmills — mind you, an establishment Loyalist company, Bushmills. But I'd noticed during visits to Northern Ireland that tribal prejudices did not extend to booze, though Catholics and Protestants did tend to drink different brands of porter.

I tried to drink slowly, but my excuse for getting tanked is that I come from a family of heavy swallowers. After four o'clock, when the light was failing and I had to look twice at things to assure myself of their verity, I saw a stretch Mercedes come round the corner by the Korean store and park in front of Jacko's doorway. Jacko emerged in a hurry, fumbling for keys. It took two keys at least to unlock the heavy steel door at street level.

I got up from the bar, from the urgings that I should prevent the extradition of Provisional IRA men and women out of the Republic of Ireland into the British sector, from the exhortations to remember dead hunger strikers. By the time I'd reached the cold evening and crossed the street to the limo, however,

Jacko was in the door without seeing me and had slammed it.

I turned back to the limo, but its windows were tinted and I could see nothing. A small man in a chauffeur's uniform, almost grotesquely broad-shouldered, rose up from the suddenly opened driver's door. He came up strangely close to me as if to intimidate me with the black-serge bulbs of his muscular shoulders.

—Can I help you, sir?

—I'm just waiting for Jacko.

—Sir, I've got to ask you to stand clear. Mr Emptor doesn't want any journalists.

The man was jostling me off the pavement, into the narrow street, back towards Coghlan's *No Extradition* bar.

I said the usual, the expected things, which sounded hollow in my mouth. That Jacko was a friend and would want to see me. The driver put his meaty little hands up and gave me an efficient shove which made my ribcage shiver and carried with it the promises of punches soon to follow.

I said, I don't want a damn fight. I'll wait over by that bar door until Jacko comes out, and if he wants to talk to me, he can. If he doesn't I'll just stand there.

The driver told me okay, to just keep there. I knew what to expect if I caused Mr Emptor any problems.

I didn't have to wait until Jacko came back downstairs. Within seconds, the well-dressed psychiatric nurse opened the back passenger door facing Coghlan's and stepped out. I could see that she was wearing a Cartier scarf.

—I'm sorry, she called lightly. I didn't realize it was you.

—Yes, I just wanted to talk to Jacko. To see how he's doing in the light of Kremmerling's death: cheated, thwarted, relieved or exhilarated?

There was something in the nurse that she could not hold in.

—We're going to Australia, she told me.

Numbed by that joyous shout, I had nothing to say.

—We're going to Australia!

—Tonight? I could ask at last.

—Yes, Jacko's just getting a few papers he needs, then he's taking us out there.

I asked if I could re-cross the street to them. The nurse turned to the driver and reassured him. I liked the confident and jovial way she did it. She was a good woman. She had a vocation for nursing. And for going to Australia.

So I crossed the street and then paused at her doorway, through which she had already re-entered the car. Sunny Sondquist was in there, holding the nurse's hand, looking tranquil but uncertain of her surroundings.

—We've agreed, said the nurse, we're going to bury that goddam sleeping bag at Burren Waters. You know Burren Waters, don't you?

Stupefied, I nodded.

Jacko emerged from the steel door downstairs with a briefcase and an envelope. He seemed as flummoxed to see me as I had been to see the psychiatric nurse. I was one item too much for his turbulent day.

—Mate, he said to me across the lid of the limo.

I said I just wanted to see how he was.

He shook his head.

—Get in, mate. I'm taking the girls to the airport. Take the jump seat in the back.

He hauled himself into the front beside his pocket-battleship driver. I sat not in the jump seat but — since she patted the leather at her side — beside the nurse. Without losing hold of Sunny's hand, she made room for me. I could smell the utterly pleasant fragrance of her excitement. She wore her expensive scarf with aplomb. Surely it wasn't a gift from Jacko? In the heightened air, I was jealous as a spouse. I sat there and let them tell me their story.

It came to me in fragments.

Jacko said, I was talking to Delia about the situation.

—Delia?

—You know, your friend there in the back.

—Yes. Delia.

—New York's impossible for Sunny. The bloody Sondquist apartment is still besieged by every wacko in Christendom.

—And now, you see, after what happened out West, she's free, said Delia.

At the word *free*, Sunny seemed to fall pleasantly, lightly asleep.

—Does she feel he got off too easy? I wanted to know.

My friend Delia nodded.

—That, certainly. But she grieved for him too. He was her bad parent, but he was a kind of parent just the same. She's been much calmer since it happened. She was dosed to the limit when you saw her four days ago. But she's on only half that dosage now!

—Have you ever been to Australia before? I stupidly asked the nurse.

—Never. This is a big thing for me. It makes some good sense. Jacko's mother will meet us in Sydney, and we'll fly across to Darwin together.

I couldn't imagine anything better for Sunny than making unexpected friends with other women like this.

—Is Chloe back in the Northern Territory by now? I asked Jacko.

—Yeah, mate, he murmured. She went back up there to keep an eye on Stammer Jack, the randy old bastard.

—I love the uninhibited way Jacko talks, Delia confided in me.

—My useless mongrel of a brother doesn't need her. He's getting on fine, let me tell you. Running things, and organizing musical evenings. Minimum security now. He doesn't need more than an occasional visit. He'll be whistling a long time before he gets one from me.

—But what about Michael Bickham? I asked, a little perversely since I already knew. Is she still running things for those two old men?

—They had a falling out.

—Over what?

Jacko shrugged, Politics. Bickham's a bitter old bastard. She sends you her love. You know, she was standing for the Federal Senate?

—No!

This was not something Chloe had told me in so many words.

—Yeah, that's what the fall-out with Bickham was about.

—She wasn't standing for the right party?

—Got it in one. Or maybe it was *too* right a party.

Bickham's people cleaned up the Aboriginals in Northern New South Wales in the 1840s, and the old bugger's still living off the income. But he's got no time for Chloe Emptor, who's had to live with them day to day and get on with them. Not that she's any model of tolerance, mind you.

—Pardon me, I said, changing the subject and nodding to the dozing Sunny, but aren't medical services pretty thin on the ground at Burren Waters?

—Darwin's only an hour away by light plane, said Jacko. There are plenty of good psychiatrists in Darwin. The bloody Flying Doctor could drop one in to her anyhow. And she'll have Delia and she'll have Chloe.

By now we had come the long dreary way across Houston Street and eased ourselves onto the reasonably free-flowing FDR Drive.

I asked, Bob Sondquist knows his daughter's going?

For I picked up here, in the expectancy of Delia and Jacko, a redolence of the day we had tried to kidnap Francis away to a cure in Tijuana.

—Well, he's totally for it, isn't he? Old bugger doesn't know what to do for her eh. And he can't go home again until Sunny's off the scene.

—A funny thing, said Delia. I think he wanted her found. But I don't believe for a minute they're ready to occupy the same house.

—Dead right, said Jacko.

But just as in the attempted kidnap of Francis, special arrangements had been made. The women were travelling business class — that was the compromise Jacko had come up with to deal with Delia's confessed mild claustrophobia and Sunny's fear of spaces. When we arrived at Kennedy, we didn't go straight to the usual desk. A United Airlines woman took us straight to the Red Carpet Club, and then, in view of Sunny's dazed condition, vanished with the women's passports and tickets to attend to their seating.

We found a quiet corner of the lounge and sat down and drank some coffee, all except Sunny who was parched and needed orange juice. This was my first and only real chance to exchange words with the more or less waking Sunny.

—Well, I offered, catching her eye, you wouldn't have thought this possible a week ago.

—No, she said, her monotone hardly muted by the hopeful circumstances.

She said, I watched a little documentary about it once. The kangaroos.

I have to say I flinched at the idea. The torture implements and implements of containment stored in the cupboard, out in the shed, and under the marriage bed, while Sunny and the children watched some cheery little segment on Terra Australis and its amazing antediluvian animals.

—The female, she said, marginally warming to her topic, the female kangaroo can carry two separate children at once, not twins, each one in a separate womb.

—Only place in the world, confirmed Jacko. Only animal.

Sunny began fiddling with the clasp of a new-looking brown handbag. She addressed Delia, the nurse.

—Do you think there's time . . . you know . . . for a call to Joyce and the children?

—Of course there is, said Delia, sitting forward. We can use my AT&T card.

—Excuse me, said Sunny, managing to stand up after some thought.

Jacko and I watched them go toward the little alcoves where the credit card booths were located, along with desks for those who wanted to do serious business here.

I asked Jacko, Is Vixen Six paying for all this?

—Not bloody likely. As far as they're concerned, they've paid their $60,000. Some of the buggers don't think they got much value for it either.

—And where is the money?

—In a trust fund. She's the only one who can draw on it eh. I wondered if Bob Sondquist would want the power to draw cheques, too. But to give the old bugger his due, he didn't.

—So, is she paying for herself and the nurse?

—God, it'd cut a hole out of the only money she has. I tell you mate, I'd better get a windfall in the near future. I've paid for three bloody Connoisseur-class round-trip tickets to Australia in the past week.

And as for a wife, so for a stranger: an expensive trip to the antipodes.

—Just over $15,000 all up eh. AMEX will bleed from the bloody ears!

I watched Delia, standing, swipe her card and make the connection and pass the phone to seated Sunny. I watched Sunny frame her words into the mouthpiece with care and hesitation, yet chancing a smile, and at one stage what looked like a stutter of laughter, speaking to Joyce and/or the children. And then tears at the end, before she hung up. I noticed then that Jacko was watching too.

—You know, I found out she tried to send half the rights money to Joyce Kremmerling. You can imagine what a defence lawyer would have made of that eh! Now it doesn't matter. It's her money. She won't need much out at Burren Waters either.

I said, There's an English company, a very well-known one, Chandler-Silver, who have an option on a book of mine. The offer expires in two weeks time, at which time they have to put up rights money for the book or let it drift. It's my agent's opinion they'll buy the rights. It's not like selling a film to Universal, but it's respectable amounts. If they cough up, I'd be honoured to make a contribution. Four, five thousand dollars say.

He could see I meant it. He leaned forward and punched me sharply on the upper arm.

—You old poofter! Keep it. I might have something coming through too. But thanks. Can you come to dinner with me and some people after this?

After the call, Delia steered Sunny to the women's toilet. I had an image of Sunny being dosed with her last pre-flight medication. They were gone a long time, and Jacko became anxious and began darting up to check the departure screen. The flight was announced as being at the boarding stage; and then ten minutes passed, and passengers were urged to proceed immediately to gate so-and-so. At last Delia and Sunny presented themselves, frankly smiling.

—Shall we go? Delia asked Jacko.

Her casual competence would not go unnoticed in the Territory, where the only competence that was respected was casual. They might never let her get away. Yet she still thought it was just a trip.

We walked them to the gate. Sunny moved as

carefully as an eighty-three-year-old with suspect hips. It seemed to me that the inertia of her black body-box delayed her even here on America's threshold. In two days she would be receiving space therapy at Burren Waters, where no door was locked. What a startling and apposite idea it had been of Jacko's to fly her away.

We saw the two young women amble down the passageway to the plane. They walked together with the easy, slow familiarity of two aged sisters who occupied the one house. Once or twice, emphatically in Delia's case, absently in Sunny's, they paused to wave.

XVIII

Outside in the growing night, Jacko flexed his $15,000-lighter shoulders as if he were soothing a back injury. I looked around for the Mercedes and its fierce little driver, but an enormous white limousine — aerialed and winged — came to us. Jacko opened the door before the driver could get around to do it, and waved me in. I found myself in a dark, plush interior. Jacko entered quickly. The driver arrived in time to close the door on him, then darted back to his position at the wheel and instructed us in all the vehicle's many appurtenances — the fax, the telephone, the bar, the television. We were collecting Mr Greenspan, he said, from the East River Heliport in forty minutes time. We should just make it.

—Is Greenspan's helicopter going to land on the roof of this thing? Jacko asked.

—Well it can, sir, in remote locations. But such a landing is not authorized for urban conditions.

—Bloody shame, said Jacko.

He flicked on the television and left the bar untouched. It was evening news time. They were still debating the Sunny Sondquist case: male rights advocates were making a martyr of Kremmerling; and feminist authors still correctly said Sunny was the archetypically punished woman and that her behaviour was utterly coherent.

—But none of the bastards know she's out of here, breathed Jacko with gratification.

The prosecution of the two San Bernardino deputy sheriffs had struck technical and forensic problems, a commentator said, and might not proceed.

Any man hounded like this, argued a male rights champion, would consider taking his life the way Kremmerling had, as a statement of bravery and dissent.

Sunny could well have perished here in New York, either of her critics or of her advocates.

—It gives a person great bloody satisfaction, Jacko told me. He switched the television off. He said, You by all means hit the bar. I've got to stay clear-headed tonight. Maybe you can tell Lucy about all this.

—About you, and about paying for the women?

—No, for Christ's sake, don't tell her that. No, about tonight's meeting. It serves as a sincere token of mending my ways. I'm offering myself to Hubert Greenspan.

Even I knew that name. Flicking channels you heard it regularly. He produced, it seemed to my lay ear and eye, all the game shows.

—You're going into games.

—Damn right. I'll keep on the doorknocks in the meantime for a basic living. But Greenspan wants to try out a new idea with me. Something like Groucho Marx: light, whimsical, wise-cracking but real money involved. Durkin might come over with me. We're toying with the idea of incorporating the doorknock thing, going into people's houses by one means or another and asking them a question. A real question though: What's the capital of Hungary? Who's the president of Austria? And they could have say, three minutes to hunt through any material they have to hand — newspapers, books, encyclopaedias. Harmless fun. Harmless, totally bloody harmless.

He cuffed the upholstery behind his head.

—You were right, he said. Now I'm missing her something bloody bitter.

* * *

We were at the heliport some time before Greenspan's helicopter landed. We waited in the little lounge, looking out at the river and squinting up at the busy, blurred lights of all the city's other helicopters, this night's only stars. At last one great, dark, clattering machine loomed, threw an intense beam onto the helipad, and then descended.

I saw a spritely little man in a white suit and an Astrakhan coat jump down in the manner of an elderly person who wants to show you how athletic he is. He then helped down a blonde woman, and then a dark-haired woman who seemed more tentative, not as accustomed as the blonde to walking out from beneath the murderous blades of the thing.

Wizened and fashionable, Hubert Greenspan, who was believed to be in his mid-seventies, introduced both women. A friend of his, he said, indicating the blonde woman. And her college room-mate.

This was, as he had warned Jacko, an informal meeting. Both the women's names flew away under the noise of helicopters, and I would not quite master them all evening.

Jacko said that on the basis of the informality of the night, he'd taken the liberty of bringing his best friend and adviser: me.

We all got into the limo together. The blonde asked me, Are you a lawyer, sir?

She had a faint Southern accent, Virginia or Maryland perhaps.

—No, I said. Nothing as grand.

I felt a palpable diminution of respect, as if it was only as a lawyer that I could achieve validity at her table.

I took one of the jump seats by the television set, and the Greenspan house-guest took another, and Jacko and the blonde woman, who can't have been much older than twenty-five years, served as bookends to Greenspan.

—Well, said Greenspan, lifting his rubicund little chin. We'll all remember this night, Jacko. We'll boast at cocktail parties that we were here. We couldn't have a better response to our initial survey.

—And it's all pure fun, said Jacko.

—My son, said Greenspan, you can at last give up being television's door-to-door salesman.

Jacko didn't mind what another man might well have considered a mild slur. He beamed not at Greenspan, but first at the blonde woman, and then at her companion. The companion seemed older than Greenspan's woman friend, seemed to be one of those ageless women who exercise, perhaps have prostheses, and work at energetic jobs.

Despite himself, Jacko was beginning to twinkle in the company of the healthy old gnome and his two handsome sidekicks.

Greenspan remarked, You seemed uncertain about your contractual situation last time we talked. I can buy out anyone as long as I know what the situation is.

This was not meant as a boast, but as paternal information.

—I don't think you'll have to, Jacko told him. A crowd called Silverarts have an option on my services. They pay me fifteen hundred dollars a month option fee.

The old man laughed indulgently, and almost with the sort of thrill which goes with the observance of microscopic life.

—This is strictly a game show option with Silverarts, said Jacko. Something they had in mind for me. But there are windows of opportunity written into the agreement, and I'm in one of them now. If we can arrange things by the fifteenth of next month, it won't cost you anything.

Jacko beamed across at Greenspan's blonde companion, whose name — I had by now learned — was Tracey.

We went to Elio's, a turbulent, fashionable Italian restaurant in the East Seventies. Jacko began to gulp the white wine. Obviously it wasn't his drinking I was to commend to Lucy, but then, I wasn't in a position to commend my own.

Anyhow, the presence of the two women and the promise of an innocently procured fortune had revived Jacko. In his shining, amicable demeanour, I could see too clearly Lucy's argument borne out yet again: that marriage was to him a casual act of kindness; that he shone his countenance equally on all creatures, a wife, a liberated slave, a psychiatric nurse, a game show producer, and in particular — as it was turning out — a game show producer's golden companion named Tracey.

We all ordered, mainly pasta. Both the women,

with ambitions to be beautiful forever, asked for the angel hair without the sauce.

—I work in production for Hubert, I heard Tracey say to Jacko. You'll be working with me.

The antipasto had barely been eaten, and we were deep into a second bottle of Pouilly-Fuissé, and — after the chastening of the past two weeks — all Jacko's demons were again at large. The older, darker of Greenspan's companions began asking Jacko about his career as America's doorknocker.

He told them his favourite stories. When Gorbachev had been in town, visiting the UN and having talks with Bush — this had been two summers ago? — Jacko had found a Texan comedian who did Gorbachev impersonations, complete with the Soviet leader's South America-shaped birthmark. The man was uncanny. Jacko had envisaged taking him to the Soviet Union and walking him through Red Square dressed in an Elvis Presley costume — just to see the reaction of the Russians, he said.

He had never fulfilled that ambition, but he'd used the man for another purpose: to test the New York real estate tycoon, Gordon Renmark. The State Department had asked Renmark if he would be available for a meeting with Gorbachev, and the New York tabloids ran away with the story from that point. If anyone could infect Gorbachev with the glories of the free market, it would be Gordon Renmark, who carried the virus in a particularly rampant form. The meeting had, in any case, been cancelled, but Jacko employed the Texan Gorbachev to turn up at Renmark Towers on Fifth Avenue for the meeting anyhow. Jacko also employed some plausible looking members of Actors Equity who resembled State

Department men, and they presented themselves at the reception desk of the Towers. Mr Gorbachev, they said, had time for a quick exchange with Mr Renmark in the lobby. The schedule did not allow for elevator-time up and down. Could Mr Renmark descend to the lobby immediately?

Beyond the glass stood Dannie and Clayton and Jacko, filming it all. Renmark, appearing in a phalanx of aides, embraced the false Gorbachev. They sat on a leather lounge chair by the security desk and began to discuss the destiny of the two great powers. The comedian, however, was incapable of playing it straight, and began to insert a few of his Gorbachev punch lines. Doubt crossed Mr Renmark's face.

By this stage of Jacko's tale, the woman called Tracey was engrossed, laughing in delight. It was chiefly for her and not for Greenspan that Jacko was displaying what he considered his triumphs.

This, one of Jacko's most favoured stories, perhaps more precious to him than the story of the Wall, concludes with Renmark looking up, seeing Jacko and the others beyond the glass, trying to make up lost ground and to be quick-witted, to be whimsical in return with the *faux* Muscovite, and, above all, trying not to be enraged. The Gorbachev meeting broke off with a mixture of bitter joking and dudgeon, and Renmark's security men emerged from the building and ordered Jacko, Clayton and Dannie to lose themselves.

Renmark's publicity office issued a statement about how Mr Renmark had known it was a joke from the start, and, being the jovial fellow he was, had clowned along. The concept of Renmark clowning along caused all of us at our table in Elio's to convulse with hilarity.

From my side of the table I watched Jacko's eyes twinkle in the old way. If it hadn't already been clear, it was now: he loved tough, glittering women. He did not love accommodating, innocent women. Hence Dannie. As with locked doors, he'd been deprived of them in childhood. Their fixity was of a different species from Chloe's, their sexuality more arduously constructed.

In any case, encouraged by the room we'd all given to his first story, Jacko went on with his tale of penetrating the Malibu Colony. He had waded across a tidal creek, he and his camera crew, Clayton holding his camera above his head, Dannie riding on the shoulders of a big technician. They had first invaded the house of an English star, who had given them something close to a welcome, for there was something in Cockneys which sympathized with this intrusion of the Colony, and the star was a Cockney. He was trying to make pancakes in his kitchen and lacked an ingredient, so he sent Jacko and the camera crew, conniving in their mischief, down to the home of a soap opera actor. Jacko carried a teacup, ready to ask for the loan of some sugar.

The soap opera star used Sunday for meditation and ordered Jacko off his sundeck, and, within two days, sued him and Vixen Six. The head of Basil Sutherland's Vixen Studios in Los Angeles ordered Jacko and Durkin to desist from molesting stars the Vixen Studios might need to recruit for feature films. The footage was never shown. Jacko had wrongly supposed people would be charmed and engaged by his brave assault on the big guns across Malibu Creek.

The laughter sounded brittler and more indulgent by the time he'd told this story, and caused me to wonder if Jacko understood the margin between the creative practical joke and buffoonery.

Greenspan said, I can see we're going to have to set someone to monitor your exuberant talent, Jacko.

His tone, though part forgiving, was also part threatening.

—Oh for the day of the bladder transplant, he said then, smiling and rising, bowing and then making his way across the floor to the back of the restaurant — a brave and even sturdy figure, a player at seventy-five in the cult of youthfully deployed forcefulness.

Jacko and Tracey fell into conversation as if he had never left. The darker woman, whose name I had never mastered, turned to me.

—You should warn your friend. Hubert won't forgive him for playing to Tracey. It's understandable. Hubert's nearly as old as the century and when he has sex he has to pump his pecker up with some kind of hand pump in his scrotum.

I stared at the woman, amazed by the image.

—Tracey's just as culpable as your pal. She ought to know better. Whereas your friend is very innocent.

The old man all in white returned, and diners looked at him admiringly as if he had handfuls of benevolence to distribute. A third bottle of Pouilly-Fuissé had arrived, and the empty second was borne away. Jacko was drinking heroically, and it must have been having its effect. We all ate our pasta, and Hubert Greenspan his sweetbreads. I rose and excused myself, looking at Jacko in the hope that he would need to come with me. To my relief, Jacko — the man who penetrated all America's doors, the knowing Man from Snowy River or Burren Waters, immune to every tide except compassion, mateship, and the sexuality of alien woman — got up at once.

We entered the men's room together.

—Thank God, he said, stepping up boisterously to the urinal beside mine, a man ready, unthinkingly, to void himself of the sort of effortless stream no doubt long since vanished from Hubert Greenspan's repertoire.

—That little blonde, Tracey. She could be my producer, mate. Can you imagine it?

—No, I can't. Not if you two keep playing to each other the way you're doing.

—Come on, he chided me. I've only just got my testosterone working again.

I told him about the warning the dark-haired woman had given me.

—Oh shit, he said, addressing the plumbing above his head. She's meeting me for dinner next Tuesday.

—If I were you I'd make it lunch. And at the end, I'd shake hands.

—Christ, you sound like one of those Marist Brothers who tried to stop me going for the groin. Why don't you mention eternal bloody hell-fire?

I was angered. I zipped up with such fury that I caught a corner of my shirt. I promptly amended that.

—Lucy's only just left, I said. Most people have a mourning period. How long was yours? Three minutes?

—Jesus, that's low, he said.

He was emphatic but not yet angry himself. I wanted to make him angry.

—Lucy, Delia, this one . . . Tracey . . . They're all just the one continuum of flesh to you . . .

—Hold hard! he warned me. I'm not thinking of begetting a sodding dynasty with this woman eh. I just want to go to dinner. And God forbid I should be so fortunate as to be allowed, through the generosity of any girl, to get in a bit of good old horizontal folk-dancing!

The truth behind my fury was that Maureen had had telephone conversations with Lucy in Australia. Arriving one humid dawn, Lucy had felt severely exposed beneath the bright, frank Australian day. Recounting it on the telephone, sending her sorrow up to a satellite over the Equator and then down to New York, she wept easily. Lucy told Maureen a great deal and confessed she was also speaking regularly to Chloe and to her own mother who had moved down to Melbourne. Maureen said tremors overtook Lucy's voice in mid-sentence. Such was the news of grieving, lovely Lucy. While, of course, Jacko laughed in Elio's.

I said, You really are an utter prick, Jacko. Despite everything. Despite the airfares for Sunny and her nurse. And you're not even a cunning prick. You're a dumb bastard! I don't know why I spend time with you, but I don't think I'll be doing much more of it.

There isn't any reason to recount his pretty explicit reply. He walked out, and by the time I got back to the table, he was saying a polite good night to Tracey and the dark-haired woman and Hubert. A luncheon date with Tracey had been openly arranged. In the meantime she wanted to be faxed the terms of his agreement with Silverarts to verify that he was available for hire. Perhaps, she said, he should bring his agent and his attorney to the lunch as well.

He didn't say goodnight to me. I made an embarrassed explanation to the company — Jacko lived in a different part of town. I thanked Mr Greenspan and left to find my own way home.

In the taxi I felt more loss than was warranted. Lucy was gone. And now Jacko. In fact, at one point I found myself reciting under my breath snatches of Jacko's holy text.

—He hails from Snowy River, up by Kosciusko's side,
　　Where the hills are twice as steep and twice as rough,
　　Where a horse's hoofs strike firelight from the flint stones every stride,
　　The man that holds his own is good enough.
　　And the Snowy River riders on the mountains make their home,
　　Where the river runs those giant hills between;
　　I have seen full many horsemen since I first began to roam,
　　But nowhere yet such horsemen have I seen.

It was raining very heavily in New York's friendless night.

XIX

Maureen and I began our plans for going home as the New York summer set in, as classes were ending in a fug of New York humidity, and the violet trolleys of NYU were delivering bashful graduates and over-dressed parents to Washington Square. Academics and writers I met along West Fourth Street and Broadway were planning summer holidays in places I had seen only in winter: Vermont, say, and Maine. Our summer place was a beach twelve thousand miles away in the mild Australian winter.

Jacko and I had talked stiffly now and then, and even ran into each other in that fairly circumscribed quarter of New York. He would always explain his lack of contact by saying that taping the quiz shows in Los Angeles kept him pretty hectic. But in fact, his timetable was no different from what it had been in the days we used to meet in the Odeon for frequent confessional sessions. He was still doing four door-knocks a week in New York. Whenever I saw his morning television shenanigans, I was impressed by the way he always looked so fresh despite all, so full of zany spriteliness. The act of intruding seemed to give him perpetual vigour.

One night during our last few weeks in New York, Maureen and I met Jacko at a black-tie dinner to open an exhibition of Aboriginal artists from Central Australia and Arnhem Land.

The male and female carvers and painters of the tropics and the desert were guests of honour at this dinner, a strainingly odd affair. I felt silly at having taken on the ridiculous duty of wearing a dinner suit. Maureen and I sat at a table with some of the thin, blue-black women artists from the Australian tropics, who wore their own dazzling batiks, and with two middle-aged sisters called Dotty and Mary Marble, who came from the Tanami Desert southwest of Burren Waters, who knew how cold the night could fall, and so wore large cardigans.

All the male artists were seated at other tables, but were not dressed so differently from the stockmen on Burren Waters, which made us stuffed-shirt Caucasians look sillier still.

All these dozen or so visiting artists had — at the start of the dinner — proceeded into the dining room to the applause of all the people in black suits and long dresses. Taking their seats, the desert and tropic painters had looked both shy and composed, tentative and worldly. I hoped the dinner crowd knew that many of them — including the Marble sisters — had achieved international repute, were used to having their work shown in cities far from home, and sometimes travelled accompanying their work to fashionable places. Some of the men in the stockmen's clothes and the Arnhem Land women in batik, whose specialties were bark paintings, were accustomed to seeing four- or even five-figure prices put upon their work.

I noticed Jacko at a table across the room from ours. His black tie was loosened and untethered, and he sat with a woman who was not Tracey, who was probably younger in fact, perhaps as young as Lucy. She leaned forward, talking energetically to her companion. Jacko grinned when her speech ended in a spate of more thorough and childlike laughter than worldly Dannie or Tracey would ever have permitted themselves.

Maureen, who thought that having got out of my friendship with Jacko with my health intact I ought to let it go at that, suggested I should use the distance between our tables as a reasonable excuse not to talk to him.

But I was pretty sure he had seen us.

So against Maureen's advice, and driven by more of a desire to plug myself back into the Emptor melodrama than I'd care to own up to, I went across to the table.

*   *   *

It was a Vixen Six crowd. Dannie wasn't there but Durkin was, together with his new American wife. Bringing Basil Sutherland's style of television to New York had made its inroads on Durkin's boisterous marriages as well.

Jacko introduced me to the girl, Angela his new doorknock producer. I made loose, over-eager, hollow promises about meeting up in the middle-future, when I came back to New York at the start of winter, when my book on China would be published, and so on. I even heartily invited the two women, Jacko's companion and Durkin's wife, both of whom I'd never seen before this evening. Such lengths I went to to pretend to Jacko, such lengths Jacko went to to pretend that we were as we had always been. We said sentimental things about the places I'd soon be in: about various Sydney beaches and places around the harbour, about eating hurriedly before the opera or ballet, or before one of Evans's plays performed by the Sydney Theatre Company in the flank of the great white building facing the Harbour Bridge. Dining at Kable's say, or Bilson's or Beppi's, or at Doyle's out at Watson's Bay. The world, including New York, might have its casual geography, but Sydney Harbour had its ordained geography, engraved — or you would have thought so from the way we were talking — on our DNA.

And then Jacko became less perfervid, dropped his voice and said, You ought to go and see the old woman.

—Chloe?

—All jokes aside, you ought to go up there. I believe it's quite a scene. Women's bloody commune. That's the other thing that's changed. Chloe says my bloody brother, Petie, has a thing going for Delia. Sunny's down to half the medication she was on when she left here. When she's not hanging around the kitchen drinking tea with Chloe, she trails behind the bloody helicopter pilot, the one called Boomer. She's become a real helicopter groupie by all reports.

This outcome, however, seemed to please him very much.

—Three women. That doesn't exactly make a commune, Jacko, I said.

—We're talking four, he said. Lucy's gone up there.

—What about the cello? I asked.

Burren Waters was not a credible venue for a virtuoso cellist.

—She's put off the cello. She's doing some paintings. Naturally I take the blame for interrupting her career.

—It could be so, Jacko, I told him.

But he didn't react. By now he expected me to champion Lucy.

—It's a question of what she wants, isn't it? If she really wanted the cello thing, she'd do it no matter what.

—Perhaps, I conceded without any enthusiasm.

—She'll probably tell her problems to some sensitive stockman too.

—Why not, Jacko? You've managed to find a few friendly ears yourself.

—Ha bloody ha. Go and see the old woman eh. Make sure you're back for the fall television series. I'm going to be a national idol.

I laughed despite myself.

—You'll be even more bloody uncontrollable.

—Damn right, son, he told me. But back to old Chloe. She's got this idea you've cut her off the way Bickham did.

—Why would I cut her off? I spoke to her on the phone just recently.

—Yeah. But did she tell you about the politics eh?

—She did. You did too.

—The Senate. She wasn't elected. But she got the wind in her sails, you know.

When I had first heard this, about the Senate, I had thought that she must have stood for the National Party, the party of rural interests. That would certainly put her on Bickham's blind side, even though all his family except him were probably members.

Now, from the airy way Jacko spoke about it, I began to suspect otherwise.

—Whose platform did she stand on?

—Some sort of cattleman's party, it was.

—Anti-land rights, I suppose?

—Well, she and old Jack always have been.

—So she doesn't want to be written off by the minor novelist eh? The way she was by the major one?

—No. That's right, mate. She doesn't.

* * *

Turning aside further still from Angela his new producer, he began to tell me his version of how Chloe came to be political.

When it began, Frank had completed his first two years in jail. And Chloe was down in Sydney most of the time still, visiting him regularly and cooking for Bickham and Khalil. Khalil himself was now rather ill with hypertension.

The first problem: Bickham chastised her in his austere way for being too attentive to Frank. And it had to be admitted, said Jacko, backing up what Chloe had herself told me, in jail terms Frank was prospering. He had been moved into low security at some timber farm in the Hunter Valley. Here he'd established a friendship with a very literary safecracker. Frank was permitted to have his sound system in his cell. His ambition on release was to attend fine arts courses three days a week at the Power Institute.

The news that came to Chloe in Sydney from Burren Waters was not so promising. One of Chloe's friends in Hector wrote and urged her to come home. Stammer Jack was more or less openly cohabiting with a woman called Muriel from the black stockmen's quarters, a young Aboriginal woman whose husband was working a long way away at the bauxite mines in the north of Western Australia, near Exmouth Gulf. Chloe called Stammer Jack, who made his normal fricative, inelegant evasions and half-denials. Almost at once, the new bookkeeper at Burren Waters, a young fugitive from paying alimony in Queensland, contacted Chloe and told her Stammer Jack was hitting the rum and had got violent with a few of the stockmen, even once swinging a punch at Petie, Jacko's man-of-few-words elder brother and Stammer Jack's most dutiful son.

This was, in a way, nothing less than she had expected of Stammer Jack. She turned homewards to Burren Waters in a fine but not unfamiliar fury, to sort out the problem her addiction to her jailed son and Bickham had caused for Stammer Jack.

She found that Stammer Jack had been keeping Muriel in the house, in the room which had once belonged to Helen, Chloe's daughter. This certainly violated the limits of behaviour she had set down for Stammer Jack when she'd gone south to Sydney. Returned to Burren Waters, she hurled Muriel's few items of clothing and possessions down the front steps, where they must have lain some time on the excessively watered green lawn of the homestead. She stamped down to the wood-and-corrugated iron shacks of the black stockmen's quarters and told one of Muriel's uncles to get her off Burren Waters and over to her husband. The Wodjiri stockmen of the old school had a long experience of such imperious demands, and said they would do it. It was an improbable assignment to get Muriel from Burren Waters to the Indian Ocean, but the stockmen and their families seemed to rally on demand to cross great dry stretches of wilderness in old Holden cars most of us wouldn't trust to get us to the supermarket. Lanky, delicate-ankled Muriel was gone from Burren Waters overnight.

Very soon after this salvage of the Emptor marriage, Petie and the helicopter pilot Boomer were surprised to find a group of elderly Aboriginal men camping by a plug of hard sandstone in the northwest of Burren Waters' cattle lease. This was one of the more notable features of the Burren Waters run, a fiefdom which was for the most part anciently flat. They landed and discovered not only that what Stammer Jack Emptor called a *bloody anthropologist* was with the old men, but that it was Doctor Fitzgerald of the University of Western Australia, the man who lived with Jacko's sister Helen in Perth.

The old men in the encampment were Wodjiri, relatives in fact of people who worked as stockmen on Burren Waters. So they certainly had some pre-Emptor connection with the land.

Soon enough — Jacko didn't tell me how soon — a notice came from the Northern Land Council and the Aboriginal Land Rights Court in Darwin indicating that a claim for the excision of a sacred site from the bulk of Burren Waters had been made by the traditional owners, the old men Boomer sighted from the helicopter.

* * *

In my time in the Northern Territory, I wondered why cattle people seemed to hate excisions. If the excision claim was validated in court, the Aboriginals involved in the rite connected to that place would have right of way into Burren Waters, and the plug of sandstone and a small amount of space around it would become Aboriginal freehold land. The votaries might start bush fires, or consort with the Burren Waters stockmen and, to quote Stammer Jack, *give 'em ideas*.

It is hard to sit inside another person's brain, but it was hard also to understand Stammer Jack's passion over this matter. His cattle run seemed so vast and the excision claims so modest in square mile terms. Those Aboriginals who sought excisions did not seem to me to be making savage inroads upon the cattle stations.

Maybe it was the principle of the thing which appalled the cattle people. Maybe it was simply that they were used to kingly occupation of large spaces.

In any case, I had heard Chloe rant about it occasionally. Miserable, vexatious bastards, I had heard her fume one night. Though on enquiry, it was not the Aboriginals themselves who were to blame, but the city liberals and the shit-stirring anthropologists who *put 'em up to it*.

Jacko himself told me he wasn't sure what mixture of pride and threat to land coincided in Chloe to make her do that silly bloody thing she did. The cattlemen of the North End and the Centre formed something disastrously named the White Defence Party.

Jacko said, If they hadn't been such blithering old

bastards, they would have at least chosen a better name.

Their manifesto said that they bore no ill-will to Aboriginal Australians. Their opposition was only to those (anthropologists, lawyers) who self-indulgently sought either to give themselves importance or to suck up to misinformed foreign opinion by indulging Aboriginal claims at the expense of the well-being of the great cattle industry. The very name of the party Chloe had joined, however, made a nonsense of such fine print subtleties.

They wanted someone in the Territory to run for the Senate. They knew they had enough support to take votes away from the established parties. They nominated three candidates. Chloe, still in a fury over the excision matter and Muriel, agreed to be number two.

Bickham wrote her a savage letter. No understanding from that quarter, said Jacko.

—You'd have thought he had more *savoir* bloody *faire*, Jacko told me. West of the Blue Mountains, nothing's easily explained in city terms. She wrote him some sort of sad but firm letter back. She got over it. After all, she got to ask him a few more questions than most people had. Anyhow, back to the first subject. Why don't you go up and see her? Prove you haven't dumped her too.

I shook my head.

—You damned Emptors don't ask for little favours.

—No. We don't, do we eh?

—See Chloe? Or the others? Who do you want to hear from, Jacko? Lucy? Sunny? Delia perhaps?

—The whole bloody *ménage* eh. Why don't you?

I could see Maureen across the room, actively conversing with one of the Marble sisters.

—It's too much to ask, I told Jacko.

Yet I already knew I was going.

* * *

The night before Maureen and I left New York for the summer, I excused myself and foolishly went down to Tribeca to say goodbye to Jacko. Ringing at his bell in the cold doorway between the mercantile glitter of the Korean grocery and the warm lights of Mary O'Reilly's, I heard an Australian voice, a woman's on the intercom.

She said, The Emptors. Yes?

I said, Oh. Is Jacko in?

—Oh yes. I'll press the button and you open it when you hear it buzzing.

Her instructions were so explicit that, quite clearly, in the more innocent world from which this voice came, such electronic arrangements were not needed. As I climbed the stairs, I wondered if it was one of the Logans, the one he said he had loved. Had she come to New York for a sabbatical now that Lucy was gone?

An athletic-looking woman was waiting at the head of the stairs, the door held open. She pointed Chloe Emptor's face at me.

—Gidday. Helen. Jacko's sister.

She closed the door behind me and took my overcoat, saying, Jesus, this New York's a bit of a shock to the system eh.

She was smaller-boned than Jacko, and when she spoke Chloe's grin appeared, dazzling and brief. She wore a track suit, but I could see the compactness of her figure. All Stammer Jack's hulking DNA had been expended on Jacko and Petie; Frank and Helen had picked up Chloe's lost beauty.

She led me through the open spaces of the loft towards the kitchen which was partitioned off with glass bricks. We found Jacko by the stove. He was wrapped in a bathrobe and was cooking omelettes with some pretensions of culinary style and much wrist-flicking. A tall, very thin man, red-bearded, fetched milk and butter from the refrigerator and was setting places at the kitchen bench. The place was so busy that there wasn't room for any air of mourning for Lucy, yet a picture of Lucy and Jacko in front of the Grand Tetons was still stuck by a magnet to the refrigerator. Either he was very busy, or else he suffered from no anguish, no nostalgia for Lucy at all.

—This is Fitzie, Jacko said over his shoulder, both hands occupied, one with the teflon skillet, the other with the egg-lifter. Fitzie and Helen are an item.

The tall, red-headed man shook my hand with little force.

—Fitzie and Helen are also bloody vegetarian abstainers, so I'm glad you're here. We can open some wine.

Jacko began cracking even more eggs and cutting up more cheddar, determined I would eat with them. Since his dawns were still devoted to trespass, he was likely to eat a breakfast omelette at any time of the day.

We sat by the window which had the view of Coghlan's. Jacko ate ferociously, talking with his mouth full. Fitzie sliced his omelette into small penitential morsels and Helen told us of her average experiences that day on the subway as if they were tales from the New Guinea highlands. You knew from the Chloe-like energy with which she told them that many people were going to hear these stories back in Australia. It was strange to see her with pale, lank Fitzie.

Fitzie, a professor of anthropology at the University of Western Australia, had met Helen in the pub in Hector, and she had followed him back to Perth. Fitzie had come to New York now to give some seminars at City College. It was on the way to City College and back that Helen had had her subway experiences.

—I'm going up to Burren Waters myself, I told her.

—Good for you, mate, said Jacko.

For Fitzie's sake and Helen's, and as a joke, he said, I think he's like old Merv. He's got a thing going with the old woman. With big Chloe. He's the bloke who got Chloe in with Michael Bickham.

Fitzie's cool, herbivorous eyes swept across me.

—That must have been a meeting made in bloody heaven, said Helen, uttering playful contempt for her mother in her mother's voice. We'll be up there too sometime over the winter. Getting ready for the excision hearing.

—Oh hell, said Jacko. Yes.

—The Wodjiri have made a claim on a place called Mongil, said Fitzie. I'm advocate for them.

—That's right on Burren Waters leasehold, isn't it? asked Jacko.

—That's right, said Fitzie. They're claiming a two square mile excision. But they're willing to let Burren Waters' cattle graze there.

Jacko began frowning.

—But the old woman tells me, he murmured, that stockmen won't be able to go in there to get them out.

Fitzie, mincing his omelette with his fork, said quietly, They'll be able to drive them out aerially if they want.

Helen said, Or wait for them to come out. Jesus, they've got cattle on Burren Waters they don't even know about.

Jacko made a mouth. It was obvious he had little time for his sister. The way he asked his loaded questions in a false-naive voice made the conversation spiky.

He put down his plate and said, Well look, you know this will upset Chloe. Why don't you talk them into picking some other spot? Eh Fitzie? Why don't you do this legal work and give evidence for another tribe?

Fitzie said, I know it's delicate as regards family and all, but the Wodjiri are my field of expertise. This is a massively important site, Jacko. It literally means the earth to these people. It'll have no commercial impact on Chloe and Stammer Jack at all. I just wish they'd yield a bit on it, that's all. It's possible to arrange these things by consensus, you know. There's no need at all for a hearing.

Jacko turned to Helen and said, You still want to get even with her, Helen.

Helen made a clicking noise with her lips and put down her plate of omelette.

—Well, said Jacko, I reckon you ought to pick on some other bloody cattle baron, rather than old Jack.

Chloe thinks her kids are poison, and this'll tend to prove her point.

Helen went through a looking-away-and-gathering-of-one's-feelings process. Then, still staring out at Coghlan's she said, This will be good for them, Jacko. This'll expand their view of the question, and Christ knows they need it. I'm not doing this out of spite. It's a case that has to be won. For everyone's sake.

Fitzie put his plate down and asked quietly, Jacko, would you prefer we stayed somewhere else?

—Shit no, said Jacko. Just the same, I don't care what your motives are, Helen. Chloe won't understand them, so it'll just seem cruel.

I wondered did he think all this would also rebound somehow on his safely removed Sunny and Delia and Lucy?

Helen said, The Wodjiri lost absolutely everything. No treaty, no money paid. *Terra* bloody *nullius*. No one's land. And now it's Stammer Jack's land and he can't afford to give up a square mile or two of it to keep a culture alive? I can't believe that!

—Yeah, well, said Jacko.

I was very pleased to stand up then and plead packing, and to finish my wine as a token of serious departure. On my way across the enormous living room towards the door, Helen came with me and told me that if ever I was in Western Australia she hoped I would come and talk to some of Fitzie's students.

It was the last I was to see of Jacko that season — in a bathrobe, gulping omelette and harried by his sister, and doing some harrying in return.

X X

I realize now that my method of re-entry into Sydney was based on a simple plan: call Evans the playwright and his wife and ask them out to dinner with Maureen and myself, and then call Oscar Mulcahy and Hefty and make a time with them. In his calm, deep voice Evans could give you a total rundown on everything that happened in Australia during your absence. He did it without malice or a skewed view, and with hardly a touch of the waspishness which had made his plays famous.

Oscar gave a perhaps more partisan rundown. Like Bickham, Oscar ran a little more to jeremiads than weighing and measuring.

To Mulcahy, of course, Frank Emptor's crimes were simply another instance of the kind of thing you could expect from the sybarites of the opera, the ballet and the theatre.

—I wish I had a hundred dollars, said Oscar, for every time I gave the bastard his last sip of Château d'Yquem.

Evans wanted to write a play about Frank Emptor. He thought it was, in its way, a riot of a story.

It was peculiar, but, once I had spoken to these two, I felt I was thoroughly at home again, in the finest, most vinegary small-large pond in the world.

While I settled into Sydney that winter I found

myself watching the Darwin and Alice Springs temperatures on the news every night. The monsoon season with its berserk humidity had long ended in the Top End, and in the deserts of the Centre the night temperatures were nudging freezing. Burren Waters was stuck between these two, on the desert's hip, on the cusp of the tropics. It was impossible to look at the map and believe that all these temperatures were affecting the four women of whom no great amount had been heard, impossible to believe that Sunny Sondquist was breathing that air.

I was slightly nervous about confessing my intention to go up there to my wife. The problem I saw was not at all that I was going to investigate what had befallen the four women; it was more that I didn't want her to believe that I was going up there purely because Jacko had asked me. Even though that was pretty much the case.

It was hard times for the newspaper business in Sydney now, since the great junk bond over-valuing of the early '80s, but I talked a magazine editor I knew into sending me back to do a piece on the Northern Territory revisited. The fee would slightly more than cover my airfare and car hire.

My wife was too used to me to be fooled by my expressed journalistic intent. Just the same, I had found the equation by which I could go to Burren Waters without anyone losing face.

I managed to get a more or less direct flight. The long air route north-west towards Alice crossed the bare plains of what was, we are told, a receded ancient sea bed. The Finke lay empty and serpentine — some experts' nomination for the oldest river on the planet.

From the window where I sat it seemed that the striations of the Simpson Desert looked sullen and heat-struck, secure in their reputation as a furnace even in winter. The question was: What had Sunny Sondquist made of this? Had the grave grey and tan of these spaces confirmed or soothed her fear of the immense?

A little turboprop aircraft took me from Alice to Hector. It touched down at Hector's airstrip amidst the scrub and the tan mud ant-heaps tall as a man. I had a car ordered, and a four-hour journey ahead of me. After I drove through Hector, past the lines of disoriented Aboriginals who spent their days on the town's pavements, I entered flat, scrubby, semi-desert country. It was country which, but for the ghost of Larson, I would have thought of as featureless.

I had forgotten to buy a supply of water in Hector, but consoled myself with the idea that the long road to Burren Waters from the highway was signposted. After three hours' driving, a great swathe of red-grey sand veered away from the highway. The signpost to Burren Waters pointed un-ambiguously southwards along it.

In this country of rubble and sand and rubberbush, you could wonder what atavistic love of cattle made the English, Scots and Irish introduce them to such an unlikely venue. But someone had told me the country had been different before the hard-mouthed, hard-hoofed cattle ran here. Elderly Aboriginals who returned to their home territories wept to see the desolation the cattle had wrought.

On the dirt track into Burren Waters, I came at last to an unmarked fork. I paused and considered things. The leftward track seemed a lesser one, so I surmised that the right one led to Burren Waters homestead. I took it, dragging my great dragon of red dust behind me. I watched it in the rear-vision mirror. How solid the cloud was, and yet it threw a red mist of some delicacy over the rubberbush, the melaleuca and the desert boronia on either side of my wake.

But even spending half my time looking in the rear-vision mirror, I began to notice how my track was dwindling in front of me. It dipped into a dry water course, but seemed to widen hopefully beyond. Perhaps I could turn there if I chose to, and return to the fork and explore the other way a little. Because the dry creek bed looked slightly sandy, I got out and let some air out of the tyres of my hired Holden. All the truck drivers who delivered beer and groceries to the remote settlements did this when faced with possible bog in dry river beds.

The act of deflating the tyres one by one, making sure with a small pressure meter I carried that it was no more than five pounds per square inch, gave me a perhaps false but certainly grateful sense of being in control of my environment. I drove into the dry creek bed and almost at once felt my back wheels begin to spin in that terrible way.

—Okay, I said. Bugger you!

I got out and was pleased to see things were not hopeless. I fetched my tyre lever and dug the front side of the back tyres free, and then I went looking for branches of acacia, breaking them loose from the bushes and laying them in my tracks. I added into the branches some slabs of rock I found in the scrub on either side of the trail. It struck me now, of course, that even if I extracted myself, it would be very difficult to make a return journey. I had to go forward. If I tried to back out, I would only embed myself more deeply. At least if I went forward I would be more visible, up there on the far side.

—You know how to behave in the bush, I told myself, and the words now felt like hot stones in my mouth.

I tried to fight a surge of anger against Jacko. He had, in a way, harried me into coming here. He'd set my mind on finding the women, and not on practical things. And I had broken all the rules. Though Chloe knew I was on my way, I had not called Burren Waters from Hector about my expected time of arrival. I had not brought water. I had no way of replacing the water which dealing with the bog had taken out of me.

When I tried to drive out of the dry bed, coaxing the engine in first gear, inviting the back wheels to take purchase, all I felt was that malicious spinning again. The stern of the car shifted sideways, settling itself deeper still into sand.

Never leave the car, they say.

The sane ghost of Larson said, Never wander away. The Wodjiri will follow your tracks from the 'abandoned vehicle, but they'll find you dead and bloated.

I got out of the car, looked at the rear and front wheels bogged to the axles, and went round to the shady side and hunched in the sand. I raised my eyes to the sky. I wanted to inform the firmament that a month ago I had been listening to the jazz saxophonist of Lower Broadway, and no one else who had stood within reach of that charming and plausible and full-throated instrument was now facing *this*. They might be sweltering in the subway, but there was a cool 7-Up in a dispensing machine available to them at the close of their small journey.

It would be beyond the belief of most of my colleagues at NYU that I had — again to use the Territorian word — *perished* so casually, in such a melodramatic way, by combining a few simple oversights.

My tongue sat in my mouth like a stone, but I made myself get the book I was reading out of my suitcase in the boot, sit down again and read. It was *Madame Bovary*, a good book to be found dead with. Dr Bovary's infatuated wife had got up in the summer pre-dawn, and left her nightcap and sleeping husband, and travelled through the pastures and the crops of summer flowers to encounter her noble lover, who was already bored with her ardent breath and many letters. This was the sort of book a person read too young, the sort of book you always said you'd read if asked, but about which, because when you'd read it you lacked the right emotional gearing, you knew you were somehow lying.

While I read a few pages of the thing, a map of the country around me built in my brain. I was certain now I should have taken the other fork, but the two roads couldn't have diverged far from each other yet. The other one might be only four or five miles eastward. Surely no one could *perish* in five miles?

Other bush questions came up, though considering them didn't give me the same sense of being an insider to the rules of the Territory that my deflating of the tyres had. Should I go now, when there might be some chance of day-time traffic — Stammer Jack or the accountant or some of the Aboriginal stock-men might have been to Hector. Or elders might be deporting a Chloe-banned woman like Muriel. Or should I wait till dusk, when it was cooler?

I told myself that I needed to rest, and I lay in the hot shade and flung poor old Flaubert aside. But my brain was driving away feverishly, sifting possibilities and settling on no option, not even in any definite way on the option of staying where I was.

A further map had formed in my head. Was there a road to the west as well? I seemed to remember one. I'd once flown with Boomer, passing a series of tracks westward, and on some of them stood the occasional stockman's huts for use during mustering. I believed Boomer had said there were rudimentary supplies there, and water tanks.

So it was not cool-headedness which kept me by my rented Holden. It was the equal pull of these two maps. I was stuck mid-way between them, in a furious inertia, like a nail halfway between two magnets. I could feel that coarse toad, the tongue, bloating to take up all available room. I saw myself leathered.

I remembered a Northern Territory cop I'd known once who had been looking for a German gone missing in a four-wheel drive somewhere west of Ayers Rock. He hadn't found the man on the first trip, nor on the second one the following month, nor on the third. But on the fourth he found him on the Sandy Blight track, a road which ran north along the Northern Territory-Western Australian border. The cop believed that the German's radiator had clogged with spinifex grass seeds, which had caused it to boil again and again, and the German traveller had used up all his water feeding the radiator. When dying of thirst, he had shot himself in the neck. By the time the cop found him the sun had completely tanned him. He sat upright, the colour of mahogany, his flesh tough as a cricket ball. From the wound in his neck, said the cop, a beetle had busily emerged.

It seemed I fell asleep, floating out in severe space, in air of such low gravity that the blood boiled at any suggestion of warmth. When I woke, the dust amongst the rubberbushes was turning mauve. I acknowledged too late that Larson was right. This was miraculous, this colour, but it couldn't be touched. It had no moist connection with my body.

—We come to things too late! I told myself aloud, but the lips were no longer wieldy enough to make the sentence.

I wanted to see my wife, so I could dissuade her from marring herself with hatred of·Jacko.

The air felt soft, the earth was dry to the last syllable of its core, and death and oblivion came clattering down to suck me away. I cried aloud for my wife and daughter. I was an antipodean martyr. I had died for mateship. The mateship of the most disreputable, casual, promiscuous and whimsical male. He had won me over by attacking the Wall with a jackhammer, and now I was dying, as men do, for the sake of casual friendship.

But so noisily and with such a clatter and maelstrom of dust.

The shadow of death perched ten yards away. It was blue in fact and had *Burren Waters Cattle Company Pty. Ltd.* written in dusty yellow on its flanks. It settled, its clatter died to a whine, and Boomer Webb, Stammer Jack's Vietnam veteran helicopter pilot, descended from it, leaving a woman seated inside.

The Emptors had influenced his idiom and he

uttered words that were not in tune with his accent.

—Jesus, you silly buggers never travel with water eh.

The blades of the beast turned languidly now. You could have stopped them with a finger. I picked up *Madame Bovary*, and Boomer extracted my two bags from the open boot.

Through my dry lips, I pushed forward a few stony words. I didn't understand myself what they were.

He said, No, listen, we can come and get the bloody car tomorrow.

Tall, and holding both my bags in one hand, he hauled me up with the other. My head hung. I could see his dusty boots.

He said, Jesus, another day out here and you could have been in big trouble.

I raised my chin by an act of will. The woman in the co-pilot's seat turned her face to me. The features were familiar. She wore an Akubra, and that confused me for a second. It was Sunny Sondquist, with some Burren Waters' protein having filled her out and put some colour in her. Her fuller hair in particular made her hard to recognize. And though I knew her so well, she looked at me without recognizing me. I would have liked to have told her that I was the one who took her to the airport, but again my tongue was too unwieldy. Boomer loaded my bags into the back seat of the machine and then unstrapped one of those hessian bush water bags from a bar above the skids of the helicopter. I could taste the sweet bore water before he had even undone the lid. I had taken two such water bags to the Horn of Africa with me, and the Africans had strapped them to the front of

their trucks and been enthused by the way the movement of the air itself cooled the water inside. I started
to drink Boomer's delightful water, and he took it
away before I was half finished.

—You'll start chundering if you have too much, he
told me gently.

He motioned me into the back of the helicopter
behind his own seat. He strapped me in while Sunny
watched, and I strove to define all that was so different about her. Of course, it was that I was the victim
now, and she was in the novel situation of looking at
me in the way the saved look at victims. She was
feeling the interest the saved feel, the well-watered.

I said, I took you to the airport the day Jacko took
you and Delia there. In New York.

She said, I wasn't too clear in the head then.

I told her my name and she nodded.

—How's Jacko, she asked, almost dutifully, as you
ask about someone you hardly know.

—He's going to become famous. A game show.
Hubert Greenspan. Jacko's been found by the king of
game shows.

—He deserves it, said Sunny Sondquist judiciously.
What did you say your name was?

I told her again. Boomer climbed into the pilot's
seat and slammed the door.

—Hi, Pudgy, he said, winking at Sunny Sondquist.

He put on his headphones, and, contentedly, she
put on hers. He let her punch a particular button and
there was that extraordinary exhaust scream. We rose
straight up and I saw the sun still high to the west,
and then darkness milling to the east. Sunny Sondquist turned to me and indicated I should put the
headphones on. When I did, Boomer said, Jesus, if

anything had happened to you Chloe would've been really ropable!

We veered away towards the shadowy hemisphere of the earth. Canted across the sky, we soon crossed another track, broad and pink in the late day.

Boomer listed the helicopter over even further so that I could get a good view of it.

—That's the road you should've taken, he informed me.

Sunny too was glancing casually past Boomer. An accustomed road, you'd think she knew it thoroughly and had for a long time.

Sunny Sondquist said something like, Give us the corkscrew.

In the earphones I heard Boomer chuckling. He asked me how I was. The water had made me queasy, but I told him I was fine.

—Okay, he said. You'll enjoy this.

The machine now slewed violently westward, away from the Burren Waters road. I struggled to keep my stomach and my consciousness. We raged upwards towards some perilous zenith. The machine baulked then, as if it had reached exactly the square metre of sky Boomer had aimed it for. This seemed to be almost a zone of silence, for the engines couldn't be heard. But then our tail tipped up, leisurely as a dolphin's, and we went gyrating and corkscrewing down the sky. And Sunny had urged this on Boomer, this mad blending of earth and sky, this crazy gyre aimed — as our ascent had been at one square metre of sky — at one terrible square metre of earth. While my brain ached and bile entered my mouth and one of my bags fell on me, I could hear Sunny laughing. For the second time in an hour and a half, I decided this was my last dusk. Whereas before I had been a martyr for mateship, now I was offered up for the sake of Sunny's liberated merriment.

In ten seconds I would find out what Larson had found out in *his* fallen helicopter. Boomer, of course, didn't intend us to hit the ground, but he had done it frequently enough before. I knew that once he had fallen on Stammer Jack's ankle.

This time, though, we levelled out and I swallowed the acid in my mouth and held my head. I could still hear Sunny Sondquist's hilarity in the headphones.

— Gets her every time, yelled Boomer.

Now we were progressing in level flight at an altitude which I surmised to be five feet above the tops of the rubberbushes. I saw the sales ring where Stammer Jack sold his quarter horses come veering towards us. Boomer climbed a little as a courtesy, so that the homestead compound would not be coated in unnecessary dust. Then we descended onto bare gravel beyond the mustering yards.

Sunny continued to sit still in her seat even after Boomer had cut the engines. They both seemed to have their ears cocked to the communally savoured whine of the rotor. When she did dismount, she came politely round to my side of the helicopter and waited for me to descend as well. I thought of how she must have treated Kremmerling with that degree of politeness, maintaining a composed air while waiting for the next torment.

— You didn't mind that, did you? she asked me.

— No, I lied. I think it cleared my head.

She covered her mouth with her hand and laughed. Her skin had changed of course. She had a good skin for this climate. Chloe's sun had turned Sunny Sondquist's arms olive.

—I wonder could I have another mouthful of Boomer's water?

She went and unlatched the bag from its bar and offered it to me. I drank again.

—Not too much, she counselled me, like a veteran of the bush.

She said, You're staying in the stockmen's quarters, just near where Lucy is.

She had the accommodation map in her head too.

Boomer and I toted my luggage past the aircraft and equipment hangars, across the red-dust square of Emptorville — at one end ·the homestead and at the other, the infinite west where Boomer had so recently tried to crash. Boomer opened a screen door and led me into the red-brick quarters I'd once shared with Larson. I went to the wash basin and drank some water from the tap with as little an appearance of greed as I could manage. I heard Boomer behind me telling Sunny to take me over to see Chloe. He himself had to go and see Jack Emptor.

—Have a beer with you later, he promised me.

* * *

As she led me up to the house, Sunny asked, Have you ever been up here before?

She put the question like an owner, as if it was startling that I had made it all this distance, and not nearly so startling that she had.

I told her I'd been a few times, that I had at one stage known Chloe better than I'd known Jacko.

—She's not so pleased with Jacko, said Sunny with a slow smile.

—No, but you should be. You're a different woman here.

Sunny blinked and looked around her. She said, I've been waiting for something like this all my life. This is what California was meant to be like except it wasn't. I'm just pleased I'm out of all that.

—Any visa problems? I asked, knowing that like America, Australia, once so open to migrants, was so restrictive now.

—Well, she said, I've got six months. And anything can happen. Chloe rang up some senator in Canberra and asked about asylum, but he said it didn't apply in this case.

We mounted the stairs, passed Chloe's library on the verandah, and Sunny knocked on the front door.

After no more than ten seconds, Chloe came, grinning.

It was the old Chloe from long before the encounter with Bickham or Frank's pseudo-cancer. She looked richly brown, and she was plump and wrapped in batik which left her shoulders bare.

—Well, she told me in a rush, look what the cat dragged in. You don't look too bad eh. Mustn't be hanging round with that self-destructive bugger Jacko any more. Sit down here on the verandah and let's have a cup of tea. They found you okay? I knew in my water that you'd take the bloody wrong fork eh.

—It used to be signposted, didn't it?

—Yes. But the bloody blackfellers burnt the sign for firewood. Going in and out of Burren Waters on this excision bullshit. Sunny, love, could you do the honours with the tea?

—No problem, said Sunny. She too sounded slightly Emptor-ized. She went into the house.

Chloe and I settled ourselves on cane furniture.

—I suppose you've come to spy for my mongrel son?

—He said you wanted to see me.

—Yes. I suppose I might have. Always a pleasure. And you're writing a bit better now. I liked the last one okay, the Chinese one.

—Thanks a million. I had to spend time in Sichuan and shit in hole-in-the-ground loos, so I'm glad it passed muster. You know you shouldn't have done it, Chloe. *White Rights Party!* Didn't you learn anything while you were in Woollahra.

—Not a bloody lot, she admitted without shame.

She squinted out at the red dust beyond the green fringes of her garden.

—I mean, was there a lot to learn eh? Bugger the lot of you anyhow! If you don't think we deserve this place, you ought to read a bit of bloody history. Old Jack's grandmother died on a wagon in the Channel Country with her eighth bloody brat. They settled a cattle lease over on the Gulf. Her husband bought her a piano, but the white ants got it within three months. You ought to read what Laurie Emptor and his wife suffered when they settled here. If *they* want their bloody excision, how is it they don't recognize my rights eh?

She sighed and settled back.

—It's like I said. Bickham's a fucking genius, the prophet Elijah eh. But I reckon he's a shit-arse human. He would have put up with a socialist child molester better than he put up with me. And a bloody shame anyhow. Poor old bastard's on his last legs. Khalil's got blood pressure. I would have cooked for them till the last, and to hell with the mongrel bastard. But it seems I'm not bloody worthy.

I found myself trying to console her about Bickham. He'd separated from friends suddenly and without giving second chances, and these tendencies had grown worse as he aged. He was a severe deity. He was, for example, a devout Republican in the Australian sense. He wanted to see the last constitutional ties with Great Britain severed, an end to the Monarch of Great Britain as head of state of Australia, and an end to Australians taking oaths to a monarch who was twelve thousand miles removed from their shores.

Evans had told me that a woman artist Bickham had been friendly with had accepted an Order of the British Empire in the Queen's Birthday Honours List in the late 1970s. The moment Michael Bickham opened the *Sydney Morning Herald* and saw that, the artist was as good as dead to him.

Similarly, an actor was invited to a cocktail party in Sydney Harbour on the Royal yacht *Britannia*. Again, the guest list appeared in the *Herald* and was scanned by that Old Testament prophet, Bickham. He never recognized that actor at public events again, and avoided productions in which he appeared. He didn't have a lot of time for the contrite though fallible heart, the old Bickham.

Not that Chloe was contrite. She and Stammer Jack were determined to fight the excision order before the Land Rights Court.

—If you call it a court. They'll come out here and set up a tent, and the bloody judge will wear shorts and socks and listen to a load of bullshit from some white PhD with a beard, probably that streak of misery Helen's involved with. And the poor bloody blackfellers will go along so as not to disappoint either of the bastards.

—That's one way of looking at it, I said. The other way of looking at it is that the Wodjiri might have been waiting all along for the bloke with a beard and the judge in knee socks to come along and answer their concerns.

She said, You've been watching too many bloody current affairs programs!

Sunny arrived back with the tea, set it down like a woman who'd had a life of light, and poured it for everyone. How I craved it. I drank it black. It was known to be the best for thirst up here, and it was. Sunny took her own cup and wandered with it down the stairs and out through the garden, now and then sipping, and occasionally touching the fronds of this or that shrub. Kremmerling, without any beneficence but by detaining her in darkness, had induced in her such powers of concentration.

I said to Chloe that it was kind, what she was doing for Sunny.

She said, Poor bloody little stray. Sometimes I think she's just going to snap in two. Goes muttering around the place. But Delia can read the signs. Delia's pretty happy with her.

—Does she still have that old sleeping bag?

—She did have some ratty old thing when she first arrived. Haven't seen it though. I wouldn't mind betting Delia burned it. But I tell you what about Sunny. She earns her keep. Bloody works like a tiger. No job too menial. I thought Yanks were different. That Delia too. Delia's a good one. Maybe after she fixes Sunny up she can start on the bloody rest of us.

—I suppose you know Sunny had a pretty savage training.

—That's right. A few things come out about that. Pretty damn strange eh. Makes me respect the mongrel bastard a bit more eh.

—Delia and Sunny. What about their immigration situation?

—Come off it! Delia and Petie are at it like bloody rabbits. Petie's not going to let someone like her go. Mind you, she's three times as bright as that great lean streak of misery you saw when you first came. And as for Boomer, I told him that if he took advantage of Sunny's confusion, he can forget about flying helicopters around here. And he was quite hurt about that, went all noble eh. I think he's very taken you know. What a pair. Lost soul to lost bloody soul.

—Well, Chloe, you're not made to be a candidate for the Senate. You're a social engineer.

—Too bloody right. I socialized the little black tart out of here soon enough, and I wasn't going to let a good girl like Delia go. You know what the gene pool is up here? Jesus, Delia's like the arrival of a bloody genetic freight train. Raise the average bloody IQ of the miserable bloody Emptors, tell you that!

We drank more tea, and Sunny wandered to the limits of the garden. She seemed to be discussing matters in a low voice with the palms and ferns.

—Does Jacko keep in touch with Lucy?

—Oh God, you tell me. Bastard's called a few times on the radio-telephone. But the radio telephone's so bloody complicated it's an excuse for not saying anything eh. I tell her to put the word on him. Tell him what's happened. But she's not that sort of girl. *She*'s no bloody social engineer. So I respect her wishes. I suppose you'll have to too.

—What wishes do you mean?

—You'll find out at tea-time.

By which she meant dinner-time.

So we sat and talked about Frank Emptor. We both found ourselves laughing over him. He had been a thief of some style.

—You know, he's really got genuine criminal tendencies, said Chloe like a boast. Everyone forgives him. Even Bickham. All the people he ripped off in Sydney, the Mulcahys and so on, he's their main dinner table story. His lawyer told me that the poor little bugger got an extra six months for that, for being bloody likeable, you know. Nothing frightens a judge like a rogue with imagination eh.

Sunny came back up the stairs from the garden to pour even more tea. It was exquisite to me since I was still dry to the core.

—Have another yourself, Sunny, Chloe offered.

—No, that's okay, said Sunny. And she hung her arm around one of the verandah posts and looked out through the garden at the land which trumped California and so clearly soothed her heart, though it did not take away her manic edge. Then she wandered off again, hatless under the sun.

I saw Stammer Jack come through the gate. He wore his Akubra with its history of sweat. Overalls covered his body and ended in his ankle boots. He came up the pathway as if he was intending to skirt past us and go straight into the house, heading for some secret business, perhaps a sip of Bundaberg rum.

—Come and say hello to our guest, you miserable bastard, Chloe told him with genuine, venomous affection. She was a woman whose marriage was mended.

—D-don't want the tea, t-thanks.

Chloe stated as a matter of fact that Stammer Jack knew me.

—Yeah, t-that's right. Last t-t-time you were here. You seen m-my son over there?

—Three weeks ago. The future's pretty bright for Jacko.

—Yeah, see. But what about poor b-bloody Lucy?

—Well, Chloe argued. He's not to tell the mongrel about Lucy. Unless Lucy gives the okay.

—That little b-bastard, said Stammer Jack. Needs his b-brains brushed. I m-might just go over there with you and get the bugger sorted out! On the one hand, l-life's not a b-bloody rehearsal, but on the other, you can have too big a c-cast!

This was the longest speech I had heard Stammer Jack make, and true as it was, I felt it was time to acquaint them with their son's virtues.

—Were you aware who brought Delia and Sunny here? Who paid their fares and so on?

—Sutherland, said Chloe. That's what they tell us. What's it called? Vixen Six. What a name! Jacko's pack of bloody clowns eh. Vixen bloody Six. What's that character's name, Durkin? Jesus!

—Vixen Six didn't pay for them. Jacko did. Roughly ten or eleven thousand dollars — because you can't buy a single ticket to Australia. Paid for the tickets out of his own pocket. And the same week another ticket for Lucy. Which was only right, of course. But the same week he was dumping Lucy, or Lucy was dumping him, he was saving Sunny.

The parents considered this together in silence. Stammer Jack was the first one to speak.

—Well, he was always generous to a b-bloody fault.

—His bloody generosity is about to be tested, said Chloe.

Chloe then called into the garden.

—Sunny, why don't you go and tell Lucy her playmate's here?

—Okay, called Sunny, putting her cup down under a fern for collection later. But I won't want to interrupt her if she's painting.

We watched Sunny dawdle off once more through the garden and out of the gate into Emptorville's full blaze of light. I felt like standing and calling a warning to her. *Careful of the light!*

—She's still under a heap of medication you know, Chloe thunderously whispered. Boomer flies her off to the psychiatrist in Darwin every two weeks. But it's a pretty good recovery, isn't it? Of course, out here, people expect you to recover and get on with bloody things. It's a therapeutic atmosphere eh. You know, she doesn't wake screaming in the night or anything. Sleeps well, eats well, works well. You'd never think . . .

—Jacko's creative idea, I said.

—Yeah, there you go, said Stammer Jack. His instincts are ok-kay. But his f-f-fucking wires are crossed.

She reached out for Stammer Jack's enormous hand, so creased, so mapped with mysterious scars, and slotted her fingers into the maw of his slack fist.

I wish Larson had been there to photograph them. The sun, which an hour and a half before had bludgeoned me by the side of my rented Holden, had begun dropping fast now. It always sets quickly above the Tropic of Capricorn. At this kindly hour, the Emptors' stubbornly retained acreage and square mileages were turning from mauve to violet, and the huge space of pounded dirt amongst the buildings — the stockyards, the homestead and the sales ring — turned violet too, as if from some internal chemistry. Across the violet I saw Lucy stiffly walking with Sunny. Sunny reached the homestead gate first and opened it for her. It was easy now to see the reason for Lucy's stiff gait. She was pregnant.

As she drew near I beheld her enormous smile, which reminded me of how she danced in the Odeon.

—Gidday, she cried.

She made it to the verandah and sat with a sigh.

—Well, she said, breathing heavily. A bun in the oven eh?

I found it hard to answer her.

* * *

Dinner came later than I would have wanted. We had to wait until after the stockmen had eaten and gone off to watch television. We ate in their dining room, which was located by the kitchen, between the quarters which Lucy, myself and — more permanently — the unmarried white stockmen occupied and the school. The table was set for eight. Chloe sat at one end, and I felt honoured to be on her right side. Lucy sat on her left. And then down the table Delia and hulking Petie, Sunny and Boomer sitting side by side, one couple (if that was a way to describe them) facing the other. And at the foot of the table but to the side, not in the spousal position, sat the ageing stockman called Merv.

I remembered the night, while Larson was still alive, that Chloe had boasted to us in mime of Merv's sexual capacity. I was encouraged to remember it because of the fact that shy Stammer Jack must have eaten a reclusive meal somewhere else. Perhaps he was now doing the books, settling to his evening drinking, or watching the 7:30 *Report* and being mutely appalled at the opinions of people who lived in cities in New South Wales and Victoria, in urban nests of liberalism where the name of the Territory cut no ice.

Everyone at the table spoke about my misadventure, which I had to recount. Boomer and Sunny ate quietly without mentioning the corkscrew. Delia, who was wearing a long sleeved shirt, complained pleasantly about the impact of the sun upon her complexion. And for her sake, Chloe said what she seemed to say to all newcomers.

—Well, no bugger sunbathes up here. It would be a sign of bloody madness. You look at the old timers. Merv, hold your arm up. See that! See that eh? Buttoned to the bloody wrist!

—I love living here, said Delia.

Like Sunny, she had the blush of this country on her. Delia continued her argument.

—If we were in New York now, we'd be stewing in humidity. I put up with it because I didn't know better things were available. Australians think they've got a bad climate. But they don't know what a bad climate is.

Chloe said, Well that's how buggered up America is eh. Americans come to a bloody hole like this and think it's paradise. Let me tell you, Delia love, if that old bastard in the homestead could be trusted, I'd swap New York with you right now. The cattle industry's rooted, and Australia's gone to the dogs.

—What would you do in New York, Chloe?

—What would I do? I'd start going to the literary bars. And I'd start writing some fiction of my own. I could write in a city like New York. I've seen it through Saul Bellow's eyes, and they're pretty good bloody eyes to see it through. Nobel Laureate, like someone else I could mention.

—You're mad, Chloe, said Boomer. The Ayatollah was right. America's the great Satan.

He was one of those disenchanted by Vietnam. Jacko told me he may have deserted during Rest and Recreation in Sydney.

—I think you're mad too, Chloe, said Lucy quietly, winking across the table at me. You can write just as well here I reckon. I'm doing more work here than I ever found possible in New York.

Now I was surprised to hear Petie chime in.

He said, Well, what Chloe's saying is the Territory's not like it was. Maybe so. But it'll do me eh. Our abattoir in town's really starting to do good business with the Saudis. If we could just sell a bit more beef to the Americans and the Indonesians, we'd be laughing.

—They've got these Arab abattoir supervisors in Hector, said Chloe. To make sure the cattle are slaughtered right. If your bloody sister was still around, she'd probably fall for one of them and go Muslim just to bloody spite me.

There was, of course, enough steak on the table to suggest the Emptors had plenty for export.

Sunny had finished working at her own lump of meat and rose with her plate in her hands. She looked around for others who had finished. Lucy was one of them.

—Pass over your plate, Mrs Emptor Junior, she told her. I'll get the dessert.

Chloe said, No, listen. You'll end up a bloody slavey like me.

But Sunny was already gone.

—Well, while you're out there, called Chloe, get the useless bloody cook to make up another pot of tea.

Petie looked at me and winked.

—We're getting all these bloody Yanks used to tea, he mildly boasted.

Delia was mopping her lips and quenching a small burp. All her movements were those of a woman who knew and had confidence in her company, a woman at her own hearth. She smiled at me.

—You couldn't drink coffee, anyhow, in this sort of climate, she said. Except recreationally. It'd dehydrate you.

At the bottom of the table, Merv had lit a cigarette and was quietly drinking, a vigilant look in his eye, as if he expected this particular company to say something really clever. Chloe watched him closely through narrowed eyes. It all seemed so easeful to me. I too almost felt as if I'd come home.

Lucy leaned over the table towards me.

—Would you like to take a preggers woman for a walk after dinner?

I said that that would be an honour.

—That's the go then eh, said Lucy. You can approve of my paintings too if you like.

* * *

. Under the three-quarter moon, the earth had softened and could be believed to be velvet. Just as when I was last here, stockmen were drinking beneath a big brush shelter, and watching a big television set.

Even from the way she walked — and discounting for the moment her pregnancy — you could tell Lucy had not had a good time of it. I noticed how her long neck was stringy, little Jacko — I presumed it was Jacko's child, but I had not heard this asserted by anyone — already plundering his mother of the minerals of her youth. Her pregnancy in its way emphasized her thinness which was of a different order from what I thought of as her New York lankiness.

—I suppose you think I'm pretty damn silly, she said.

—Why?

—Well, I'm up here, swearing everyone to bloody secrecy. You'd think if I wanted to keep it secret, I'd clear out.

—You ought to consider telling Jacko.

—I'm sort of disappointed you think it's Jacko's?

—Well, let me say, I wouldn't blame you if it wasn't.

—Well, it's bloody Jacko's. But women who get pregnant to stop things busting up are a bit of a cliché, aren't they?

—Anything that works, in my opinion.

—As soon as I found out, I came up here. It wasn't

visible then. I said that as soon as it began to look visible I'd go back to Sydney eh. But the thought of *that* fills me with horror. In Sydney I'm an angry woman, and I don't know what to make of myself. So you won't report back to him, will you?

This was a gentler form of Chloe's accusation that I was a spy.

—I ask you to imagine what my life would be like if my wife and your friend, Maureen, found out I had leaked embargoed information to Jacko.

She laughed at that, remembering Maureen.

—If I stay here, she said, and he turns up, I won't be able to tell whether he's here to see Chloe or me. I really ought to go somewhere else. But . . . Chloe's a bit of an addiction with me. And Sunny . . . at least I can look at Sunny. She doesn't need me here of course. But I think I need to see her around the place. Because . . . believe me! . . . she's not nearly as well as she looks. Walking wounded eh.

—Does Jacko talk as if a reconciliation's still on?

—Well, that's what he tells me, every time he calls on the radio-telephone.

—I wouldn't give him too long, I advised her.

It was as near as I could come to telling her what I knew of Jacko. If she could have somehow seen a video clip from the dinner at which Jacko had made his unwise moves on Hubert Greenspan's mistress, she could hardly have been surprised, though she would have been enlightened.

—Do you think he's fit for marriage with anyone? Lucy asked.

—Jesus! That's a terrible question to ask me.

—But just do me a favour and say whether you think he's fit for it.

In such a deep night, north of Capricorn, amidst such impending and inhuman spaces, I did not want to say something that would torment her and spoil her small, human sleep.

—I think he could certainly be educated to marriage.

She laughed the old, rich Odeon laugh.

—Like Stammer Jack's been? Anyhow, that didn't hurt you too much eh? Lowering the mateship barrier.

—I think he could be educated and coerced. Your brand of education seemed to me to go very, very gently with him.

—Well sorry. I thought I could influence him. I was hard on him in private. But not in public you know. In public I think it's disloyal to kick up a fuss. I thought that when my parents bunged on public scenes. It didn't seem to help them much. If I did act up, it'd work the other way with him. He might take it from some other woman. Look, come and see these paintings of mine.

She was pleased to drag me away from the dusty plaza and the whole subject. She led me to her room in the brick stockmen's quarters. It was nondescript, but it had two beds. On one of the beds and around the walls and either side of the wash basin lay a number of canvases and sheets of board.

I thought they were very competent, lively impressionist and abstract versions of the Burren Waters landscape. Since she was working on technique, they were repetitive, like Monet's water lilies or haystacks. Worked over and over, in all conditions of Burren Waters light. She'd managed to turn the Emptor house into something more mysterious than itself.

I told her I thought they were wonderful.

—Come on, she said. You're just saying that.

—What would I know anyhow. But I like them enormously. Any for sale?

—I'll give you one.

The truth was I wished I could have conveyed how startling this display of her work seemed; a real phenomenon in the lee of her leaving Jacko.

—I don't know; it really keeps me occupied. You can't get that result out of playing the cello eh. It keeps me so busy. The paintings don't satisfy me in retrospect, when they're lying around the room, but making them satisfies me.

I could understand that. Compared to the imponderables of writing and music, painting was a sort of busy and absorbing art.

As we stood looking at the canvases, she asked, So, is he living with Dannie?

—Didn't you know they fell out so badly over the Sondquist business? He behaved with real style, and Dannie hated it. As far as I know he's not living with anyone. I don't want to raise any stupid hopes, but he misses you in his way.

—Oh yeah. In his way eh. Got to be careful of that way. I suppose I'll stay up here and give birth to the child, and still expect everyone to keep it a secret.

Putting my arms around her for no more than a friendly — probably a paternal — hug, I believed I could feel, through the flesh of my small paunch earned in distant bars with Jacko, the beat of her child's heart, or maybe just the pulse of its energetic growing. The heart of a riotous, reproduced Jacko. She carried that beloved enemy.

* * *

I asked her that night if she wanted to come back to Sydney with me, and try the city again. She could stay at the beach with Maureen and me. But she said no.

Three times, as far as I remember.

Back in my room, I lay on my bed fully clothed. When you grew still at Burren Waters, you *were* aware of an edginess in the atmosphere. The place was on a cusp, where water-laden air from the Timor and Arafura Seas ran up against the super-dried air from the Tanami and other deserts. You couldn't sleep at ease unless you were used to these ionic complications. Besides, I was woken from my first few minutes dozing by the muted voices of women outside. What did these voices mean? Was something being plotted? Punishment of Stammer Jack? Of Jacko? Of me as a subscriber to the same chromosomes?

I had reached a paranoid hour.

In the end I fought off the leadenness and dropped my feet to the floor and — against a terrible weight of gravity — rose to go and see where these persistent voices came from.

It was Chloe and Sunny Sondquist. Both barefooted, they trod the mauve dust of the homestead square. They were pretty clearly delineated by moonlight. Chloe wore a mumu, Sunny a light floral dress. As they strolled, Chloe would sometimes lag, as if the air was getting at her, but would catch up. I could hear that it was Sunny doing most of the talking. They passed the hangar where Boomer's corkscrew beast slept. As they drew level with the sales ring, Sunny reached back and linked arms with Chloe, and the two smiled at each other. Sunny kept talking, but you'd hear the occasional rumble of Chloe's sentences — waivers, questions, counsels.

They were sisters under the constellation of Capricorn, under a sky bright as lunacy. They strolled across the dust, and now they were a daughter and mother, the one dragging the other off to a shop to look at a dress. I heard Chloe say *Bloody hell!* and laugh.

They were heading back to the homestead now, along the line of the stockmen's quarters, the cookhouse, the office. I stepped back into my room a little. They would pass my door. I have to admit I had tears in my eyes, for Sunny the maimed daughter of course, but for Chloe's maternal kindness too. The crazed senate candidate had become something else, something supra-political, under the uneasy moon.

Sunny was chatting away in a subdued voice, but as she passed my door, I heard what she was saying.

—Legerdemain — L-E-G-E-R-D-E-M-A-I-N. Anodyne — A-N-O-D-Y-N-E. Polymorphic — P-O-L-Y-M-O-R-P-H-I-C . . .

My wife in particular loved returning to New York in its first chill, the last of its summer humidity. The leaves in Washington Square were at that stage investing themselves in their last brave flare of colour. Maureen found the East Village, which purists said did not exist, a genuine community. The manager of Shakespeare's bookshop knew her, as did the Korean dry cleaners, and the Italian-Americans in the postal service at La Guardia Place. There were people in Dean and Deluca's who welcomed her back. She knew the actress who made the gourmet sandwiches in Mercer Street, still under-employed at the end of the summer, still waiting for the summoning voice.

When we went back to the Grand Ticino for the first time, the *maitre d'* welcomed her like a cousin from Trieste. And if she shopped at night at the local general store, again Korean, the managers would send their second oldest chunk of a son to get her home safely.

In the sorts of magazines which told you what was coming up on Fall television, Jacko's picture appeared and re-appeared, but I only heard from him once, when he left a recorded message saying that unhappily he would not be able to come to the party for the launch of my book on China, the one on whose revisions I had worked all the previous New York winter.

Jacko was clearly in California a great deal, being produced by Tracey perhaps. Since, in a sense, I had gone to the Northern Territory at his bidding, and since I might have died of thirst on the errand, I felt chagrin that he didn't seek me out for a report.

The book was published and was featured on the front page of the *New York Times Book Review*, for, as people liked to say then, what that was worth.

In November there was a further sequence of recorded telephone conversations, as if he were calling at times he knew I would be out. My wife and I were invited to his launch party in Los Angeles, the launch of the game show that is. The invitation came inconveniently late and, though my wife urged me to go if I wanted to, I decided against it. I had begun another book, and two days of flying and a night of wildness with Jacko did not seem to me to be best for it.

So the television season began, and Jacko's show was madly successful in the seven-thirty time slot on Wednesday night, in the meat of the week, the primest of prime times. I watched the credits and found Tracey's name listed as Executive Producer. I left a note for him at the bar of Mary O'Reilly's, the sentimental non-IRA bar above which he lived.

—I know you're on the other side of the country all the time, I wrote, but if ever you have time, I'm not averse to having a drink.

I hoped that did not seem like pleading. I wanted to tell him how Sunny and Delia were, even if I were forbidden to tell him the full story of Lucy. The fact that he did not urgently call to ask me about Lucy —

whether I'd tell him the truth or not — made him seem more trivial to me by the day.

He still did the doorknocks, getting past all barriers, transcending them this way and that. Basil Sutherland reputedly paid him a fortune for doing three doors per week. Social commentators speculated that people wrote to Jacko begging to be included in his raids of the suburbs. He did the taping of his game show over three days in California — I quote a newspaper — and perhaps a day of that was spent practising his material and his timing. He had remarkably talented people willing to play his quiz game. Jacko picked up a small but renowned English comic, an Oxford graduate, who would answer ten questions in a row correctly, and then, at what passes as centre stage, Jacko would lift him in his arms and turn him upside down, like a wolfhound jovially cuffing a kitten. This image became talismanic in all the advertising for the show.

—It's not his success that's making him avoid us, I said to Maureen.

—I wish it damn well was, she said.

I got a call from him one Wednesday morning, when I was still working on the beginnings of the new novel.

—Aren't you supposed to be in California on Wednesdays? I asked.

He had none of the liveliness of a man whose mad show would take viewers by the scruff of their sensibilities at seven thirty that night.

He said, We've got some episodes in the can. I need to see lawyers this afternoon. Do you want to meet in the Odeon afterwards?

—I've got a workshop at seven, I told him, just to

show that he couldn't expect to be put, on a whim, at the top of my list.

—Four then. What do you say?

—You still drink at the Odeon? I asked him, making it hard for him, wondering how nostalgia for Lucy must lie in ambush for him in that place.

He seemed to understand what I meant too.

—Jesus, mate, he protested. I know it's got memories eh. But it's just around the corner after all.

All right, I said, trying to sound grudging, but avid for the hour.

* * *

At four, Jacko and I had — as usual — the barman to ourselves. The gritty residue of daylight invaded the floor where Lucy had danced in her 'waistband', singing in her helium-childish voice.

Jacko was seated at a table, whereas all our former mid-afternoon Odeon confidences had been at the bar. This afternoon, however, the Great Intruder wanted his privacy. He had lost some poundage since last I saw him and had an untouched glass of white wine in front of him. This was close to being a penitential drink in Jacko's case. To show that I would not be allayed by social boozing, I ordered water. All this must have confused the barman.

—Okay, he said when we had settled. We know where we are, don't we? You're pissed off at me for not calling. But you don't know how busy I've been. The time I've had free to ask you about the women, I've been utterly rooted. And I know something about them anyhow, from phone calls. On the other hand, you went up there under your own steam. I know that. I saw an article on it in the in-flight magazine of some airline. Makes Burren Waters sound pretty bloody picturesque eh. Not half as picturesque as it is in reality. You had the grace not to mention Sunny or Delia or Lucy. So ... my apologies. I'm a silly prick who doesn't deserve his friends, and so say all of us.

—I did go up there, and I covered my expenses. But I would have preferred to be at home working on my new book, and damn the whole troop of you!

Jacko gave a throaty laugh.

—Come on. You can't tell me that. You were dying to find out what happened to all the girls. Come clean eh. You've got a mill and this is your bloody grist. You can't tell me what happened to Sunny isn't astounding. Out of the box in San Bernardino County, and into Burren Waters. Bloody astounding!

—And there's a more plebeian mystery too, I told him. How well Chloe gets on with Lucy.

—That's no surprise, said Jacko. Women are amazing that way. They have a common cause against bastards like me and the mongrel bastard. Maybe he and I've got a lot in common, even though he probably doesn't think so. Listen, are you going to take this high moral tone all afternoon?

—Maybe not, I conceded.

—I can tell it's a bloody strain for you, said Jacko.

—It's not a strain. I was always a partisan of Lucy's. Whenever you mention Burren Waters, you put Sunny first. You've got to expect me to wonder how normal that is.

—Blood-ee hell! Give me a chance. I've got enough answering to do in the next day or so.

He merely wetted his lips with his chardonnay. It

was as if working for a network had made him a more seemly drinker.

—Bloody Silverarts've taken an injunction against my game show, he told me then. They say that I was still legally under option to them when I signed on with Hubie Greenspan. It'll be heard downtown tomorrow. In the meantime the network has pulled tonight's episode because they don't want to be sued retrospectively. You wouldn't believe it, but you're looking at a man people have been distancing themselves from all day. My bloody agent made me sign a sheet of paper indemnifying him for the advice he gave me at the time!

—But you had legal advice about it too, I argued.

—Jesus, and I still do. Up to the bloody ears eh.

—Silverarts can't possibly win, can they? They're not within their rights?

—Well, both Greenspan and I got advice which said I was clear to make a new contract. But now, after this writ, the lawyers are all at once more cautious. They're looking at me like someone who's just been told he's got bloody cancer.

For the first time since I'd known him, Jacko covered his eyes from daylight with both his hands. This I found prodigiously affecting, and I reached out and held him by the inner elbow — a large gesture from one Australian male to another.

—They've joined the injunction with a damages writ for three million dollars against me and eight million against Hubert. It's legal opportunism, but it could work. If the injunction sticks tomorrow, I'll have to file for Chapter Eleven bankruptcy. And I won't last more than a month as a bloody popular idol.

—They can't win, I stated in a flush of brotherly conviction. Surely.

—Well, we'll see eh. If they don't, we'll come back here tomorrow night or the next and have a total shit-heap of a party, I tell you that.

The idea of escaping the damages writ and re-assuming his godhead made his eyes glitter in a way that had very little to do — I believed — with egotism as such, and more to do with the childlike intentions of mischief which had first brought him to New York and carried him over thresholds. I asked him if there was anything I could do, as if in some sense I could be a buffer against the sometime shame and modern day expediency of Chapter Eleven.

He looked at me, weighing me.

—You're going to stick around till the bloody last. Is that it?

—Well, I confessed to him, I'm a novelist. I'm certainly going to be an interested observer, which is as close to friendship as a novelist would want to claim.

—Bloody good, he said. Let's get really pissed.

His eye was moving along the bottles on the lower shelf by the Odeon's mirrors. The bottles which said Black Bush and Laphroaig and Calvados and Metaxa.

—No, I said. No. I've got my class.

He held up his hand.

—Listen, mate, I understand.

* * *

The next morning the story of the injunction was in the *New York Times* and on morning television. Even *Morning Manhattan* ran it.

I went downtown by the subway from West Fourth Street and though, through my brushes with the media, I thought I knew what to expect, I was astounded by the crowds of journalists and camera crews in the corridor leading to the courtroom where the injunction hearing was taking place. The court-room gallery was already full — men and women with the intense grains of the street in their faces and wearing old bits of clothing, and young, lost-looking men with halitosis who had a folder with everything ever written about Jacko in it. For this is the truth of stardom, temporary or transcendent: only the demented, the manic, the lost, have time to tend the altar.

I found half of a seat amongst them all. I stood with them as the judge entered, a hard-nosed looking fellow of about fifty years.

The case opened with the calling of the chief executive officer of Silverarts. He argued that the contract Silverarts had with Jacko entitled them to be contacted if Jacko envisaged availing himself of the windows of opportunity. That contact had never been made.

The man then indicated Silverarts' plans for Jacko, plans for a gradual acceleration of career which would have pitched him at a level of stardom far in advance of the mere game show notoriety which Hubert Greenspan had planned for him. While Silverarts worked on production plans for Jacko Emptor, it had, after all, consistently continued to pay Jacko Emptor a monthly fee for the past two years. The concept of that fee was that Mr Emptor would keep Silverarts apprised of his intentions and of other offers.

I saw Greenspan and Tracey in court. Greenspan laughed briefly in Tracey's direction, or perhaps into the breast pocket of his Zegna suit, at Silverarts' low estimation of game shows and their renown for quality.

Greenspan's lawyers then did a powerful, probing job on the president of Silverarts: taking him through the option agreement, clause by clause; getting him to identify the windows of opportunity; trying to have him contradict himself on the matter of the liberties Jacko was thereby entitled to. By the end of a morning of this I was feeling hopeful for Jacko.

But Jacko's agent, called to the stand just after noon, was a grievous disappointment to the Greenspan-Jacko camp. I had met him before at parties at Jacko's place. He was a thin, ageless man, a competitor in half and full marathons. Silverarts' lawyers did not have to wait long for him to utter the decisive sentence.

—I reminded him of the existence of the option agreement, as was my duty as an agent. And I told him that he needed to be very careful about the Silverarts agreement and his duties under it.

—But did you advise him to go with Greenspan?

—I said ultimately it was up to him.

—But is it true that you had him sign an indemnity agreement, exempting you from liability?

The agent said yes, it was so. He had the indemnity agreement with him. He produced it. Throughout the court you could hear Jacko saying, Oh Jesus, as if this were something he had forgotten. You could hear Greenspan snorting.

Greenspan's lawyers, joined in action with Jacko's, argued that it was a nuisance suit, that Silverarts' agreement with Jacko was of dubious legality and violated his constitutional rights to enter contracts. The president of Silverarts could not produce any convincing documentation — other than a few speculative letters — for his claim that Silverarts was actively working on a project involving Jacko. The idea that Jacko had somehow damaged *them* by working for Greenspan was fatuous, and their injunction writ was opportunistic and meant to create the basis for a damages settlement.

The judge sent us all to lunch. In the corridor, I stood on the edge of the sizeable group which included Jacko and Greenspan.

—You didn't tell me you signed an indemnity, Greenspan marginally complained.

—I did it to set the bugger's mind at rest, said Jacko.

I was aware of the curious bewilderment in Jacko's eyes. There was still that much of Burren Waters in him: he did not expect to suffer for technicalities.

Greenspan said, I wish you'd told me.

Tracey looked at the distempered wall and pursed the corners of her mouth. Jacko's agent appeared and walked smoothly past, but Greenspan detained him by the elbow.

—Do you generally sell out on your clients like that?

The man pulled himself free and shrugged.

—I can only lead my clients to water. I can't be expected to drown with them.

Greenspan told the agent, I've put five million dollars development and promotion into Jacko. I wonder about your intentions.

—That's your prerogative, said Jacko's agent. It's

all speculative at the end of the day, isn't it?

—Oh hell, said Jacko, but it was more in despair than in fury.

—If I can manage it, Greenspan told the agent, I'll ensure that before the end of this year you're wearing your anus like a necklace.

—Are you threatening me, Mr Greenspan?

—Well, as they say, I hope it's more than a threat.

—It's a big industry, said the agent.

He turned his eyes to Jacko.

—Jacko, I'm sorry it hasn't worked out.

—Bloody hell, said Jacko, nearly beyond protest.

By mid-afternoon the judge granted the injunction against the screening of Jacko's show. Jacko was not to participate in any game shows, other than those produced by Silverarts, for the next three years. He was free to go on making his living through door-knocks and current affairs.

That night, when those who had not heard the news tuned in to see Jacko, they found a re-run of a comedy show instead. Jacko drank vodka in the Odeon with me and a young lawyer, and his new segment producer on *Morning Manhattan*, Angela, whom I had met briefly at the start of the summer. She was a robust looking young woman from Wisconsin who had gone to Rutgers on a swimming scholarship. Her manner was not unlike Lucy's — very country, not New York gritty.

At one point in the evening when Jacko and I both stood at the urinals, Jacko said, Jesus, couldn't be permitted, could it? Jacko Emptor, wealthy *and* a star. Just couldn't be permitted. Would've fucked the universe some way or other.

Back at the table Angela, his new producer, said,

Better watch it, Jacko. You might be wiped out for the morning.

—Are you doing a show tomorrow morning? I asked Jacko.

Jacko put his head in his hands and then laid his brow down on the table.

—As per contract, he told me. To keep the bread and butter on the table. I think it would be a good morning for the Bronx. Despair within, despair without.

He turned to the young country girl.

—Will you come home with me and make sure I get up?

Angela reached out and put her hand on his wrist but didn't say yes or no. She didn't want word to get back to her mother perhaps, or maybe she intended to get him to his door and then leave him to sleep until the wake-up call.

Next Jacko turned to me.

—Then you'll come out too in the morning eh?

—But why me?

—Solidarity with the bloody downtrodden, said Jacko. Besides, you stay in that apartment of yours all day and keep writing, and you'll be mad as a cut snake.

—Like television people perhaps? I suggested.

—All jokes aside, he said. You're my fucking sage.

—I'm your fucking stooge, I said.

And Jacko said a garbled Biblical-sounding verse he may have heard when he came down from Burren Waters to Sydney to go to boarding school at the age of fourteen.

—So shall the wise man appear foolish . . . Eh? Eh?

—You've got that bit right, Jacko.

I had the embarrassment still ahead of me of arriving home having drunk too much in a bar in which, yet again, I was the oldest person, and then of admitting that I would rise before dawn at Jacko's bidding.

—This is madness, I said.

I was no closer than I had been before our estrangement to working out why I obeyed Jacko or why I wanted to.

* * *

As I have already confessed, I was by now used to the process of waking with the night's sins not quite burned away in the blood. There is first the sense of having awakened in hell, beyond the ambit of Divine Grace and mother love. Then the stirred and abused brain begins to coruscate with the unabsorbed residue of the night's alcohol, and a curious, fatuous, reviving energy sets in, which will leave you stark-eyed by mid-morning yet strangely equipped for the flippant demands of dawn.

The limo picked me up first. It was the hour when cities are still and pensive, the night's crimes behind and the day not yet marred. At five-fifteen berserk thoroughfares like Houston and West Broadway were vacant except for the trucks bringing the countryside's bounty into the city.

At Thomas Street, one mere ring of the bell brought Jacko suited, coated, in his porkpie to the car. He was accompanied by his producer. I deliberately did not look to see if Angela was wearing the same clothes as last night under her coat. She was such a pleasant girl, and I might one day get into a situation where I needed to claim ignorance in front of Chloe or Lucy. She packed Jacko functionally into the back with me, and checked if she had brought everything Jacko needed downstairs. This neo-Lucy was foolish if she thought she had a chance with Jacko. Someone should be *in loco parentis* to tell her, but please God not me, not this morning.

On the one hand, I assured myself, she seemed a smart enough girl to work it out herself. But on the other, Lucy hadn't, not until great grief had been done.

—I appreciate you being here, cobber, Jacko told me. I know your missus doesn't approve of me any more.

Most polite Manhattanites, even honorary ones like me, avoided the Bronx. It was a mystery you did not want to enquire into. Stories returned from there and fantastically lodged in the pages of the *New York Times* or the *Post* or *News*. Brave documentary teams kitted up and plunged into it. Safe in numbers, people went to the baseball there, to see the Yankees, but skittered home as soon as the result was clear. It was the Third World just across the Triboro Bridge, inhabited by a race named the underclass. As Livingstone had disappeared in Kenya, Manhattanites could disappear in the Bronx. There had been novels about the mishaps which could befall the best people who mistakenly took an exit here.

This morning Jacko and Angela and I were taking one by design. We ran all too briskly at this hour along the FDR and made the crossing, in fact, at the 138th Street Bridge. We found ourselves almost at once in the Grand Concourse, a superb nineteenth-century *faubourg*, designed a hundred years past in the belief that the Bronx would ever flourish as a centre of bourgeois urbanity.

No street on Manhattan stood up beside the Grand Concourse. Park Avenue was a boring conduit by comparison, Fifth too narrow. We took a turn at a shopping centre with steel and mesh chain shutters, and turned again into a narrow street of old apartment buildings. Here burnt-out cars sat hunched in the gutters, and black-lipped windows spoke of someone's dangerous fury.

—Jesus, said Jacko. You could rent a few blokes from Actors Equity, put 'em in camouflage, give 'em Armalites and do a documentary on Belfast up here.

—We might do that, conceded Angela, but her smile was tight and she was watchful.

With another right turn and then a left, and a few other little dodges, the driver soon had us lost in streets where apartment blocks had given way to houses, which stood in their own gardens of litter and weeds. The front car seat, set in the garden as a form of *al fresco* settee, was one of the area's favourite items.

We were pleased to see the microwave truck with *Vixen Six* marked on it and the technicians standing by its back door drinking coffee with good old Clayton.

Our car drew up.

—You got a gun, driver? Jacko asked the chauffeur.

—Better believe it, sir.

—Good to know, said Jacko.

We got out and Jacko and Angela had a conference with Clayton.

—House on the corner's burned out, said Clayton. I don't know which of the others. Good if we could find an honest Bronxer who'd talk about what it's like out here.

—Or a dishonest bloody Bronxer.

Jacko nodded across the street to a house whose windows were boarded up.

—Give that one a miss, said Clayton. Crack house.

—That's the one though, said Jacko. Isn't it? Haven't done one of those . . .

—Don't be stupid, Jacko, said Angela.

—Didn't you hear the judge yesterday? He said no more fucking game shows, boys and girls. But I'm game for that bloody place.

—Jacko, reproved Angela.

—You'll come in with me, Clayton.

—I might. But will the cable man?

Jacko put a hand on my shoulder.

—My mate here won't mind pulling the cable. He's been in war zones in Africa.

Angela said, Clayton, I really don't want you two to do this.

Jacko turned to me, stooping to look me in the eye.

—Will you handle the cable for me? Can't ask the blokes on the truck. Or I can, but Angela's under a duty to tell 'em they won't be covered by insurance.

—I'm not covered by insurance, I argued.

Yet I was utterly and irresponsibly ready to go. I was strangely and exultantly ready. The last of the night's toxins were urging me and would be burned up by such an exercise. I had the same self-indulgent but delicious sense of inevitability, of lightly playing with fire, as when I had climbed in a dawn party to the front trench-line in the Horn of Africa four years ago. Since I knew there was a sort of indecency in

these euphoric impulses, I said nothing further. I
stood still. Yet I knew I might be used by Jacko.

Jacko, Angela and Clayton went to talk to the
technicians at the truck. I could see people nodding,
Angela shaking her head. I should back her up. If I
added my judgement to hers, it could no longer be
argued — as Clayton and Jacko were arguing — that
her caution was purely a female thing. But Clayton
had already shouldered his camera and Jacko was
being wired up.

Angela cried, I'm coming anyhow. I'm your
producer.

But Jacko kept saying no. This was a special case.
There was a time Dannie hadn't come, and everyone
knew what a hot shot she was. The bitch.

—When didn't she come?

—It was when I took on an apartment block in a
cherrypicker.

—We ought to talk to Durkin.

—We'll talk to Durkin in a second. We'll tell him
we're just doorknocking in the Bronx.

He pointed at Angela, Don't bugger this up, love.

I had been in a demented state. Now I remembered
Lucy. The unborn child entered as a factor into my
primal thought.

I walked closer and put my hand on his coated
shoulder to signal I wanted a last word before we
tried this grotesque thing. Because he presumed that
I had something cautionary to say, he took some time
to turn, and when he did I saw a certain weariness in
his face. He pointed to the cable which snaked out of
the truck and was connected to Clayton's camera.

—It's pretty much like dragging a hose. You make
sure it doesn't snag on the gates or on the doorway.

Keep it right up to him, feet of it. Clayton's got to
have plenty of cable behind him to allow freedom of
movement once he's inside. Okay?

—Okay. But listen, I have some news.

He was not going to suffer equivocation. He lifted
the plastic cable and put it in my hands. He was
distracted then by something he heard in his ear:
Durkin was talking to him from the studio.

—No, he said, with that peculiarly beefy, resonating laugh. The mike on his tie would have conveyed
his words to Durkin.

—No, Eddie. She's exaggerating, old son.

He listened further, and Clayton swung his camera
to film the house across the street. This of course
would allow Durkin to see the proposed target of
today's doorknock. I could dimly hear Durkin protesting in Jacko's ear.

—Eddie, Eddie, said Jacko soothingly. Where's the
well-known Durkin sense of humour?

—And then, Look mate. You can boss me around,
but unless you get out here within five minutes . . .
Listen, don't go soft on me . . .

Angela, paler even than all our foolishness could
possibly have made her, yelled, Ninety seconds, to
Jacko.

—Durkin says pick another house, she added.

—Who's robbing this bloody stage coach, Jacko
called jovially.

—Oh Christ, she cried, since Durkin was giving
her orders, telling her to stop Jacko, telling her not
to go in with Jacko, and that time was so close. Early-
riser Jacko-ites waited along the great littoral to be
told where Jacko Emptor was this morning, to see his

frantically wakeful face, and to be encouraged to believe he would do anything.

Jacko began walking briskly across the road.

—Come on, Clayton, come on.

And to me, Keep that cable up.

I heard Clayton murmur, We're on.

We went in the wire gate and up the path and to the door. I was sure we weren't meant to proceed at such a pace. Generally Jacko's broadcast began in the street and then moved to the door after the first commercial break. We were galloping to make contact with the residents. I hauled on the cable just to stay near him.

By the three steps leading up to the little front porch, Jacko turned to Clayton's camera.

—We're in the Bronx, my friends, and we've got a funny one here.

He mounted the steps and put his shoulder to the front door.

—Feel this door, he invited us.

He did a rat-a-tat-tat on it and it dully and metallically answered. Thud, thud, thud.

—A security-conscious neighbourhood, ladies and gentlemen.

He put a hand to his ear.

—Oh, oh, my producer-in-chief, Ed Durkin, wants us to get out of here. We can't get out, Ed. If these are people of any professional standards, they know we're here already.

Jacko took one of his gloves off and began to hammer at the door, raising an unresponsive yet resonating thud from it, somewhat like Buddhist temple bells.

Angela had appeared on the pathway, careless of

maintaining the illusions of television. She was calling, Jacko, Durkin says No! Come on!

If she could be reckless, then perhaps I was entitled to be also.

I went up to him, holding my cable, and, whether in shot or not, said, Come away, Jacko. Listen, Lucy's carrying a child.

—What? he said.

I told him again. It took no time. But all through it, he kept knocking and knocking, and we could all feel, in that frozen morning, the imminence of someone opening to him.